About the Author

Kimber A. Harvey was born in San Jose, California, and currently resides in the Sierra Foothills.

Her love of books began at an early age. Even as a toddler, she preferred to take books to bed, leaving stuffed animals and toys discarded on the floor.

Her natural talent for writing began at around age seven when she wrote her first book (all four pages of it) about a horse that could outrun the wind.

Although *Filling in the Blanks* is her first novel, Kimber has shared her writing talent in many other ways; writing columns for a small local newspaper, with a poem titled *Under Heaven* published in an anthology, winning college writing competitions for short stories *Bordering on Obscenity* and *Pieces of Me. She* won the Coveted Dead Bird Award for Best Title with *Beating the Clock* from the San Joaquin Sisters in Crime, and she self-published *My Favorite Recipes* cookbook for her family—twice.

After earning a Bachelor of Arts degree in Psychology and a Master of Science degree in Counseling, she wrote two nonfiction books to ensure affordable access to professional mental healthcare for everyone with:

Inner Awakenings: Navigating the Emotional Black Hole Inside and *Preparing for the Journey Home.*

While she writes nonfiction to support mental health healing and recovery, her passion is writing thrillers, suspense, and mysteries, or some combination thereof.

With a Criminal Justice Counseling Specialist Certificate of Advanced Study, knowledge officers and investigators shared with her, coupled with her years of education, training, and experience in mental health, *Filling in the Blanks* has many twists and turns that will keep readers guessing.

Keep an eye out for the sequel to *Filling in the Blanks*, entitled *Beating the Clock*, which is currently in the works.

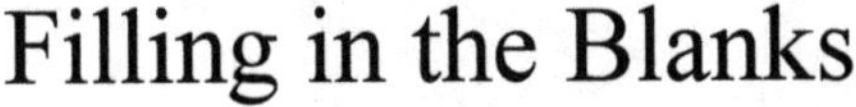

Filling in the Blanks

Kimber A. Harvey

Filling in the Blanks

Vanguard Press

VANGUARD PAPERBACK

A CIP catalogue record for this title is available from the British Library.

ISBN 978 1 83794 011 0

Vanguard Press is an imprint of
Pegasus Elliot Mackenzie Publishers Ltd.
www.pegasuspublishers.com

This is a work of fiction. Names, characters, businesses, places, events, and incidents are either the product of the author's imagination or used in a fictitious manner. Any resemblance to actual persons, living or dead, or actual events is purely coincidental.

First Published in 2024

Vanguard Press
Sheraton House Castle Park
Cambridge England

Printed & Bound in Great Britain

I'd like to dedicate this book to a precocious little girl who loved to read. But even though she was given every advantage, she lost her way, and is no longer here to enjoy her mother's first novel.

I want to acknowledge all peace officers and members of our armed forces who, with honor and integrity, readily put their lives on the line to keep us safe.

A special thanks to Sergeant Perry Speelman and Officers Brian White and David Miller with the Denver Police Department Metro SWAT/K9 Unit.

These men were not only diplomatic in sharing their knowledge but were also obliging in answering a plethora of questions, both in person and through email.

These officers, along with all the men and women who put their lives on the line to protect our way of life, will always have my gratitude for their fidelity in service and personal sacrifice.

CHAPTER ONE

The Danger Zone

Jason Maxwell Colt, aka Colt
April 2021

Jason Colt sucked in stinging breaths.

Each inhale like icy needles piercing the fleshy part of his bronchi, while every exhale expelled his body heat into the night in little white puffs.

The frigid air seemed thick enough to coat his lungs with frost, restricting their capacity to expand fully.

April was not the time of year for a middle-of-the-night run, particularly with patches of snow and ice still littering the ground.

With the tails of his jacket flapping wildly behind him, the light rain quickly penetrated his clothes. Shivering intermittently, he managed to keep going thanks to a reserve of adrenaline powering his energy. Intermittent shivers might have dropped him if not for the burning fever that alternated with the chills.

It was amazing how quiet the mile-high city could be. The din was just part of the city's music, but the racket that filled the city to engage the mind and congest the ears—was silent.

No horns were blaring from impatient drivers, no screeching sirens to demand the right of way, and no jackhammers to sing their deafening dah-dah-dah, dah-dah-dah, song. No enticing aromas from the various restaurants to lure diners or music that drifted its melody into the night from the dance clubs. No rowdy laughter was heard from the bars hours after the bartender shouted, last call! And no alarms set off by intruders shattered the night.

Even the popular LoDo District and Larimer Square areas had watched the last of their clientele retreat home. Only the winds were left to whistle through alleyways and playfully skip a Starbucks coffee cup along the curb on the empty street.

The quiet exposed him.

Without the city's racket to mask his feet pounding the pavement or the crunch of ice, he was an easy target. In situations like this, situational awareness and observation were as necessary for survival as the Glock 19s holstered on his hip.

It was late. He hadn't clocked out yet and would likely get an earful about unauthorized overtime from Billings when he returned to the station. But he would gladly risk pissing off the boss to find his partner.

Pushing on for what seemed like miles, he listened intently for any sign that he was still running in the right direction, aware that time was running out.

With muscles burning, his frustration mounted, knowing that the perp had gotten away from him and knowing that if he slowed his pace, he might be too late to save his partner.

Where the fuck are they?

After using his sleeve to wipe away the mist clouding his vision, a heaviness settled over him that interfered with the natural rhythm of his stride.

Before starting his shift, Jason had fought the urge to hit the snooze on his alarm. He was amazed that he'd slept more than twelve hours.

After a week in bed, he was sure he'd taken enough time to recover from the flu and was determined to go to work.

As the hot water soothed his body, he rested his forehead on his crossed forearms and allowed the high-pressure shower head to beat the soreness out of his deltoid muscles.

Jason had always been strong and healthy. On the rare occasion when he caught a cold, an over-the-counter medication usually was enough to keep him going.

But this time was different.

Without warning, the flu weakened him so much that he had to call out of work. Even though he didn't want to surrender, without energy, he couldn't fight. He couldn't remember ever being so sick for so long.

Unwilling to move from under the warm, pounding spray, his mind wandered. He remembered being late meeting up with the guys at their favorite pub the week before. When he walked into the bar, Dean and Kade were finishing their game of pool.

After pouring a glass of beer from the pitcher, he ended up sipping the same glass most of the night, never finishing it, which wasn't like him. Worse, he'd only taken a few bites of his favorite bacon cheeseburger, which meant that he'd already been infected days before.

But the following day, he woke up feeling woozy, surprised to find himself dripping sweat and lying on damp sheets.

He was unbearably hot despite kicking off the covers sometime during the night. When he got up to check the thermostat, he noticed weakness in his muscles. And before he'd reached the hallway, chills had begun to shudder through him, soon accompanied by other symptoms.

But once the flu hit, it clung to his body like static electricity and refused to let go, even after he spent a week in bed.

Though he'd gotten stronger, he could feel remnants of the flu hanging on. Pulling himself out of his reverie, he turned off the water and pushed himself through the rest of his routine, preparing for work.

Bypassing the heavier M&P 9mm luger Smith & Wesson and the Sig Sauer P-226, he grabbed the Glock 19s from the gun safe on his way out of the house.

At the substation, he took his time catching up with the team. Still a bit under the weather, Colt hoped for a calm shift as he went out on patrol.

Cruising by the surplus store, he looked for the small group of kids who had a habit of cutting class to loiter around local businesses.

To run wild until minutes before parents were expected home at the end of the day.

Sadly, truancy leads to higher dropout rates, teen pregnancy, drug abuse, petty theft, graffiti, vandalism, and gang recruitment. All of which had become a problem for working parents, businesses, and the city.

The Gang Reduction Initiative of Denver was developed to keep kids safe, drug-free, and out of gangs.

As a volunteer, Jason hoped to encourage the kids to enter the program before they became a statistic. But they weren't at their regular hangout behind the surplus store.

Hoping they were still in the area, he decided to walk through the park to see if they had changed locations.

Walking through Cheesman Park, Jason noticed a regular sleeping on one of the path benches. Curled up in a fetal position with his back to the world was John Marshall.

Touching his shoulder gently, Jason said softly, "John. Hey, John. It's late, and you should go home and warm up. Maybe get something to eat."

It didn't take much to check on his friend. But if John had tied one on, it would take him more than a few minutes to rouse himself.

While he waited, Jason scanned the park, hoping to see the kids parked at one of the picnic benches.

Having no luck, he looked at the trees, pleased to see that the branches no longer held a dusting of snow.

To Jason, the trees announced the change of seasons, from the wet, cold, and white winters to the warmer and much more colorful displays of spring, to the cooling shade provided by thickly leafed boughs in the heat of summer, to a kaleidoscope of colors with the chillier winds of fall.

He was looking forward to when the cottonwood, sugar maple, and thundercloud plum trees woke up from their winter slumber with buds ready to burst into leaves—followed by a showier display of the Catalpa's bloom of orchid-looking blossoms.

It seemed somewhat magical how the trees revealed, with their unique display of color, when spring had come and winter was ending.

Turning his attention back to his friend, Jason sighed. Even though it had been years since the sharpshooter had taught him how to use a weapon, it was hard to watch the strong Marine shrink into the old man on the bench.

A result of injuries that hadn't been sustained while he was a soldier at war, but by the loss of love.

Charles Adams, John Marshall, and Sam Albright had served with Jason's father overseas. The bond of friendship created during their deployment continued long after their discharge. Good men with honor, courage, and commitment were always faithful. Passing down the core values they believed to their children.

John was away at a conference when a faulty electrical wire in the garage caught fire in the middle of the night. Everyone inside the house, as well as the neighbors, were sound asleep when it started. It wasn't until the house was fully engulfed that anyone noticed. But by then, there was no way to save John's family.

John and Sally married right after high school. Their daughter Denise came much later in life and was lost to him at only fourteen.

John's mother had just moved in with them after her doctor recommended that she not be left alone. John, not wanting to put her in a nursing home, had just bought a larger house.

He blamed himself for the tragedy. He'd been the one to insist they buy a bigger house so his mother could move in but neglected to check the batteries in the smoke detectors before he left on his trip.

John had always been a genuine, caring man. But he changed after losing his wife, daughter, and mother in the fire. It was more pain than even the love of his closest friends couldn't help heal. No matter how hard they tried.

Unable to take his own life and take the chance of not meeting his family "someday on the other side." John started drinking. Most days until he passed out.

At that point, the group set up a trust to pay rent on a small guest house at the back of a property near the park and a tab at his favorite diner. It wasn't much, but it provided John protection from the elements and a way to feed himself. And since Jason worked close by, it wasn't that difficult to check on him.

Traffic was usually heavy at that hour. Honking horns and screeching brakes as cars jockeyed for position on the crowded streets. Most of them rush to be with loved ones after a hard day's work.

After the funerals, John had gone to the office but couldn't stay focused. Soon, he began drowning his pain in a bottle, unable to face life without the woman or the little girl that he had devoted his life to.

As the sun started its slow descent behind the mountain range, shadows blanketed the figure.

The scene became a contrast between the dark, silent figure on the bench and the high energy of downtown life.

With a gentle shake, Jason said, "Come on, John, you need to go home before you freeze. We're in for another cold one tonight. Maybe more snow if we can trust the weather forecast."

The only movement was the soft breeze playing with the tendrils of white hair peeking out of an old Broncos cap.

A knowing hit Jason hard enough to drive him to his knees. "John!" As he turned the man over and searched for a pulse, he realized that John's wish to join his family had been granted.

Pressing the key on his epaulet mic, he called the death into dispatch.

While waiting for the coroner, Jason looked to the Rocky Mountains that bordered Denver to the west. A spectacular sailor's sky filled with reds, pinks, and purple illuminated in an aura of gold that seemed to melt over and behind the majestic peaks as it followed the setting sun.

Bowing his head and feeling emotional, Jason whispered, "Sometimes life is just so damn unfair. I'm sorry that life was so unkind to you, old friend. I pray you'll be at peace now."

He watched as the sun inched its way below the horizon, dousing its flame below the horizon, leaving only darkness in its wake.

As the park lights sizzled on to cast a dim glow over the darkened form, the moon's glow took the sun's place in the sky.

Waiting to the side, he watched the team process the scene and package his friend for transport.

After giving his report to the coroner's office detective, he returned to the substation to write up his report.

Exhausted with several hours left before the end of his shift, he stood in front of his locker, staring as if in a daze. He was still contemplating how he should handle the situation when Jax walked in.

"Hey Jason, you okay?"

"Huh… um, yeah, fine."

"Well, you don't look fine. You look lost, staring into your locker like that. Are you sure you're okay?"

"Yeah. Just thinking about something."

"Well, I heard you were sick last week, and honestly, you still look like shit. Are you thinking of going home?"

It had already been a tough shift. And although Jason wasn't sure how he'd deliver the news— he wanted to be the one to tell Charles. It would be a blow no matter who delivered the news, but it might be a little easier coming from a caring friend.

But Jax had pretty much said exactly what he'd been considering.

The problem was that he was still struggling to wrap his head around John's loss and wasn't sure how to break the news to the man who'd been a second father to him.

Accepting that he needed more time, Jason decided to finish his shift. He thought it would be better if he delivered the news in person, when he had a clearer head, and preferably after a few hours of sleep.

Not wanting Jax to see his discomfort, he said, "Nah. I've been out for a week already, and I'm feeling better. It's about time for Stryker and me to get back to work."

"Okay. Well, hey, try to take it easy out there. No point in pushing it."

"Yeah, okay, thanks, Jax."

After taking another cold tablet to get through the rest of his shift, he got settled in the cruiser, and said, "Okay partner, we can go."

Parking in their usual spot near the closed Gas Mart, which had closed. They sat in the cruiser, checked license plates, and screened the area.

Jason wondered if there was ever a good way to tell a person they'd lost a friend. It was hard enough for him to understand why bad things happened to good people, even though he saw it all the time.

Jason decided to get out of the car and stretch his legs.

Walking up to the station, he checked the doors. Everything was locked tight. Using his flashlight, he searched inside—everything looked good there, too.

But when he heard a grunt and turned to his partner, he was given the signal.

Moving carefully down the side of the station, Jason remained vigilant. Recognizing the threat, he pulled his weapon. Just as he went for his cuffs to make an arrest, all hell broke loose.

Stryker took off after the first suspect moments before Jason was knocked to the ground.

Sweat ran into his eyes and blurred his vision.

His nose was running again, whether from the frigid air or because the cold meds weren't working. Whatever the reason, the buildup of snot made it difficult to breathe. His vest was overly tight, constricting his chest like a python, slowly crushing the life from him.

The tail of his wet jacket slapped loudly against him as he ran, indicating that he was moving fast. Yet, it felt like he was barely moving.

His limbs felt like they were loaded down with weights, draining what little energy he had left.

He flew past rows of brick and stone buildings lined the streets like sentinels—straining to hear any sounds that might lead him to his partner.

Shadows shifted into menacing shapes along the edges of his vision but vanished when he looked directly at them to dissolve into the crevices of the buildings.

A tingling sensation crawled up and down on nerve endings. A warning?

He froze for a moment and looked around. No. He was getting jumpy.

The more immediate concern was the problem with his radio.

The radio was top-of-the-line with radio encryption. The signal, within city parameters, was prime, yet there had been no response to his call: the only sound he'd heard since was the crackle of static.

The last echo of his partner had quieted, but Colt pushed himself toward the remnants of those last distant sounds.

Frustrated with himself for getting winded, he worried that the pounding in his head might impede his ability to hear essential signals in time to take necessary action or avoid potential dangers.

Questioning if he'd passed the mark, he slowed his pace.

His instincts had never failed him before, and he hoped they wouldn't let him down now. Admittedly, his senses, generally on high alert, were compromised.

He sensed the change as fatigue began to infiltrate his system.

Even the whistle and roar of the wind became a nefarious whisper meant to misdirect him.

The perp with the long black ponytail, the one with the gun, got away. Since he'd interrupted acquiring potentially profitable weapons, the perp might be seeking revenge, hiding somewhere, waiting for the right time to kill a cop.

Angry with himself for letting the perp get away and exhausted beyond reason, he listened for any clue as he committed the description to memory. The skinny jeans and brown hoodie under a black jacket that didn't hide the snake tattoo wrapped around his trigger finger that would help identify the guy later. Colt had gotten a quick glimpse of it when the guy was struggling with the crate.

Where the hell is my backup?

That's when he heard it.

A muffled sound reached him along with the wind that rushed past his ears, but in time to slam himself against a building.

A high-pitched barking, close by.

He gulped air to catch his breath and grabbed his mic to wheeze into it, "Denver 1…102K requests backup… Officer… on foot moving down M... need assistance… alley at 14th…. I repeat, Denver 102k needs assistance… now!"

But the only response to his call was static. Shit. What is going on!?

His only hope was if one of the officers covering him at the station had followed him.

He could have sworn his last call had been confirmed. *So, what happened? This whole shift has been nothing short of a cluster fuck!*

Echoes of barking reverberated from the alley, followed by the sound of something metal creaking that seemed to be coming from behind the building.

In the late 1800s, after a fire consumed most of Denver's downtown district, a brick ordinance was developed to prevent the whole city from being reduced to ashes. Many of those buildings remained part of Denver's vibrant cityscape.

He leaned his weight against the rough brick to evaluate the area, needing a tactical pause to catch his breath and assess the situation. The information gained through a man's observations could safely guide him through a minefield.

Moving toward the entrance opening, he peeked into the darkened cavity of the alley just as screams pierced the silent interlude. But just as quickly as it started, the screech, hiss, growling, and yowling of alley cats soon faded away into the night.

With a quickened heartbeat, Colt tried to ignore the tickling sensation that ran across his flesh, the hairs standing up on the back of his neck, and the warning dancing along every nerve fiber in his body.

While taking a few deep breaths to stop his empty stomach from heaving acids into his throat, a deep guttural vibrato echoed into the night from the alley entrance.

Using the sleeve of his jacket, Colt wiped sweat and snot from his face.

Then, using the shadows for cover against the building, he cautiously moved closer to the sounds in the alleyway.

At the entrance, with his Glock in hand, he peeked around the corner of the building into the void and realized that he'd be moving blindly until his eyes adjusted. But the perp had to be close. The barks were louder and more aggressive.

No high-pitched sirens or flashing colored lights fragmented the night; he was on his own.

With every muscle contracted in anticipation of warding off an attack, he squinted, pressuring his eyes to see into the darkened corridor. Then, I tried to concentrate on the growls and threatening barks that reverberated down the passage.

With one final glance around and sweating profusely, Colt took a deep breath, rubbed his eyes to clear them, and moved as fast as he dared into the dark opening.

After entering the wide, dark mouth, Colt quickly hugged the brick wall and moved further into the alley. It was darker than he'd expected, and his eyes hadn't adjusted.

Gusts of wind raced into the alley behind him and, while trapped between the buildings, surrounded him, snarling before rushing off in a chorus howl down the passageway.

With his heart racing, Colt whispered to himself, "Where the fuck is my backup?"

With his back and shoulder against the brick wall for cover, he moved into position at the precipice of the anteroom.

Turning the upper part of his body to peer into the opening, he did a quick sweep of the area for a position of advantage.

From what he could tell, the space was enclosed by three commercial buildings. It appeared wide and deep enough to hold a large commercial vehicle. At the far end between the two buildings to the east was a good-sized gap.

But without even the small sliver of moonlight that had hidden behind a dark cloud, the varying shades of pitch and shadow messed with his eyesight.

When the deep vibrato in the space grew louder, he repositioned himself behind the wall.

I must be getting close.

Before rushing in, Colt took a second look.

A weak light over the backdoor on the building to the left, along with the stars above, provided the only light—defused light.

The sliver of moon peaked around the building but couldn't penetrate the depth of the hole.

Two commercial dumpsters, a few pallets near the back door, and some unidentifiable debris scattered on the ground. But between the variegated shades in shadow, it was hard to confirm whether anyone besides the person on the dumpster was hiding in the space.

With his eyes better adjusted, he entered with his gun drawn and caught a glint off a chain-link fence pole located between the buildings.

It enclosed the space, leaving the perp only one way out.

The barking was so much louder in the enclosed space, magnified by an echo that bounced off the buildings.

With just enough light to see the perp's silhouette hiding behind the metal lid of the dumpster, which he was using as a shield against the dog. Colt quickly pointed his flashlight at him to see more clearly.

Sunken dark cavities peeked over the lid under a pasty furrowed white forehead, and above that was wavy orangey-red hair.

When the light hit the man's eyes, they were darting around the alcove like a trapped animal searching for escape. Logically, this had to be the other suspect. But for a moment, Colt was confused. He didn't remember seeing red hair at the scene.

"I give up! I give up!" the perp squealed.

Little drops of sweat ran down Colt's forehead into his eyes, the burn making them water.

Blinking several times to clear his vision, he kept his stance, refusing to take his eyes off the perp.

With hackles up, the dog growled and barked, unable to get on top of the dumpster with the lid up without falling into it. With each jump, the dog snapped at the perp, who was just out of reach behind the lid.

Colt was on edge. The guy with the ponytail and the gun was still a possible threat.

"Police freeze!" Colt ordered in a hoarse but demanding voice. "Any fast moves and my partner will attack. Do you understand?"

Lifting his head above the lid, the perp cried, "Okay, okay! Just keep that… crazy thing away from me!"

As he lifted his head, a long-pointed nose, beak-like in structure, was accentuated in the dim light of the alcove.

Sunken cheeks, accentuated by sharp cheekbones and dark pinhole craters left by atrophic scars, were a contrast to the pale face.

With a better glimpse of the guy, there was a split-second when the guy looked familiar, but Colt couldn't place him. "Stryker Aus! Stryker. Aus!"

Stryker stopped jumping, looked at his partner, and then went to sit beside him, panting happily.

Still trying to catch his breath, Colt held his weapon tightly in his sweaty hands, worried he might lose his grip.

"Okay. You can get up now."

Standing, the perp didn't look much taller than the lid he still held in front of his body. Estimating Colt figured somewhere between five-five and five-eight.

"Good. Now, slowly put that lid down," He ordered, "And don't let it slam."

The weight of the Glock was getting heavy.

The variegate shades of ash and coal shadows blended with the darkest obsidian recesses to conceal and distort everything.

He was straining his eyes, which gave him a headache. He couldn't help but flinch when the lid slammed into place.

Looking up quickly, the perp squealed, "I swear, I couldn't reach any farther!"

"That's all right. Just keep your hands where I can see them. And don't make any fast moves, or my dog will take you down."

"I swear, I won't move."

Even though he was grateful to have Stryker with him, he also knew his partner's limitations. Mainly because he couldn't shoot or drive a car.

And without backup, they were both severely compromised.

Keeping his eyes and gun trained on the perp, Colt moved his left hand to his mic. Just as he bent his head toward the mic and opened his mouth— he was hit with the power of a shot on the right side of his neck. The impact threw his body off-balance to the side.

His arms shot out from his body while he fought to keep his footing.

He missed the grin that spread across the perp's face or his partner's startled response. And he wasn't aware that when his right hand reflexively flew to protect his neck, he'd tossed both his gun and flashlight into the air.

He barely registered the penetrating sting until it turned into hot, burning knives shooting through his veins, exploding on impact with his brain.

Blinking to clear his undulating vision, he barely caught a glimpse of Stryker turning to snarl at someone behind them just as his knees buckled and he hit the ground.

It was strange how disconnected he was when his head hit the hard ground. The pain is delayed. Moments later, a stabbing pain penetrated his haze, making it hard not to feel the waves of aftershocks that tried to break open his skull.

Images, sensations, and sounds seemed disconnected. Too broken up to understand. Whispers echoed around him like phantoms, encouraging him to leave the chaos behind. Unable to move, Colt began to sink into the earth.

As his body dissolved into the ground, a rude tug on his shoulder forced him onto his back, which reawakened a succession of white-hot, rippling waves at the back of his head and down the side of his neck.

Moments later, something heavy and cold hit the palm of his hand.

Unintelligible voices spoke gibberish into his ear while a cobra wrapped around his hand and began to squeeze.

From an echo came a blast of sulfur burning his nostrils while, at the same time, a comforting warmth spread across the palm of his hand.

Too exhausted to fight the void trying to consume him, he no longer worried where the strength to fight had gone.

Just as he began to drift off, a sharp pain on the side of his neck pulled him back. An unfamiliar sensation, a suction, just before the side of his throat exploded.

Jason Colt watched his body float away without him.

It seemed like he was holding onto something but couldn't remember what it was or why he needed to hold on.

So, he let go.

Somewhere, an echo, like the slapping of running footsteps on pavement, bounced around in Jason's brain until there was nothing left but a deafening quiet.

CHAPTER TWO

The Meeting

Matthew Braxton Colt, aka Mac
November 2020

Heading home after an unusual day, Matthew Colt assessed the snow melting in patches on the road.

After the mild flurries predicted the week before turned into a significant snowstorm, an army of snowplows was commissioned to push the fluffy mounds into snowbanks on the sides of the highway.

Unfortunately, what hadn't been cleared or melted since then would hide the black ice—a possible metaphor for his situation.

Still filled with adrenalin after what he'd accomplished, he held onto the steering wheel tightly and tried to focus on the road while staccato images of what he'd achieved in the last few weeks played out in his mind's eye.

Before that first meeting at the Morales mansion, he had been looking forward to meeting the man behind the voice on the phone, even though he had found it hard to believe that the job was as big as the owner had claimed.

He never passed up the chance for a big job. A lesson he learned while working with his father. It was how his father retired young and had Matt take over his business.

The advertisement blazoned across his van and hat broadcasted COLT PLUMBING wherever he went. Bright white lettering made with PVC pipes and fittings set on a wavy blue background fooled the eye into seeing letters floating on water.

Matt considered it advertising genius, even if he said so himself.

Since then, he'd made a good living as a plumber. But in the last few years, he'd been too busy. After this last job, he planned to take time off and take Sofia on a dream vacation. The one they'd talked about for over two years. She deserved it, and if he were honest, so did he.

When he'd stepped from the van that sunny October afternoon, he had no idea what he was walking into. The home he'd been asked to provide a bid for turned out to be a mansion.

The immensity of the two-story monstrosity seemed misplaced in the rural setting.

Like an immense weed springing up in the garden of Eden.

Transported from a southern plantation, it starkly contrasted with its rugged surroundings.

Like most antebellum homes, it was based on Greek Revival architecture with thick columns and a square, symmetrical floor plan.

As Matt walked up the front steps, a small, over-dressed butler opened the front door and said, "My name is Henry; please follow me."

Without another word, Matt was led through a massive foyer with an ornate double staircase that snaked up opposing walls in a sweeping arch to a second-floor landing that connected them.

Intricately crafted iron ivy tendril balusters appeared to grow up and around the curved mahogany posts and handrails.

An overly large chandelier hung from the foyer's center. Thousands of stalactite crystals illuminated the mahogany handrails. Large canvas artwork was placed gallery style on the curved walls above the wide staircase.

They walked across Carrara marble floors inlaid with streams of gold.

A little intimidated since he had just come from a job and was in his work clothes, Matt covered his discomfort by saying, "You guys have a real nice place here."

The butler made no attempt to answer, just gave a curt nod, and continued through the foyer into a corridor.

Glancing into a room as they passed, Matt was surprised at how fancy everything was. Not that Matt knew anything about decorating, but he was sure that Sofia would say it was "too foo-foo."

The Parisian rugs picked up the gold streams in the marble as if weaved right out of the floor.

Matt had never seen anything like it.

Two matching hunter-green leather tufted sofas sat facing each other in front of the most ornately carved fireplace Matt had ever seen. Without realizing it, he'd stopped to stare at the room until the butler cleared his throat to indicate that Matt shouldn't loiter.

As luxurious as everything seemed, it seemed unlikely that the job was as big as his conversation with the owner had suggested.

The owner, Mr. Morales, asked to speak with Matt in person. He insisted that it was an urgent matter that required an experienced plumber.

Mr. Morales informed him that the last plumber had left the system barely operational and had not bothered to finish the job.

Several toilets had overflowed repeatedly, and he wanted the whole system evaluated, repaired, or upgraded immediately.

But so far, the house looked relatively new, maybe ten or fifteen years old, and well cared for, making the job they had discussed on the phone seem excessive.

The mousy butler hadn't said a word since he had given his name and asked Matt to follow him.

The corridor ended at a formal dining room big enough to double as a conference room.

In the center of the room was a large rectangular table surrounded by twelve richly upholstered chairs. The thick glass top was nestled in a rich mahogany bed that rested on a labyrinth of metal scrollwork easily noticeable through the clear glass.

A smaller version of the foyer chandelier hung from the recessed ceiling.

Rays of light poured into the room from the large picture window, refracting and bending the light through each crystal, casting a kaleidoscope of rainbow-colored prisms onto the walls and ceiling.

Most homeowners met Matt in more casual clothing. A few had even met him in PJs. But sitting at the head of that ornate table was a morbidly obese man in an expensive suit.

His almost cone-shaped shaved head looked too small for his round face, plump lips, and thick neck.

In front of Mr. Morales sat a set of rolled blueprints. His plump hand resting on them somewhat protectively. Tiny black eyes sunken into caverns of fleshy cheeks appraised Matt as Henry escorted him to his seat.

A strange sensation ran down Matt's back as he pulled out the chair and sat down. Feeling out of his depth and possibly underdressed by the homeowner's standards, *I just hope I put on some deodorant this morning.*

He worried that his clothes might soil the delicate fabric on the chair since he'd just finished replacing a water heater earlier that morning when he got the urgent call from Mr. Morales.

Mr. Morales's face lit briefly as it folded into a smile that deepened the creases around his eyes. "Please get comfortable, Mr. Colt. I have so much to go over with you… and time is of the essence."

Matt tried to calm his racing heart. He never got nervous with new clients, but it was evident that he was now; he just couldn't figure out why.

Pushing his discomfort away, he said, "You mentioned on the phone that this was a new system? Your home doesn't look that old, so I'm not sure why a new system is necessary."

With a flick of his hand, Mr. Morales dismissed the comment. "I just wanted an upgrade and was instead given a downgrade."

"Well, I'll need to know exactly what the plan was and how much work was completed. As I mentioned on the phone, time could be wasted trying to figure it out. So it would be helpful if I could contact the last plumber…"

The smile quickly disappeared from the owner's face, his tone deepened, and his accent thickened as he interrupted Matt. "…That's impossible. I do not want anything more to do with that business."

Surprised, his throat dry, Matt said, "Okay, well, the blueprints should help. Still, it would be best if you were prepared, Mr. Morales. There's a good chance we'll need to turn off the water for several days. Without consulting the previous plumber, the troubleshooting time will be extended."

As Matt reached for the blueprints, Mr. Morales placed his hand protectively over them and said, "First, I need to make something clear."

The smile had left his lips, and its absence had somehow darkened the man's eyes. "I hope you understand. So far, the only people who know the layout of this house or this compound, besides the staff, are the people who built it. I'm a very private man and wealthy enough to maintain my privacy and security. I'm sure this is a concept you are familiar with. I was informed that you have worked for other homeowners who appreciate confidentiality."

Matt felt that strange chill on his backside again. He knew that people with money could be a little paranoid, but he struggled to understand why the owner was so intense.

Matt smiled, hoping to put the homeowner at ease. "Of course, let me assure you that I would have no reason to share the layout of your home. I respect my customers' privacy and understand the need for security. I have spent years building my business, and my reputation is important. I have no reason to disclose anything about your home."

After a long silence, Mr. Morales remained quiet, so Matt continued, "I'm not sure what more I can say to put your mind at ease."

Mr. Morales sat quietly for several minutes while he appraised Matt. He already had a complete file on Matthew Braxton Colt, or Mac, as his friends called him. The private detective had given him a complete dossier on the man: where he grew up, his time in the service, his wife, Sofia, and son, Jason, who, it turned out, was a cop. He even had Matt's tax returns and a list of his recent customers.

But he wanted to meet the man in person. A file couldn't provide the true measure of a man – the scent of him. No, only a face-to-face meeting would do to incite his instincts and warn him of potential danger. He depended on them to guide him, and they were usually right.

"Do you share information with your family? I only ask because we all share things with those closest to us that we wouldn't think to share with others.

It's reasonable to assume that you might share information about your more… interesting clientele."

Matt knew that was true. He shared everything with Sofia. But he quickly decided it might be better if she didn't know much about this job. "Well, I can agree with that. But it's different with business. At least the way I work in my business.

"Don't get me wrong; I share most things with my wife – we don't keep secrets from each other, but I've never been a gossip, and in truth, my family isn't that interested in plumbing.

"Sofia does the books for our business, so she'll know that much. But at the end of the day, all she wants to know is how my day went and if I've input the hours and expenses for each job so she can keep up with the job cost reports.

"Look, Mr. Morales, the way I see it, I'm here to do a clean job and get paid. That's about the extent of it. If you need more than that, I might not be the right man for you."

Yes, Morales thought, *the information I was given is correct: Matthew Colt is work-driven. I think the pay will ensure his silence.*

Taking the rubber band off the roll, Morales began unrolling the blueprints. "Then I'll take you at your word. Let's go over the immediate problems, shall we?"

The blueprints clearly outlined the plumbing layout in the house and provided a diagram of the septic systems and leach fields.

Looking at the plans, Matt thought, those two systems for the main house should be more than sufficient to manage the sewage flow, especially in a house this new.

Having a game plan in mind, Matt said, "I doubt that your septic tanks need to be pumped, so I'll switch the leach field lines first, then troubleshoot the most obvious problems.

"If the problem is in the pipes, I'll open everything up and send a snake camera to check the interior of the pipes. Roots can crack and penetrate pipes, although that usually takes a few years."

But Mr. Morales wanted more than clean pipes. "That's fine for cleaning things up, but I have a list of things that I want fixed. As well as upgrade the whole system."

Matt checked the list: "I can see that. In addition to the repairs to the current systems, it looks like you want to replace the current water heaters with tankless heaters with circulating pumps in dedicated zones.

"Along with smart showers in the master and guest baths and chair-height smart toilets in all bathrooms.

"Have I missed anything?"

"Yes. I also want the pipes relined with epoxy to seal any leaks. For my garden, I'm adding a system to divert grey water from the laundry, showers, and sinks into a filtered storage container that has already been placed.

"You will need to connect that system to the drip lines in the garden. I'd also like a timer placed on it to create a watering schedule."

"Sounds like a good water conservation system," Matt said more to himself than the owner.

Then, to his host, "I'd like to look at some of the problems you spoke of on the phone and see where the last plumber was working before I prepare a proposal for you."

The chubby hand disappeared under the thickness of the table. Within seconds, the wiry man named Henry reappeared. "Please show Mr. Colt the problem areas in the house. I will be in the library for the next hour or so if I should be needed."

Then he looked at Matt. "I'm afraid this is where our meeting ends; Mr. Colt. Henry is a trusted employee. He knows more about these troublesome things than I do.

"As I told you on the phone, money is no object.

"Please let Henry know your findings and when you can begin. By the way, Mr. Colt, I'd prefer you to handle the job alone. I realize that might not be possible, but the fewer people who have the layout of my home, the better."

But before Matt could respond, he was escorted out of the room.

Matt knew he couldn't manage a job this size alone. Just the troubleshooting and repairs would require a team, but he'd write that into the proposal later.

He walked behind Henry through the house in silence.

As they passed through the kitchen, a plump woman, her bun of black hair held back by netting, was at the stove managing several dishes. The amount of food she was preparing indicated that more than one guest would be arriving soon.

Slowing his step, he inhaled the intoxicating fumes in the kitchen and watched the cook drizzle a silky white sauce over pasta in an elongated bowl. She created a divot in the center of the pasta and filled it with a thick layer of scallops simmering in an aromatic garlic sauce. She then spooned a bit more garlic sauce over the top.

She placed the bowl under a heat lamp and returned to the massive marble island, where she began working on an asparagus salad.

A toweled basket sat at the counter's edge, bulging with giant cheese bread rolls. He could see the bits of cheese in each one.

The aromas made his mouth water and his stomach rumble, and he couldn't help thinking, *It's too bad I wasn't invited to lunch.*

She didn't bother to look up as they walked through the kitchen, but Matt noticed a shift in her posture when Henry returned and indicated with a grunt that Matt should follow him.

The laundry area and servants' quarters were behind the kitchen.

Henry said, "Mr. Morales would like you to inspect the plumbing in all areas of the house. He wants nothing missed. The situation has proven to be very uncomfortable for all of us. And we need the house to run smoothly."

Matt spent an hour touring the house. He took notes of each problem and compared them to the pipe layout on the blueprints, added materials and equipment he might need to a sheet held securely on a clipboard.

The master suite encompassed the north wing on the first floor. It had a dedicated system, and it was huge. The bath was almost the same size as the bedroom and held every amenity available, including a sauna.

He would need to test everything, including the main pipes.

The second floor consisted of six bedrooms with an open loft library between them where the staircases met. Each bedroom offered a private guest bathroom.

Carrying the blueprints with him as they went, Matt tried to calculate what he might need for the job.

The house was enormous, but he couldn't make sense of it. The plumbing had different systems — different zones, so it was confusing that more than one system would have a problem.

The longer the tour, the more Matt understood just how big the job was if the several pages on his clipboard were any indication. This job would require his whole team and a few subcontractors for trades he wasn't licensed to perform.

Carrying his clipboard as he followed Henry, he swallowed hard to clear the frog in his throat. He didn't want to lose the job, but he needed to ensure Henry understood that he couldn't do the job without his team.

"Look, Henry, I'm afraid this job will be much more extensive than anyone can do alone. I know Mr. Morales is a private man, but based on what I've seen, I'll need my whole team—especially with the spec sheets Mr. Morales gave me for upgrades. I wouldn't even attempt a project of this size alone. Too many things could go wrong, and I can't be in two places at once.

"And from what I've seen so far… troubleshooting will be a bear. The problems… well, they just don't make sense. Two systems aren't even connected. Even if there was a problem with one, it couldn't affect the other. So, until I can figure that out, I'm not sure what to think.

"I hate to say it, but I'll have to bring in my team or advise you to find another plumber."

"It will be discussed with Mr. Morales. In the meantime, I'll show you the issues in the basement and the staff cabins. We've had to move a few men around due to the problems out there." Henry shook his head as he walked to the basement stairs. "It's not been good for morale."

The cabins were on yet another system separate from the main house. But from what he was shown, the repairs would be easier to resolve.

Once they'd gone through the cabins and garden, Henry escorted Matt to his van and said, "I'll need you to leave the plans with me. I'm sure you understand."

Shocked, "Um… okay, I guess. That's not how it usually works. I'll have to look them over again to ensure I haven't missed anything."

Matt opened the blueprints on the porch railing. He compared each room diagram against his notes to ensure he hadn't forgotten anything, then handed the plans back to Henry.

As Matt jumped into his van, Henry said, "Please email your proposal as soon as possible. Mr. Morales wants this done right away."

Just as Matt started the van, he saw an armed sentry in his review mirror move behind a tree and wondered what he was getting himself into. Some environments were controlling, and some pressed down on you with a weight so heavy and oppressive that it just felt that way.

Matt only knew that his energy had abated since entering the Morales estate. Consequently, he headed home instead of to his commercial building to finish the day. He needed to see Sofia.

Walking into the kitchen, Matt gave Sofia a quick squeeze from behind. She was cooking dinner and preoccupied when he kissed her on her neck. "I heard you come in; how'd it go?"

Matt wasn't sure he wanted to worry her with his concerns. Instead of answering, he hung his coat on the back of a kitchen chair in the nook and grabbed a beer. "You want a beer, hon?"

She smiled at him and said, "Sure, I'll have one with you."

At the small table for four, he watched her cook. It was like watching a conductor with a baton. With a flick of the wrist, she instructed spices to blend with meats and sauces.

Sofia had always moved with a natural grace, fluid and easy, even as she added ingredients, chopped and diced. Cooking was one of her favorite things to do, and she was a fantastic cook, even without a recipe.

Matt wondered if telling her about the job was a good idea.

Sofia had always been intuitive, but she might intuit his misgivings about the place if he started talking about it. She usually left all business decisions up to him, but if she heard about the sentry, all bets were off.

Colt Plumbing had always been profitable. Yet, it was rare when they could walk away from it for an extended vacation, even when his foreman, J.D., kept things going. So how could he pass up a big job that might give them that kind of breathing room?

Not to mention, it would end the year with a big bang. Put extra into the retirement account, give the boys a little Christmas bonus, take her on that trip to Hawaii, make the beginning of the following year less stressful.

Maybe even buy her the diamond stud earrings she'd admired the last time they'd gone to the mall.

I'd be a fool not to take it.

Matt rubbed his left temple, a gesture he was prone to do when getting a headache. Instead of sharing his worries, he said, "Hey, hon, you mind if we eat a little later? I have a big proposal I want to work on. Can you keep supper warm for me?"

She took a swig of her beer, smiled brightly, and winked. "Of course, just let me know when you're done." Then, with a little shimmy, "It's just beef stew, so it can s-t-e-e-e-w for a while. Nothin' that can't wait while you do your thang."

Matt went to her, turned her to him, wrapped his arms around her waist, and pressed her gently against the counter with his body.

Face to face, he said, "You keep lookin' and talkin' like that, sweetheart, and nothin's getting done, and no one's eatin' — grrrrrr!"

Wiggling his eyebrows only elicited more giggles.

Giving her a big kiss that ended in a dip, he went to his home office to work up the bids for Mr. Morales. He needed to be careful. It would be easy to lose money on a project of this size, and he wasn't about to let that happen. To protect the business, he included a clause for unexpected problems outside of his control and change orders requested by the owner. Then, he put the upgrades and the cabins on two separate bids.

He finished with a sentence in bold type and read it out loud: "This proposal is only an estimate and is subject to change."

Matt leaned back in his chair and propped his feet on the desk while he reviewed the tour of the Morales property in his mind.

The house was massive, but he was confident his crew could handle it. Still, there was something. Maybe it was something about the meeting - the compound… he couldn't put his finger on it, but it was something.

And whatever it was, it was bugging him.

He couldn't shake the feeling that something was… was what?

By the time he finished reviewing the proposal, his head was throbbing. Rummaging through his top drawer for the small bottle of Tylenol he kept there when his eye caught the leather journal Sofia had put in his stocking one year for Christmas.

She'd inscribed the inside page with a sweet sentiment, 'My dearest Matt, man of my heart, journaling is one of the truest forms of release. I hope you will use this small gift to organize your thoughts, plan our future, note romantic ideas, and honor that little rascal inside of you by documenting your humorous wit. You have so many wonderful qualities, and I love every one of them, Your Loving Sofia.'

Opening the journal, Matt began sketching what he'd remembered of the blueprints and what he'd seen of the compound.

He had a talent for sketching, and the truth was that drawing helped him relax.

Whether he wanted to admit it or not, something about the job made him tense, and staring at his sketches wasn't providing any answers.

After a few minor changes, he was satisfied with his drawings, but he thought they needed context.

Drawing was a whole lot easier than dealing with his emotions. He struggled with how best to describe his trepidation. It started when the door was opened before he'd had a chance to knock. But how do you describe uneasiness without evidence of a problem? People would probably think he was paranoid if he tried to explain it.

Questioning himself, he wondered how meeting a man for the first time could give him the heebie-jeebies. How would he even describe that sensation? What made the hairs on his arms and the back of his neck stand up?

He decided to note what he'd seen—the opulence of the place, the men, Henry, the armed sentry, and Mr. Morales.

Before he set his pencil down again, he noted, I just can't put my finger on it, but there's something about that place that's -?

Taking the Tylenol, he shrugged it off and thought, *Oh, for Pete's sake! I'm not planning on socializing with the man. We'll do the job and get out of there with a big fat check!*

Not wanting to worry Sofia if she found the journal while doing the bookkeeping, he pulled the third drawer out of his filing cabinet and set it on his desk. The drawer was heavy with the year's completed jobs. And it would be too much for her to bother with.

After placing the journal in a manila envelope, he duct-taped it to the interior back of the filing cabinet, replaced the drawer, and closed it. The journal was thin, but the extra bulk had made the drawer a little harder to close.

Sofia had been right about the journaling. It did feel good to get his thoughts out of his head and onto paper.

With his task completed and the Tylenol working, he was just about ready to eat. After a quick scan, he emailed everything to Mr. Morales and set off to enjoy a delicious dinner with his beautiful wife.

CHAPTER THREE

The Alley

Jason Colt
April 2021

Jason fought to reach the surface.

His heart boomed its objection.

An increase in lactic acids set his muscles on fire – a sequence precipitated by a lack of oxygen that caused his lungs to punish him with brutal, unforgiving spasms.

Refusing to heed the warnings, he kept his jaw clenched tight. To inhale meant accepting death, and that wasn't an option. He was determined to fight as long as he could, even as carbon dioxide grew like a parasite in his blood until it killed him.

With a Herculean strength of will aimed at his limbs, blind and drowning in mud, he concentrated on his unresponsive muscles until he felt a tingle, then a twinge. And with a surge of hope, he propelled toward a surface he couldn't see.

With his right arm straining to break the surface and his body stiff with tension, he opened his mouth and choked on his first breath.

Gasping and choking in gulps of frigid air, he was pulled into a dazed consciousness while electrical shocks ran through his nervous system. Disoriented, he opened his eyes and tried to sit up.

A thick soup of fog highlighted with a soft glow began to swirl. The movement made his head spin and his stomach churn until the sensation of falling forced him roughly back down. With labored breath, he remained as still as possible and waited for the spinning to stop.

The cold ground penetrated wet clothes while a stabbing pain threatened to split open his skull and expose his brain to the biting chill.

The residual smell of burnt cordite mixed into a toxic brew with urine and decaying garbage.

He became aware of a warmth dissipating in his right hand. From the weight and size, it had to be his Glock. That warmth meant that the weapon had been fired. But that didn't seem possible because he couldn't remember pulling the trigger. Then, another smell came to him that he couldn't readily identify.

He began taking deep breaths while he fought to remember what had happened, where he was, and why he was there.

As the fog cleared, he turned his head and saw a dark lump on the ground next to him. Unsure what it was, he closed his eyes tightly to clear his blurred vision. His heart dropped when he recognized that the lump was Stryker.

Letting the weapon fall from his weakened hand, he reached toward his partner, placing it on Stryker's side. He was rewarded when he felt for the slow rise and fall that would indicate life. Stryker was breathing.

As his mind cleared and his breath came more naturally, he felt his strength returning. With effort, he attempted to readjust himself. To move closer to Stryker.

"Bad idea," he groaned as a wave of dizziness forced him to stay still.

Movement made his head throb, and his stomach leapt into his throat with a small amount of its sour, acidic contents fouling his mouth.

Swallowing hard, he focused on breathing and tried to remember. As he relaxed, his vision cleared, and understanding hit.

He was still in the alley.

Keeping his movements small, he scanned the area around him. Between patches of impenetrable darkness, variations in the depths of shadow, and the smells, something provoked him. There was a menacing air to the place. Threatening. But he hadn't seen anyone. And even with limited movement, he should hear something.

Then, it reached him, an… underlying metallic odor that most cops knew all too well… blood.

His backside was almost numb. He was soaking wet and freezing cold but didn't think he'd been shot in the back. Running his hands over his torso, he didn't find any holes.

“Okay. So where’s it coming from?”

Slowly, Jason rolled onto his side and lifted himself onto an elbow for a better look, but everything was hazy.

His body felt incredibly heavy as he pushed himself up enough to sit on the ground. After rubbing his eyes to clear them, he tried to focus. Several feet away, there appeared to be a darker shape within the shadows lying against the side of the dumpster.

Thinking it might be someone he could send for help, but still a bit dizzy, he got on his hands and knees and crawled a little closer.

Still unable to tell what it was, he slowly moved in closer. Focused on the shape, he was startled when his hand slapped down into something wet and sticky.

He automatically pulled his hand from the puddle; what the…!

He wiped the slime onto his pants.

He looked at the dark form and understood that it was a body.

Sidestepping the puddle, he moved closer. The body was in an unnatural position against the dumpster. Like a rag doll tossed negligently from a bed to the floor. The body twisted strangely.

His heart tripled in rhythm as he attempted to find a pulse while choking down the bile that had climbed up his throat when no pulse was found.

Although his eyes were already accustomed to the darkness, the dark sockets made the face appear skeletal as they stared back at him from that perverse, upside-down position.

The neck was bent, the head turned as if looking at him from the ground.

The lower part of the body was elevated above the head, held in place by the dumpster. One leg had fallen at an odd angle toward the head, with the toe of the Air Jordan shoe almost touching the forehead.

The arms reached out from the body in opposite directions. One straight above the head, the other down and slightly tucked under the side of the body.

When he realized the body was actually the suspect, he quickly backed away from the corpse and sat on his heels, trying to comprehend what had happened.

“Jesus! What the hell happened?”

Stryker began to whine from behind him and tried to stand with a yelp. Like Jason, any movement caused Stryker pain.

Looking back at his partner, Jason said, “It’s okay, buddy, just be still for a minute. Trust me, don’t push it – or it’ll hurt way worse.”

Confused, Jason briefly wondered why Stryker seemed to be hurting in the same way he had. Without an answer, he returned his attention to the body, hoping to remember something. Only nothing came to mind. His memory was blank.

He tried his mic but only heard static. Feeling defeated, he wondered softly, “Even if my calls go through, how do I explain this?”

Hearing his partner moving with a whimper, he turned and asked, “Stryker, you all right, buddy?” Crawling toward Stryker. “I know it hurts, but don’t worry, I’m here; I’ll help.”

As he moved toward his partner, Stryker crawled on his belly toward him. With his ears flattened against his head and panting between groans and whimpers, he hadn’t gotten far by the time Jason reached him. Patting Stryker on the head, Jason pushed his hand underneath Stryker’s vest and buried his fingers in the thick winter coat, checking for injuries. Placing Stryker’s head in his lap, he rubbed his ears to soothe him and tried to recall the protocols for similar situations.

His radio wasn’t working, so he couldn’t call for backup, and he couldn’t leave a crime scene unattended. *So now what?*

He must have been knocked out, only he didn’t remember hearing or seeing anyone besides the perp. The one with the ponytail must have snuck up behind him while he was distracted.

When he woke up, he’d been hurting all over. It had been hard to tell the locations of any injuries.

The back of his head was throbbing. It eased when he sat still. The matted hair made it hard to tell how deep the cut was or if his skull was cracked. But the pain started at the back and radiated through his head.

He’d obviously been hit in the head from behind, but the pain on the side of his neck didn’t make sense.

Using just the tips of his fingers to explore it, he noticed a bump about the size of a walnut. Firm, hard, angry. Even the gentlest touch made it throb.

To forget about it, he focused on trying to remember what had happened. Even a small amount of information might help him explain it to Sergeant Billings.

An image popped into mind when the beam of his flashlight hit the perp's red hair. He kept it in his left side pocket, which reminded him that his cell phone was in the side pocket.

Shoving his hand into the pocket, he found it empty. *Damn!*

Disappointed but determined, he quickly searched his remaining pockets.

Empty.

With his phone and flashlight missing but still a bit shaky, he tried to search the alcove. A dead end that allowed the winds to gather abandoned garbage against the buildings.

The north building had been the JC Penny warehouse until they moved locations and abandoned it.

The building to the west had a door with a light over it.

A row of empty wooden pallets stood against the east building, which belonged to an import/export warehouse.

He scanned the alley again, hoping to find a clue, but the depth of shadows provided shelter for cockroaches.

As the ringing in his ears subsided, a siren filled the night just as a cruiser entered the narrow mouth of the alley.

Jack Hanson turned off the siren and parked. The cruiser's bright headlights were blinding. Colt looked away but gestured for him to hurry.

He seemed unsteady on his feet – drunk. His hair was sticking up, and his uniform was a mess.

Leaving the lights on, Hanson used the car radio to call in their location and went to meet Colt in the alcove.

"What the hell happened to you? You look like hell?"

Colt waved him over, knowing the narrow entrance would make it hard to see the body. As Hanson came closer, Colt pointed at the body and said, "Honestly, I don't know."

Hanson blinked at the body, then looked at Colt and whistled. "Jesus. Who is that guy? Is he dead?"

"Yeah. But he didn't used to be. And I have no idea what happened or who he is." Colt just shrugged. "At first, I thought I recognized him, but I can't place him."

Hanson put his hand on Colt's arm and asked, "Are you all right? I'm serious. You don't look so good. Shit, Colt, have you been drinking?"

"Nah, but I think someone used my head for batting practice."

Hanson pulled his flashlight and passed it over Colt, then kept it on his face. "Hey, you mind? You're blinding me, and my head already feels like it's about to explode."

"Just taking inventory." Hanson checked the body for a pulse, then moved away to search the area around the body.

He didn't see a weapon on the guy or anywhere near the body.

Colt tried to clear his head, "Jax, I swear I have no idea what happened!"

Hanson looked at Colt and shook his head. "Damn, I hardly recognize you. You're a mess! Your hair's sticking up in places, especially at the back. Your gear is missing, and your uniform looks wet. And what the fuck is that on your pants?

"Looks gross, dude. A mix of something. And is that blood on your pants? Do me a favor: step back, take a pace – maybe two. You smell like you took a bath in urine!"

Without waiting for Colt to move, Hanson took a few steps away, "Did you call it in?"

"Huh? Oh, yeah. But no. Trust me, I've tried. Something's wrong with my radio, just static. But didn't you hear me? Isn't that why you're here."

"No, I was out on patrol getting ready to clock out when I got the call that everyone was looking for you.

"I heard something went down behind the Chevron, and you took off after a perp. No one's heard anything since, so Billings has everyone out looking for you.

"I was driving past and thought I'd check out this alley when I spotted you."

Hanson clicked his mic and called it in again. "Hey dispatch, what's up? This is Officer Jack Hanson. I found Colt. What's taking so long?

We're in the alley behind the old J.C. Penny warehouse. Call the sarge, the ME, and the forensics team, too. And I do mean A-SAP!

"We have a DB here." After he got confirmation, he said, "Okay, Colt, the team should be here soon. Before they get here, you might want to hand me your gun. We don't want a newbie to get excited.

"You know that Protocol requires securing an officer's weapon immediately after it's been fired. Both for his protection and the protection of the public's."

Colt reached for his gun, but it wasn't in the holster. "It's not here! Shit."

"Okay, don't freak out. Let's look around; I'm sure we can find it."

"You don't understand! I've been trying to find my flashlight and my phone, but somehow I've lost everything!

Moving back toward where Stryker sat watching them, Colt saw his gun lying on the ground. "Oh, good. It's over here!"

Rushing to pick it up, Hanson said, "Well, don't touch it for fuck's sake! I'll take it. Where's your flashlight? Do you remember if you dropped it?"

"Not sure, but it's got to be around here somewhere."

"Look, when the sarge gets here, I wouldn't say too much if I were you. There's a dead man over there, and if your gun's been fired… well, it doesn't look good. So be careful what you say. Wait until the debriefing and until your rep shows and…"

Before Jack could finish, two cars pulled up behind his cruiser, and four officers were quick to move into the alcove.

Without thinking, Colt touched the sore spot on his neck and grimaced. Not much he could say, but "Okay… thanks, Jax."

As more officers arrived, the work of securing the scene began. After what he'd been through and the added activity surrounding him, Stryker was getting agitated. A deep growl rumbled through the alley. Standing by Colt, his legs trembled a little, but his growls deepened.

"Stryker, Nyet!" Colt scolded, grabbing Stryker's collar. "It's okay, boy, settle down, it's okay."

Colt reached into the big pocket for a leash, but his hand came away empty. Something else that got away from him.

Just as he let go of Stryker's collar to look around and search through his jacket pockets, a rookie got into Colt's face and started talking trash. "Looks like you got one of 'em, huh? One less creep for us to track down and book, huh?"

Stryker pounced. Already agitated and in pain, he was primed. Colt grabbed for him, yelling for him to stop. But Stryker wasn't listening, and Colt's timing was off, which gave Stryker enough time to attack the rookie before Colt could intervene.

Still impossibly weak, it took everything he had to pull Stryker off the rookie.

Colt's hand got in between the two, and he was bitten a few times before he was able to get his partner under control.

From several feet away, Christopher Grayson screamed, "Keep that stupid dog away from me!"

Still agitated but more controlled, Stryker turned on Hanson, who jumped out of reach to avoid one last snap of canine jaws.

Holding tight to Stryker's vest, Colt barked at the rookie, "What's wrong with you? Don't you know that you never walk up on a handler like that in front of his K-9? Especially when he's been primed at a crime scene. What's wrong with you?"

Even in his compromised state, Colt noticed several hands move to the butts of weapons. Most officers wouldn't dare shoot one of the department's K-9s. Like them, Stryker had a badge and was an important part of the team. But Stryker had attacked one of them, which had put all of them on guard.

Before Grayson responded, his Field Training Officer grabbed him.

The rookie had already been written up for reckless behavior—it was his last warning. One more, he'd fail his training and would be officially terminated from the department.

It would be a bit more complicated to fire him since he'd been injured while on duty.

Frustrated with the situation and his charge, the FTO said, "Jesus, Grayson, when will you learn not to step in it?! Come on, I'll take you to the hospital, but just get a clue already – will you?"

As Grayson limped to the cruiser, a few began mocking him.

The rookie had trouble making friends, and he wasn't much liked. But their sneers only inflamed Grayson, "You think this is funny? Well, I think it's funny that none of you cowards stepped in to help."

Tugging, dragging, and pushing with a hand full of his coat, his FTO interrupted, "Just shut your trap and move your ass into the shop before something else happens — like you getting your ass kicked."

The reprimand only elicited louder laughter.

Sergeant Grant Billings arrived just after Grayson had been bitten and was irritated to find that his crime scene had been compromised.

As the ranking officer on the scene, he was responsible for anything that happened once his people showed up. Not only were there way too many cops milling around, but now one of their own was leaking blood everywhere.

Raising his voice enough so that everyone would pay attention, Billings said, "Anyone just standing around needs to leave. We don't need this many people here.

"Cruise the surrounding area and look for witnesses, but don't come back; just put what you find in your report or call the Watch Commander.

Grant Billings was a retired Navy captain. He was used to giving orders. However, he'd been up all night contacting the military about the artillery his officers had confiscated behind the gas station.

Then, instead of going home to bed, he had to send teams out to find his missing officer. Worse yet, he still hadn't found a decent cup of coffee.

He really wasn't in the mood to babysit at the moment.

"Those of you actually doing something, finish what you're doing and secure the area."

Pointing at two officers who had arrived right after Hanson and were still holding crime scene tape, "I want you boys to secure the scene at both ends of the alley.

"We don't need that tape here. No one could have come into this area without coming down that alley first.

"I want one of you to stand watch at each end of that alley. Make sure the media has a wide birth – no cameras… period! And for God's sake, don't say anything to them.

"No one comes in or out of this area but the forensics team. Is that understood? I don't need any more people fucking up my crime scene!"

As the officers dispersed, Billings turned to Jason. "Officer Colt, control your canine before someone else gets bit and hand over your weapon!" His tone had deepened with his agitation.

Hanson intervened. "Hey, Sarge, I've already confiscated Colt's weapon. I can check it in as soon as I return to the station."

"Not necessary. I know you only stayed on to help look for him, but you can go clock out. I'll take it from here. I need to wait for… hmm, I guess he's already here. Good. Detective Jacobs will take the gun once he's done reviewing the scene. Then you can go home."

Colt was struggling to keep his thoughts straight. Between the pounding in his head and his threatening stomach, he ached to go home. But Stryker needed to be taken to the kennel before he bit anyone else. It was proving difficult to hold onto Stryker's ballistics vest when he kept jumping at people, especially since Colt was losing strength.

Billings had been with the K-9 unit long before Colt had joined the department.

He was an expert handler and would understand Stryker's agitation. "Hey, Sarge, Stryker's really been through hell tonight, and he's kind of unpredictable right now. I can't find his lead, and before anything else happens, he needs to be secured."

"Hanson, do you have a lead, maybe a muzzle in your shop?"

"Yeah."

"Give it to Colt so he can restrain Stryker, then take Stryker back to the kennel. Jesus, Colt, what the hell happened to your lead?"

Billings rubbed his temple; a headache was breaking through. Frustrated as he looked around the cluttered alcove, he said, "I'll tell the team to look; maybe they'll find it here somewhere."

As Jack came back and handed the lead and muzzle to Colt, Stryker snarled at Jack. The growl grew into a deep-throated rattle. A rumbling like far-off thunder as his hackles rose.

"Nyet! No, Stryker." Grabbing the handle on his partner's vest, Colt attached the lead to Stryker's collar and pulled up hard. "Sitzen!" With a heavy heart, Colt put the muzzle on his partner.

Hanson watched Colt put the muzzle on Stryker. Colt looked defeated and sad when he handed his partner over.

Sergeant Billings said, "Take Stryker to the department kennel and tell Jennings I want him examined as soon as possible."

Stryker fought the leash as he was pulled down the alley and pushed into the cruiser.

His aggression, especially toward Hanson, was out of character because he'd been part of Stryker's training since he was a pup.

As he watched Stryker, Colt felt his gut clench.

"Okay, Colt, we've secured the scene. Can you think of anywhere else we should secure?"

"Just the area behind the Chevron station."

"Yeah, I got that.

"Do you realize how long we've been looking for you?

"You were on foot. When we didn't hear from you… we had no way to track you. All we knew at that point was that you were chasing a perp – no way to know if you were down.

"So what happened? I mean, after you took off?"

Colt tried to unscramble his thoughts. "There were two guys moving crates. It looked military, so I called for backup, pulled my piece, and identified myself -- told them to drop it.

"I reached for my cuffs when backup arrived. That's when the hooded guy took off. I sent Stryker after him and went to cuff the other one. But before I got my cuffs out, he charged me, knocked me down, and took off. I went after him and yelled to my backup to secure the scene.

"But within a few blocks, I lost him.

"I'm not sure where – maybe somewhere around Walnut. I looked, but he had disappeared.

"Anyway, after I lost him, I headed in the direction of Stryker barks.

"It took a minute to get why down here, but I found him holding the DB over there. Colt gestured in the direction of the corpse. "The guy was on top of the dumpster, holding the metal lid like a shield. Stryker couldn't get to him."

"I pull my piece and call Stryker out. But when I click my mic to call it in – I'm hit. The last thing I remember was queuing my mic."

Subconsciously, Colt touched the sore spot on the back of his head, "I must have gotten hit from behind cause I didn't see anyone else around."

"Okay, so why didn't you call it - then!"

"I did, Sarge, but all I got was static. I needed to find Stryker before one of those guys shot him. I swear, boss, I tried calling in – a few times!"

"Okay… we'll talk more about the radio later. Then what?"

"When I woke up, I couldn't breathe. It was like I was drowning. My head was pounding, and it felt like my arms had weights on them. I was barely able to move, so I just stayed put, trying to pull myself together. It took a while even to remember where I was.

"When my vision cleared a bit, I looked around and found Stryker next to me. He was down — out cold. At first, I thought he was dead, but then I felt him breathing. It was weird cause he struggled to come around just like I did.

"That's about when I saw something by the dumpster and found the guy DRT. I checked for a pulse, but he was PNB. But he was alive and breathing last I saw him."

"I can't say what happened to the guy, but I did try to call dispatch – it just didn't go through. It did work at the station. But something must have happened when I went after those guys because nothing worked after that."

Rubbing his stomach, "It's been a weird... actually, sarge, weird stuff has been happening all shift."

"What? What's been happening?"

"Well, first, I find John Marshall dead in the park. He was a good family friend before he lost his family. Finding him like that hit pretty hard.

"Then I see those guys behind the station with WMDs. I mean, shit, sarge, how often does that happen? And, like I said, the problems with my com.

"Then I get knocked out and find that perp down with no clue what the hell happened to him. Can't think of another word for it – not an everyday occurrence, that's for sure."

"Sounds like a rough night.

"The part I don't get is the part about your coms not working. The com range is excellent within the city limits… so it isn't sitting right with me.

"No one has heard from you since the gas station. So when did you call it in?"

He pressed his palm against the side of his head. “I know. I mean, a few times… I never had a problem with my radio before, but…”

Colt couldn’t finish. The tumbling in his stomach finally blew up into his throat and exploded out of his mouth, just missing Billings’ boots.

“Shit. Okay. You’re just making a mess here. We’ll talk more once we get you checked out. Maybe the doctor can figure out why you blacked out. But I gotta say, Colt, you look like shit, and this whole thing smells bad.”

Just then, Detective Jacobs arrived.

CHAPTER FOUR

Chicanery

Becca Ellawyn Kennedy
January 2021

Becca relaxed, enveloped in her overstuffed floral watercolor print chair with green gingham trim, staring through the large picture window in the living room.

The majestic Rockies surrounded the front of her property, and she enjoyed relaxing while admiring their splendor.

They soothed her mind and made it easier for her to think through her troubles.

She'd positioned herself one county away from her target. In her mind, she was on a covert mission and had to stay under the radar if she hoped to keep the lifestyle she'd created.

The morning was bright, crisp, and clean after the storm that had threatened to enter the house the night before. She woke to fresh snow covering the floor of her twelve-acre property and clinging to the boughs of the quaking aspen and lodgepole pines.

The landscape was magical — a true winter wonderland. The scene's tranquility reminded Becca of one of her favorite family vacations. They'd all gotten lost in the pure magic of the place.

Snuggling down into the comfy cushion under the colorful Afghan she'd made herself, she took another sip of the dark hot chocolate with marshmallows.

The warmth of the fire and the quiet morning were just what she needed. This morning, she was determined to relax and enjoy the magic of watching what was on the other side of the glass.

From the first time she was asked what she wanted to be when she grew up, Becca knew she wanted to help animals. Even as a baby, she had been drawn to animals.

Her mother often repeated the story of the first time she'd found Becca with animals.

Arianna was visiting a friend. Becca and Joss had fallen asleep in the car. So, Arianna put down a blanket on the living room floor and let the twins sleep while she and her friend continued their conversation in the kitchen.

But when Arianna went to check on them, Becca wasn't on the blanket. Arianna searched the room, but when she couldn't find Becca, she started to panic, worried her daughter had been kidnapped.

Soon, both Arianna and Josie were racing through the house.

It was a comfortable summer day, and they'd left the front door open to enjoy a warm breeze through the screen.

Fearing the worst, Arianna ran and flew open the screen door. But just as she was about to race outside, out of the corner of her eye, a movement caught her attention.

Becca could almost hear her mother say, "And there, hidden behind this large recliner in the very corner of the room, was my little rascal sleeping peacefully with her little arm lying on a low-rimmed cardboard box.

"I didn't realize that she could crawl that far.

"When I went to get her, inside the box was a litter of kittens nursing while their mother cleaned them.

"It was just so precious, and I will never forget it."

Becca worked hard to achieve her dream of opening a veterinary practice and acquiring a home she could decorate, just like she used to talk about with her mother.

In order to make her dreams come true, she saved her allowance and money she earned from part-time jobs while in school and persevered through years of education.

The only time she put her dreams on hold was to help out when her mother was sick.

Becca's first memory of healing was when she was eight. She'd found a bird with a hurt wing flapping around on their front lawn. After weeks of tending to the poor thing, she was overjoyed when it was able to fly away.

That experience had been so rewarding that she often brought home strays or helped friends care for sick animals.

She still experienced that same sense of wonder and joy each time she was able to save one of her patients. Being a caregiver was one of the qualities she liked most about herself.

Keeping her mind focused on new techniques and experiences of healing distracted her enough to keep her mind from boarding a runaway train of thought that many times took her down a very dark and lonely road.

When her mother was diagnosed with breast cancer just after Becca's fifteenth birthday, Becca was the one who took care of her. Their father had to work, and Joss had to focus on getting caught up with her schoolwork.

With her learner's permit, Becca was able to drive her mother to her appointments, fix the family meals, and look after her younger brother, Garrett. She even did the grocery shopping and became a crutch when her mother was too weak to walk on her own.

Becca didn't regret any of it because her mother lived another seven years before her body succumbed to the disease.

Becca looked around at the beauty of the newly painted and furnished room. She'd decorated it herself, and she had to admit, it turned out amazing—better than she'd hoped.

A combination office library across the wide hall complimented it nicely.

Since adolescence, she'd dreamed of a place like this.

Decorating was something she shared with her mother, who was an interior designer.

While her mother was confined to bedrest, Becca would sit on the bed, and they would talk about remodeling and decorating until her mother became too tired to continue. While her mother slept, Becca would cut out the pictures from magazines that her mother liked and glue them onto construction paper. Then, she put them into a binder to share with her when her mother woke up.

While away at college, Becca continued the ritual. She spent most of her time alone while her roommates were out partying.

For Becca, school wasn't about partying or popularity, even though she was pretty enough with her long brown hair with natural auburn highlights, dark blue-green eyes, and long legs.

But partying and hanging out with the guys on campus just wasn't her scene. For Becca, studying was her priority. After hours of hitting the books, she'd spend her time searching for the perfect accent piece or the best paint colors that she could share with her mother when she went home for the holidays. For her, that was much more fulfilling.

In fact, she still had the four-inch binder filled with decorating ideas. That scrapbook was Becca's way of staying connected to her mother.

As she viewed the room, she wished her mother could see it. She loved the colors of teal, tan, blue, and green in the tiles that surrounded the fireplace face, which matched perfectly with the pops of color in the overstuffed two-toned velvet sofa.

Velvet was the perfect fabric for a home with animals because of its tight weave.

The back and sides were upholstered in a large floral watercolor pattern in shades of green, blue, maroon, tan, and teal. The cushions were made in eye-catching solid hunter-green embossed velvet—a striking combination that made the sofa a real statement piece.

Built-in bookcases on each side of the gas fireplace held pictures and mementos.

Becca picked up one of the frames sitting on the shelf closest to her. It held the last picture she'd taken with her mom and Joss.

Becca stared at the images of the two women she loved most in the world, and a tear fell down her cheek.

Tears stung as she remembered that special summer day during their three-week family vacation in Italy—a time when she and Joss had their mother all to themselves.

Their father and Garrett had left early that morning to go fishing, leaving Becca and Joss to spend a girl's day with their mother. Getting pampered at the hotel spa and honoring Arianna's new hair growth, the girls surprised their mother at the salon with matching hairstyles. After lunch, they went shopping at the chic boutiques in Piazza dei Mulini, where they found matching sundresses and sandals.

When the family met up late that afternoon at a café near the beach, their father asked a waitress to take a few family photos. Then, he insisted they go onto the beach so he could play cameraman while Joss, Becca, and Arianna playfully posed like models on a runway.

Holding the picture, Becca reflected on how playful and young they all looked -- especially her mom. In it, they were giggling and hanging onto one another like schoolgirls. The dark circles had disappeared from under Arianna's eyes, and her flirtatious smile was contagious.

So bright and full of life.

Memories flooded back like mini-movies featuring each special moment of their vacation: holding hands as they walked into the sea on the Amalfi Coast, the beauty of the Sistine Chapel that took their breath away in Vatican City, and the gondola tour of Venice.

They'd filled each day with adventure, fun, and laughter, and she had an album full of memories, which was all she had left of those remarkable women.

However, the one she held was one of her favorites. It had been taken just a year and a half before the cancer had stolen Arianna from them during Christmas break.

Joss had just been accepted at the Auguste Escoffier School of Culinary Arts - after studying abroad. And Becca had just finished a rewarding semester at U.C. Davis.

No one could have asked for a more loving parent. Arianna always made sure she was available for her children even after working a long day. She was proud of her children and enjoyed sharing in their interests.

She encouraged their passions and dreams: Joss, with her gourmet cooking and ability to sew just about anything; Becca, with decorating and her love of animals; and Garrett, with his love of science and sports.

Young and playful, having had the girls when she was only nineteen and Garret before she turned twenty-four, she made sure that there was always something to keep them busy on the weekends.

Arianna made everything an adventure.

She thought it was important to teach her children that learning could also be fun.

Whether hiking in the mountains with sketch pads to draw the landscape, filling their pockets with colorful little rocks they picked out of creek beds, sunbathing or napping under the shade of a tree, or enjoying the treats they'd baked the night before after eating a picnic lunch, rock climbing, putt-putt golf, bowling or going for a swim at Sloan Lake. Arianna did her best to teach them something on every excursions.

And at home, they'd tend their family garden and harvest what they'd grown for dinner.

Becca still had the jar of colorful rocks they'd gathered during their adventures prominently displayed on one of the bookshelves.

The emotional pain hit too hard to keep under control when she got lost in the memories.

Becca had come home early for the holidays. Her parents and Garrett had put up most of the Christmas decorations after Thanksgiving but had waited for the twins to come home from college to find the perfect tree to decorate as a family.

Christmas was always two weeks of family fun.

A special time that Brendan and Arianna Kennedy set aside just for family. It was one tradition that they'd practiced every year.

It was a magical time filled with ice skating, skiing, playing in the snow, watching Christmas movies, decorating the tree, playing games, and baking tons of cookies for neighbors and friends. And at night, Mom's special hot cocoa with Dad telling stories by the fire.

But they all agreed that their favorite game during the holidays was Undercover Mission, a unique game invented by Arianna and Brendan to teach the kids the importance of giving.

The kids were each given credit cards with a set spending limit for their holiday purchases.

The object of the game was to keep all purchases hidden while spying on the other players. Once deduced, each player wrote down the gift and the person it was for on Christmas cards they sealed in an envelope and put on the tree. The cards were opened after presents and stockings on Christmas morning.

All gifts were secretly wrapped and hidden until Christmas Eve, when they were put under the tree.

Just before bedtime, they each opened one gift before sitting around the fire with cocoa to listen to Dad read *The Night Before Christmas*.

On Christmas morning, the detective who made the most presents correct matches of gift and recipient had the power to choose the family vacation the following year from a preselected list.

Those were some of Becca's favorite family memories.

But that Christmas, while playing Undercover Mission at the mall, Arianna fainted and was rushed to the hospital. The cancer had returned with a vengeance, and the doctors had no time to save her. It didn't seem possible, but three days after Christmas, their mother was gone.

Arianna had made arrangements for her funeral when she was first diagnosed with cancer, so everything was taken care of, leaving nothing for them to do but grieve her loss.

After the funeral, their father disappeared into his work. He never said, but Becca knew that the intensity of his grief made it difficult for him to be around them. The twins looked so much like their mother that it had to be hard for him to look at them without thinking of the love of his life.

Brendan fell in love with Arianna the first time they met and had been devoted to her ever since.

He often told their kids that she was made just for him.

When the semester started after the holidays, Becca returned to school and let her schoolwork consume her.

It was only a few short years later that Joss was gone, too.

Looking through the picture window, Becca swallowed her grief and allowed anger to replace it. It had been bad enough losing her mother, but it was the injustice of how it was handled that made her crazy.

Anger, any anger, was better than the intensity of pain triggered by the emptiness and loss of the two most important women in her life.

When angry, she had the strength to keep moving, to fight and keep the pain at bay.

But when she gave into the grief even for a minute, the emptiness overwhelmed her. Sapped her strength, and making her lose hope of avenging Joss.

Radar and Scout bounded into the room after romping in the snow. Thankfully, the thick mat in the laundry room covered a large enough area that most of the dirt on their wet paws was left on the mat.

With their big doggie grins and wagging tails, they pushed at her hands with cold, wet noses, competing for her attention. And they always seemed to know when she needed to smile.

"You guys are just way too cute for your own good."

They were like a magical tonic that easily changed her mood and interrupted her negative thoughts.

Closing her eyes, she took three slow, deep breaths like the therapist had shown her.

Feeling better, she said, "Okay, okay. You want my attention. Maybe a little lovin', too, huh?"

After ruffing up their fur and nuzzling them, she tossed the ball until they got tired and laid down for a nap on the floor.

The truth was that the boys made it impossible to be upset when they were around.

She had the life she'd always wanted: a practice and a beautiful home that she'd remodeled and decorated herself. So, instead of focusing on what was missing, she focused on the gifts in her life.

It always helped her through the days when the pain caught her off guard.

After years of education and training, but she'd finally opened her practice. But not before, she'd looked at more than fifty homes and several practices. She'd just about given up finding anything when she'd stumbled onto this small farm.

The timing couldn't have been more perfect.

She was driving by and saw the owner putting up a for sale sign. Even though the property was isolated several miles from town amongst just a scattering of other parcels and on a main road, she stopped on a lark, figuring that she wouldn't be able to afford the place anyway.

But while talking with the owner, she discovered that it wasn't on the market yet. Even more surprising was that the property was purchased from the original owner years before.

At that time, the only structures on the property were the small farmhouse near the front and the barn across from it.

While Dr. Taylor and his wife lived in the back portion of the house, he used the front section to start his veterinary practice.

As their family grew, he built the larger house nearer to the center of the property, remodeling the old farmhouse into a full-service veterinary clinic and surgery.

Where he practiced for almost forty years.

The clinic boasted a reception area, a small kitchenette, three examination rooms, a small lab with a medication dispensary, and a surgery with a recovery bay.

In what had been an old pantry, four large dog kennels supported several smaller kennels on top.

Between them was a solid layer of metal sheeting.

After retiring, Dr. Taylor and his wife decided to travel for a few years before relocating to Colorado Springs, closer to their children and grandchildren.

Once Becca shared her plans for establishing a veterinarian practice, Dr. Taylor was happy to sell her the place, knowing the animals in the area would be cared for.

What he didn't know was that it was perfect for another reason, too.

It was close enough to the target to investigate him while living far enough away to make it hard for him to expose her true identity.

She immediately started renovating the clinic when she took possession.

She removed walls to increase the usable space.

Merged the lab and medication dispensary, created a small grooming and bathing salon, and added a recovery bay next to the surgery.

Although the reception area was a little smaller, the indoor/outdoor boarding room had increased.

The updated bathroom lost the tub, while the kitchen received small but new appliances and built-in bench seating around a small table.

The wall behind the reception desk was made of safety glass that provided an open view of the cattery.

Although similarly designed for function with slide-and-hide examination tables separating the upper and lower kennels that sat on top of supply drawers.

The canine area was next to the grooming station.

It had larger kennels and cabinetry with a door to the training arena.

A frosted safety divider ran between the canine and feline areas.

The newer, higher-cost items included a new computer system, scale, endoscope, binocular compound microscope, digital X-ray, and anesthesia machine.

Since the clinic was in a more rural area, Becca added a shaded indoor/outdoor boarding kennel and training arena where her assistant exercised the dogs and where new dog owners could take lessons from a dog trainer for a fee.

The remainder of the work improved the aesthetics. Paint and colorful displays showed off the products that she sponsored.

Looking through the picture window, the clinic was humbled by the colossal giant peaks towering in the distance to the west, with their whitecapped crowns.

Forested ridges and rough crags interlaced along towering embankments, pristine waterways, and lush valleys; the Rocky Mountain majesties reigned supreme.

The generous old barn sat catacorner across the driveway from the clinic, and it had doubled her clientele with five large stalls, each having access to a paddock, the main arena, and a four-acre horse pasture, she was able to board livestock.

Even though the update on the barn had been put off for over a year after the clinic became profitable, it was the only large animal surgery within a hundred miles.

The renovation of the main house was her biggest undertaking because the house was originally designed with a closed floor plan, which made the space feel disconnected, and the walls separating the rooms blocked the light.

Becca preferred an open floor plan, so the first floor had to be completely reconfigured and engineered.

Inspired to create a gourmet kitchen for her twin Joss, who loved to cook and bake, she expanded into the enclosed patio.

That allowed her to enlarge the kitchen with plenty of cabinets, create an extra-large pantry, a six-seater breakfast nook, a full laundry and mudroom, with a grooming station for the dogs.

The upper cabinets were painted white with mullioned glass doors, while the lower cabinets had walnut flat panels. The countertops were made of Calcutta-inspired gold-veined quartz.

To add a pop of color, the base of the large prep island was painted a dark teal blue, creating a stunning focal point in the middle of the space.

The kitchen was equipped with professional-grade appliances and had all the kitchen tools, cookware, and essentials that Joss would have loved.

Even though she took pride in how well everything turned out, it still bothered her that Joss and her mother couldn't share in the vision, creation, and enjoyment of it all.

But then, the injustice of what happened to Joss seemed to taint everything. Even on her best days, it was hard for Becca to hold onto happiness when she still hadn't gotten Joss the justice she deserved.

Staring out the picture window, she tried to remind herself that the story hadn't ended; no fat lady was singing, and she was still breathing. She would still vindicate her twin.

Sometimes, it just seemed like justice was taking too long.

She'd been working herself ragged and without a break since moving into the newly renovated house. It was like pulling teeth just to acquire the tiniest bit of knowledge about her sister, let alone get anything on the target. But she was determined to uncover the truth.

And for the first time since she'd confirmed that Joss was dead, she had what she needed to put her plan into action.

It was time for retribution.

CHAPTER FIVE

The Crash

Matt
November 2020

Matt woke with a start.

In the dream, he was on a tightrope. With each unsure step, his legs wobbled, and the rope swayed. When he dared to look down, he saw only a pit of darkness. Yet, he was aware of something that waited there for him to fall. It was the sensation of falling that had awakened him.

Hearing the soft sound of Sofia's breath had calmed his thudding heart. The dream had been a warning to stay vigilant.

Not wanting to disturb her, he lay still in the quiet and reviewed his plan.

Soon enough, the birds would begin their morning serenade to the sun — a song that Sofia had long since made her alarm clock.

It was his last day at the compound, and he was eager to be done with it.

And yet, it was risky to take anything for granted. Things could still go wrong, so he needed to stay vigilant. If everything went the way he hoped, the impact would prove significant—he equated it to preventing cancer from spreading.

As Sofia began to stir, he rolled onto his side and wrapped his arms around her, pressing his body against hers, and whispered, "Good morning, beautiful."

She turned and snuggled against him, not quite awake, "Ahh… you're so warm." Then she looked up and smiled, "And I feel something else that feels nice and warm, too."

Unable to resist, he kissed her with all the desire he felt. That morning, he took his time, first enjoying her in bed and then again after they moved into the shower.

After a very satisfying shower, while he dressed for work, he couldn't help but look at her. Even with her wavy brown hair sopping wet and no makeup, it was hard to take his eyes off of her.

And when she looked at him with those round hazel eyes that changed color with her moods, from browns to golds, to amber or olive. The way she was looking up at him now, with the same depth of love as when she was a young bride. She sat on the edge of the bed with nothing on but a towel loosely wrapped around her.

When their eyes met again, Matt still couldn't believe how fortunate they were to have found each other.

She was as beautiful as the day they married. Her love had never wavered through his deployment and endless jobs.

He was a lucky man.

Their anniversary was coming up, but he couldn't wait. He wanted to give her the diamond earrings that evening after meeting with Clay. He felt a need to celebrate.

Then again, he wasn't sure he could wait that long. "Hey, Hon, how about… we go grab lunch somewhere nice… if I get done early and before my afternoon appointment. How does that sound?"

"You know I'd love that. But please don't rush; that road you take home is dangerous this time of year with those switchbacks and sharp turns. Even a careful driver like yourself has to watch out for black ice this time of year.

"How about, instead of lunch, we have a nice dinner somewhere instead. Maybe have a cocktail or some wine with it… what do you say?"

"I say, you're the best. Tell you what, you decide on whatever sounds good and make reservations for around seven." A big grin spread across his face as he added, "That should give me enough time to go to my appointment and get home in time for another shower."

Changing tactics when he caught the worry on her brow, he said, "Hey, don't worry so much. How about I try to call when I'm on the way? Just keep in mind the cell service in that area is spotty.

“And don’t forget my promise to take some time off after this job is finished. I’ve already spoken to J.D., and he’ll be covering things while I spend some quality time with my woman.

“I just hope you’re ready to spend some quality time with your man.” Wiggling his eyebrows up and down, he gave a little bark that made her giggle.

“Whose worried? You just make sure your motor’s running hot. I have plans for you.” Smiling, she did a little shimmy with her shoulders, and the towel fell to her waist, revealing her breasts—no longer a shy little bride.

Bending down, he gave her a quick kiss and, in a husky whisper, said, “I’ll love you forever.”

As he jumped into the moving billboard he called his plumbing van, he was already looking forward to finishing the day and happy that he’d once again soothed her worries and left her with a smile.

Just before the turn into the compound, he had a moment of hesitation. The consequence of getting caught meant that he might not see Sofia again.

Pulling over, he focused on the intense specialized training that had prepared him for completing some pretty sketchy operations.

Although his skills might be a tad rusty, he had strategies for survival, analysis, planning, land navigation, and escape.

His tactical skills with weapons, intelligence collection, communications, reconnaissance, and unconventional warfare gave him an edge.

He gained each skill by practicing them over and over again until they became second nature.

If all went well, he’d finish connecting the last few pipes, run a few tests, grab the devices, and collect his final payment.

But no matter what happened, he had to remain calm.

Quieting his mind, he took a minute to prepare himself mentally before entering the compound, visualizing the successful completion of the job, and driving away unharmed.

Then, completing the job by handing the tapes to Clay.

For Matt, it was more than a mission. It was his duty as a Marine, retired or not… Semper Fi.

At the compound, Matt checked and rechecked each zone, taking the time to explain to Henry what was done and how it worked.

Plumbing talk bored the man to the point that he walked away without a word. But that morning, Matt couldn't seem to shake him.

The cabins only needed a quick check and a brief explanation.

After that, Matt directed Henry to the new outside equipment to avoid going straight into the main house.

He tested the new equipment and showed Henry how to use it—then spent time on the importance of maintaining them.

"I've shown you the backwater valve and the cleanout plug, but I'd like to demonstrate how the new high-tech grey water recycling system works. I was happy with how well it turned out, considering it took a few days just to set up the lines and connect them to the solar system and backup battery. This thing should keep running for years without a problem.

"Of course, the manufacturer is responsible for the equipment warranty since it was purchased by Mr. Morales directly.

"My warranty only covers the labor for the installation. Still, I think Mr. Morales will be pretty impressed with it."

Matt explained in detail the non-warrantied work, listing repairs he'd made that were left unfinished by the previous plumber.

Then, he did the same with items warrantied by him on the old and new systems, including the upgraded materials he'd provided for the job.

The more he spoke about couplings, connectors, fittings, and adapters, the more unhappy Henry seemed. Matt knew he was bored. The deception was just a tactic to get rid of the man so he could collect the DEA's equipment.

When they entered the mansion and walked into the kitchen, Matt noticed the time and was disappointed that he'd have to pass up his lunch date with Sofia.

He checked the plumbing in the laundry and kitchen and then headed upstairs to go through the guest bathrooms.

As they moved through each room, Henry checked off the items on his list while Matt made a mental note of where the cameras had been moved so he could update his drawings when he got home.

Perspiration began to collect under his arms and at the natural curve of his lower back. At least he'd kept his jacket on, which would hide it.

Time was running out, and there wasn't much left to do. With Henry still glued to his side, Matt explained, "Our last stop will be the master bathroom.

"Boy, that was the real surprise. I mean, considering the quantity of debris in that line. That blockage had to be intentional, no matter how you look at it.

"I will need to spend some time in there before I finish for the day.

"If you have any questions, you can ask them while I work."

As he finished his statement, Henry was called away and, as usual, left without a word.

Relieved to be rid of his companion, Matt moved quickly to collect the devices. With the camera probe, he checked the new interior lining and, as he retrieved it, grabbed the mini recorder before Henry returned.

Once secured under the tray in his toolbox, the only recorder left was in the basement pipe. After a last check for leaks, he'd grab it, seal the pipe, and clean up.

Once the inspection was completed, he set the toolbox on the passenger's seat, stored his gear in the back, and grabbed the clipboard from the center console that held his last bill.

Happy to be finished with the job, he headed to the library.

Standing uncomfortably in front of Morales seated at his desk, Matt explained, "The lines to the septic have been cleared, and the septic was pumped, so you shouldn't have anything to worry about for many years.

"I've walked Henry through every system and left him with instructions regarding the maintenance of the system to keep things running smoothly.

"Every system we worked on from the main house, staff cabins, and the garden have been double-checked and are under warranty.

Of course, I can't warranty the established lines or the work done by others. It's all detailed in the packet I just handed you. If there are any problems, just call Colt Plumbing, and we'll take care of it."

Mr. Morales nodded and handed Matt a thick envelope of cash, which continued to be his preferred method of payment.

Matt found that it held not only the last payment but also a substantial bonus.

"Thank you, but a bonus really isn't necessary."

When Mr. Morales looked at him, his black eyes seemed colder—darker than before, filled with contempt that was eerily incongruent with his words. "You've done a good job, even completing the job on time.

"You're a man of your word. There's only one thing more valuable to me… loyalty."

A cold shiver ran down Matt's spine. "Okay then! Well, thank you. I'm sure you'll be happy with your new and improved plumbing system."

Matt couldn't be sure, but the man's voice seemed accusing.

***

Minutes after Matt left, a squirrely-looking redhead stepped from behind a beautiful gold silk hand-painted Chinese screen.

"Well, Billy, did you take care of our little problem?"

A devious clown-like smile made a slit across a pale white pot-marked face. His dark lips, almost purple, replied, "You betcha, boss. I wasn't a mechanic for seven years for nothin'."

Lowering his voice, he gestured toward the door, "I mixed a little brake line cocktail for our friend there and poked a little hole—a slow leak, so he doesn't know what's happening right away.

"And just in case that doesn't do it, I loosened a few screws on the steering arm.

"I doubt he'll make it too far. Not with patches of ice still on the road."

Morales glared at the photograph of Matt leaving DEA headquarters and said, "For your sake, Billy, I hope he doesn't."

***

Matt jumped into his van, excitement mixed with anxiety, adrenalin mixed with dread.

He'd done the right thing weeks before, when he'd reported to Agent Thomas overhearing Morales order a hit on a dealer.

Clay had studied Matt's service record prior to their meeting.

He explained how Morales had been under surveillance for years but managed to evade them. "He's smart, sociopathic would be a better characterization. He has managed to get others to do his dirty work. Some underling is always willing to take the fall for a payout.

"His lieutenants live a good life, and he makes sure they're covered, too. So, we haven't been able to secure an arrest warrant on even one of them.

"We know who the major players are, but just as soon as we think we have good intel -- something happens. And we're left looking like a bunch of idiots. We need evidence. Hard evidence."

But Matt didn't have any.

"Look, Mac, it comes down to this. I believe you. Your testimony would help, but it's not enough.

Morales can claim that you overheard a TV program, for Christ's sake! We need proof that can't be discredited or overturned in court."

Several minutes pass while Clay looked over the information on his computer screen.

Finally, he asks, "How would you feel about going undercover? You're a civilian. You have a contract that gives you access to the Morales compound.

"You won't be infringing on any civil rights or liberties like an agent would be, so you can't be held responsible for anything you overhear, and Morales can't claim he was framed.

"Any information you get could help take down the whole cartel.

This goes way deeper than the problems we have here in Colorado. We believe that what Morales does not only crosses state lines but international boundaries.

"Your record shows that you were trained as an Intelligence Specialist with a focus on espionage."

"Yeah, that's right.

"I have your record here, but can you tell me about any training that is not listed?"

"I was trained to be invisible, collect intelligence, and kill when necessary."

"Well, your country needs you. The DEA needs you."

"I know I took a pledge to protect this country, and my loyalty hasn't changed. But you need to understand that I'm much older now, and I've been out of the military for years."

"I'm not worried about that. Once skills are ingrained, they're never forgotten.

"Besides, we can keep an eye on you and try to pull you out if it gets too dicey. But as you know, Mac, any mission is risky. Morales is a dangerous character, and if you're caught, there's no doubt that you'll be killed."

Matt didn't respond right away.

He turned to stare out the window, thinking of Sofia and how she would react to hearing that he was back in the trenches.

She gave up so much during the years I was in the service. Living with the possibility, the fear that the knock on the door would inform her that she was a widow.

How can I do that to her again?

Still, he couldn't just walk away and live the rest of his life knowing that he might have stopped a threat but didn't.

Taking a deep breath, he turned back to Agent Thomas. "I'll do the best I can to get what you need. But I'm watched all the time, so I won't be able to rifle through desks or break into safes."

"Look, Mac, whatever you can get us is more than what we have. Just rely on your training; we'll provide whatever equipment you need."

The road from the mansion descended to the base of a canyon that connected with the I-70 freeway. However, the cliff drops were steep on that bypass.

In the winter, the roads were more treacherous.

Matt knew the road intimately since he'd driven it twice a day for several weeks, and after all that time, the mission was almost over.

As he drove, he calculated the time he needed to shower before his appointment with Clay at the DEA Headquarters in Centennial, Denver.

Their last meeting had been several weeks prior, and even with the office more than an hour from the compound, it was a risk.

So Matt tried to make it look like he was there for a plumbing job just in case word got back to Morales. Grabbing his clipboard, he went to the back to pull a few supplies that he tucked into the toolbox and then walked into the building like he had nothing to hide.

Distracted with thoughts of their last meeting, he hardly perceived that the van had picked up speed. The light pressure he'd distractedly applied to the brakes had little effect on reducing his speed. Discovering that the truck wasn't slowing as expected pulled him out of his reverie.

He pressed harder on the brakes, careful not to panic and cause a skid.

The wind whistled as the pressure intensified in the canyon, making it seem like it was pushing the van. The speed increased even as he pumped the brakes.

At a more level turn, the van slowed and took the next switchback more comfortably. Downshifting to slow down, Matt searched the road in front of him for black ice.

At the next switchback, the road dipped again. The steep descent caused the van to pick up speed even in a lower gear. Tapping the brakes did nothing. They weren't responding.

After another sharp corner with wheels sliding on patches of snow and plumbing tools banging around in the back like artillery, Matt realized that the van had been sabotaged, which probably meant that Morales had somehow discovered that he was working with the DEA.

He knew that if he couldn't slow down, he might not make it around the sharp curve just over the rise. Even if the incline reduced his speed for a few minutes, it would accelerate again on the other side just before reaching the curve.

I have to keep my head.

Having been in sticky situations before, he knew that fear could shut down a man's ability to discern a situation and respond to it effectively.

In war, once you lose your head, you lose your life. And that just wasn't an option. He had to survive for Sofia. He needed her as much as she needed him. If there was any chance to keep the van on the road, any chance to survive, he had to keep his head.

The breaks were gone; if he turned off the engine, he might lose what was left of the power steering, and that was really all he had left, even if it seemed to be slipping.

Downshifting again, he pumped the brakes.

Nothing.

He downshifted one last time.

Thankfully, it was just days before Thanksgiving, so there weren't many vehicles on the road. Knowing that no one else would be hurt in the crash was a bitter-sweet comfort.

But, if he survived, he might not be found for days. At this time of year, hypothermia would kill him if his injuries didn't.

He'd forgotten how adrenaline acted like jet fuel racing through his veins at high velocity, cruelly intoxicating and oddly provoking.

But he was running out of time.

He took several deep breaths to calm his thudding heart and white-knuckled the wheel while he slowly pulled up on the emergency brake.

Hearing the clanging behind him, he was glad he'd listened to Sofia and installed the safety metal screen behind the front seats that stopped the supplies currently being thrown around like ping-pong balls from knocking him out.

As the van started to climb the slope, his thoughts returned to Sofia. She would be preparing for their big Thanksgiving Day bash, which she loved to host every year.

She had started cooking days before the party, which usually lasted well past midnight.

The steering was slipping as he tried to maneuver close to the mountain wall.

While trying to calculate an alternative to going over the cliff. A seemingly inevitable conclusion to the downhill roller coaster ride he was about to take. A clear, high-pitched metallic ping was followed within seconds by a loud thud from somewhere under his feet, and he lost the steering completely.

He had one chance.

Grabbing the toolbox with the recorders and tapes, he opened the driver's side window and threw it as far as he could. He was reassured when he heard it crash against the mountain wall, knowing that the tapes would help Clay.

Then, waiting until the last possible second, he said a quick prayer.

The truck slowed as it crested the top of the rise, and without a second thought, he opened his door and jumped. Hoping he wouldn't be crushed by the truck. He tucked to roll before hitting the ground, but at that velocity, he rolled to the edge of the cliff.

As predicted, the truck picked up speed until, at the turn, it catapulted off the side of the mountain like a missile. Everything seemed to slow down when he caught a glimpse of it. For just a moment, it seemed to hover in the air.

Then, it disappeared as gravity forced it down with an earth-shattering crash.

The first impact ripped a yearling from the ground. As it continued down the incline, it flipped and began to roll. The plumbing supplies made a terrible racket that echoed through the canyon as it tumbled down the slope.

With an ear-splitting scream of metal when it slammed into a large boulder, its torturous demise echoed through the gorge. The impact ripped open the side and broke open the back doors, turning the otherwise innocuous items into shrapnel that impaled everything around it. Gas splashed from the ruptured tank over the hot manifold and, in a flash, was ignited.

When Matt hit the ground, it knocked the wind out of him.

But the propulsion pushed him too close to the edge of the cliff, and he couldn't stop the inertia before he fell over the edge.

Tumbling over sharp rocks and branches, he caught a snippet of his logo on the van before he slammed into a tree. A low-hanging branch impaled his side, but he didn't feel it; he'd lost consciousness after his head slammed into a rock.

***

Sofia hadn't been out of the house since the funeral. She couldn't bring herself to go anywhere. It was too hard to imagine being outside in the cold, wet snow without Matt egging her into making a snowman.

They'd had flurries a few times, and there were remnants of it collected in long, broken swathes along the freeway. Sofia was reminded of the danger that lay hidden under the patches of snow that was probably responsible for her husband's death.

A thought crossed her mind that maybe she could suffer a similar fate and join her one true love. But as swiftly as the thought came, it deserted her. Such a thing was against her beliefs regardless of how much she missed him.

At the grocery store, she felt out of place.

They'd always done their big shopping day together. At the check-out counter, Matt would tell some silly joke to make the cashier laugh. His silliness had always made doing mundane chores fun.

At home, he'd carry the groceries into the house, and she'd put everything away. A well-oiled machine in the easy manner they worked together.

But remembering how good things had been just made it that much harder for her to do those things on her own.

Without Matt's crazy antics, life lost a lot of its color.

The thought of going to lunch or a movie with a friend no longer interested her. Many friends and neighbors worried that her grief had turned into severe depression. Many had suggested that she see someone. But Sofia discounted their counsel and remained isolated.

J.D., had offered to buy the business, but Sofia couldn't bring herself to sell it. Instead, she asked J.D. to run it, giving him an increase in salary.

Both the freezer and pantry had been stocked days before the accident, but with Matt gone, she hadn't needed to go shopping or cook a large meal.

Besides, she'd lost her appetite.

She loved spending time with her son, but she had a few things she needed to discuss with him. To make things more palatable, she invited him for dinner, texting that she'd be making one of his favorites - chicken tetrazzini.

So, with a list in hand, she drove to the store with Matt's voice telling her to just get up and get it done, in her head. He was a go-getter who hated to leave tasks looming. It was one of the things she loved about him, one of the things she missed about him.

Pleased that she'd finished her errands so quickly, Sofia entered the kitchen and set the armload of heavy bags on the kitchen island.

Sofia sipped a glass of cold water at the sink as she wondered how best to explain to her son that she needed his help to clean out his father's office.

Since she continued to manage the books for Colt Plumbing, she needed to complete the end-of-year bookkeeping and get it to the accountant, but she couldn't bring herself to do it.

The idea of closing last year's books felt like she was closing the book on Matt.

And she wasn't ready for that ending.

Still, it was challenging to go into a room that was primarily Matt's domain to do the billing.

Even if she could bring herself to box up last year's receipts and bids, she couldn't manage the heavy wood furniture by herself. *Besides, it's time that I do the redecorating like we planned.*

Leaning back against the counter, she congratulated herself for being ready to get it done, just like Matt would have wanted.

As she set the glass on the counter and turned, she noticed the open sliding glass door.

Tiny hairs rose in unison on the back of her neck and on her arms; at the same time, a thud came from the back of the house.

Pulling her cell from her purse, she punched in 911 but then hesitated. *Hold on. It might be Jason coming early for dinner.*

Her heart was racing.

But he wouldn't leave the back door open like that... would he?

Taking a deep breath to calm herself, Sofia quietly moved down the hall toward the noises with her finger resting on the call button.

The office door was slightly open even though she knew that she'd kept it closed when she wasn't working in there since Matt's death.

Peeking into the room, she saw two men with black hoods searching Matt's office.

The tall one was unplugging Matt's old computer.

Pressing the send button on her phone, trying to stay as quiet as possible, Sofia turned around and ran.

Halfway through the kitchen, but before she could reach the garage door, one of the men caught up with her to send her flying across the kitchen floor until she slammed headfirst into the pantry door.

Her phone slid across the floor in the opposite direction.

She could hear him coming for her.

Towering over her, he bent down and yelled with spittle splattering her face "You're not supposed to be here!"

"Hello?"

He saw the phone and stomped over to it, enraged when he saw who she called. His voice roared through the house: "She called 911! We have to go! Now!"

Throwing the phone at her, he pushed up his sleeves as rushed back to grab the front of her top, pinching her skin, and picking her halfway off the floor, "You fucking bitch!"

Terrified, she couldn't move, could barely breathe with the fabric being tightened around her throat. Registering a little too late, the fist that came slamming into her face.

"Hello. 911. Are you still there?"

CHAPTER SIX

In the Line of Fire

Sofia Isabella Colt
January 2021

Having left work in a hurry with only a short explanation to Billings and still wearing his uniform, Jason bolted from his cruiser and ran into the emergency room.

When they'd called him on the radio, all dispatch had told him was that his mother was taken to the hospital. After losing his father, Jason wasn't ready to lose his mother too.

Rushing into the Emergency room, he went up to the front desk, bypassing a patient with a blood-soaked rag on his arm waiting to be admitted, "Can you tell me where to find Sofia Colt? She was brought in about thirty minutes ago."

Looking a little confused at the sense of urgency in his voice, the Admission Clerk said, "Oh, you must be here to take a statement from the woman who was assaulted at home. But what's the rush officer? Is a suspect in custody or something?"

Reflexively, Jason held his breath to stop himself from yelling and lowered his voice. "I'm sorry, what did you say? She was assaulted? At home?"

Confused, the clerk said, "Yeah, isn't that why you're here?"

For a minute, he just blinked at her while his stomach dropped to his feet and his heart closed off his throat. "Huh? No. I'm Jason Colt. I was told that my mom was brought to the ER. Can you just tell me where she is? And if she's okay?"

As her smile faded, her fingers flew over the keys. "Sure, just give me a minute. Well, it looks like she was admitted just a short time ago --

not much here. I'm sure they're taking good care of her. Why don't you go get some coffee, and I'll let the charge nurse know you're here."

An hour later, a young nurse walked into the waiting area. "Mr. Colt!"

Jumping up, "I'm Jason Colt. Is my mother okay."

"I'm sorry to say I don't have much to report. The doctor has seen her and ordered some tests."

"Can I see her?"

"Not right now. We're still conducting tests, and it takes time. The doctor will speak with you after he's had a chance to review them. I'd recommend grabbing a bite at the cafeteria. It might take some time."

Three hours later, the nurse walked Jason through the large double doors. "I can take you to your mother now. The doctor wants to speak with you both." As she turned to leave him in the doorway, she added, "Go ahead and get comfortable; the doctor will find you when he has something to tell you."

At first, he thought he'd gone into the wrong room. The bed looked too big for the petite woman lying on it.

Staring at her from the foot of the bed, Jason wanted to hit something.

Both of her eyes, nose, and the left side of her face were swollen. The left eye looked swollen shut. There were stitches along her left cheekbone. A vertical cut on her lower lip. And her left arm was in a sling.

Her face appeared darker around her injuries, a precursor to the ugly bruises that would develop over the next day or two. Her natural olive complexion, more characteristic of her Mediterranean heritage, seemed pale.

Unfortunately, he knew that those were just the visible injuries. He didn't want to think about what injuries might be hidden from view.

Although her physical injuries would heal, her home had been invaded, diminishing her sense of safety—psychologically traumatizing, especially when living alone.

Beside himself, he struggled to speak softly, "Mom... you asleep?"

"No, sweetheart. Just resting my eyes."

When she opened them, he could see why. Red-rimmed, bloodshot and swollen. And although it was nearly swollen shut, at the corner of the left eye he could see a bright red hemorrhage.

It angered him to think of her in pain. "Jesus, Mom! Who did this to you?

Looking at her son, she tried to smile, but the cut on her lip made her wince. "Jason, please don't. I'm alive, and that's all that matters. Now, please sit down so we can talk. It hurts a little to look up like this."

Grabbing a chair, he placed it next to the bed. "Okay, Mom, sure. But can you describe them, tell me what they looked like?"

Closing her eyes, "Jason, you know how much I love you…"

"Huh? Mom, I know. You don't have to say..."

"Jason, don't interrupt. Now, just sit down, and let me say what I want to say. I need you to listen."

Sitting down, worried that he'd upset her, "Okay, Mom. I'm listening."

"Since waking in the ambulance after that… that monster attacked me, you're all I've thought about. And before anything more happens to this family... I just couldn't stand it if I didn't say… what's important."

Reaching for the cup of water on the overbed table, she paused to take a sip.

"Jason, I don't want you running off half-cocked trying to find out who did this.

"After losing your father and then seeing me... well, I can only imagine how I look -- your emotions must be running high. When emotions are high, we are more vulnerable. And that Italian blood running through your veins only intensifies it.

"We're a passionate people, Jason, but that can be dangerous for a cop.

"I know you've looked into Dad's accident. But I need your word that you'll stay out of it.

"I mean it, Jason. I don't want you anywhere near this.

"Those men are dangerous, and God only knows what they were looking for in Dad's office. You could be their next target. And right now you're too close… too wounded."

Tears leaked from under closed eyelids. “Jason… I just, I can’t… bare… to lose you too. I need you to promise that you won’t get involved. Promise!”

He knew that determined tone. She wouldn’t rest until he agreed. Worse, he knew she was right. “You won’t lose me, Mom. But okay. I promise. Just please don’t be upset.

“Tell you what. How about I promise to stand on the sidelines if you promise to take it easy and let me help you at the house until you’ve healed up a bit?”

With a slight grin to avoid opening the cut on her lip and flinching at the painful reminder, she said, “Now, that sounds like a smart plan for both of us.”

“Great. But I’m worried about you. I won’t sleep right until those creeps are found and are put behind bars…” He lifted his hand to stop her from interrupting and said gently, “My turn, Mom.

“Don’t worry. I’ll honor my promise and let the detectives handle your case.

“But it’s hard to see you this way.

“Your arm’s in a sling, and even though I don’t know the extent of your injuries, you look pretty bruised up.

“I know that you’re perfectly capable of taking care of yourself, but I think I should stay with you at least until you can manage comfortably on your own.

“Besides, you’re always saying I should visit more.”

Just then, the doctor walked in. “Hello, Mrs. Colt. Do you remember me? I’m Dr. Horowitz.”

Sofia nodded.

“And you must be Jason. I know you’ve been here for several hours. So, if it’s okay with your mother, I won’t keep you guessing any longer.”

“Of course, doctor. Please tell us what you’ve found. But please, call me Sofia.”

“Well, the good news is that you’re healthy and strong… Sofia. And honestly, it’s a good thing you take care of yourself.

“Still, I’d like to keep you overnight for observation. You’ve suffered quite a few injuries, so staying overnight would be best.

"You've suffered a mild concussion. Nothing too serious, but I'd rather err on the side of caution. There's a nice little gash on your scalp that has a few stitches which might itch. The nurse will see to the dressing while you're here.

"I didn't see anything too concerning in that left eye, but I'd rather have a specialist take a look before sending you home. In the meantime, I'll have a nurse put a patch on you. It would be best if you didn't use it. There's no sense in taking chances with your sight.."

"You have a cracked rib and three more that are bruised on the right side. And a hairline fracture in your forearm… in the ulna about here." He touched his arm to show her where. "Thankfully, it didn't break.

"I've ordered a light cast to ensure it's not reinjured while healing. In the meantime, try not to use the arm.

"The good news is, as long as there aren't any complications, I'll release you tomorrow afternoon. I know we're managing the pain right now, but I'll need to reevaluate your pain level before you leave.

"You'll need to rest as much as possible once you're released. The more you rest, the more quickly you'll heal.

Once the doctor left, Sofia said, "Well, not the best news, but not the worst either.

"So, to finish what I was saying... I hope you know how incredibly proud I am of the man you've become.

"Not a surprise since you've been a delight since birth.

"No mother could ask for a better child. The joy that you've brought into my life, into both our lives… well… you've been our greatest blessing.

"I know you miss him; I do, too. But he'd want us to move on. As he liked to say, the world stops for no man.

"Life gets shorter with age. At a certain point, time moves into hyperdrive. So, while there's still time on the clock, it's important to share what's in your heart.

"Your dad was better at that than I am. I tend to get too mushy… too emotional. But your father was a man who loved life. He lived to find joy in everything.

"It was his truest wish to make those he loved… feel it. I plan to follow his lead because every day of life we're given is a gift."

A tear fell down the side of Sophia's face.

Jason wasn't sure what to say. It was a lot to take in, and it had been a long, emotional day. But he leaned in closer and held her hand. "Honestly, I was so lucky to be given such loving parents. Some kids are never shown affection. And don't sell yourself short, Mom. You always say what's in your heart and what's on your mind - just like Dad. You're the best mom any son could want, and I love you."

Holding her hand in both of his, "Now, will you please tell me what the hell happened?"

Sofia described how she'd been distracted because it was the first time she'd gone shopping by herself since they lost Matt. "That's why when I noticed the glass door open, I didn't act right away. I thought it might be you.

"But I did manage to call 911 and run into the kitchen before he grabbed me… damn, I just remembered, the groceries are still in the car.

"Jason, please go to the house and put them away for me. In this weather, nothing should be spoiled. But if they keep me overnight…."

"Don't worry about it, Mom. I'll take care of it."

He kissed her forehead. "By the way, I put some magazines on the bedside table in case you get bored. But why don't you sleep for a bit while I take care of those groceries? Is there anything you need from the house? Anything I can bring you?"

"Some clean clothes would be nice. Just something comfy like sweats."

As he stood to leave, he stopped. "Mom, you said the guys wore masks, but can you remember anything else about them? Like height, build… maybe eye color or a tattoo?"

Sofia thought about it for a minute. "I'm not sure about eye color – dark, I guess. The mask made it hard to tell.

"Hmm, I only got a quick look… but now that you mention it, I think I did see part of a tattoo… when he pushed up his sleeve as he came at me.

"A hook of some kind… with sharp points… kind of jagged. It was on his left forearm. Oh, there was color… um… a bit of blue… and I think I saw some red, though I suppose it could have been part of his clothing.

"I'm sorry, son, that's really all I remember."

"No, Mom. That's good. Real good. It should help narrow things down.

“You just rest up like the doc said. I’ll take care of everything at the house. If you remember anything else, just write it down.”

Driving to the house, Jason called a security company he knew was good and scheduled a home evaluation for the next day.

Then, he called to take a week off work.

There was no way he’d leave his mother vulnerable to fend for herself.

***

Whoever said March comes in like a lion and out like a lamb never lived in Colorado. The temperature had changed from freezing that morning to springtime warmth in the afternoon and back to a winter chill at dusk.

One minute, Becca was shivering with a blanket next to a fire; the next, she was in the backyard with a jacket, enjoying herself playing ball with Scout and Radar.

Once the dogs were worn out sleeping nearby, Becca sat at her desk and checked her schedule, trying to figure out how she was going to keep things running smoothly at the clinic with both Alice and Sarah out sick.

After two days with a full schedule and no help, she was running on empty. She needed to hire another person soon.

Sifting through applications and resumes, Becca hoped to find a seasoned large animal technician to oversee the barn hospital and a part-time assistant to help at the clinic.

Realizing that training a new tech would take time and that it could be up to a week before her staff returned, Becca decided to cancel all but emergency patients for the next week.

After several calls apologizing for the inconvenience, most of her clients agreed to postpone their appointments for a week or two.

What Becca didn’t know at the time was that this sudden change in circumstance would give her the time she needed to find trouble.

CHAPTER SEVEN

Guilty till Proven Innocent

Jason Colt
April 2021

The April winds left a bite in the air that made it feel more like January. Billings was glad that he'd been awake enough when he left the station to put on his gloves.

As Jacobs walked up to him, they shook hands. "Colt, you remember Jacobs from Homicide. He'll be following up with forensics and turning any evidence over to IA. We're hoping he can figure out what happened, and I'm hoping he'll be the one to clear you."

Still bent over, Colt used his sleeve to wipe the remnants of vomit from his face and lifted his hand in acknowledgment. Still distracted by the back-flips in his stomach and a headache that threatened to crack open his skull.

Detective Jacobs was a decorated officer who was often mistaken for Danny Reagan from the TV show Blue Bloods. However, he wasn't just Wahlberg's doppelganger; Jacobs had characteristics similar to the character Wahlberg played on the show.

Looking at Detective Jacobs, Billings continued, "I've got to take him to the hospital for tests. If he spews one more time, I might lose it myself."

Jacobs gave Colt a once over as Billings continued, "He says he doesn't remember much of what happened, and he still seems disoriented… might have hit his head on something. I'll have the hospital bag his clothes and gear for the lab.

"One strange bit: he said his com hasn't been working, so I'd like his equipment checked out.

“Between us, I can’t see how that could happen. Never had communication problems before— but I guess it wouldn’t hurt to confirm.”

Jacobs reminded Jason. “Colt, you know the drill. Once the doc clears you, you’ll be debriefed and asked to write an incident report. If there’s nothing else, I think you guys should get going. Colt looks pretty bad.”

As they turned to leave, Jacobs asked, “Did you do it? Did you shoot that perp?”

Fearing he might spew again, he swallowed hard and looked at Jacobs. “I never even thought to shoot the guy. I was only holding my gun on him. I couldn’t see if he had a weapon while he was hiding behind that lid. It was just too dark to tell.

“I had hoped to take him in. Maybe see if he’d squeal on his weapons supplier. Those crates behind the station looked authentic.

“But I swear I can’t remember much after I called Stryker out. And everything since then... seems like a crazy dream.”

“Well, it’s real, all right. Maybe the docs or some tests can tell us something that supports what you remember. While there, try to remember more if you can for the debriefing.”

Jacobs walked away to speak with Simon Smothers, the forensic specialist in charge of the scene.

Smothers was an odd character who always carried a physician’s black satchel with him. It gave the impression that he was a doctor going on a house call instead of the lead forensic scientist for the department.

Although Smothers was short in stature, had a barrel chest, wore a black suit and tie, had an undercut hairstyle, and a kaiser mustache half hidden under a bulbous nose, which reminded Jacobs of a commander in the Gestapo, it was his comportment that exuded authority wherever he went that put him in charge, which never sat quite right with Jacobs.

Regardless of his appearance, Smothers was the best. Highly intelligent and surprisingly kind, he always followed the evidence until he uncovered the truth. Even when it took more time than Jacobs thought it should.

Smothers took great pride in his trade, even when he was dragged from a warm bed into the cold night. It gave him considerable pleasure to find those sometimes microscopic puzzle pieces that told him the story of what happened.

He didn't trust people on principle because, as far as he was concerned, science didn't have an agenda.

Jacobs filled Smothers in on what little information Billings and Colt had given him.

Smothers considered the information while he monitored the forensic team. "That's not much to go on, but let's play devil's advocate for a minute.

"If he were drugged, it wouldn't be unusual to have a lapse in memory.

"And if someone put the gun in his hand and pulled the trigger, there should be a void in the GSR on his hand, the weapon, or his clothing.

"There might be fingerprints in the residue if the person wasn't wearing gloves. However, it can be hard to get a good print because of skin elasticity, perspiration, or exposure distortion.

"If gloves were worn, we won't find any fingerprints. However, we might find a void in the GSR.

"But hey, even a partial print can provide a lead. And either way would indicate that he wasn't alone at the time of the shooting."

Signaling Jacobs to follow him, they stood close to the body. "Then there's the bruising to consider.

"When we're in a rush like perps are when committing a crime, anxieties increase and intensify. Without realizing it, there's a tendency to use more force.

"And that extra force leaves pressure marks.

"The bruises can take a while to form. Days even. That's why they are so often missed.

"We'll just need to be diligent while collecting evidence from his person."

The gen-pop doesn't realize that, even when wearing gloves to avoid leaving fingerprints, the pressure necessary to force a weapon into someone's hand can leave evidence of foul play."

Jacobs rubbed his hands together. The cold never sat right with him. Pulling winter gloves from a pocket, he asked. "So Colt might be innocent after all?"

"Maybe. Give it a day or two. Give my team time to process the scene. Each of our labs will focus on their specialty: weapons, radio, clothes, tests, and fluids.

"But, whatever I collect from his person, I will personally oversee.

"There's also another method I can use to check for bruises that aren't visible yet. We can require him to be rechecked in a few days and follow up.

It might be a long shot, but without saying it, Jacobs hoped Smothers would find something to prove Colt's innocence. "Just send me a text with whatever you find. I hate to think that one of ours is a bad egg. Either way, the truth needs to come out."

Smothers nodded, "Yeah, well, here's the problem on that score. Proving innocence is a lot harder than proving guilt. Remember, even these days, circumstantial evidence can convict an innocent man.

"My team hasn't found a gun anywhere near the perp. If Colt shot him, it looks like an unjustified shoot… murder.

"But we have a long way to go before we can confirm anything.

"And until we can find and verify evidence, it would be wise to keep an open mind.

"For one thing, what's the motive here? Did Colt know the victim?"

Jacobs added, "Yeah. And what has me scratching my head even more is, what happened to the canine? The incident with the rookie. But why is he suddenly so aggressive… and with cops he knew?"

Jacobs was pensive, "Yeah, and Colt was off, too. Did you see the back of his head? "

Taking a deep breath as he looked at the body, Smother's said, "Well, it's early yet. We've only taken a few pieces out of the box; we're a long way from figuring out the whole picture in this puzzle.

"But don't worry. I'll go to the hospital as soon as I'm done here and see what else I can find out.

"The evidence will lead us to the truth."

"Well, please keep me in the loop. If he's innocent, we need to make sure we don't miss anything that might clear him. And if he's good for this, we need to make sure he can't do it again."

With that, Jacobs left the scene in Smothers' capable hands.

***

Jason was silent on the ride to the hospital, doing his best to stop his stomach from jumping into his throat.

Even with his wits were slowly returning, he had a strange heaviness in his limbs. Not only was his scalp sore, but the pounding wasn't helping his sick stomach. His hair was matted and sticky with blood on the back of his head.

Since he needed to preserve whatever evidence might support his innocence, he tried to sit still and keep his head off the headrest. But that just put more pressure on his already sore neck.

He wanted to bring the memory of what happened into his consciousness. But no matter how hard he tried, he couldn't remember what happened after calling Stryker out. And at the moment, that was even fuzzy.

Someone else must have been in that alley with them. Nothing else made sense.

Maybe the other perp found them and hit him from behind while he was distracted. But if that were true, why shoot Stryker? Why leave them alive? Why not just kill them both and eliminate the witnesses?

The more he tried to remember, the dizzier he got until vertigo took over, and he threw up again, only this time all over Billing's floorboard.

"Jesus, Colt! What the fuck is wrong with you! You didn't look this bad at the station. I just hope whatever you got isn't contagious."

At the hospital, Sergeant Billings asked to talk privately with the doctor while the nurse helped Jason fill out the admissions paperwork.

Billings and Gates grew up in the same neighborhood, and Billings trusted him.

"This one's grave, Nathan. It has the potential to turn into a fucking media feeding frenzy. Cop bashing has become the new American pastime. At this point, it could be a fucking game show. I've already come up with a name for it, The Blame Game, where you can win a get-out-of-jail-free card even if you're a repeat offender.

The strategy is simple. Just break the law and find a way to blame a cop and bingo! You win a big settlement from the city.

"It used to be that if you did a crime, you did the time. Period. Failure to comply with a lawful order, and depending on the judge, noncompliance, insubordination, or belligerence could cost you jail time. Attempt to assault an officer, and you deserved whatever you got.

"Now, it just doesn't matter what criminals do. They get a free ride while cops are put in jail.

Like being a cop is so damn easy. I'd like to see how the average citizen would respond if their life was on the line and they were forced to make a split-second decision without making a mistake.

"It just pisses me off. Too bad there's no way to force accusers to prove they'd respond any differently if presented with the same life-threatening scenarios we deal with every day."

Not quite finished writing up his notes on his last patient, Nathan looked up. He'd heard it all before, until that piece about a game. "Hey, Grant, that's not a bad idea."

"Huh? What's not a bad idea?"

"A video game. Only a more realistic one. What are they called… immersion games?"

"I'm not sure what they call them, but we have something like that in the department. It's a shooting simulator to help us better assess real-life situations.

"I'm not sure that it would help the public understand our position. There are plenty of shoot-um-up video games out there. But they don't discourage violence; they increase it. I don't know about you, Nathan, but I never had to worry about someone coming to my school with a gun."

"Well, okay, I'll give you that. But what if there was a way to make them more real? Add an electrical shock or a hard thump like when hit by a paintball—a non-lethal consequence.

The biggest problem with video games is the disconnect between action and consequence. Any game that encourages killing without conscience desensitizes the act of killing, but feeling pain for killing indiscriminately might influence change."

"I see what you mean, but I'm not sure it would be safe or legal. And even if it was, no one likes consequences, so I doubt it would be very popular."

"Yeah. You're probably right."

"But hey, at least you're trying to find a solution. I sure don't have the answers. Experiencing video games, TV, and movies at a physical level might provide a change in the general population's perspective. Pain is a good teacher.

"Unfortunately, a criminal mind is different, and I'm not sure anyone will ever get through to them. The prisons are full, and don't get me started on the recidivism rates.

"Sometimes it seems like they're breeding the good out of the world... criminals, I mean.

"But, you know what gets me, Nathan? What keeps me awake some nights?"

"No, but I could probably guess."

"What happens when they outnumber us? When criminals are voted into every key office, and there's no one left to stop them?

"There are bad cops, too. Shit, I know there's bad in any profession. But if things don't change soon… the shit will only get worse."

"Come on, Grant. I know it's been bad for you guys out there. But it's hard to believe that it's gotten that bad yet."

"No, not yet. But think about it. Why would anyone want to work at a thankless job that puts their life at risk and then rewards them with jail time for a bad decision?

"My God, even repeat offenders have better odds than that.

"Today, if a perp gets hurt or killed while a cop is trying to do what they're trained to do, the cop is made at fault for excessive force. It doesn't matter if the perp has broken the law or even if he assaulted the officer.

"What happens when those screaming to defund the department today call for help tomorrow, and no one responds?"

Nathan placed a hand on Grant's shoulder. "Don't worry so much, my friend. Remember, I may not be out on the street, but I'm the one who stitches up these guys. I get it.

"Anything more you want to tell me about your cop?"

Feeling a little better after dispelling some of his frustration, Grant sighed, "Not really—at least not specifics. But I was hoping that you would do a tox screen on him. He's been acting strange – loopy, kinda zombie-like. And unless he's an accomplished actor, something's really wrong with the guy.

“You might want to wait, though. Smothers should be showing up any minute. He can be a pain sometimes. You remember Simon?”

Nathan nodded.

“Don’t get me wrong. The man’s thorough… a perfectionist. He has about every gadget out there, and his reports are clean. But he can be a bit of an ass when it comes to his investigation. Just do us both a favor and post-security outside that room.

“But he’s not very good at sharing what he finds until he’s damn good and ready. And I need to know.”

“Sure. And I’ll let you know what we find.”

Billings bowed his head and lowered his voice. “Yeah, this one’s tricky. I was his training officer. And I don’t need eyes on me because he’s a bad egg.

“How do you kill someone and not remember doing it? Anyway, just keep me in the loop.”

“Okay, Grant. Give me a chance to check him out, and I’ll text if we find anything. But tests take time, so try to be patient.”

***

When Smothers arrived, with two techs rushing behind him trying to keep up, he found a security guard staring at his phone in front of Jason’s room.

Walking inside, the first thing he noticed was that Jason was alone. However, his clothing had already been removed, and the bag with them was left on a prep table nearby.

“Frustrated that the hospital still didn’t recognize the need for his protocols, Smothers hoped that the evidence hadn’t been compromised.

CHAPTER EIGHT

Finding a Friend

Jason Colt

Jason was startled by the intensity of the nightmare. His body jerked, and his arms shot off the bed as if he were falling.

Unfamiliar sounds surrounded him in a hypnopompic state.

Seeing a form beside him, he reached for the ghost of his partner, only to have his hand go through the specter and intensify his horror.

In a cold sweat and disoriented, he fought for consciousness.

The beeping monitor at his bedside kept tempo with his heartbeat. It had been that noise that had reached into the dream to change its course.

Back in his childhood neighborhood where his mother still lived, Jason stood in the street and watched the movers unload their truck in the driveway at the first house entering the cul-de-sac.

Growing up in a cul-de-sac without many kids his age was tough. And asking his mom to arrange playdates was embarrassing. So, Jason spent most of his time alone. That is, except when his parents would get together with Dean's parents. That was the best because Dean was his best friend.

Jason hoped a new kid his age was moving into the neighborhood, which was why he'd been watching the men for so long.

When he saw one of the men pull a rad bike out of the van, he got excited. He reminded himself that, even though it didn't look like a girl's bike, sometimes it was hard to tell. But man, he hoped it wasn't a girl's bike.

Going around the side of it, he planned to peek inside. If he saw toys, he'd know if the kid was a boy. Just as he got to the garage, a voice said, "Hey, what ya doing?"

Jason spun around to face a boy about his age and height. The boy was skinny, had skin the color of the hazelnuts, dark curly hair, and the lightest green eyes Jason had ever seen. The best part was that the kid was his best friend and he was wearing a Colorado Rockies baseball cap.

Trying not to act surprised or excited, he said, "Um, just lookin'. Hey Dean, I didn't know you guys were moving here. Why didn't you tell me?"

"I wasn't sure where we were moving. My dad just said we were moving closer to you guys. I just figured I'd sneak on up and surprise you when I saw you. Was it a surprise?"

"Yeah, but I wasn't scared or nothin'. Super cool, though. Now, we can hang out all the time instead of waiting for our folks to get together. It seems like I haven't seen you in forever."

"Yeah, my mom took me to see my grandmother in Idaho while Dad was on a big case. But guess what?"

"What?"

"Dad gave me a nickname."

"Why?"

"Cause nicknames are cool, man. Anyway, so, like, one day, Dad grabs me as I'm running down the hall. He's laughing and says they should have named me Dash. Then, he's like, maybe we should make it my nickname."

"Okay, but why Dash?"

"Because he says I'm always dashing around. I can't argue with that, I guess.

"Only I think it'll fit me better when I'm older.

"See, I'm gonna fly jets someday, and they're way fast. It'll fit me much better then!"

Slumping his shoulders and looking at his feet, Jason said, "My dad just calls me Jason. I don't have a nickname unless you count my mom calling me Lovebug. I mean, it's okay for her to say, but I wouldn't want anyone else saying it.

"Geez, Dean, I've never been called—nothin' as cool as Dash."

"Well, that's not really true, 'cause you know what? Colt's a really cool name. So, why not make that your nickname?"

Jason looked up at his friend and smiled. "Hey, you're right, that does sound cool! Never thought of that before. Okay, call me Colt."

After shaking hands on Jason's new nickname, they spent the rest of the day riding bikes and playing with matchbox cars.

Fast-forward memories of times shared on fishing and camping trips, riding bikes, playing games, swimming, going to camp, family gatherings, and barbecues, from childhood to adolescence to adulthood.

They both loved basketball and played regularly since they grew tall enough to hit the basket.

They tried out for every sport offered at school until they found their best game. Both sets of parents attended every game as their supporting cast.

In high school, Jason chose baseball, and Dean chose football, and by then, he had filled out and was built for it.

They graduated high school early and, after college, joined the Marines together. Colt fought on the ground while Dash provided support in the air.

When their tour was up, they eventually joined the Denver Police Department.

At six-foot-five, Dean had grown taller than Jason by a full two inches. An imposing figure with broad shoulders and chest, along with thick, well-defined muscles. But it was his round baby face and beautiful light green eyes that softened his intimidating size.

Jason slept peacefully until the dream promptly changed again. He was patrolling the Union Station area in downtown Denver. He was on his own for the first time and eager to prove himself.

It wasn't the best part of town, but it was a perfect area to train newer officers.

As he turned the corner on Eighth Street, Colt saw a dealer in the process of a sale. He'd seen the guy before, but the one time he chased him, the guy had gotten away.

It was his job to stop the criminal byproduct from violating, or in this case, corrupting, the rest of the population -- and a kid no less.

To Colt, that was way out of bounds.

After parking just out of sight, he moved in.

The darting eyes and exaggerated movements typical of most dealers were absent. After the handoff, they stood and had a conversation. Even more surprising, they didn't seem to notice him walking up.

Excited that a bust might gain points with his sergeant, he checked his bodycam and jumped into action.

But just as he made his move, they both saw him coming and ran in opposite directions. "Shit!"

Figuring he'd worry about the kid later, Colt went after the dealer, weaving in and out of the congested downtown traffic.

After playing cat and mouse for a few blocks, he thought he was closing in when he lost sight of the guy. Frustrated after searching the area, he decided to walk it off, figuring he'd have a better chance of relocating the dealer on foot.

Leaving the cruiser parked where it would be a good deterrent, he called in his location and his intent to walk a beat.

By the time he got to Zuni Street, he'd managed to walk off most of his frustration. But the hot summer rays were beating down on him, and sweat was saturating his vest. In search of some shade to cool off before heading back to the station, he found a welcoming spot under the I-25 overpass.

Leaning on a pillar under the overpass, a nice breeze helped cool the area and was just enough to give him a little relief from the hot July day.

Musing about catching the guy, he was distracted.

With cars roaring by on the freeway above him, Jason tried to replay how the dealer got away. If he could figure that out, he might be able to catch him. And there would always be a next time.

His Sergeant had mentioned, at one of their meetings, that someone had been hassling the homeless living at a tent camp near the overpass. Apparently, the guy was threatening them and taking what little they had.

Dealers were a dime a dozen. Take one down, and two more pop up in his place to provide an escape for those who can't deal with life's hardships. Sad though it is, people always find ways to numb out. For some, it doesn't matter if they find it legally or illegally.

To Colt, hooking a kid on drugs was one of the worst types of depravity.

While unsuspecting parents worked, their unsupervised kids on summer break often ended up in trouble. Luckily, there were programs like the GRD that helped keep kids off the streets so they didn't end up recruited into gangs or getting hooked on drugs.

Colt committed the boy's image to memory. If he saw him again, he would make sure to have a heart-to-heart with the kid.

If only he could be in the right place at the right time when the unsuspecting dealer wandered into the area, not only could he save that kid but many others like him.

Looking at his watch, he realized that it was almost time to call out for the day.

Just as he turned to walk back, a break in the hum and rumble of traffic noise that had been masking a muffled sound caught his attention.

He scanned the shadows under the sloped abutment where the bridge met the concrete support pier and waited for another break in traffic. That's when he noticed a pile of trash in the shadowed space not a quarter mile from a haphazardly constructed cardboard camp.

Listening intently, the short lull in traffic allowed him to hear a crinkling sound followed by a high-pitched squeal.

Still uncertain, he advanced slowly toward a pile of kitchen trash bags with his hand on the butt of his weapon and unhooked the strap, "Who's there? I can hear you, so just come out!"

As the roar died down, he was close enough to decipher a low whimpering. Rushing up to the heap of garbage, his eyes fell on one bag with a tear. As he reached for the white bag, it moved, and a high-pitched cry came from inside.

Ripping the bag open, Colt pulled out a small puppy. It was wet and shaking, with bugs hopping off it.

Colt experienced a mixture of emotions: gratitude that he'd found the pup in time and anger at whoever had thrown a living thing away to suffocate in their garbage. Such cold-hearted cruelty was unconscionable—intolerable.

No matter how often he was exposed to it, it wasn't easy to accept that people like that existed.

The department kennel was located in the warehouse district and had a full-time veterinarian on staff.

Dr. Mills had been with the City for most of his career. He was a wise but fun-loving man in his fifties. Colt had heard that he had a tender spot for animals, and if anyone could save the little guy, Dr. Mills would find a way.

On his way to the kennel, Colt called his Sergeant to report finding the puppy and to sign out.

But for all Colt's confidence in the doctor's abilities, Dr. Mills didn't offer much hope. "I hate to say it, but he's pretty weak, Jason. God only knows how long he was in that bag before you found him. I'm surprised he didn't suffocate, even with a rip in the bag.

"I'll do some tests, but I can't give you any guarantees here. The one thing I can say for sure is that this poor little guy is way too young to be away from his mother."

But Jason refused to be discouraged, "Please, doc, do whatever you can. Someone just threw him out with the trash! Alive for God's sake! I swear if I knew who did it, I'd arrest the heartless SOB for animal cruelty."

When the puppy began crying for his mother again, Jason gently put his warm hand over his body and continued to rub the top of his head with his thumb. "Geez, Doc, the little guy has been through it, you know? I don't know if you can save him, but I was hoping you'd at least try."

Looking at the small pup, Dr. Mills said, "Okay, I'll see what I can do, but we've got to be realistic here; even doing all I can, we could lose him.

"I figure he's maybe three to four weeks old—young enough that he still might need to be stimulated to eliminate. Caring for a pup this young is a lot of work, and he'll require constant care.

"My staff can try to bottle-feed him every few hours, but someone will have to stay overnight, and that's not cheap. You'll have to cover the expense because he's not part of the department's program.

"Look, even if he makes it through the night, he could still get a respiratory infection, especially after being in that bag. Not to mention, a pup this young is more vulnerable to viruses, kennel cough, and the like.

"And even if we save him, there's just no way to tell how long it might take before we could let you take him home.

"It's a tough call… and an expensive one. Are you sure about this? I can't even provide an estimate."

"Yeah. I'm sure."

Colt looked at how his warm hand comforted the pup, quieting him, and shrugged. "It's too late for me, doc. I'm committed to the little guy. I couldn't give up on him now if I wanted to.

Just think how scared he must have been. And how hard it was to be alone and in an unfamiliar place without his mom. Just imagine how hard he had to fight to live!

"Even if there's only a small chance to save him, I'm willing to pay for you to try."

"Well, okay. We'll clean him up and see if he makes it through the night. If he does, then tomorrow, we'll work on building up his strength. Right now, all we can do is wait and see. But he is a fighter."

Thrown into darkness, his heart pounding and his breath rapid, his arms involuntarily shot out from his body concurrently with his legs in a hypnic jerk.

Whether his body was trying to slow the freefall that he was experiencing or minimize the trauma upon impact when he hit the ground, he would never know.

He was asleep.

When he woke, he was in the alley, shivering on the frigid, wet ground in saturated clothing years after he'd saved that little pup.

Turning to a dark form lying beside him, expecting to touch soft fur and feel life in the rise and fall of breath, he was unprepared for the emotion that overwhelmed him when the form evaporated, and his hand fell heavily to the ground.

Unable to see clearly through a blur of tears, his arm swept the ground - searching. The anguish of loss compounded and left him with a depth of emptiness so vast that there seemed to be no end.

Emotions he'd kept at bay since his father's funeral suddenly rose to the surface with an intensity so fierce he lost all strength to push them away.

It was too much. Where was Stryker?

Tears slipped from out of the corners of his closed eyelids to slide unheeded into his dark sideburns.

He needed to stop his brain from throbbing and the sharp pains radiating from there down into his neck and left arm. He struggled to open his eyes, but the alley was too dark.

It was hard to tell if he was awake when his arms and legs jerked out. It wasn't until Jason sat up and looked around the room that he appeared awake.

But just as Billings opened his mouth to speak, he noticed that Jason's eyes were closed only seconds before he fell back onto the pillow, holding his head -- groaning.

He'd sat there waiting and watching in the corner of the room hidden in shadow, quietly observing.

Admittedly, seeing Jason writhing in pain, it seemed unlikely that he was faking. Then again, appearances could be deceiving. No one knew that better than a cop.

Besides, that wasn't why Billings had come. He had questions that needed answers, and before anyone else got to him, Billings wanted to know what Jason remembered.

***

The night nurse woke him to take his vitals and to let the lab tech draw another blood sample. But that part didn't make sense since they'd taken several samples in the last twenty-four hours. What were they looking for? And if they hadn't found it yet, why did they keep trying?

The lights were too bright, and he couldn't keep his eyes open. All he wanted was to go back to sleep and remember.

An hour later, Jason woke to a beeping sound. It took a minute to grasp that he was in a hospital bed with medical equipment making strange noises around him. With eyes closed, he searched for the call button. But he couldn't tell if he was in a dream or a dream within a dream.

Something had happened… but he'd lost it when the nurse woke him.

As the medical staff completed their duties, he thought about what the doctor had said the night before, "I know you want answers, but we haven't found why you passed out in that alley."

"The flu and the cold meds might have weakened you, and it probably didn't help that you exerted yourself running after the suspect.

"Of course, that wound on the back of your head—which is the culprit for the concussion. If nothing else, it explains the dizziness, headaches, and lapses in your memory.

"Have you been able to remember anything more?"

"No. Nothing. I still have some dizziness and that headache. It's not pounding as bad, but it's still raging. Is there any way I could talk you into another dose of that painkiller they gave me last night? It really helped.

"And is there a way to turn down the lights? They burn my eyes."

"Hmm, you're still sensitive to light, huh?" Using a penlight to check Jason's pupils, he looked at his watch. "Well, okay, I think we can fudge it a little. It's almost time anyway, and it's a low enough dose. I'll have the nurse administer it after we're done here. It'll help you sleep.

"I'd hoped that your sensitivity to light and your headache would have dissipated by now. I'll put in an order for another CT scan.

"Can you turn the other way so I can examine that knot on your neck?"

Jason turned his head and gritted his teeth while the doctor took his time prodding and poking him.

A sharp pain shot into his arm and head simultaneously as if pierced with a tiny double-ended switchblade.

When Jason jumped, the doctor pulled away, "Okay. We'll just leave that alone for now. It seems a bit larger and is still too sensitive. I want to follow up with another MRI. Don't worry. I just want to make sure everything's okay.

"The good news is that your lungs are clear, and the flu has run its course. You're in great physical shape, so I think you'll heal up in no time."

Nothing made sense. Even if the flu and meds were partly responsible for his blacking out, it didn't explain how the suspect was killed. If no one else was in the alley, how did he get a concussion or that knot on his neck?

He was worried about Stryker.

No one seems to believe me. And there's no way to prove that when I woke up, Stryker was knocked out beside me.

The next afternoon, after a two-day hospital stint, the doctor agreed to discharge him. Thrilled that he was finally going home, he didn't initially realize that once he was released, he'd be taken to department headquarters to be debriefed.

Only without a memory and few answers.

Wanting to provide the answers to the questions he knew he'd be asked but unsure of how to explain it all, he began making a list of what he could recall. He needed to have something to offer before Billings showed up.

The last thing that Jason could remember, and that wasn't all that clear, was instructing the perp to get down from the dumpster and reaching for his mic.

He remembered telling Billings something at the scene, but he couldn't remember exactly what he said.

Jason had always liked Billings. Not only because he was a great sergeant, but Jason thought of him as a friend. And yet, when he'd visited the day before, Billings had been different toward him. His questions made Jason wonder if Billings was on his side.

It was a relief when Earl Howard, his union rep, showed up and put a stop to it.

The debriefing was sure to be more of an interrogation than the simple interview Jason had hoped it would be. Internal affairs was bound to lead the charge with its typical accusations.

At least that horrible pounding had been dulled, making the headache tolerable. So, whatever was asked, he wouldn't have that distraction.

But how do you prove you're innocent, especially when you have no memory?

He considered some of the questions they'd ask, "Did you do it? What did you do before you started your shift that day? Are you having problems at home? Have you been under a lot of stress? Did you take any drugs or medication in the forty-eight hours before your shift? How are your finances? Do you have any relationship issues?"

That's when Jack popped into his head.

I may not remember much, but Jack knew how sick I was. He can vouch for that much, at least. I'm sure he reported seeing me take my cold meds, and he was the first person on the scene. They've probably already debriefed him. I hope he told them how unsteady I looked. At least he'll be able to back me up on that much.

His mind raced with what-ifs. Then, it hit him: he hadn't seen Jack since he watched him drag Stryker away that night. It seemed odd that Jack hadn't visited, considering that those closest to him had.

His mother had brought him clean clothes, the book half-read on his nightstand, and the writing utensils he was using. Dean and Kade had called and then visited. He'd even got calls from Jeffreys and Anderson on his unit. And Billings—well, at least he'd shown an interest.

So, what happened to Jax?

As he considered the possibilities, the walls in his room seemed to close in.

He'd worked several cases side-by-side with Jack. They'd trained their dogs together until Max got sick, and Jack had a new canine he needed to train with.

Jack might not have been a close friend, but he was a colleague. "So, what's the deal? Did someone tell him to keep his distance?"

A few hours later, a nurse woke him. "You need to wake up, Mr. Colt. The doctor just signed off on your discharge order. I've called your sergeant, so you need to get dressed before he gets here to pick you up."

After the nurse left the room, Jason picked up the notepad from where it rested on his chest after he'd fallen asleep.

Hoping it might trigger a memory, he took a minute to read what he'd written before dozing off. But nothing new stood out. With a sense of foreboding for what was next, he whispered to himself as he began to dress, "Why can't I remember?"

CHAPTER NINE

The Interrogation

The drive to department headquarters was a blur. What he hadn't expected was his insides dropping when the Crime Labs aluminum panels came into view.

Preoccupied with intermittent headaches and without any recollection of what happened that night to the victim, Jason knew his debriefing wasn't going to be pretty. Not that a shooting debriefing was ever easy. But it would have helped to have some idea of what happened.

Department headquarters and other government buildings, including a new modern crime lab designed to look like a DNA molecule, are secure in an expansive complex that covers an entire city block. The concrete buildings are bound with light tan stucco.

As Billings parked in the underground parking structure, Jason wondered if he was entering hostile territory. Although he'd been comfortable entering the complex for the last few years, he suddenly felt like an outsider.

It was hard not to speculate if his colleagues would condemn him or if they would hold off on judgment and give him the benefit of the doubt since many had worked with him.

Billings didn't move after he turned off the car. Jason didn't move either wondering what Billing's had to say. "Jason, I wasn't going to say anything, but you need to be careful what you say in there.

"Sometimes honesty isn't always the best policy. Especially, when you don't remember anything.

"That's all I wanted to say."

Walking through the thick, bulletproof glass double doors into an antechamber, Jason found it difficult not to feel guilty about something, especially since his sergeant was leading him to an interrogation room.

Set into the wall directly in front of the entrance doors was a teller's window, surrounded by bulletproof glass.

A distinguished-looking man with a full head of neatly combed white hair sat behind the glass. Sergeant Reynolds had been with the department for thirty-five years and had no intention of retiring. Three years earlier, after being shot during a convenience store robbery, he was put on a desk where he was happy to stay until he retired.

Reynolds knew every cop in the department by name. Recognizing Billings and Colt immediately, he pressed a hidden buzzer, releasing the interior side door latch while not missing a beat, helping a woman with her paperwork.

Neither man said a word as they walked down the corridor lined with pictures of past police chiefs. Nothing could be said that would ease the tension.

The sounds of confused activity seemed to be amplified in the corridor. Phones ringing, combined with unintelligible voices, filled the passage.

Passing the patrol division, Colt felt that he was being watched walking past the open door.

A group of patrol officers had stopped talking to level their eyes on him. He knew they were just curious, but it still stung.

He knew those guys and thought they knew him.

As they continued down the hall, Colt stopped for a second in front of the detectives' unit. Most of the noise was coming from that division. Detectives working active cases were either on the phone, in conversation with another detective, or reviewing case files.

Bolted to a side wall was a row of plastic chairs where a few people were waiting. A large city map on the back wall behind the desks caught his attention. He knew that the red pushpins that littered the map marked the locations of homicides that were being investigated.

Montgomery, the detective who had agreed to take a look into his father's case, was on the phone. When he glanced up and saw Colt standing in the doorway, he just shook his head and went back to jotting down notes.

Getting the message, Jason did a quick scan of the large room.

As he became aware of several eyes looking at him, Jason wondered if they'd already placed one of the red pushpins for the perp and if they suspected him of murder.

Billings nudged him, and they continued down the long walkway.

They passed a corkboard that took up a large section of wall. It held a secured ringed clipboard with a stack of the FBI's ten most wanted, in chronological order. The stack's thickness attested to the increase in the number of serious offenders.

A No Smoking sign above the FBI's most wanted list and a faded Alvin and the Chipmunk's 'It's not cool to do drugs' poster had been there since Jason started with the department.

Jason felt increasingly uneasy as he heard muffled voices coming from the end of the interrogation corridor.

As they entered the room, he began to sweat.

Seated around a rectangular table, drinking what appeared to be coffee, the men filled the room with the noise of their conversation as much as with their bodies.

He didn't know all of them, but the two that seemed most concerning for the future of his career were Lieutenant Jackson Bernard, who was in charge of the K-9/SWAT Unit under Captain Alverez, and Sergeant Hank Chambers from the Internal Affairs Division.

Jason had heard about Chambers through the department grapevine and knew that he'd been responsible for dozens of investigations. He had a reputation for being hardnosed while pursuing the truth but was also known to be fair.

Jason had never met the man, but Sergeant Chambers was easy to identify. At a husky six-foot-six inches tall, with short black curly hair, thick, bushy eyebrows, and a beard, he resembled a lineman stuffed into an expensive suit.

Jason had also heard that once Chambers thought a cop was guilty, he made convicting the cop his life's mission. A corrupt cop was worse than the criminals they apprehended, both in the eyes of the department and the law.

While Billings greeted the group, Jason caught Alan Jacobs, the senior Detective from the Homicide Division, giving him the once-over.

Jason had met the doppelganger only once, but he had heard that Jacobs was like a dog with a bone when it came to uncovering the truth.

He just hoped the man was on his side.

On the other side and at the end of the table sat Earl Howard, his union rep, and Edward Mills from the Denver Police Protective Association.

Two trays with pitchers of water and an upside-down tower of paper cups sat within easy reach at the center of the table.

Even circumstantial evidence could ruin a cop's career.

Innocent until proven guilty didn't apply to cops. Not if they wanted to stay a cop. Police were held to a higher standard. Any doubt of innocence, even if acquitted of any wrongdoing, would mark the officer as a pariah for the rest of his career.

But as big and intimidating as Chambers appeared on the outside, he had a big smile and bright eyes and was quick to laugh heartily.

And Colt couldn't help it; he liked the guy right off.

Lieutenant Jackson Bernard cleared his throat and started the recording. After introducing everyone in attendance, he began, "For the record, the discharge of a peace officer's weapon, especially one of my officers, must be investigated to keep both civilians and officers safe.

"It's even more critical when a discharge results in the death of a civilian; we must assess whether a criminal violation has transpired or if the discharge was accidental to maintain the department's integrity, which is more challenging in the current climate.

"Even though the crime lab is on it, this isn't an open-and-shut case. There are way too many unanswered questions in this case, so be prepared, Colt.

We'll be asking a lot of questions, but we also need you to share what you remember about that night.

"When I learned about the incident, I immediately notified the Homicide unit. Detective Jacobs will be the lead on your case until he uncovers the truth, which is why he's here today.

"Once I've finished, I'll hand it off to Sergeant Chambers from Internal Affairs. He will oversee the investigation and report all findings to the Commander of the Major Crimes Division, the Office of the Independent Monitor, and he'll update the Chief.

"To ensure fairness and accuracy, this proceeding is being recorded. I assume that everyone in attendance will professionally conduct themselves.

"As you know, peace officers are expected to cooperate; refusal would result in immediate termination. However, to ensure an impartial discovery, you have been provided advocates to protect your rights. Earl Howard and Edward Mills are with the Denver Police Protective Association.

"Do you have any questions before we begin?"

His father's words echoed in his mind. "It's okay to be scared, son, but never run from fear; it's always best to face it head-on so you have a chance to defeat it."

Colt's heartbeat quickened. Inhaling deeply, he replied, "Yes, I mean no. I don't have any questions, Lieutenant, and I'm willing to cooperate." Taking another breath, he tried to sound more confident: "Regardless of any discipline, I have no problem waving my constitutional rights under the Fifth and Fourteenth Amendments."

Looking around the room at the men seated around him, he quickly continued, "Seriously, though, I have no problem telling you everything I can remember. But I need you to know that there are holes in my memory. Holes that, no matter how hard I try, I can't seem to fill.

"The doctor said I have a concussion, but there's a chance I'll start to remember with time. But I'd like it on the record that I wouldn't have discharged my weapon unless there was an imminent threat…"

Brushing away the rest of Colt's statement, Lieutenant Bernard said, "We'll get to that. For now, stick to what you can remember from when you saw the suspects behind the gas station. When you've finished, we have some questions."

Colt rubbed at the tender spot on his neck and closed his eyes. The nasty headache that had plagued him in the hospital was making a comeback.

Bernard continued, "After reviewing what you can recall, we might have a better idea of what happened. You might even recall more during the review. Regardless, the lab will be able to corroborate or disprove your story. So, let's just take this one step at a time. We can sort out your memory lapses as things develop."

Colt rubbed his head, trying to relieve some of the pressure that was brewing. "Right. Like I told my sergeant, I'd just parked my cruiser in front of the Chevron station to make my rounds. I check out the businesses in my jurisdiction every night before the end of my shift. I had just checked the door at the station, and everything was good.

"That's when Stryker picked up on something. At his cue, I moved to the side of the building and caught a noise. It sounded… like something scraping across the ground, and I went to…."

Bernard interrupted. "You reported that your equipment wasn't working."

"Yes, sir. But that was a bit later."

"Right. Go ahead, finish what you were saying."

Colt rubbed his temple. "Um… right… okay. There were these two guys. At first, it was hard to tell what they were doing. They were wrestling with this large box, but I wasn't close enough to make it out.

"I didn't want to jump the gun and scare them off, but I wanted to know what they were up to. So I just watched.

"The guy with his back to me had a long black ponytail, and the other one wore a hoodie. I make out their faces.

"As hoodie struggled to lift his end of the box, I saw what it was… and it had a twin already in the bed. I called for backup, identified myself, and told them to drop it.

"I knew that if they loaded the second box, they'd take off."

Interrupting, Bernard asked, "At what point did your backup arrive?"

"Huh? Oh yeah, um… okay, hold on… let me think… I was holding them for all of two minutes, maybe, and I'd just unleashed Stryker… when I saw lights.

"I ordered them to drop it… lock their hands behind their heads, and went for my cuffs… no, hold on… that's not right.

"They weren't on the ground yet when the cruiser pulled up… they were still standing when Hoodie took off… and I sent Stryker after him. I… caught a glimpse of the cruiser doors opening in my periphery just as the other guy charged—knocking me down.

"I yelled at backup to secure the scene and went after him…"

"Why not let your backup go after him?"

“I’m not sure… um, I think I was closer. I thought they might try to circle back… for the weapons, or at least go for their truck.”

“The truck was stolen.”

The statement interrupted Colt’s train of thought. He was doing his best to remember, but he couldn’t keep up. “Huh? Stolen?”

“How long did it take from the time you called it in till your backup rode up?”

Jason felt like his head might explode. It was hard enough trying to remember exactly what happened without being interrupted every few seconds. “Umm… I was watching them…”

Earl interrupted this time, “Look, Lieutenant, he’s obviously struggling here. I think we’re forgetting that he just got out of the hospital.

“He’s getting confused and keeps circling back, trying to answer the first set of questions. If this keeps up, we could be here all night. I think we should let him finish telling us what he remembers. Then he can fill in any blanks by answering your questions.”

After a brief pause, the Lieutenant nodded, “Okay, go ahead, Colt. You were saying.”

After filling a cup with water and drinking half, Jason continued, “I don’t remember what I’ve told you.” Taking another sip, “Oh yeah, so at first I thought they might be rearranging their load… like maybe something had fallen. So I stood back watching them for a sec… to make sure.

“Hoodie was struggling to lift his end, and the other guy, I’ll call him Ponytail, was trying to hang onto his… end… and that’s when I recognized it. The crate, I mean. Same as those we used overseas.

“It was an MK… shoulder launcher. I spotted the other crate already in the vehicle then, too.

“I moved behind the building to call it in so they wouldn’t hear and rabbit. After I got confirmation… I… right! That’s when I unleashed Stryker! Damn, I knew when I mentioned it before it didn’t sound quite right… the timing, I mean.”

Looking up, he saw an inpatient look cross Bernard’s face. “Yeah, sorry. I can’t say for sure how long it was. It didn’t seem like it was too long… minutes after my call, maybe when the team rode up.

“I pulled my weapon and ordered them to drop the crate, drop to the ground, and lock their hands behind their heads.

Interrupting again, lifting his hand to stop Earl's protest, Bernard asked, "What type of vehicle was it? Was there anyone inside? Were there any other vehicles or maybe a witness?"

Colt's head was swimming. "I think the truck was black, maybe dark blue; if I were to guess, I'd say it was an F150.

It was dark, and the tailgate was down. I couldn't see the manufacturer's logo or the plate. I wasn't at the right angle.

"I must have missed whoever sold the weapons to them… but no. I didn't see anyone inside the cab, but then, like I said, it was dark."

Bernard added, "Except when your backup arrived."

Colt nodded, "Huh? Oh yeah… that's right."

When Bernard raised one eyebrow, Colt continued, "Right… so as soon as I took a step, Hoodie took off. That's when I sent Stryker after him. I kept my weapon trained on Ponytail, but before my backup parked, the guy charged me — hit me hard enough to throw me off balance, and I hit the ground.

"I jumped up, but I couldn't believe it. I mean, he was a short guy, skinny even. I probably outweighed him by at least thirty pounds.

"Anyway, after chasing him for a few blocks, I lose him, but while I was searching, I hear Stryker. So I change directions and went to find him.

"I called it in… or thought I did. I can't remember if I got a confirmation from dispatch."

"Well, no calls were logged after that, but we do have information from that call.

"Colt, this department has a call system that is continually updated. There is no way, especially within the city limits, that your radio malfunctioned. There weren't any interruptions, and nothing was wrong with your equipment. We checked. So, what prevented you from calling in?"

Earl objected, "Lieutenant, please…."

"…Just let him answer. There are just some things that can't wait. He can always retract his statements later."

Colt swallowed hard. "Nothing prevented me, sir. The radio just wouldn't work. I swear I don't know what happened… but my calls wouldn't go through. I know it doesn't make sense, Lieutenant. All I know is that I tried to call in several times, but I only got static.

"Maybe the frequency was hacked. I really don't know. I can only tell you what I experienced and hope someone can figure it all out later."

"All right. For now, we'll put it on the back burner. Just tell us what you believe happened, and we'll go from there."

"Okay, so… I searched the area, but I couldn't reacquire Ponytail—and I looked!

"After hearing Stryker, I thought I should find him before Ponytail shot him."

"He had a gun? You didn't say anything about a gun?"

"Well, I didn't see it until I was chasing him. It was SOB carry, partly concealed by his clothing, but I caught sight of the grip sticking out of his waistband as he ran. After seeing he had a weapon and losing him, I was worried about my partner.

"I called it in—but my focus was on protecting Stryker. By the time I caught up to them, Stryker was trying to get to Hoodie, who was on top of a dumpster.

"It was hard to see him because he was hiding between the wall and the dumpster's metal lid… holding it up like a shield so Stryker couldn't get to him.

"The alcove was dark, the night only providing a sliver of moon nestled too high in the sky and partially blocked by a building.

"Totally insufficient to penetrate that hole.

"The only light was a soft glow from a fixture over a doorway to the west. Even my Stinger didn't help dispel the pitch black very well.

"I couldn't see what the suspect was doing behind the lid. I couldn't be sure he wasn't packing like his friend.

"All I could make out were bits of red hair.

"Stryker was making all kinds of noise, so I called him out and ordered the perp to get down."

"Things moved pretty fast after that. "He stopped, unsure how to explain what happened next.

When no one spoke, he continued, "Well… I remember reaching to que my mic… but… I don't know what happened."

Lieutenant Bernard was more encouraging when he said, "That's okay. Just tell us how you remember it."

Colt stopped to pour himself more water. He was exhausted, and his head was throbbing again, so he emptied his cup and continued. "Well… okay, but I'm not sure it's what you want to hear.

"The next thing I know, I'm waking up on the ground, freezing. I'm not sure if I can accurately describe what it was like to wake up on semi-melted patches of ice, shaking uncontrollably while dripping with sweat, as if under a summer sun. Something sharp was trying to cut its way out of my gut while fireworks exploded in my head. But that wasn't the worst of it. I can handle pain, but when I couldn't breathe… now that was the first time in my life that I felt terror.

"I was drowning in… something. A substance that I can only describe as… thick mud. My lungs… burned and began… convulsing… the only way I can describe it. Like they'd burst open.

"I fought to reach the surface… and finally… finally… took a breath."

He had to stop. He was breathing too fast, nearly hyperventilating after reliving that horrible moment. And in front of witnesses. The heat of a blush made its way over his face.

Downing more water, he looked at his lap, trying to pull himself together.

Their blank expressions pushed him on. "I know, I know. If I just blacked out, why would waking up be so… so… intense? If hit from behind, where was the weapon? And how would any of that affect my breathing? I've been trying to answer those questions myself. I just don't have any answers."

As he glanced around the room, the blank facial expressions made it hard to tell what any of them were thinking.

"My eyes couldn't focus. Everything was blurry. I couldn't think right. My brain was in a fog. When I finally opened my eyes and turned my head, there was a blurry lump next to me—it turned out to be Stryker. But he wasn't moving. He was out cold but breathing.

"At one point, I tried to sit up, the pain in my head… man, but it was the vertigo that forced me back down.

"I'm not sure how long it took before my eyes cleared. At first, I didn't recognize where I was, but when I was finally able to move around,

I noticed a dark form against the dumpster. I say form because that's what it looked like—just a darker shape in the shadows.

"At that point, I'd totally forgotten about the perp. I was dizzy, trying to get my bearings, and since I couldn't stand, I crawled. Near the body, my hand slapped into something wet and sticky. It was gross, so I wiped it on my pants. It didn't register what it was then, but it had to be his blood.

"When I got closer, it looked like a body dump. All twisted up like a life-size ragdoll that was dropped on its head and got stuck with its lower body held up against the dumpster.

"I think I was stunned, but it hit me that it wasn't moving. I searched for a pulse, but there was no sign of life.

"It really freaked me out, if I'm honest.

"As my thoughts cleared more, I worried that I'd disturbed the scene and was stressing about how I was going to call for help. That's about when Stryker started moving."

Colt's headache went from throbbing to pounding. "Um… I hate to ask, but I really need a break."

Without waiting for an answer, he took two of the painkillers the nurse had given him when he was released. "I still get these terrible headaches. If we could take just ten minutes or so to let my meds kick in, I'd appreciate it."

After all parties agreed, Colt went to the restroom and splashed water on his face. He was hoping he could get through the rest of the debriefing without throwing up.

Once everyone returned, Bernard restarted the recorder and asked. "So, did you recognize the body was the same perp you'd seen at the station? And what did you do next?"

"Well, like I said, Stryker started moving around, so I crawled over to him. The poor guy was in a bad way, and since I'd just been through it, I was sure he was suffering. I know I tried to call in the DB, but I can't remember exactly when.

"Although it had to be before Hanson drove up. I'm still not sure how he found us, but I was sure glad he did. I was pretty messed up. So when he asked for my gun… that was the first I'd even thought about it."

Chambers piped up, "Wait a minute— back up a sec. Where was your gun during all of this?"

“I really don’t know. Last I remember, I was holding it and my Stinger on the perp. It wasn’t until Jack asked for my gun that I realized it was gone. I must have dropped it… maybe when I reached for Stryker. Anyway, Jack kept it.”

Bernard asked, “Jack was the one who picked it up.”

Jason nodded, “Yeah, I saw it, but he grabbed it.”

Chambers followed up, “Why did Hanson pick it up? Why not leave it for the forensic team?”

Colt shrugged. “Um, I’m not sure. I don’t remember him saying exactly. I guess he thought he was securing the scene.”

Bernard and Chambers exchanged glances, and Chambers continued: “So if I’m to understand this, you’d completely forgotten about your weapon?”

“I must have. I couldn’t think straight… even after Jack got there. I was worried about Stryker… he’d only just started moving around shortly before I heard Jack drive up.

“My stomach kept jumping into my throat every time I moved. My head was pounding like a mother… so hard I’m surprised… anyway it took me a minute to stand.

“But there was no way I was going to let my only hope of getting help get away, so I went and waved him over.

“But yeah, dealing with all of that, I guess I forgot to check for my weapon. Oh… and there was this sharp pain on the side of my neck… it was swollen.”

“A sharp pain on your neck?”

“Yeah, it hurt like a mother… still does. Anyway, the doc found a hard lump.” He pointed to the swollen area on the right side of his neck, “…and he took a few pictures, so if you have any questions, he’d know. I have no idea how it happened. But Jack could confirm the shape we were in when he found us.”

Colt moved to the edge of his chair. “And that’s about it… all I can remember before everyone started showing up.

“Was anyone else in the alley with you before Hanson arrived?”

Colt’s brow furrowed as he stopped to think. “I didn’t see anyone, but I really can’t say for sure.

“I’ve had a few blurry images jump into my dreams. But so far, nothing that makes sense. Just blurry, undecipherable scenes that jump around, sometimes with mumbled voices—arbitrary and impossible to grasp without some context… that’s about it.”

“But there’s no way I would have killed that perp in cold blood. That’s just not who I am! Something must have happened that I can’t remember!”

“Okay, relax. Tell us what happened after Hanson got to you?”

“He checked the DB and asked for my gun. That was the first time I noticed that it wasn’t in my holster. We retraced my steps, and he picked it up. That’s about when the team arrived and began securing the scene.”

“About what time was that?”

“I really have no idea. Jack might know. He called it in.”

“Okay, we can check the log for times.

“Let’s change direction for a minute. Stryker attacked a rookie named Christopher Grayson at the scene. Is that correct?”

“Yeah, but Stryker was provoked, and he was just as sick as I was. He’d barely gotten on his feet when Grayson came up on me. If he felt anything like I did, Stryker was hurting.”

“A lot was going on by then. Several guys had showed up and were moving around. With all the commotion… Stryker was already stressed.

“But that rookie was out of line. He got in my face—at a crime scene when my canine was primed.” Disgusted, he asked, “Who does that?”

“Stryker growled… tried to warn him, but the guy wouldn’t back off, and before I could grab him, Stryker attacked.

“Look, he was just doing his job… protecting me like he was trained.

“It took me a minute to pull him off the guy... but like I said, that rookie was out of line; no other cop would be that dumb. Ask Greyson’s training officer; he was pretty pissed at the guy.”

Lieutenant Bernard’s left eyebrow raised, “So you’re condoning what Stryker did to Officer Grayson?”

“No. But you know how the dogs are trained. Once they’re keyed up, it takes a minute to settle them. Ask any of the handlers. They’ll tell you the same. We all get bitten sometimes—even in training.

“But you can’t blame the dog for doing what he’s trained to do.

"Look, there were several cops around, and Stryker didn't attack any of them. The rookie brought on the attack. I just don't think Stryker should take the blame because Grayson was showing off and acting a fool."

"Has Stryker been more aggressive lately?"

"No. In fact, besides training, he's never bitten an officer before. And he's less aggressive than the Belgian Malinois. Nothing was wrong with Stryker until that night."

"Okay, but is he a threat now? That's what we need to determine. Has anyone been able to get close to Stryker other than you?"

"He's been socialized with the other handlers on the K-9 unit, but he's most familiar with Jack Hanson. We trained Stryker and Max together since they were pups." He was getting emotional and needed to change gears, "By the way, how is Stryker doing? Did the Vet find anything?"

Hank Chambers interceded again, "After Officer Hanson took your weapon, what happened next?"

With his question left hanging, Jason replied, "About the time we found my gun, other units were pulling up. It got busy after that. I was focused on Stryker. He was still recovering, and all the activity was agitating him. If he felt half as bad as I did… well, anyway, after Stryker bit Greyson, his training officer took him to get checked out."

The room was quiet for several minutes. Until Bernard asked, "Do you realize that the DB in the alley was Billy O'Leary?"

A chill covered Jason's body from head to toe in an instant, tingling his scalp and sending goosebumps down his spine and along his arms.

He knew the guy seemed familiar, but everything had happened so fast that he hadn't been able to place him. Still, how could he have forgotten that scum bag?

Shaking his head, he could barely get the words out, "What! No. I mean, I thought he looked familiar, but I couldn't place him. It was dark, and he was mostly hidden in the shadows behind the lid."

"Yes, but you knew him, right? You were the last officer to arrest him, isn't that correct?"

"Yes. I just didn't make the connection. I was so damned focused on my radio. It hadn't been working, and I wanted to call for backup. But yeah… I can see it now. That's who it was all right." He shook his head.

"I just can't believe I didn't recognize him. Son of a bitch!"

Colt's chin hit his chest. Worrying his hands, he shook his head. "That red hair should have reminded me. I didn't think I'd ever forget that guy. I was so happy to get him off the streets—you know?"

His dark hair fell into his unfocused eyes as he stared off, searching the past. "I'd seen him hand off to addicts a few times that first year. I got close enough to chase him, too. But I'd lose him after a few blocks. He would just… vanish…" *snap* "…gone just like that.

"It really frustrated me at the time. I couldn't figure out how he pulled it off. Still, it was one hell of a good lesson.

"Billy wasn't like other dealers, who always had their heads on a swivel, eyes darting around, and all nervous-like. Billy didn't even try to hide what he was doing. He didn't have to because he had that little secret.

"It took a few more losses before I finally caught onto his game."

"What game? What are you talking about?"

"The sewer tunnels. That's how I was finally able to arrest him. I finally figured out his disappearing act, you know, like a magician, one minute right in front of you, and the next, poof—gone.

"I figured it out not long after I caught him selling to that kid… couldn't have been more than eleven or twelve. Man, I was pissed… had to walk it off when I lost him that time. I didn't think anyone could be that depraved…"

Pausing, his eyes grew wide, and his jaw dropped slightly, "Son of a bitch! I'll bet that's how Ponytail disappeared. Man, it didn't even occur to me. How did that escape me?

"Damn, it had to be a side effect from those damn cold meds."

"You were sick taking cold meds, that shift?" Bernard asked.

Earl Howard interjected, "Uh… hold up a minute, Lieutenant. I'm not sure how relevant that is at this juncture."

Colt pushed the hair out of his eyes, "It's okay, Earl. If I did anything wrong that night, it was probably coming into work sick. I admit that it was a bad call on my part. But at the time, I'd already been off for a week.

"I'd never had a negative experience with them in the past… still, hindsight being 20/20 and all, I was pretty sick."

This time, it was Chambers who asked, "What do you mean by side effects?"

"Well, until now, I'd barely considered them. I did ask the ER doc, but when he didn't give them much weight, I didn't either. He said my flu had just about run its course anyway.

"It would have been a shit shift no matter what after I found John dead in the park. I spent about half of it just waiting for the coroner and finishing the paperwork.

"John was a family friend who had lost his whole family in a fire. Anyway, I was sad, sure, but health-wise, I felt okay. I just didn't want to go home, where I'd just think about it all night.

"And I wasn't ready to inform the family at that late hour. So, I took a second dose of the cold meds in my locker to work the rest of my shift.

"A while later, my head started feeling foggy. Then, my muscles started getting fatigued. Between chasing Ponytail and running for what seemed like miles, I didn't think about what was happening. It wasn't until my nose started running and my eyes… were watering that I even wondered why the meds weren't working.

"For maybe a second, I thought it was weird that the meds weren't controlling my symptoms anymore."

Continuing his line of questioning, Chambers interjected, "Do you remember when the symptoms started? Was it before or after the situation at the gas station?"

"I couldn't say with any confidence exactly when they started, but it had to be sometime around losing Ponytail. I was briefly confused by how easily he lost me."

"Okay, continue with what happened after that."

"Like I started to explain about Billy, if you have one of those weird-looking keys and a little strength, you can lift those sewer covers enough to jump down and hide in the tunnels. I wouldn't recommend it. The stench is overwhelming. Still, it's a great way to vanish if a cop is chasing you.

"Once I figured out how Billy vanished into the sewer, and by the way, he only needed to be out of sight for a minute, I was able to bring him in."

Then, it hit him, pushing back in his seat; he challenged, "Hey, wait a minute! I thought he was doing four to six. How the hell did Billy get out of jail so early?"

CHAPTER TEN

A Few Pieces of the Puzzle

Six hours later, after answering the same questions repeatedly and feeling like they were trying to trip him up, Billings finally had a patrol unit to take Jason back to his truck at the substation.

Minutes later, he was parking at the Denver Police Department Kennel/Training Facility and Clinic. The stress that had knotted his muscles was slowly melting away, picturing a relaxing night at home watching a movie with Stryker.

When he entered the empty lobby, he asked, "Hey, doc, how's it going?" But as they met in the center of the room, Jason's smile slowly faded. It was obvious that the vet had been waiting for him at the front desk, and if his furrowed brow and slight frown were any indication, it didn't look good.

Jason didn't want to think the worst, but he wasn't going to prolong the agony by waiting to hear about it either, "What's happened? Is Stryker okay?"

Dr. Keith Jennings placed his hand on Jason's shoulder and said in a soothing voice, "No—nothing like that. Your boy is fine. I have a few things I need to talk with you about."

Sitting in his truck a few minutes later, chewing on what he'd been told, Jason was ready to punch something.

While listening to the insane department mandate, he'd somehow managed to stay somewhat calm. It was a touchy situation, and Keith was just the messenger. It had to be hard for him to relay that kind of news, especially when he had to tell a friend. Logically, he knew that Keith was a good guy just doing his job.

He'd been understanding and compassionate, calmly listening to Jason's protests while he did his best to be reassuring. It couldn't have been easy for him either. They had become friends in the last few years, shortly after he saved Stryker's life at only a few weeks old.

Stryker attacked an officer, so the department impounded him until they completed their inquiry.

Being told that Stryker wasn't permitted to go home was hard enough, but the punch in the gut, when told he wasn't even allowed to see Stryker, nearly took his breath away.

The fiery passion of his heritage burned in Jason's blood at the persecutory injustice that both he and Stryker faced.

The city, always busy and loud, made it difficult to think. Yearning for some peace and feeling beaten and thoroughly wrung out, Jason headed home.

Daylight was rapidly shrinking in the shadow of night, settling over him like a wet blanket. A chill had worked into his bones that even the truck heater couldn't ease. The shivering provoked memories of the alley, making him yearn for a hot shower.

Driving toward the mountains, highlighted by the sinking sun, usually provided him a sense of serenity, but now, they were darker, even unfriendly.

Jason was worried about what might happen to Stryker; his future depended on the results of the inquiry.

At home, Jason warmed himself in the steaming hot shower. With his head bent between his arms, he allowed the shower massager to pound the painful tension out of his deltoids.

Enveloped in the water's heat, his anger grew. He had rarely spent a night without Stryker sleeping on the floor next to the bed. And they'd been together almost 24/7 since Stryker was a pup in training.

Jason was tortured. Too much had happened, and Stryker wasn't just a dog or even a partner; he was family. He would have never imagined the department restricting his access to Stryker. What possible purpose could it serve? It was impossible to understand their reasoning, especially after what they'd been put through in the alley.

Angry at his incapacity to remember, he worried that the key to redeeming them from suspicion, indictment, or prosecution was lost somewhere in his memory. That meant that their only hope was locked in his mind. He either needed to find a way to remember or put all his faith in the crime lab to uncover a clue that would explain what happened to them and free them from the nightmare.

If Stryker were found unfit, he'd probably just be forced into early retirement. Unfortunately for Jason, things could be much worse. If found guilty, he'd not only lose his job—he'd go to prison for murder.

"Why is this happening?"

Getting into bed, Jason slowly lowered his sore and tired body onto the firm mattress. It had been an exceptionally long day, and he was drained. He desperately wanted sleep to take him away, to enter a world free from the nightmare that had taken over his waking hours.

An hour later, after tossing and turning, he sat up. The pain medication helped to reduce the pounding in his head, but he found it difficult to relax enough to fall asleep when his mind wouldn't stop speculating.

Too wound up to allow sleep to take hold, he closed his eyes and tried to replay what he remembered about that shift—when a thought hit him. Tossing off the covers, he jumped out of bed and went into his den.

The older house had a traditional floor plan. Instead of a large great room, it had a living room in front and a family room at the back. Shortly after moving in, Jason converted the front room into a den by adding a couple of anchored bookcases against one wall.

In a small nook between the bookcase and a deep picture window, he placed an old leather recliner and arched floor lamp.

On the other side of the room was an L-shaped solid oak desk along with matching filing cabinets. However, the iMac computer, modem, and printer kept on the desk were missing.

Jason had placed each piece of furniture precisely as it had been in his dad's home office, hoping it would guide him. And if he was honest, those meager possessions comforted him during all the days and nights he'd spent investigating how Matthew Colt died.

Above the desk, a magnetic dry-erase board had held the names of people Jason suspected might be connected to his father's death. Next to that was an evidence board that had held the photos and documents from the crash.

At least that's where everything he'd collected used to be.

While Jason was still in the hospital, the department received a subpoena to search his house. The techs had taken everything, including his computer. He hoped to get everything back as soon as the crime lab processed them, but it was unlikely his things would be brought back any time soon.

Against the wall behind his desk was a long folding table. Under it sat the boxes he'd picked up from storage on his way home.

When he'd put the boxes in storage, the plan was to go through them within a week. But every time he had planned to go and "just get it done," as his dad would say, he'd find a reason to put it off.

Dash had told him that he was in denial, saying that investigating Matt's death was only extending Jason's grief.

Billings told him that he was on a fool's errand and would end up driving himself crazy trying to find answers to a senseless tragedy, that he should just accept what happened and move on.

Kade just tried to distract him with outings and women.

But Jason couldn't let it go. He had a gut feeling that there was more to his dad's death than a simple accident. He believed that the investigators had missed something, and he needed to know what it was.

And as hard as it would be to go through his papers, Jason hoped he'd find something that would help him regenerate the information. Since he was put on suspension, he had plenty of time. He just needed to quit with the excuses.

Leaning back in his father's office chair, Jason returned his attention to the empty evidence board.

Something had triggered a memory just minutes before; what was it? He struggled to recall what had briefly tickled his tired mind and wondered at how quickly it vanished.

***

The sun began its climb, waking the birds to sing good morning. Squirrels chattered back and forth as they chased each other through the trees. A hawk screeched victory as her talons latched onto a small rabbit and soared home with food for her young. Troops of ants marched over rough terrain carrying more than ten times their body weight. Life had begun its work for the day.

The scent of fallen leaves and wet pine from an early morning rain drifted on the breeze through the slightly open window.

The sounds and smells of nature were soothing yet insistent.

The fireplace's heat had ebbed throughout the early morning, leaving a comfortable warmth as the remaining coals crackled.

Becca fought the morning's attempt to arouse her. She'd had a hectic week, and last night at the casino, she'd had an intense encounter with her past.

It was her day off, and she wanted to rest, play with her dogs, and rethink things.

She felt content in her semi-consciousness, at least while cocooned under the warm covers. But the boys were awake. With tails wagging, they raced to the bed, nudging her with wet noses, hoping to get an early breakfast.

"Come on, guys, it's too early! The sun's barely up. Go outside and play for a little while. I'll get up in about an hour or so."

With that, Radar and Scout headed for the laundry room and their doggie door. They would play until Becca called them for breakfast.

Turning over, Becca sighed deeply and tried to let sleep claim her once again. But lying perfectly still wasn't helping; her mind was already active.

Thinking about the night before, she sighed. She'd barely made it out of the casino without being identified. Her disguise was childish — too easy to see through. She needed a better disguise and a better plan. If Erika Stevens, an old high school classmate, could recognize her after all these years, anyone could.

Jumping out of bed, Becca went to the kitchen to grab a cup of coffee and feed the dogs before going into her home office.

When renovating the old farmhouse, she had turned the front parlor into a library and home office equipped with what she needed to run her practice.

She liked finishing the workday in comfort. For Becca, comfort was listening to her playlist playing softly in the background while Radar and

Scout were curled up close by. It just made the administration part of her job more manageable.

After finishing the orders to restock the clinic's supplies, Becca began searching the Internet for ways to change her appearance. Her first attempt at a disguise had been an epic failure.

She'd chosen it because it was out of character, it was in her closet, and it would hide her identity.

But the spiky blond wig with streaks of pink, cut to look like one of her favorite singers, black leggings, oversized maroon mini dress, jean jacket, and lavender Ugg boots, made more outrageous with several gold necklaces, a clip-on nose ring, hoop earrings, and multiple rings on her fingers, weren't able to fool everyone.

But Erika had spotted her and seen right through the disguise. "Oh, my God, Becca, you look just like you did when we were in high school getting ready for Boyd Reynold's party! The only difference is your hair! I thought you were going to be a vet or something, but you still look like a kid."

Looking around, hoping no one had heard the loud shrill of Erika's comment, Becca, thinking fast, said. "Well, I was supposed to meet a friend for a costume party, but she got sick, and since I was already in the area, I figured I'd just stop for a drink — but I was actually on my way out, my dad just called and said he's on his way to my house so I need to run.

"Have fun." With that, Becca quickly walked away before Erika could say another word in that over-the-top way of hers.

After several failed attempts, she'd gotten better at reacquiring Mark.

Last night, she had followed him to the Ameristar Casino in Black Hawk but was forced to leave after watching him for only half an hour. During that time, he hadn't spoken to anyone but the blackjack dealer, which, for her, meant the night had been a bust.

She was looking for proof that he was the one who killed Joss and followed him, hoping to identify his supplier, believing that with a little more proof, she could force the useless detective Myers to reopen her sister's case.

She'd managed to sit just a few yards away from him in that ridiculous costume. But when he suddenly got up and headed her way, she ran like a scared child, almost knocking Erika down in the process.

That experience had been a wake-up call. An omen portending doom if she continued on her current trajectory. She needed a way to hide her identity so that even her own family wouldn't recognize her.

A silicone mask was too bulky, hot, and uncomfortable, not to mention they were way too obvious. Besides, she wasn't dressing for Halloween. And looking young or hip wasn't enough to conceal her identity.

Most young women stood out, "Okay, so, what subgroup of the population is rarely looked at twice?"

That's when Mrs. Connors, Ruby's fur mom, came to mind. She was the perfect age to emulate in her late sixties and dressed just like most women her age. But looking too old could also bring unwanted attention if she didn't play the part right. "I can't appear too feeble, too rich, or poor; I just need to fade into the background."

No. She didn't need to look old, just older.

She'd watched enough cop shows to know how to change her identity. She'd get a new PO Box outside of her county. Her current box was at the local post office, which was way too close to home to use for both her business and surveillance needs.

To make her new disguise more legit, she planned to get a fake ID—no more hiding in the shadows. From now on, she would blend into the background and find out the truth.

With the help of a YouTube instruction video, she'd teach herself how to apply SFX makeup, and with practice, she hoped to stay under the radar.

Her new name would be Lily Jane White—a mix of names from her mother's favorite actresses. The names were a bit old-fashioned, which fit into her disguise nicely.

She snickered to herself and thought, *I'm going full-on spy. It might be dangerous, but if I can get justice for my sister, it will all be worth it.*

A little sting of doubt crept into her thoughts.

She'd worked hard to create the life she'd always wanted, and she didn't want to lose it: her home, her practice, and her clinic.

Should Mark Payton and whoever he was working with discover that she'd uncovered their little secret before she could turn over what she had and bring them to justice, they would kill her just like they had Joss.

Then again, if she didn't even try to avenge her twin – she wouldn't be able to live with herself anyway.

Making a list of supplies, she began shopping. The SFX order included nose and scar wax, spirit gum adhesive, liquid latex, a character crème makeup wheel for shading and age spots, and SFX makeup removers.

She found a perfect ash and platinum wig with long wispy bangs cut into a respectable bob that was similar to Diane Keaton's style. The long bangs would help hide her younger facial structure and eyes.

Dark brown colored contacts and a pair of glasses would conceal her round blue-green eyes.

Studying clothing popular for women in their sixties, she purchased a maxi dress, a floral cardigan lightweight coat, a few scarves, two collared blouses, two pantsuits with elastic waistbands, and a calf-length wool coat.

Finally, to disguise her body, she bought foam padding to sew into the clothes, adding weight to her stomach, hips, and back.

With everything purchased, she spent the rest of the morning watching videos on how to apply the SFX makeup.

At the far side of the bookcase in her office, just out of view of the large picture window, she pushed a hidden button. The click that followed opened a section of the bookcase, allowing entrance to a small room.

During the remodel, she'd had the overly large front room made smaller to accommodate a narrow hidden room. It wasn't on any blueprint since it was added after the county inspector had already signed off.

Since the room was longer than it was wide, she had a wall of built-in bookcases installed to square it off, but the new space only shortened the room by six and a half feet.

The contractor thought that the hidden space was a panic room because of the metal barrier installed between the office and the small room. But Becca used it to protect the evidence she'd collected.

If the target ever figured out who she was, at least the evidence would be secure.

The walls were painted with duck-egg blue magnetic chalkboard paint, which made them perfect for writing on or for hanging maps or pictures with magnetic pins.

An Edison fire-rated gun safe and a tall filing cabinet sat against the back wall at the back end. Inside the safe were several weapons purchased at different gun shows. She'd taught herself to shoot each weapon at a small gun range two counties away.

The filing cabinet held all the evidence she'd uncovered over the years. It wasn't much, but it was more than the bumbling detective had bothered to look for.

Entering the room, she checked off two more items on the list and smiled. The list was getting smaller.

Then, she grabbed one of the pictures hanging on the wall, took an envelope file from the filing cabinet containing one of Joss' journals, and returned to her desk.

She remembered something Joss wrote in her journal, and if her memory served correctly, it might help narrow her search.

It pleased her that the drawing from the journal and the picture she'd taken of Mark from a distance would have been an exact match if the image had been clearer… and the drawing had been in color.

CHAPTER ELEVEN

The Escape

Colt was called into the captain's office a month after his interrogation. Billings was already seated in front of the desk, and the hangdog look he was wearing told Colt that what was coming wasn't good.

Captain Luis Alverez was seated behind his old, scarred desk, covered in stacks of files. An old computer sat angled in the left corner near the wall, and Colt spotted his employment record on the screen.

Everything in the room looked old and worn except for a new ergonomic desk chair the captain had purchased at his own expense.

Captain Alverez cleared his throat. "Colt, take a seat. I've been going through your personnel file, and I've learned a few things. For example, I knew that you've trained with Stryker since he was a pup and that you both are part of the K-9 unit.

"But what I didn't realize was that Stryker is on loan to the department and that there is an agreement that he will be returned to your full custody when he's retired. I wasn't aware that the department accepted K-9s on loan, so I've had to check on the legality of our current situation.

"I've also read the complaint your attorney filed with the department. In it, you claim that Stryker is being held without legal representation, that he hasn't been allowed to see his handler — yourself, which you believe is the cause of his aggressive behavior, and that by all rights, Stryker is your legal property. Because of these reasons, you are requesting full custody of him. Is that about it? Is that still your position?"

"Yes, sir!"

"Well, were you aware that since the incident with Officer Grayson, no one, not the vet who has taken care of Stryker since he was a pup or Hanson, who helped train him, has been able to get close without the threat of being bitten?"

"Well, no. But Cap, I think two critical issues are being overlooked. The first is that Stryker suffered a trauma while on the job. The second is that since that traumatic experience, he's been kept from me—the person he feels safe with.

As I mentioned in my complaint, I'm Stryker's handler. We live and work together, and he's used to a routine that mainly involves me.

Jack mentioned that Stryker wouldn't let the vet examine him after the incident, which seems reasonable considering what he'd been through. He was agitated even before anyone arrived at the scene.

"I heard that Stryker had to be muzzled to be examined, and he tried to bite Jack.

"What I don't understand is why I'm not allowed to see him. If you'd just let me spend some time with him, I'm sure I can settle him down.

Everyone who has ever been around him knows that he's a good dog. Whatever happened in that alley has really messed him up, and until he feels safe… well, he's not himself."

What Colt didn't mention was that Jack had agreed to check on Stryker and report back to him. But there was no way he'd throw Jack under the bus by bringing that up.

Jason had met Jack in Afghanistan during a gun battle in the middle of the desert. After his squad was deployed to escort a convoy of supply trucks through hostile territory. Jack was part of the ground supply officer's unit in charge of transporting the supplies to Kabul.

Unfortunately, the Taliban had other ideas, which included stealing the supplies and killing every living soul in the convoy.

It had been one hell of a fight.

They'd been trapped for two long days while insurgent snipers picked them off. In the end, they'd lost several men before they were able to track down and kill the last member of the cell with the help of air support.

Captain Alverez cleared his throat. "Because this is an ongoing investigation, you shouldn't be told anything, including anything related to Stryker."

Colt tried to keep his temper in check.

Too much had happened. Between losing his dad, his mother's assault, dealing with the worst flu of his life, John's death and that awful night in the alley, the pressure of the debriefing, learning about Billy, the strange nightmares, and being kept from Stryker, his anger had been simmering just under the surface.

Anger had never been a problem for him before, and this was definitely not the time. Being insubordinate to his Captain, even while on suspension, would only make things worse.

He could howl at the moon later, but for now, his Captain was looking at him and waiting for a reply. Pushing down the anger, he finally responded, "I'm sorry about that, Cap, but the bottom line is that Stryker needs help, and so far, no one seems to know how to help him. Why not let me try?"

"Look, Colt, with your suspension, we have to do everything by the book. IA is all over this, and until you're cleared, this is just how it has to be. Honestly, we're lucky you haven't been arrested."

Sighing, the captain continued, "But that's not why I brought you in today."

Colt held his breath, fearing what was coming.

"Dr. Jennings couldn't find any physical injury to explain Stryker's behavior. And because he bit an officer and then tried to bite Jack at the kennel, he's been designated as a high-risk canine…"

Colt interrupted, "…but he was traumatized!"

"Colt, let me finish. I know this isn't easy, but the fact remains he's a trained threat — trained to attack and kill, if necessary. If the wires somehow got crossed in his brain, no matter how it happened, he might bite a civilian, maybe even kill someone. That's why we haven't been able to let him return home. The department can't be liable for something like that."

Colt jumped out of his chair and pleaded, "Cap, I'll take full responsibility. I'll sign whatever legal documents you want. He's a good dog, I swear! He needs me. If you'd just let me see him, I know I can help him get past this.

"Please, Cap, don't give him a death sentence until you've at least given me a chance to help him. He's never been away from me this long! Just give me an hour to work with him at the kennel. I know I can help him... just please don't let them do this!"

"Colt, sit down. It's not my call; this came directly from the Chief, who, by the way, gave me an earful after he got an earful from the mayor's office and passed it down the line.

"I'm sure you've heard that Grayson has a beef with us now that he's no longer with the department. He's filed a lawsuit claiming that he was targeted and bullied and that Stryker attacked him because of that.

"It costs the city a lot to fight these things, wasting valuable resources we could really use elsewhere.

"The only concession the Chief was willing to make was with the timeframe.

"Dr. Jennings recommended giving Stryker at least three months. In his report, he cited a few cases like Stryker's, in which most canines, after a trauma, tended to have symptoms slowly subside over three months.

"If Stryker doesn't show improvement by then, the Chief has ordered that Stryker be put down. I'm sorry, Colt; I know how much he means to you, but there's nothing more I can do."

A month had passed since that meeting with the captain, but Stryker hadn't improved enough. There were signs that his aggression was softening. He was allowing Dr. Jennings into his kennel. However, he still got agitated when other handlers attempted to work with him.

Leaning back in his dad's old office chair, Jason couldn't concentrate. Time was running out, and he felt his heart drop every time he thought about it.

Too many what-ifs kept him up most nights. What if Stryker didn't show improvement in time? What if he attacked a civilian? What if he got Stryker back but then was found guilty? What would happen to Stryker if he was in prison?

First, he needed a plan to save Stryker. Then, he needed a backup plan in case he couldn't take care of him.

What he was thinking was risky.

He really needed help, but he struggled with the thought that he might put those he cared about in danger. An accomplice was just as guilty.

And yet, there was no way he could do it all alone.

After struggling with what to do for half the night, Jason finally sent a quick text to Dean to meet at the cabin.

The two men had grown up like brothers.

Their parents had been close friends since before they were born. So, they'd spent many summer vacations at the cabin, which they considered their own special hide-out.

Located off the beaten path and far from Denver, the cabin remained a secluded and private place.

The land had been in the Adams family for generations.

Over the years, the cabin became a great place to enjoy the outdoors with family.

When it was passed down to Dean's grandparents, they built the cabin as a retreat. And by the time Charles took possession of it from his father, the cabin was in need of some TLC.

Charles wanted there to be enough room for their growing family, which by then included the Colts.

So they all pitched in to fix it up, adding two bedrooms and a detached garage. After that, they spent many of their summers at the cabin.

Years later, after being discharged from the military, Dean and Jason upgraded and remodeled the cabin as a surprise for the family.

It took several months and a few subcontractors, but they enlarged the back deck, opened the floor plan, and added a bathroom.

They installed double-paned windows throughout, had the cabin rewired with a new electrical panel, and, with Matt's help, repiped the house.

Once the big projects were done, they painted the interior and installed shiny new appliances, cabinets, and countertops in the kitchen, as well as new light fixtures and sconces.

For Dean and Jason, the remodel had been an excellent way to decompress after their stint overseas. And the downtime spent fishing, watching sports, barbequing, and learning how to brew beer hadn't hurt them much, either.

Jason parked his truck out of sight on the curved driveway out back. He remembered when he and Dean had helped build the garage the summer when the whole family, his and Dean's parents and grandparents, had spent an entire week together.

As soon as Jason opened the screen door, Dean walked up with a concerned look on his face and put an arm around his shoulders, "Hey brother, how you doin'?"

After setting his bags down, he patted Dean on the back. "Man, am I glad to see you! It's really been hard. I mean... damn." Shrugging his shoulders, "...let's just say life is kicking my ass right now. Let me drop this mess in the room and grab a beer. Then we can talk."

"Okay. You get settled and meet me on the dock."

While Jason put his things away, he worried that he was about to put his best friend in a compromising position. But he'd gone through every scenario, and this was his last hope.

Sitting in the chair next to Dean, Jason grabbed a beer from the ice chest. After drinking nearly half and staring at nothing in particular, he finally said, "I want you to know that this is hard for me. You're one of the most important people in my life—but I think you know that. And I hate to ask... but I really need help."

Without even a pause, Dean said, "You know I'll do whatever I can. But first, you need to talk to me. What's going on?

"You were kind of out of it at the hospital. And the last message just said that you're not allowed to see Stryker. So just spill it already."

"They're gonna kill him, Dash! The order came down from the Chief. The Cap told me that he's only willing to give Stryker three months to recuperate, and time's nearly up.

"He's worried that Stryker's a risk to the public.

"I've tried everything. Charles filed a motion to let me take Stryker home, but as long as they feel he's a threat, it's a no-go.

"He only has till July fifteenth—three weeks from today. If he doesn't show improvement by then, the Cap said they'll put him down.

"No way, I can let that happen. I have to figure something out. I've come up with a few ideas, but you're better at strategy, and I'm way too close to this to think straight.

"I know it's asking a lot, but will you help me come up with a way to save him?"

Shaking his head, Dean replied, "That's messed up... don't even have to ask.

"What I don't get is why you're being so weird about asking. Shit, man, Stryker's been a part of the family since way back. And we help family... period. You know that.

"I swear, brother, sometimes you get lost in your head. So hear me and write it down so you don't forget… I'm here. I always have been and always will be.

"We're family, so stop with the worry, okay?

"We'll figure something out. Shit, Stryker's one of us—and he doesn't deserve to be put down. I think of him like the family dog. Hell, he belongs to all of us. So, just tell me what you're thinking."

Standing in front of the full-length mirror, Jason stared at his reflection. His face and hands were covered in the camo paint he'd mailed home before completing his tour.

Charles had done all he could legally, leaving what little time remained to save Stryker.

Words from an arrestee came back to him, "Aw, come on, it's easy for cops. You guys break the law all the time—and then go hiding behind the badge. And this here is easy money. A little bonus for just looking the other way."

But Jason hadn't taken the bribe. The truth was he'd never thought of taking advantage of his position as an officer. He'd just spent too much of his life respecting the badge.

And yet, standing there looking at himself, knowing what he intended to do was illegal, was tearing him up inside.

That nagging small voice of guilt cautioned him again. A warning that what he planned to do… he'd regret.

Talking to his reflection, "What choice do I have? It's all so wrong! Keeping me away from him was cruel… to both of us. But… killing him is just so… undeserved… so wrong... it's inexcusable!"

He was being forced to choose between the law, which had his loyalty, and the life that had his heart.

Jason asked the man in the mirror. "What kind of choice is that?"

Going through with his plan meant breaking his oath to his badge, his integrity, his character, and the public's trust.

In other words, dishonoring the thin blue line.

To Jason, the thin blue line represented a barrier between law and order and the chaos that would transpire without it.

The thin blue line flag was a symbol that indicated their bravery, loyalty, courage, and solidarity, consistent with the ideals of justice and freedom—the field of stars, the citizenry that every officer vowed to protect.

But he wouldn't be taking a weapon, and the only person who might be injured was Jason.

While scrutinizing himself in the mirror, he went over the plan one last time. He wasn't nervous about the mission; he'd been sent on plenty of them while in the military.

But this was different. He wasn't at war fighting an enemy for his country, and what he was about to do wasn't sanctioned by his government or his conscience.

The black paint surrounding his dark blue eyes would subdue reflections and distort the color. The balaclava hood would hide his face. Form-fitting black gloves covered his hands up to his wrists while allowing him to use his fingers more freely.

Jason had always had a strong sense of justice and believed he was one of the good guys. As a kid, he'd wanted to be a superhero.

As he stood in front of the mirror, he asked his reflection, "What kind of person will I be after this?"

He was pleased that the black turtleneck and matching black Levi's would make him nearly invisible at night.

A nervous laugh escaped him when he noticed the stark contrast of his bare white feet. "Yeah, some criminal mastermind I am; where the hell are my boots?"

Pacing back and forth, Jason went over the plan he and Dean had made at the cabin.

He'd told Dean to stay away during the escape. He didn't want to risk ruining Dean's life in addition to his own, and he refused to let Dean take the fall with him.

But Dean had pushed back. "Dude, what are you talking about? You're not going to stop me from having your back, so quit being a jerk."

Jason was quiet for several minutes. "Look, Dean, it's illegal.

"If I'm caught, not only will Stryker's fate be sealed, but I'll lose my job, maybe even do some time.

"I'm taking a big risk here, but it's my risk to take.

"You're already doing enough. But at least you can claim ignorance if I'm caught at the cabin. I won't ask you to risk anything else."

"But you're not asking, I'm offering."

"Okay. But honestly, that just makes it harder.

"I appreciate you caring enough to put it on the line like that, but like you said, we're family, and I think our family has been through enough.

"I can't put you at risk if things go wrong, so please don't push it! I mean it, brother; I couldn't take it if this ended up costing you. Letting me stay at the cabin is enough… it's enough, okay?"

They hadn't talked since the day at the cabin but had agreed that it would be best if Dean worked on gathering intel.

They needed to know how Billy wiggled out of finishing his jail sentence. There was a reason he got an early release.

Dean would track down Jason's old street snitch to see what intel he might have—maybe get a lead on who Billy's supplier was.

Jason didn't disclose the details of his plans to Dean. He wanted his friend to have some deniability.

He hated getting Dean involved, but it sure felt good to know that his best friend had his back.

Sitting down on the bed, Jason slipped on his black socks and worn combat boots, with Dean's parting words still in mind. "You do what you have to do, brother, and I'll watch your six."

After their strategy session, Jason purchased a 2001 black Jeep Cherokee with tinted windows from a private seller.

When he met with the seller, wearing dark sunglasses and a ball cap, he felt like a spy. But Dean was right about the importance of hiding his identity.

To make it difficult for anyone to trace the purchase, he paid cash and held off sending the transfer of title to the DMV until the mess he was in was cleaned up.

Then he could sell it, or if it came down to it, leave it in a high-crime area with the transfer of ownership papers inside.

He waited to take it home until after midnight when his neighbors would be asleep so that the Jeep couldn't be connected to him.

Then he spent the weekend making sure it was mechanically sound, adding a lift kit, steel bumpers front and back, wide grab tires, an LED light kit, and a winch.

To hide the license plate, he splattered mud randomly along the back bumper and tires along with part of the plate to make it look like he'd been four-wheeling and got stuck.

He chose the Fourth of July weekend when most of the city was otherwise engaged in countless parades, backyard barbecues, art festivals and breweries in the RiNo district, restaurants and clubs in the LoDo district, or going to the Fireworks Games at Coors Field.

The stadium would be packed with families excited to stay after the game for the fireworks show.

With the rest of the city busy with mass gatherings and patrols focused on keeping those areas safe, it also limited his risk of getting caught.

The kennel's security system hadn't worked in years, and due to budget cuts, getting it fixed had been at the bottom of the department's list.

Then again, there was always the possibility that it had been repaired—just one of the many unknowns he'd have to deal with when or if it came up.

Jason hoped the plan would give him enough time to clear his name and prove that they were wrong about Stryker.

If the vandal was caught after his tag and initials were found in the lobby, some good might even come out of it, especially if he was made to remove graffiti around the city as punishment.

The tagger had been brazen enough to deface patrol cars with his signature red pig with a diagonal slash across the face.

Considering the current environment, it wasn't a harmless act. It was another call to arms. That would add to the growing threat to police.

But the department had ignored it, deciding instead to cover its patrol vehicles with an anti-graffiti coating that was more cost-effective than repainting them.

Sometimes, a little payback can make a wrong right.

The DPD kennel was located in the old warehouse district. Since it was located in a commercial area, there was little chance anyone would hear the dogs barking when he broke in.

The warehouse, along with two others, had been seized as part of a criminal property forfeiture after a major drug manufacturing and distribution bust led to the long-term incarceration of the owners.

Because of its location, the size of the lot, and the department's need to grow the unit, the building and grounds were transformed into the new canine clinic.

Handlers had access to the indoor/outdoor training areas during business hours, regardless of the weather.

Jason drew the layout and highlighted the exits; there were several, including an emergency exit at the end of the enclosed kennel, wired to alert both fire and DPD.

The lobby had the main entrance and a side door. Past the lobby, there was a door in the hall, one accordion-style glass door in the indoor/outdoor training arena, and a door near the kennels that had access to the main yard.

He needed the closest entry point to the office to check the alarm panel and decided to enter through the side door from the main yard.

That meant cutting through the chain-link fence and crossing the massive training yard, which was about the size of a small football field, all without being seen.

Inside the main yard were two sizeable fenced-off areas where handlers could focus on agility and obstacle training.

There was also a junkyard area used in various scenarios for training the dogs to search for suspects, drugs, or bombs, with the rest of the yard used for bite suit training and exercise.

From the office, it was a straight shot past the examination rooms and the indoor/outdoor training arena to the kennels at the back of the warehouse.

To keep the staff busy, he planned to release some of the dogs.

Depending on the number of dogs being housed, he'd leave the pups in the lobby, a few yearlings in the indoor training arena, and the dogs he was familiar with in the yard. Leaving the rest in their kennels.

Because a bite suit was too bulky to drive in, he'd sewn padding into the arms of his shirt and pant legs just in case any of the dogs, including Stryker, got aggressive. Knowing that the whole thing would be blown if he left a blood trail.

In his backpack was a set of lock picks, heavy-duty bolt cutters, his PVS-14 night vision binoculars, a headband flashlight, and a can of bright red spray paint that he'd taken from his parent's garage.

He had stocked the cabin with enough supplies for the duration and withdrawn enough money from his savings to last for a few months, figuring that if he couldn't prove his innocence and find redemption for Stryker by then, they'd both be out of options.

He'd waited until his neighbors were asleep and the crazy traffic had died down after the fireworks.

And it was time.

Finally, he was about as ready as he might ever be.

Pulling the black knit cap over his face, he grabbed the backpack off the kitchen chair and headed for the Jeep.

No one was expected at the kennel until eight o'clock the following day. With any luck, they'd be long gone way before then.

CHAPTER TWELVE

Meeting the Enemy

"Do sit down, Doctor; I want a full report. I'm sure what you have to share will be entertaining. At least for a little while, and we might as well be comfortable."

The accent was barely discernible except for the occasional rolling of the Rs and accent on the As.

The man behind the sizeable handmade mahogany desk imported from his homeland was seated on a made-to-order, thickly padded chair with hidden shocks that silently absorbed his weight as he shifted.

He was wearing an Armani suit, the lines expertly placed to hide his rolls. His thick arms lazily reclined on the highly polished surface.

The only jewelry he wore was a simple gold band on his pinkie. It had been his mother's wedding ring, although he'd had it for several years, and his skin had begun to bulge around it.

He considered himself a fantastic host, just like his father. His demeanor appeared relaxed and calm, but anyone who knew him would never drop their guard. Hidden underneath the smile was a serpent, always ready to strike.

When his father was arrested in 2002 for conspiracy to obstruct justice, Christian decided to distance himself from his father's reputation, mainly to avoid the connection to the Magluta name. His father, Sal Magluta, was a famous cocaine drug mogul who had run a cartel out of Florida.

Unfortunately, at the time, he was still in law school, learning how to protect his interests. He wasn't about to let sentiment threaten what he was building for himself. So, he changed his name from Christian Magluta to Francisco Manual Morales.

The room was a bit ostentatious, but it showed off Francisco's wealth and his ornate style just as he liked.

Two hand-carved grand oak double doors adorned the entrance. The walls held floor-to-ceiling built-in bookcases crammed with books and journals that he had never bothered to open any of the treasured volumes on the shelves.

The abundant lips curved into a smile as he asked, "Can I offer you something to drink?"

On the other side of the room was a fifty-inch stone fireplace with a fire dwindling in the large firebox.

The wing-backed chairs, deep-seated sofa, and overstuffed chaise lounge were upholstered in variations of dark greens and gold brocades and within easy reach of side tables in rich wood tones.

Just behind Mr. Morales, to his left, sat an artfully designed gemstone globe on a brass stand that reflected the room's light off an ocean of lapis.

Francisco's guest was a short, thin, Hispanic man. His long black ponytail slicked back tightly against his scalp with pomade.

Francisco had always felt that the hairstyle was distasteful and unappealing. It made the man's hair look oily, as if he hadn't bathed in days. But that was only one of the many things Francisco didn't like about the man.

Still, the chemist was brilliant at his craft, which is how he'd gotten his moniker. And although Francisco was loath to admit it, the man's talents had proven irreplicable, at least for the time being.

Keeping his eyes mostly averted, the Doctor responded with his best formal English. "Thank you, that would be most welcome. A shot of brandy is sounding good on this cold afternoon."

The Doctor had been summoned to the room many times but had never felt comfortable in the over-done room. Too much of a sweet thing gave a person a toothache. He'd always loved libraries, but this one was more like a museum.

He was more comfortable in his cabin and lab, where he could run his experiments and engage in his extracurricular activities.

Standing in front of the desk with the fireplace at his back, he didn't think it was the heat that was making him sweat. To avoid any appearance of fear, the doctor removed his jacket and neatly placed it on the back of the soft Italian leather chair.

The luxurious chair belied its deceptive design. Its shortened legs gave the host a distinct height advantage, allowing him to look down upon his guests—an unnecessary intimidation for those who knew his capacity for doling out violence.

For Emanuel Xavier Sanchez, who was already smaller than most, the towering threat was superfluous.

Francisco recruited Emanuel, a well-paid chemist at a lab in Houston, into his cartel and gave him the designation of the Doctor. The alias was required to maintain his anonymity.

The acquisition of the Doctor proved to be Francisco's most advantageous and profitable after the doctor created a substance he named Charm.

However, unbeknownst to Francisco, the recipe for the drug's chemical composition was incomplete. This was an intentional oversite that ensured Charm would always be connected to the doctor's preferred alias, the Wizard.

The title was given to him while he was imprisoned in Mexico. It denoted his skills as a sorcerer, enchanter, and magician—skills he perfected while incarcerated until he was able to escape from behind iron bars and his native country unnoticed.

Born in a remote area, his parents traveled from city to town to find work and had never bothered to record his birth with a local church or with the state.

They'd never been cruel to him, but they were often neglectful. Leaving him alone for long periods in the backseat of their beat-up old car or, if he was lucky, with strangers.

Still, it was painful when, within months after celebrating his fourth birthday, they sold him to a dealer, a man named Jefe.

Whenever Manuel spilled milk or dropped something, Jefe would retell the story of his parents begging him to buy the boy. "I am not surprised that you are like this. You are so stupid; you are incapable of learning even simple things."

"They begged me to buy you—for nothing more than a fix. You were such a burden that even your parents didn't want you. I only agreed because I needed a houseboy and thought that someday you could run my errands. But no, you are too pathetic.

"Yes, this is true. But, your parents, they were trash. You know this. Then, seeing tears well up in the boy's eyes, he'd smile and say, "I feed you and give you a place to sleep, and what do I get? Nothing! I've been robbed!

"But one day, you will repay me. I will see to it."

After being beaten frequently when crying for his parents, wetting the bed, or moving too slowly, Manuel feared that even being near Jefe was enough to upset him.

That's why he spent most of his time on the soiled mattress, which took up most of the floor space in the closet that was his room.

The box of things his parents had left with him still sat in the corner of his tiny room. It held his clothes, several books, a dirty stuffed bear wearing a colorful poncho, an old but colorful Loteria game with missing cards, a small wooden truck, two small plastic dinosaurs, and a ball.

The ball was the last birthday present his parents had given him, and it was his most treasured possession. But he only dared play with it after Jefe was asleep, fearing it would be taken away if he accidentally made too much noise.

Manuel missed his mother the most. Even though she left him alone a lot of the time, she was always kind to him. She would play games, cuddle, or put him on her lap and teach him songs.

She taught him the alphabet, numbers, colors, and even how to spell his name.

And every night, she made an effort to read him a story. Sometimes, she'd even make one up for him.

Even now, he liked to look at the alphabet she'd written on the inside back cover of one of his favorite books before he fell asleep.

When he was six, Jefe began calling him Pendejo, "You are worth no more than my animals—my possessions. And I will only feed you if you do as you are told. No more spilling, eh? You are old enough now to understand this."

That was the last time his birth name was ever mentioned. From then on, Pendejo was used so often that if his birth name hadn't been carved on the underside of the little wooden truck, he might have forgotten it.

He was almost eight when things began to change.

He was surprised when Jefe unexpectedly gave him clean sheets and blankets. A week later, he was allowed to watch TV at night as long as he stayed quiet.

The day Jefe replaced the dirty clothes he'd grown out of with new ones, he made Manuel take a bath while he watched, saying, "You need to be clean to put on new clothes, and anyway, you're old enough now to understand the importance of going to bed clean."

Jefe also instructed him on how to wash himself with particular attention to his genitals.

Manuel didn't understand why Jefe had started treating him differently or why he was suddenly friendly. He just knew he liked it.

It was almost like having a parent again.

And when Jefe started letting him watch cartoons, Manuel even started liking him.

It wasn't long after that when Jefe started watching cartoon tapes with him at night. But they weren't any kind of cartoons a kid would want to watch.

They were confusing, explicit, and gross and made Manuel uncomfortable.

Innocent with no basis of understanding, he had no idea that the man was grooming him.

It wasn't until the sexualized cartoons were replaced with pornographic movies that Manuel couldn't watch. He'd sit with Jefe with his eyes closed or looking at the ground so he didn't have to see.

One night as he watched a spider make a web, Jefe grabbed his hand and placed it on his erect penis.

Shocked, Manuel tried to pull away, but Jefe pinched his fingers together so hard it brought tears to his eyes.

Unable to fight the man, Manuel had no choice but to let Jefe put his hand around his penis and use it to pleasure himself. Once he was satisfied, he went to bed.

Disgusted, Manuel knew he had to leave.

Sitting on his mattress on the floor of his closet, he cried quietly, waiting to hear Jefe's snoring before going into the bathroom to bathe.

Then, he gathered his few belongings in the new pillowcase, used half a loaf of bread to make sandwiches, moved a chair to unlock the deadbolt, and quietly slipped out the back door.

It was dark.

Manuel was scared and alone.

He didn't know anyone and had no idea where to go.

After wandering the streets, he noticed a group of kids and decided to follow them. That was the night Manuel became one of fifteen thousand street kids in Mexico City who faded into the shadows.

Before long, he realized that most kids slept during the day to avoid predators like Jefe, who prowled the streets at night.

They stayed in groups and scattered when adults approached them.

Emanuel had never gone to school and had never had a friend. Although smart enough to survive by watching others, he didn't know how to make a friend.

Still traumatized by his experience with Jefe, he spent several months following a group of older kids at a distance, making sure he stayed hidden.

Many of the street kids would dig through trash or sell themselves for food, but Emanuel found other ways to stay alive.

After watching families go into restaurants, he discovered a healthier way to eat. He would walk in behind a large family scanning tables and head to the restroom to wash up.

On his way out, when no one was looking, he'd pick up leftover food from uncleared tables and discretely put the food in a bag he had secured inside his pants.

Over time, a few kids taught him how to beg for money, which made life easier for a while. But if the bigger kids caught him, they'd steal it.

When he learned how and where to hide it, he used it to buy clothes at a thrift store. As he got older, he learned to save enough to splurge on a motel.

Even in the most run-down and dirty motels, he could at least take a shower and wash his clothes in the tub, letting them dry overnight.

He would get a soda and binge-watch all his favorite TV shows. More importantly, in those cheap motels, he could sleep peacefully throughout the night.

When older kids told him he could make better money selling drugs, he knew that the bullies would steal from him, so he declined.

After living on the streets for a few years, he got up enough nerve to follow a few kids to school. Watching through a window as the teacher taught a lesson. He'd even walked around a little before a man stopped him and started asking questions.

Terrified they'd contact Jefe, he managed to run away.

All he wanted was to be like other kids, and that desire drove him to find another way to get an education.

That's when he learned about the library.

Over the next several years, he taught himself to read by sneaking into the local library and spending most days in the children's section practicing letters and words until the librarian closed for the night.

The librarian, Cecilia Sanchez, was so impressed with his desire to learn that she helped him with lessons when things were slow.

When he was old enough, she taught him how to find the books he was interested in, and over the next few years, she became a surrogate mom to him, bringing him food and teaching him English and French.

As his reading improved, she introduced math, and finally, in his teens, she introduced chemistry, which became his favorite subject.

Mrs. Sanchez encouraged his interests and even purchased an age-appropriate chemistry set for him to practice with when he wasn't in the library.

The worst day for Emanuel came when he went to her station to say good morning, and a new librarian had taken her place.

She told him that Mrs. Sanchez had been killed in a car accident but refused to answer his questions.

When he tried to explain that he spent the days at the library, she just shooed him away, saying, "You need to hurry, or you'll be late for school."

***

Francisco's perpetually swollen lips smiled again as a chubby index finger hit a button on the desk.

Within seconds, Henry walked through the large double doors. "Henry, I think we'll each have a Bloody Mary and make it a tall one."

"Of course, and I'll use your favorite peppers to spice it up just as you like!" Receiving his cue, a slight nod of the head coupled with the slight closing of plump eyelids, Henry left as silently as he'd entered.

Francisco suggested, "While we wait for our refreshments, why don't you narrate how our little game played out last night? Were all the players in their places? Did it go well?

"The anticipation is killing me, or should I say, Billy, huh?" A gleam of humor shone in his dark eyes, and a short chuckle escaped him.

Proud of his success, Emanuel began, "Well, before I get to the juicy parts, you should know that there were a few hiccups that I think you should be aware of.

"First, there was a little difficulty with our friend at the hospital. Although he was interested in the trade, it took him a week longer than anticipated to get the succinylcholine.

"A most frustrating imposition since the delay left me little time to test the dosages that could have compromised our plans."

"Then, I had to figure out a way to manipulate Billy so that he would agree to participate. That's when I came up with the weapons trade idea. I knew our men would recover our product on the back end, so we wouldn't lose anything if the weapons got confiscated.

"I led Billy to believe that he might have a chance to play with the weapons as a bonus incentive to the money, and he agreed. I think there was just enough mystery and excitement to interest him. And the healthy payoff cinched the deal.

"Then I instructed him where to go if we were caught and that he'd be safe if he made it to the deserted alley.

Henry returned with their drinks, balancing the heavy tray carefully. Setting his burden down on the side of the large desk and leaving the full pitcher on the silver platter, he placed the drinks in front of each man, bowed, and retreated as quietly as he'd entered.

"And whoever came up with the idea to put that bum out of his misery was a genius. His death totally threw Colt off his game."

Francisco nodded, "Yes, well, that was my nephew. He deserves all the credit there."

"Well, it definitely provided the time we needed to put a tracker on the dog's collar in case Billy ditched him. While Colt was finishing the paperwork on the dead bum."

"Wonderful… what happened next."

"We'd received the weapons shortly before I got the call that the target was on the way. Still, with so many unpredictable variables, anything could have gone wrong.

The Doctor topped off their glasses and then lifted his in a salute. "A stroke of genius on your part, sir! With so many variables clouding his thoughts, it was easy to manipulate the course of events!"

A smile broke over the fat face. "Yes, I must concur. My mother always said patience is a virtue; of course, let us not discount my precocity for making the impossible possible."

"My point exactly.

"The crates were bulky and difficult to manage. We had just loaded the ammo box, and I stalled for a few minutes arranging it.

"Go on, my friend, you whet the appetite! I'm truly starting to enjoy these revelations."

He stopped briefly to refill his glass and savor the spicy nip in the cocktail. "What really tipped the scales was the combination of factors. The drug in his cold medication and the residual effects of the flu, and maybe even his grief."

"After Colt told us to drop it, Billy took off while I purposely stayed behind to run interference.

"The one uncertainty at that point was if the dog would be released. We could only guess.

"In truth, I hadn't expected the other unit to be so close, so I had to improvise. And as soon as he released the dog, I charged him, knocking him off his feet."

The Doctor took another sip of his drink before continuing, "People often misjudge my strength due to my size, which gives me an advantage.

"Colt landed hard but jumped up, giving me barely enough time to run out of sight and into the drain I'd uncovered earlier. I heard him looking around, but he couldn't find me. My magic still works pretty well, eh?

When Francisco didn't respond, the Doctor continued, "Anyway, it was a good thing our man carried that ultrasonic radio jammer. I heard Colt trying to call for help a few times, but his radio was useless.

"Again, I must bow to you, sir; your idea to use the jammer was inspiring."

The smile spread slowly. "Yes, I thought it might be. Go on, Doctor. The picture you paint is amusing. Tell me about this drug that can kill." He leaned back in his chair, drink in hand, his eyes glazing over as he listened to the Doctor's narration.

"At that point, I must admit that a director on a movie set couldn't have been more pleased with how well each player was acting out his part.

"Colt must have headed for the dog after he lost me.

"But the time he'd wasted was enough to give me the time I needed to beat him to the location."

Reaching carefully for his drink, Emanuel took a big sip before he continued, "There was the possibility that our shooter would miss the injection site. He only had seconds to hit a small area of about two inches square on a moving target. It would be a hard shot for anyone, even a sharpshooter with a laser sight, to land it exactly where I'd instructed.

"Not to mention that he was a bit too close to the target. Any closer, and the syringe would have shot through his neck.

"The drug is a neural muscular blocking agent that produces muscle paralysis. It was a difficult choice, but it worked out.

"Still, I had to calculate every possibility; otherwise, the side effects might have ruined our plans. Unfortunately, I was left with an unknown variable for interactions with medications unaccounted for.

"Luckily, he is in perfect health."

Emanuel moved closer to the edge of his seat as he lowered his rising voice. "I know cutting down the dosage was a risk. It took longer to knock him out. Even so, we did complete our tasks as planned and were able to leave without any witnesses.

"Succinylcholine is usually administered in a hospital so that counteracting medications can be administered to reduce side effects and prevent death from muscle paralysis that can stop breathing. Without the countermeasure, the aftereffects can be pretty traumatic.

"The patient may feel as if they are drowning or suffocating and end up hurting themselves if they panic.

"Typically, symptoms only last about six minutes. But one minute is terrifying when you can't breathe.

"Other side effects include confusion, dizziness, blurred vision, severe headaches, nausea, and muscle spasms.

"But the best part is that it affects memory.

"Making it perfect for our game.

"Since it is rapidly metabolized in the bloodstream, it's difficult to detect unless a gas chromatography-mass spectrometry is performed, which wasn't indicated in this case."

Francisco's smile had grown, even as his eyes were nearly lost in the fullness of his raised cheeks, "Perfect. After his snooping, he needed to be cut down to size."

The Doctor's confidence grew. "It was a perfect night for the drug. The cold helped to slow down the oxygen consumption in his tissues, so he suffered only minor respiratory distress when he came out of it."

Recounting the story increased his excitement, and his voice started to rise. "I'm fond of this particular agonist; before I prepared the dose for the target, I had planned on testing it on a few of my little ones…"

"Doctor!" Francisco interrupted. "Please spare me your sadistic interests! Just stick to the topic at hand."

The smile that had previously cracked the fully jowled face was gone, replaced by a frown that took possession of the folds of flesh. The eyes that had sparkled with excitement had lost all light focused on their source of irritation, turning dead black with a squint.

"Now, please continue. What about the mutt?"

He needed to calm himself; he was getting too excited, which usually antagonized the fat man.

Taking a long drink of his Bloody Mary, he prayed that the drink wasn't laced with strychnine. He was well-versed in Francisco's specialties since he'd helped develop them.

Continuing, he said, "Yes, of course, I forget myself." He placed the empty sweating glass on the platter and hoped the alcohol would quickly relax him.

Inhaling deeply, he continued, "Once the agonist dropped him, the dog turned on our boy, ready to attack. It was as if time stopped for several seconds.

"I thought for sure he'd be bitten before he could reload. But our boy was quick, already had the thing primed and ready, and before the dog could attack, he took a few steps back and shot him.

"To be honest, I was a little surprised at how fast the Ketamine tranquilizer worked."

"Billy was there, but he was on top of a dumpster. The dog was jumping up and down, snapping at him. But Billy managed to hold him off with the lid.

"Colt called the dog and ordered Billy to get down. That's when he tried to use his mic again.

"While his neck was exposed, our man fired the dart, hitting precisely where I'd asked.

"As the dog turned and growled, he hit the dog with the small dose of ketamine I prepared especially for him. The whole thing went off just as we planned, with everything falling into place just as we intended.

"It took a few minutes longer than anticipated, but as soon as they were down, our boy emerged from the shadows.

"Billy was smiling like a Cheshire cat. But before he jumped off the dumpster, our man put the target's weapon in his hand and pulled the trigger.

"It took just a few minutes to kill Billy, gather the darts and the tracker, and set the scene to ensure Colt would be blamed.

"We were gone before the first siren!"

Unbeknownst to Francisco, the Doctor had painted a story that he knew his employer would most enjoy while hiding the fact that he'd videotaped the whole event to enjoy in private.

For several minutes, Francisco sat with his eyes closed and his fingers steepled against his chin. Then, without a word, his hand moved to the buzzer.

Henry arrived within minutes. "What may I get for you?"

"Please set an additional place for lunch; the good Doctor will be joining me. Oh, and don't forget to refill our glasses; the drinks you've made are delicious and will go nicely with the spicy crab cakes and stuffed bell peppers that cook is preparing."

CHAPTER THIRTEEN

Growing Pains

It was the summer during her third year at UC Davis School of Veterinary Medicine while living in California that changed Becca's life forever.

After the semester and fulfilling her obligations at a local shelter, Becca was finally able to fly home for the rest of summer break. Joss was expected to meet her as soon as she finished with her obligations.

But Becca had only been home for a little over a week when an officer came to the house to inform the family that Joss had died of an overdose.

Inconsolable, Becca struggled to accept that her twin was gone. Nothing the officer had told them made sense.

After the funeral, her father encouraged Becca to return to school. Flying with her to California to help her get resettled.

But as the weeks went by, Becca continued to struggle.

Even when she made it to class, she just couldn't concentrate or keep up with her studies, so she began staying in bed all day and skipping classes.

Her roommate tried to tempt Becca with various activities, but when she stopped eating, Violet finally called Becca's Dad.

"Mr. Kennedy, this is Violet… um… Becca's roommate. I wouldn't have called… but where I come from, folks help each other. And… well, I've never seen her like this.

"She's always so energetic, and… well… I hate to say it, but I think Becca is in a world of hurt.

"Since she came back from summer break, she's been cutting classes and staying in bed most days.

"I know she lost her sister, and that has to be the worst... and I'm really sorry for your family's loss... but well, I know it's not my place to say… and I mean no disrespect, but something's wrong with her… with Becca I mean.

"I'm near positive that… she's… well, she's stopped eating. I think you need to come out here and see for yourself, sir. I'm sure she just needs… well, I truly don't know what she needs. But family always makes me feel better.

"Anyway, I thought you'd want to know."

After thanking Violet, Brendan quickly made arrangements to fly out the next day. But he was just as much in the dark as the roommate. He hadn't even dealt with his grief yet and had no idea how to help Becca with hers.

It was times like these that he missed Arianna the most.

Finally, he did what came most natural to him – he researched.

He knew that loss was hard, and he accepted that losing a sister would be tough, especially because she'd also lost her mother only a few years earlier.

What he didn't expect was the research which showed that twins experience loss much more intensely due to the deep connection they share or that surviving twins often experience the loss as a tangible piece of themselves having been cut away.

They often develop survivor's guilt, blaming themselves for what happened, for not protecting the twin, wishing that it would have been them, or believing that if they'd been there, they could have prevented the death.

The trauma of loss, the symptomology, could become debilitating.

Joss was Becca's twin, but not just a twin—her identical twin, and he discovered that identical twins experience that type of loss as a persistent and unrelenting pain.

The good news was that he'd found an organization near Becca's school that specialized in grief counseling for twins and provided individual and group treatment.

After contacting the clinic and arranging assistance for Becca, Brendan felt a little better.

Later that evening, as he packed, he wondered if the not-knowing had made it harder for Becca since they hadn't heard anything about the investigation.

He learned years before, while Arianna was still being put through tests, that it was the unknown that created anxiety and wondered if an update might help a little, at least until he could get to her.

That's when Brendan called Detective Myers on his cell, hoping for an update that might help Becca. If she thought that the police were making headway on the case, it might give her some hope.

He explained the situation to the detective and asked him to speak to Becca. "I think if you would give her an update, it might help."

Unfortunately, he had no idea just how hearing from the detective might affect her.

George Myers, the lead detective, along with Susan Hawkins, the coroner, had ruled that Joss had died of an opioid overdose.

Instead of an understanding or empathetic call, Myers was firm and deliberate, "Although your sister was found in an unusual place, there was no indication of foul play. And the coroner ruled it an unintentional death. Meaning that your sister died

"And since the cause of death was ruled a drug overdose, there is nothing left to investigate. So, Ms. Kennedy, we've closed the case."

Becca couldn't believe it, "What? But that's impossible. Joss couldn't have overdosed—at least not willingly. My sister never used drugs, so how can the case be closed? You must have missed something!

"You need to find out who did this! You can't close the case!"

But Detective Myers replied in a firm tone, "Look, the case was closed because addicts use higher and higher doses that eventually kill them.

"No one did this to her. Addicts basically kill themselves, so there's no point in reopening the case. I know you don't want to believe your sister was an addict, but you need to let her go and move on.

"There's nothing more I can do."

His words had not only wounded but had enraged Becca to the point that she refused to allow his assessment to stand.

To him, Joss was just another addict, which simplified his job and probably the coroner's too.

For the life of her, Becca couldn't understand how the cause of death had been determined so quickly and how the case was closed before it had barely opened.

That's when her rage took over.

After hanging up, she jumped out of bed, surprised at the strength that bubbled up from deep inside, and came out in a scream.

Joss loved life. She woke up excited for the day's adventure, and even as a child, she loved to laugh. As a teenager, Joss used to say, "Who needs drugs? I'm a natural high."

She was such a happy, playful, and creative person, and Becca would never believe that Joss had needed or wanted drugs. Convinced her twin had been murdered, Becca found a new purpose, and no matter how long it took, she would uncover the truth.

By the time Brendan showed up the next day, Becca was out of bed and ready to start going to classes.

To stop her dad from worrying, she agreed to go to therapy. What she didn't tell him was that she was on a mission to find her sister's killer and that she wouldn't rest until the job was done.

While completing the requirements to become a veterinarian, Becca did her best to uncover anything that might explain what happened to Joss.

She interviewed her twin's friends, who said that Joss rarely had more than two drinks, even when she went to a party. Which Becca already knew.

Becca interviewed teachers, dormmates, neighbors, and classmates, but no one had seen anything that indicated that Joss had used drugs.

During Becca's residency program, she hired a private investigator who found what he called "inconsistencies" in her sister's case.

It turned out that Hawkins was a coroner Myers called in from out of town. That should have sent up all kinds of red flags since the county had a coroner on staff.

Becca knew that Myers was lazy by his sparse notes. However, the PI's reports indicated that the detective was an alcoholic who had three previous infractions.

Joss's closest friends were outraged to hear the case had been closed, so they put together a petition requesting that the District Attorney look into the mishandling of Joss's case.

After she read that report, Becca requested that the body be exhumed. She insisted that a local medical examiner and very respected pathologist by the name of Ella Tanner do the second autopsy.

However, an additional impassioned request was still required to receive a copy of the doctor's report.

That's when Becca found even more inconsistencies: an injection site at Joss's left deltoid.

But Joss was left-handed.

There were no other track marks or needle scars anywhere on the body that might indicate a long history of addiction. The only other marks were the new grouping on the inside of the left elbow.

Multiple defensive bruises were also on the forearms, face, and body, not listed on the initial report. They indicated she'd fought with an attacker shortly before death. She'd suffered skull fractures and a broken index finger on her right hand; none of those items were listed on the initial report.

Because of her findings, Dr. Tanner listed the death as suspicious. And because she ruled the death suspicious, the file was forwarded to the district attorney's office.

Since then, Becca spent the last few years collecting information. All she needed was a little more evidence to insist the District Attorney go after her sister's killer.

It all started with inquiries. She was asking questions, hoping to find information about Joss that she didn't already know.

Joss's best friend Tara only knew that Joss was seeing "some guy" off campus and that she'd kept the relationship secret. Unfortunately, Tara had only seen them together once, and that was by accident on the way to the restroom during a concert at Red Rocks.

She had nearly bumped into them, but since Joss was cuddled up against him laughing, she didn't stop longer than to say a quick hello.

Tara described the man as tall with dirty blond hair and dark eyes.

It was Becca's first real lead. The first bit of information Becca hadn't known about her twin.

Joss had always loved to write, and Becca had a good idea where Joss hid her journals. But when she'd packed up Joss's room, she hadn't seen any journals.

That's when she went back to search the room.

The hard part was trying to understand why Joss hadn't confided to her friends or, more importantly, to her twin, anything about the guy she was dating.

Why the big secret, Sis?

Luckily, Myers hadn't bothered to go through Joss's things, or the journals may have been lost, and Becca found them quickly.

As she studied her sister's journals, she looked for anything that would corroborate Tara's description. Any hint of the man's identity. Clues that Joss may have hidden in the pages of her journals.

Something her killer may not have known was that, as much as Joss loved to write, she loved to draw even more.

In fact, in the weeks before her death, Joss had drawn several portraits of one man, and each image was framed by letters.

As Becca tried to decipher them, she discovered that the names correlated to places she'd been taken on their dates.

Under one of the last portraits in the journal was the name Mark Payton. Only the frame wasn't in block letters like the others. This one was cursive doodles.

In the four journals that Becca found, there wasn't one mention, not even a hint, that Joss was into drugs.

The only secret in her life was the man named Mark Payton.

Determined to find out more about the mystery man, Becca searched for him on Google, looking up old newspaper clippings at the library, and after months of frustration, running down one rabbit hole after another, without having any evidence that there was a rabbit.

After buying the property from Doc Taylor, Becca impulsively went to Red Rocks. She wanted to visit the place Tara mentioned when she saw Mark with Joss and the location mentioned in Joss's journals where they went on a date.

She was totally blown away when she passed by the man, who was identical to the drawing and had a woman wrapped around his arm.

That had been her first real connection to the mystery man, and she wasn't about to let it slip away. She kept her distance and followed them.

Tara was right. He was tall, over six feet—with dirty blond hair shaved close to the scalp on the sides and a wind-blown mop on top.

The boyish hairstyle looked like the one Justin Bieber was famous for when he was young, which was probably one of the reasons Joss had been attracted to him. Whether Becca wanted to admit it or not, he was handsome.

Keeping her distance, she followed them to a black Ford F150, a bit surprised that the young woman didn't get in.

Instead, he left the young woman standing in the parking lot with nothing but a quick hug, discarding her like one might a worn-out pair of jeans.

Clearly, Mark was no gentleman.

Staying a few cars behind, Becca followed him to a Whole Foods Market in Lakewood. Since most people bought groceries close to where they lived, she took several pictures of his truck and casually made her way out of the parking lot, happy with her successful reconnaissance.

With another piece of the puzzle uncovered, she would wait until she could get closer in her new disguise.

A few weeks later, she easily reacquired him at a place called the Game Train. A few days after that, she knew his routine pretty well.

He spent a lot of his spare time in Black Hawk, going to the casinos. But for some reason, he never stayed very long. After a drink and a little time at the blackjack tables, he usually left within an hour of arriving.

And that little detail had to be important; she just needed to figure out why.

After days of practicing with YouTube videos and being pleased with her new disguise, she began spending most evenings at the casinos.

The new look made her fade into the background. Now and then, she'd walk in with a group of seniors just to ensure that she looked the part.

She was just waiting for Mark Payton to lead her to the proof she needed. Then, everything she'd gone through in the last few years would be worth it.

After watching him for a while, she wasn't surprised to discover that he collected women like trophies, even though she hadn't seen him with the same one more than a few times.

As time went on, it infuriated her to watch the way he mistreated women. Attentive and charming one minute, the next tossing them aside. To the point of being dismissive and cruel. He seemed to enjoy making them feel insignificant and devalued. Probably the same way he mistreated her sister.

On a few occasions, after watching him act exceptionally cruel, she was forced to leave before she did something stupid – like run him over.

Near one in the morning, Mark casually strolled into the casino, laughing at a beautiful girl wrapped around his arm.

She didn't look eighteen and had way too much makeup on her face. Her black mascara was smeared in blotches around her eyes, and her bright pink lipstick sparkled to the left of her lips and chin as if it were melting off her face.

Her skirt was short enough that when she bent over, her skimpy leopard print underwear was on display.

A near fall down the steps made her laugh uncontrollably as her escort grabbed her moments before she hit the ground.

As they walked through the casino, Mark seemed to be half-carrying her. Just as they passed Becca, the girl tripped over her three-inch heels, which required another save from her escort, along with another fit of laughter.

The girl was obviously high, and Mark was enjoying her childish behavior. It took all of Becca's self-control not to yell at the poor girl to run before he tossed her away like trash, as he'd done to Joss.

Watching them made her heart pound so hard that, for a moment, she struggled to breathe.

The idea that he could enjoy himself at all when her sister was gone was torture. But to corrupt such a young girl—put a young life at risk, was just more perverted than she could stand.

Standing ready to walk out, she quickly reconsidered.

No one was watching; no one cared, which meant that no one would think to save the girl, and Becca's conscience wouldn't let her leave that vulnerable child alone with such a vile man.

Hiding behind the machines, she held onto chairs as she followed the couple through the casino, moving to a row of slot machines where she could observe them at the blackjack table.

Once she was within hearing range, she stopped at a machine behind them to calm herself with one hand against her chest and the other holding onto a machine; she was breathing too fast.

She wasn't paying attention.

To onlookers, she would appear to be an older lady in distress.

A passing cocktail waitress moved to her side and asked, "Are you all right, mam? Can I bring you some water or something?"

"Huh? Oh, no, no… um, I'm okay, thank you… young lady. I just need to sit here a minute. I got myself all excited when I saw my favorite machine was available, that's all."

With a quick backward glance, the waitress went about doling out drinks.

Becca took her last deep breath and smiled.

Her disguise had fooled the waitress, and that little success had calmed her. She no longer needed to worry about being recognized by Erika or anyone else.

And she was closer to uncovering Mark's game and getting the evidence she needed to put him away for Joss's murder.

***

Jason slowed the Jeep and stopped two blocks away from his destination. He'd decided to use the sewer system trick he'd learned from Billy.

He'd discovered the manhole just yards away from the kennel during his previous recon.

Slowly lifting the lid, he scanned the area around him before pushing the lid out of the way and moving down into the dark hole.

The sewer was pitch, and the stench was overwhelming. But there was no turning back. Switching on the headlamp to keep his hands free, he found the tunnel opening and hurried to the manhole cover near the kennel.

When he crawled out of the sewer, he was glad for the headlamp. There weren't many streetlights in the area, and without the headlamp, he would have struggled to see well enough to cut through the links in the fence.

Squatting down at the fence, Colt cut through the chain links. If he triggered an alarm, he wouldn't know about it until he was inside. And that would be too late.

Once through the fence, he scanned the yard and rushed across the ocean of lawn and around the sectioned-off obstacle courses.

The janitorial staff had left hours before, but he took a few minutes to look through the backdoor sidelight to make sure nothing moved inside the building.

The dogs had been quiet up till then, but as if on cue, they all started barking at once; "Jesus, I forgot how loud they can get."

He knew the command to quiet them. If that didn't work, he had plenty of treats and rawhide chews to keep them busy.

As he rummaged blindly in his pack for the picks to open the door, tiny beads of sweat broke out on his brow. Frustrated, he tore off his glove and tried again.

But when his fingers touched the leather sheath, he was momentarily transported back to the morning when he unwrapped the inappropriate gift from his father.

His astonished expression at the sight of the picks had triggered fits of laughter from Matt until tears shimmered at the corners of his eyes.

"You should see the look on your face, son." And after hiccupping another guffaw. "Priceless! Sofia, where the hell is the camera? That was one for the books!"

"Matthew Colt, I swear you go too far. Now stop all this foolishness; let's have dessert. I've made a nice cobbler… would you like some ice cream with it?"

Matt winked at Jason and, still laughing, said, "Did you say something about dessert?"

When he jumped up from his chair, she realized what he was up to, quickly moving out of reach with a little giggle as he pursued her.

"Come here, my love. I'll show you foolishness. Let me show you how foolish this old man can be!" His last words were emphasized with a few growls and barks, which was all it took to send them all into fits of laughter.

Matt had always been the goofy comic to Sofia's straight-man routine. The perfect duo, they made marriage look easy, even when they argued, which was rare. Jason had always admired what they had and hoped to have the same someday.

Later, while drinking his mother's famous Christmas hot chocolate, his father said, "This stays between you and me, kid. I got those well-worn picks from an old friend of mine. He never said where he got them, but he implied they came from a famous thief who forged them himself. I figured it would give you an edge. A better understanding of what you're up against with these criminals. Knowledge is power, and that way, no surprises… and hell, son, I thought it might be fun."

That had been their last Christmas together.

Matt was killed before they could enjoy another.

The racket the dogs made urged him to focus on the task at hand, but they were making him nervous. He'd never even thought of breaking the law before, and it went against everything he believed in.

As his dad had recommended, Jason learned about the picks and practiced until he knew which picks worked best for each type of lock. What he didn't realize was the stress involved while trying to break in.

Each pick was inserted into a slim pocket. Putting his glove back on, he took a deep breath, opened the case, and made his choice.

Jason fumbled first with one pair of picks and then another. When the lock finally released, he put the picks back in their slots, closed the case, grabbed his pack, and moved through the door.

Standing inside with his back against the wall, he re-engaged the lock. Standing in the shadows, he grabbed a flashlight from the backpack and turned it on. Moving quickly to the office, he found the alarm panel and was relieved when the bright green light smiled back at him.

The noise level had increased; the barking was more insistent and less playful.

Working his way through the hallway and down to the kennels, he raised his voice above the din, "Nein!" pause, "Aus! Nein!" After three attempts, the dogs began to quiet down.

As he moved to the area of the kennel where young recruits were kept, the dogs barked intermittently and had to be reminded to stay quiet. As he made his way through the cages, he talked to them, saying their names as he handed out a treat. The canines who knew him stayed calm with wagging tails, waiting for their turn to get a treat.

Corralling the pups into the reception area was a bit more challenging than he anticipated. Much more interested in playing, the pups were too distracted by one another to listen to commands. But once they were all in the main lobby, Jason was able to finish his task.

Using a can of neon pink spray paint, he drew a pig similar to the one painted on the cruiser. Then he signed it with the prankster's initials.

He released the older canines into the outdoor kennel area to enjoy the night air, figuring that they didn't go outside as much as the others.

After he unlocked the dogs' cages, he only had one thing left to do: find Stryker. The first time he called out, he was answered by three loud barks, and he quickly moved toward that low timbre.

At Stryker's cage, Jason bent down to talk to his friend through a tight throat, "How you doin' buddy?" He was more emotional than he'd expected—his relief at seeing his partner and best friend after so long apart got to him.

With unshed tears, he released the latch and stepped inside to give his friend a big hug. When Stryker placed his paws on Jason's shoulders and licked his face. Any doubt that Jason had about Stryker's recovery, vanished.

Taking time for their reunion, Jason sat with Stryker and told him the issues they were dealing with—just as he always had. After a few minutes, the other dogs quieted to listen.

Finally, Jason looked at his watch and said, "Okay, buddy, how would you like to get out of here? The last of the partyers should be home by now, so the roads will be clear."

Stryker wagged his tail as he followed Jason from the kennels to the side door.

When Jason unlocked it, Stryker rushed past him into the yard. Running from one end to the other as if saying, I'm free!

When Jason caught up, he gave the hand signal for Stryker to follow him. As they slipped through the small opening in the fence, they just needed to make it to the Jeep without being seen.

As he turned back, thinking he should connect a few links to keep the dogs in the yard, he saw two older dogs that had followed them through the fence.

He was worried they'd get lost, so he commanded Stryker to stay and retraced his steps.

Once the dogs were back in the yard, he threw a few rawhide chews and waited until the dogs were settled with their treats before turning to leave.

Then rushed to the manhole and helped Stryker down into the sewer. The water was low, although that didn't improve the smell.

Moving quickly through the tunnel, it didn't take long before they were back on the street and making their way to the Jeep.

While driving through the city, Jason removed the mask and used it to remove the camouflage from his eyes.

Stryker hadn't shown any aggression. He didn't growl or fight during the frenzy of their crazy escape. He'd walked out of the kennel at his side without one issue.

Looking over at his passenger, he saw a happy dog. In fact, looking at him now, sitting in the passenger's seat, Stryker had a huge grin, smiling with his tongue lolling out the side of his mouth.

"I knew they were wrong about you, boy; now we just need to prove how wrong they were about both of us."

Stryker looked at Jason, panted, and, with the same smile, turned to look out the windshield.

CHAPTER FOURTEEN

Making Connections

Colt sat heavily on the soft leather sectional, feeling like his bones had turned to rubber.

The cabin had always been a serene place. Out in the middle of nature, where the hardest thing to do was relax.

It was where he'd learned to fish, boat, and swim. Not to mention the years of barbecues, hikes, games, and camping out on the back porch with Dean.

After the remodel, Dean purchased comfortable but rustic furniture so there would be plenty of room for everyone. Although it made the place more cozy, Jason couldn't get comfortable.

Massaging his temples, he slowed his breathing, trying to stave off yet another headache—this time, a tension headache. He couldn't shake the shame he felt. Breaking the law—even for a good cause like rescuing Stryker, was just something he never thought he'd do. Those actions were in total opposition to his morals.

But what troubled him even more was the possibility that he could put the Adams family in jeopardy, either by making them accomplices or by harboring a fugitive.

If Dean were caught with him, it would ruin his career, and if he and Stryker were caught, he would go to jail, and Stryker would be euthanized.

Jason had his ups and downs like everyone else, but nothing as extreme as what he'd been dealing with since his father died.

The stress over the last eight months was weighing heavily on him.

Stryker padded into the room and nudged Jason with his nose. Seeing the goofy grin was all it took to pull Jason back to the present. "Well, at least we're okay for now, huh, boy?

"And you're right. You've been locked up long enough. How about we take a walk to the dock and watch the sun come up? On the way, I can throw the frisbee, and you can sniff it out. How does that sound?"

Between the bark, wagging tail, and rush to the door, words just weren't necessary.

Wanting some bonding time, Jason made sure to mix playtime with structured work time, putting Stryker through his paces. He wanted to see if Stryker would get aggressive.

They worked and played hard most of the day, and by the time the sun set, they were both ready for bed.

He'd already answered multiple questions, and he was doing his best. What did they want from him?

Accusations were flying, and they were pushing for a confession.

But he had nothing to confess, did he? He couldn't remember.

What reason did he have to want Billy dead?

After hours of questioning, Lieutenant Bernard asked, "Were you aware that we found Billy's DNA and his partial fingerprints underneath your father's van?"

Like a punch in the gut, the air was driven from Jason's lungs. His jaw dropped, but he didn't speak. His eyes widened, then blinked as he tried to grasp the significance of what had been said.

Stunned, speechless, and in utter disbelief, the minutes ticked by as Jason tried to process what he'd heard.

It didn't matter that he was innocent. If Billy had killed his dad, it gave Jason motive, and it didn't matter that this was new information to him.

All the questioning looks and disappointed expressions suddenly made sense.

Then he felt something warm in his hand, but when he looked at it, nothing was there. Still, he felt the warmth and weight of a gun; it had been fired.

They were waiting for an answer—expected an answer, only he didn't have one.

In the silence, the pressure grew.

Finally, he took a deep breath and asked, "What?" He couldn't prove it, but he answered honestly, "No! I didn't know that! But how…I mean, Jesus, how did… oh, did forensics finish the second report?"

The room was utterly silent, and all eyes were on him.

Staring into the void, he began speaking more to himself than to the others in the room. His voice was soft as he tried to work it through, "How is that possible? Billy was a drug dealer. I caught him -- arrested him.

"But my dad? He was the most moral man I've ever known. A happy, hard-working, well-respected business owner – a plumber. And he adored my mother."

Swallowing his hurt, "I swear, I don't see the connection or how that's possible. It just doesn't make sense."

He looked around the room and, in a stronger voice, said, "I'm telling you, I had no idea about any of this. I can't think of one scenario where Billy and Dad's paths would cross! They lived and worked in different areas -- I just can't see it.

"Maybe if Dad had his truck serviced somewhere Billy worked-- maybe? But even that's a stretch. I just don't see it.

"Besides, the guy is brainless. Yeah, he did some nasty stuff. But he didn't have the brain power to plan a murder. What motive did he have? And when would he be anywhere near my dad's truck?

"So, to answer your question, no. This is the first I've heard of any DNA or a connection between them! And just to be clear, it never would have crossed my mind.

"Last I heard, Billy was in jail. But it doesn't matter because how would I know if he got released? And why would I set him up if I didn't know about the DNA? And how could I have done anything while I was so sick?

Hank Chambers cautioned, "We have more than you think. While you were in the hospital, we collected evidence from your house.

We know that you were investigating your father's death. Can you tell us what made you suspicious about the accident?"

"Well, to set the record straight, I never kept what I was doing a secret. My Captain knew all about it.

"And if you knew my dad, you'd understand why I needed to know what happened. It was partly due to what he experienced as a kid.

“He told me about it when he taught me how to drive.

“His best friend in elementary school lived across the street, and Dad spent a lot of time with him, often going with the family to the drive-in movies.

“One night, they were running late, and the mom was upset, complaining they’d miss the beginning of the movie.

“There were five kids, my dad, his friend, and siblings, stuffed in the backseat, and they weren’t wearing seat belts.

“When the light changed, the dad hit the gas at the same time a drunk driver in a FedEx van ran the light.

“Dad didn’t remember the impact, but he woke covered in blood and had to crawl over the mangled bodies of the family to get out of the vehicle. He was the only one who walked away from the car.

“Before he started learning how to drive, his father showed him the newspaper clippings about it.

“The driver had apparently had too much to drink at lunch. He rammed two vehicles: the one my dad was in and a dully truck. My dad, the passenger in the truck, and the FedEx driver survived.

“The driver ended up hanging himself in prison because he couldn’t live with knowing he killed seven people.

“After that, my dad didn’t take chances. He could drive just about anything, but he was cautious.

“That’s why I was looking into his accident. It just didn’t make sense that his accident was because he was driving recklessly.

“Captain Alverez helped me get a copy of the first report. It indicated that there were no skid marks, no attempt at slowing the vehicle, and no significant evidence of skidding. But that didn’t make sense because who wouldn’t try to slow down on switchbacks and with the possibility of black ice?

“It didn’t feel right from the get-go, but after reading that report, I knew something was really off.

“I knew he’d never intentionally leave my mom. Plus, he was a happy guy. He had no reason to kill himself, which left only one other possibility. Someone had intentionally caused him to crash.

“I just needed answers.

"Some guy with road rage, or if dad was speeding, maybe he was running away from someone and lost control.

"But that first report didn't show any evidence that another car was involved. In fact, there wasn't an investigation. It looked like an accident, so that's how it was listed.

"And that's where I got stuck, where my investigation stalled. I asked that a forensic team complete a more thorough investigation, but I haven't heard anything yet."

Chambers turned the page in his notebook, "Okay, I concede that your reasons to investigate were reasonable.

"But isn't it possible, Officer Colt, that you discovered that it was Billy in the alley that night and suspected he was the one responsible for your father's death? And that while having him in your sights, you decided to take advantage of the situation and exact your revenge?"

"No. That's not possible. As I said, the perp seemed familiar, but I couldn't place him. It was too dark to make an identification, and he had that lid in front of him to keep Stryker away.

"And at that point, I was still trying to catch my breath."

He finished the glass of water in front of him. "Look, if you've confiscated my notes, then as far as your questions about Billy are concerned, you can see that he wasn't part of my investigation.

"I'll check my email when I can to see if there's anything new I haven't seen, but I swear I had no idea he was involved until you just told me!"

"That may be, but the connection provides motive." Chambers said, "Look, the investigation is ongoing. Still, this may be your last chance to come clean—maybe get a reduced sentence.

"Is there anything you can tell us to secure your defense? Is there anything else you can remember from the alley?"

"Hey, wait a minute. If I had taken the shot with that metal lid in front of him, wouldn't I have hit the lid… or something? In that situation, isn't there a possibility that I would have taken more than one shot under the circumstances?

"How many shots were fired? What did forensics find?"

Chambers didn't like Colt asking questions. "How about we just stick with what you do know instead of getting ahead of ourselves like this."

"Okay, but to be honest, I'd had a pretty rough shift before I ever got to the alley.

"It started when I found John, a family friend, dead in the park. It didn't help that I was getting over the flu. And I admit, with hindsight being twenty-twenty and all, I should have never come into work that night…"

He looked around the room. "Anyway, after writing the report on John, I took another dose of Sudafed to keep my symptoms in check for the rest of my shift."

"Chasing the suspect… then trying to reach Stryker before something happened to him… was distracting enough.

"But even if I had recognized Billy that night… to me, he was just a dealer. A guy to arrest for breaking the law, and that's how I would have played it.

"And like I said, after I told the guy to get down… things get fuzzy. Sometimes bits of a memory come in, kind of like a shattered snapshot, but that's about it.

"Trust me, I want to remember what happened so I can clear my name. I'm hopeful because the doc said I might remember more as time goes on.

"But I have nothing more I can tell you right now except I had no intention of shooting anyone, and I had no reason to shoot Billy, regardless of how it might look."

Chambers took a few moments looking through his notes before responding, "Well, until the investigation is over and you are either cleared or convicted, you need to stay close.

"If you leave the area, you'll be treated like any other suspect. Are we clear?"

"Yes, sir!"

Hearing his voice startled him awake.

There was something in the dream that he needed to remember, something he knew he hadn't said during that debriefing, something he wasn't even aware of while being grilled.

The harder he tried to remember, the more the dream faded away. Frustrated that he couldn't remember and hadn't gotten any closer to exonerating himself or Stryker, he headed over to the office nook in the corner of the living room to unpack his new laptop.

He was still trying to reproduce the information the department had confiscated. He'd memorized most of it, but copies would have made it much easier to verify.

The first officer on the scene was Colorado State Patrol officer Kipling Roberts. In his report, he stated, 'A passerby anonymously called in the accident, but there were no witnesses on arrival.

'A one-vehicle accident, hazardous driving conditions of melting snow and black ice present. No skid marks were visible, even in areas where the road was clear of show for at least a half-mile leading to the accident site.

'It appears that the driver took a sharp curve too fast and lost control. At that high rate of speed, the vehicle propelled off the road and landed in a gulley.

'At some point, the vehicle impacted a large object that broke open the back doors and ripped open the right-side panel. The gas tank must have ruptured and ignited, causing a fire to engulf the van.

'Most of the damage was located around the gas tank at the back and the right-side panel, with evidence that the fire went through the interior of the vehicle. The flames must have been extinguished by rain before I arrived at the scene.

'The driver didn't survive the flames. The body was unrecognizable, still smoldering several feet from the wreckage.'

However, when Jason tried to get a copy of the 911 call later, no such call on that day could be found.

Jason contacted Officer Roberts, but after insisting on being called Kip, he didn't have anything more to offer than, "It was pretty cut and dry. No other vehicles. It's all there in my report."

There had to be more than that limited report provided.

After that, time seemed to stand still while Jason waited for the crime lab to complete the second investigation.

Powering up Dean's old desktop computer, Jason looked over his notes. It bothered him that after the accident, in January, there was a breakin at his parent's house where his mother was assaulted. It was just too coincidental. Suspicious even.

That report stated only that Sofia Colt had arrived home to interrupt a home robbery and was assaulted before she could run away. When questioned later at the hospital, she stated that the thieves wore masks, making identification nearly impossible.

When officers arrived, the only indication of a robbery was in the home office, which had been tossed. However, nothing of value has been reported stolen.

That April, Billy was dead, and Jason was the prime suspect.

Life had taken an ugly turn for the Colts. But it was all too coincidental.

And it all started with his father's death.

Stryker made his way into the living area from the kitchen. Patting him on the head, Jason said, "Well, it's just you and me, boy, and it's do or die. No more procrastinating. If I can't figure this out, we'll both be in a world of hurt."

The new investigation he'd requested had taken months and would have taken longer without his captain requesting to take over the investigation from another county.

After the debriefing, without a computer or his phone, he had to go to his mother's to check his email and was happy to see a copy of the forensic report that had been emailed to him while he was in the hospital.

Opening the second report, he went over everything it contained and felt vindicated.

Billy's DNA and fingerprint evidence were found underneath the soot on the vehicle's undercarriage. Luckily, the fire hadn't been hot enough to distort the metal or corrupt the evidence.

They'd also found evidence of tampering, missing bolts on the left control arm cross brace, and residue of a substance other than brake fluid in the line determined to have caused the vehicle to crash.

The unusual brake fluid mixture was also found two miles from the incident.

Billy had worked as a mechanic until he started selling drugs. But it was one thing to know how to disable a vehicle and another to use that knowledge to kill someone.

On his rap sheet, Billy O'Leary had been arrested for public intoxication, petty theft, and possession. He'd even done a short stint, but he'd never been pulled for a violent offense.

Tampering with the van was a deliberate act that required planning, and he just couldn't see Billy having the brains or balls for it.

Someone had to put him up to it.

So, who and why?

Jason felt that if he could just find out where they crossed paths, he might get some answers. Otherwise, there were too many holes and no real motive for why Billy killed his dad.

The GPS report provided a map with Matt's locations prior to the accident.

Unfortunately, the report was emailed after Jason learned Stryker's fate, which completely changed Jason's focus.

Now that Stryker was safe, Jason was ready to look at the report. He clicked the link, and the map on the day of Matt's accident popped up.

Jason had wondered why his father had been so far away from home that day. His mother said that he'd been working on a Job in Blackhawk, but the GPS showed an address in Central City.

Still, the accident occurred in the area where Matt was working. Logically, that was where he needed to look.

To build a strong enough case against Jason, the detective needed to find the connection between Billy and Matt as much as Jason did. If there wasn't a connection or a motive for Billy, then what motive did Jason have for killing Billy?

Jason had hoped going through everything would trigger a memory of that night. He didn't see how he could prove his innocence if his memory remained unreliable.

As day turned into night, a programmable timer turned on a lamp at the far end of the room, startling him, "Shit, I've got to get a grip!"

Stryker lifted his head, hearing Jason's voice, but he didn't get up.

Looking at the bankers' boxes stacked near the built-in desk, Jason realized that he was lucky that the boxes had been in storage and not confiscated with the rest of the stuff from his house.

A few weeks after the robbery, his mother called, "Please don't be upset with me, but I think it's time to clean Dad's office, and I'd hoped you'd be willing to help.

"I miss him terribly, but I can't sleep through the night thinking about those awful men and what they were doing in Dad's office.

"It haunts me.

"I can't stop wondering why they didn't go into any other room in the house! My brain won't stop trying to make sense of it."

Although it was unlikely that the thieves would go into an office without looking into the usual places for valuables, he wanted to ease her fears. "Maybe they didn't have time to search the whole house, Mom."

"Does that make sense? I mean, if I'm a thief, wouldn't I want to look for the valuables first? Money, jewelry, then electronics?

"Things that I could grab and sell quickly?

"Where do most people keep their valuables anyway? I wouldn't think the first place a thief might look is in a home office at the other end of the house."

He could hear her sigh, "I've looked through every room in this house. Dad's mad money is still on his dresser in our bedroom; that's about two hundred dollars, Jason!

"My jewelry is still safe in my jewelry box.

"The smart TV you got us for Christmas two years ago was right there, pretty as you please, in the living room where you installed it.

"Jesus, Jason, that's the room where they broke in.

"My laptop, which is only a year old, is still on the kitchen counter, and they walked right past it.

"Jason, nothing of value was touched.

Seeing that it was useless to try to alleviate her fears, Jason tried a different approach. "You're right. I can see why it might be hard to sleep trying to figure that out."

"So why didn't they take those things? Why didn't they go into any other room in the house? What the hell did they want in Dad's office?

As far as I know, there's nothing of value in there.

"And why wear masks if they didn't expect me to be home?"

Jason heard both fear and anger in his mother's voice. But her arguments were sound.

Sofia was a passionate woman who expressed herself with animated hands and facial expressions as much as she did with her words.

Listening to her, he realized that she was feeling helpless. He was feeling a bit helpless himself.

He'd never been good at expressing his emotions, but he didn't want to make things harder for her either, "Agreed. I wish I knew what to say, Mom. And I have no idea what those guys were looking for. I wish I could find a way to help you feel safe again.

"The truth is that we may never understand why they broke in.

"But you're right. It is time we clean things up. I'll come over tonight, and we'll box everything up, okay?"

She was quiet, and he heard her sniffle a few times before she responded. "Honestly, I'm not sure it will help, but I have to do something. Thank you, son."

That evening, after a delicious lasagna dinner with garlic bread and a Caesar salad, they got started.

After a few hours, they managed to go through the desk, sort through, and gather the documents Sofia needed to give to the accountant.

As Jason began on the next drawer in the filing cabinet, Sofia said, "This is tedious. My neck's getting stiff, and I'm going cross-eyed, checking the numbers and looking at all this paperwork. I need a break. I'm going for a soda; do you want anything?"

"Now that you mention it, a cold Dr Pepper sounds good about now."

While Sofia was in the kitchen, Jason noticed that one drawer of the filing cabinet hadn't closed all the way. As he pulled out the drawer, he found a large manilla envelope stuck to the back with a piece of duct tape.

Curious that nothing was written on it and wondering if it had been intentionally hidden or if it had just gotten stuck, he started to open the envelope but stopped hearing his mom walking down the hall.

Knowing she was tired, he decided to worry about it later and quickly stuffed it into a box with the rest of the files.

When Sofia returned, Jason said, "Mom, I think we're both pretty tired. There's still a lot to go through, and I don't think we can do it all tonight. Plus, if you want to put your new desk in here, I'll need to get Dean to help move the furniture.

"Tell you what. I'll put this first batch of boxes in Dad's storage. We can always look through it later, or better yet, just let me take care of it. Most of this stuff is old bids, anyway.

"I'll get Dean, and we'll fix this room up so it's more comfortable for you. What do you say?"

"That sounds good." Sofia agreed.

Since then, there had never been a good time to look through the boxes—so it was time.

When he and Dean went back to box up the rest of the office, they didn't take much time to look at the files. But now Jason wondered if that had been a mistake.

Was it possible that they missed a clue hidden somewhere amongst all those documents?

He'd barely looked at his father's computer—the one the thieves hadn't been able to take before Sofia surprised them.

In fact, her assault had been another incident.

Could three misfortunate events affecting different members of the same family be a coincidence? Jason didn't think so; it was just too personal.

And how did one prove a gut feeling anyway?

Jason hoped to find something to substantiate his gut, beginning with the contract of the last job Matt worked on.

Between Matt's computer and paperwork, there had to be something to guide his next step. If nothing else, there was certainly enough to keep him busy for hours, if not days.

His mind flip-flopped between the trauma each member of his family had suffered.

He had looked death in the face and had overcome those fears while still in the military, but this was different. This enemy was invisible.

Feeling a bit drained, the unanswered questions swarmed his mind like angry bees buzzing with cryptic threats.

In moments like this, Jason yearned to talk to his father.

Overcome with emotion that seemed to erupt from an unfamiliar place, tears fell unheeded down his face.

CHAPTER FIFTEEN

Getting Insight

Jason believed that if anyone could give him solid advice, it would be Charles.

Charles had been Matt's best friend for as long as Jason could remember. They'd met while fighting overseas and had built a strong friendship during their time there.

When they went to college, they spent most of their free time together. When they met their wives, Charles was Matt's best man when he married Sofia, and Matt was the best man when Charles married Desiree.

He was Dean's father and a second father to Jason.

Once Desiree and Sofia met, they became fast friends, creating a strong bond of their own.

The couples spent most weekends together. So, it was inevitable that Dean and Jason would become close.

Even better, the boys grew up with four loving parents.

Jason walked into the reception area at the law offices of Adams, Marshall, and Wright, hoping Charles would prevent him from being indicted.

It had been a while since he'd spoken to that man who had been a father to him. He just hoped he could find the words to explain.

Julie looked up as Jason entered the office. With a smile and shake of the head, she said, "Now look who the cat dragged in. We thought you might come by sooner or later. Charles has been worried sick about you; he'll be glad you finally decided to show up."

Julie had worked for Charles for fifteen years as his secretary. But as his cousin, she was part of the Adams family.

The chiding didn't escape Jason. "Hey, Julie. I meant to contact Charles right after… but it's just been crazy. Is this a good time?

"Of course!" Hitting the intercom. "Jason's finally made his way to you, Charles."

The quick response was, "Well, don't make him wait; tell him to come right in."

Jason entered the office, and Charles moved quickly to greet him in his customary bear hug. The man had always been affectionate, but his size betrayed his gentle nature.

But at that moment, it was just what Jason needed.

Charles was like a giant out of a fairytale. A bear of a man who would lift the boys high above his head and spin or wrestle with them on the ground, always letting them win. And whenever they were scared, he'd wrap them up in the safety of his arms.

And even though Jason was a six-foot-three grown man and was happily dwarfed in the strong arms.

"Jason, it's so good to see you, son; I've been worried that you'd try to tackle this whole thing yourself. I'm so glad you came to your senses. Sit down, sit down. Do you want something to drink? I've gotta say, son… you look a real mess."

Leave it to Charles to point out the obvious.

Jason sat down in the leather chair in front of the desk and set his backpack on the chair beside him.

Before coming, he had tried to figure out a way to explain his error in not coming sooner. But it was hard to explain something he didn't completely understand himself.

Still unsure what he should say, he leaned forward and laid his arms on the desk. "I have so much I need to tell you, but first, I need to apologize for not calling you after I found John. I should have been the one to notify you, and I'm so sorry.

"I had planned on coming to the house the next day… but well, with everything that happened.

"Anyway, a nurse told me that you stopped by the hospital when I was sleeping, and I would have stopped by, but..."

Charles waved his explanation away, "That's all in the past. You're here now, and that's all that matters."

"...yeah, well, I really appreciated what you tried to do for Stryker, and I should have called after our last appeal failed. It's just that... it's been hard.

"I've really been fighting with myself. I really don't want anyone caught up in my mess. With everything that's happened and with what I've been accused of... I've just been afraid of putting anyone else in the line of fire."

Seeing Jason's haunted look, Charles said, "I'm not surprised. You've always been conscientious. Nevertheless, you know me. I never shy away from a fight, and I will always have your back. So let's agree that from now on, no matter what the problem is, you'll come to me. Do we have a deal?"

With a nod, Jason said, "Yeah. And honestly, you've always been there for me. It's just been crazy, and I was hoping I'd make more sense of things before I brought you in on it.

"I think this whole thing started with Dad's accident."

Charles's brows drew together along with his frown as Jason continued, "I'd hoped to come up with a better way to tell you, but I haven't, so I'll just say it.

"Dad was murdered."

Charles tightened his jaw, but he didn't interrupt.

"I still haven't figured out why.

"But the men who broke into the house and assaulted Mom must have been looking for something in Dad's office. Because, like Mom said, nothing was stolen.

"I'm telling you, Charles, nothing has made sense since Dad died.

"Shit, just look at what happened to mom. To John. And what's happening to Stryker and me? It's all just too coincidental. And if that's not enough, there's even more that's pretty hard to swallow.

"Which is another reason for not wanting to bring anyone I care about into it. I found out that there's a connection between Billy, a drug dealer... and... dad."

"What? Not the man killed in the alley?" His voice deepened.

"Yeah. Like I said, nothing makes sense.

"When I was released from the hospital, Billings took me to the station for debriefing. Not that I remembered a whole hell of a lot. But near the end of it, it seemed clear enough that they thought I set the entire thing up to kill Billy.

"Then, before I can begin to process all that, my Captain informs me about Stryker. So yeah. It's messed me up pretty well. And I'm not handling anything very well."

"I can see why." Charles leaned back in his chair. "Must feel pretty overwhelming."

Jason bowed his head and brushed the hair out of his eyes, "Honestly, I'm not sure. Sometimes I'm just numb; other times I'm mad as hell."

"So much has happened, and I can't figure it out… it's all so confusing. Every time I think I've figured one thing out, something else comes up to confuse what I thought I knew."

"Well, don't worry about all of that. I'll do what I can to help so you're not carrying this by yourself. You know that there is nothing I wouldn't do to protect you. You're family. So let me share the burden."

Hitting the intercom, Charles said, "Julie, cancel all my meetings for the day."

"Already done, Charles. I knew that's what you'd want as soon as Jason walked in."

"Nice work, Julie, as usual! Thank you."

Turning back to Jason, "Okay, son, let's order some lunch, and you can tell me everything you've uncovered. Two minds are always better than one."

After placing their orders, they moved to the large table to wait for their Chinese take-out.

While they waited, Jason looked at the man who had been a second father to him and asked, "So, how much do you know about Dad's death?"

"Well, I read the police report, if that's what you mean. Like you, I wanted to understand what happened, but I was pretty disappointed. Like you, the conclusion that Matt was driving too fast didn't make sense."

"Yeah, that sounds like the first report. It took pushing for a more intensive investigation for them to find that his work truck had been tampered with."

Charles raised his voice slightly and asked, "What?! His plumbing van? Where did you hear that?"

"I know—crazy. But after I read the first report, I knew that there had to be more to the accident. I figured they'd missed something. Dad would have never driven like that. There was just no way! Something else had to be going on. Only I couldn't figure out what.

"It took a little pushing and help from my Captain, who negotiated some cooperation from Gilpin County, but a second forensic team was finally sent out.

"And surprise, surprise, guess what they found?

"There was fresh brake fluid on the road about a mile before the accident site, from a small puncture in the brake line, and matched the brake fluid on the road to the fluid in the van's master cylinder.

"But that's not all.

"The left steering control arm wasn't connected. The grooves and scrapes in the metal show that the arm was disconnected for a distance, dragging on the ground before the vehicle left the road.

"The CBI's report states that the vehicle was deliberately sabotaged, causing vehicular homicide. The conclusion noted that it took malice aforethought to puncture the brake line, along with a knowledge of mechanics, to cause the steering malfunction.

"They found partial fingerprints and some blood on the undercarriage that were matched to Billy O'Leary.

"Charles, Billy murdered Dad!"

His voice caught slightly, and unshed tears filled his dark blue eyes, "I can't even imagine how scary that was for him."

A cloud darkened Charles's features. Stunned into silence, unable to look at the pain on Jason's face, he looked down to add a few notes.

Charles had always been full of joy and humor. Like Matt, he was fun-loving and playful and rarely got angry, but when he did, it showed.

At hearing how Matt suffered, the intense pain Charles had carried since losing his best friend merged with an equal amount of anger at the injustice of what happened to him.

Those emotions were coupled with a deep need to protect the boy sitting in front of him.

"I didn't have a clue about any of this until my debriefing when they told me about the report. It wasn't until I could use Mom's computer and opened the email that I got the particulars. I planned to forward everything to you, but I wanted to be able to tell you in person first.

"It's a lot to take in.

"I wanted the truth—really thought I was ready for it, but I was wrong. I had no idea how bad the truth would hurt." Jason shook his head.

"It really messed me up, and I couldn't let on to Mom. It would have devastated her. So I swallowed it until I could figure it out in private. I know I have to tell her; I just don't know how."

Charles looked up, pushing his own emotions aside. "Don't worry about that right now, son. I think you did the right thing to keep it from her, at least for now. She's still grieving pretty hard, and she's gone through a lot.

"I fear more may be coming since now they have a motive for you wanting Billy dead."

"I know. But I swear, Billy's name never came up. They wouldn't say how he got an early release. But for Christ's sake, Charles, he was supposed to be in jail!

"And now that I'm a suspect, no one is willing to give me any information. But what really bugs me is how Dad even knew a scum bag like Billy. Where the hell did their paths cross, and why would Billy want to kill him?"

Corralling his emotions, Charles set his pen down and shook his head. "No wonder you're struggling. I'm having a hard time with it, and I wasn't put through all the rest with the department.

"You said they haven't charged you with anything yet, right?"

"No. For now, I'm on administrative leave while they complete their investigation. I don't think they have enough evidence— too many holes.

"But there's so much more that has my head spinning.

"If Billy was responsible for Dad, who attacked Mom at the house? Are those two incidents related?

"It seems like they should be, and yet, the description Mom gave doesn't match Billy at all.

"I just can't seem to connect the dots.

"Then there's what happened to me. I hate to say it, but I think it might have started with John.

"Finding him like that hit me pretty hard… but it was also… off. I can't really why. Hell, I was pretty sick, but it almost seemed… staged."

Charles lifted his eyebrows, "What do you mean staged?"

"I don't know. That's the problem. I don't seem to know much of anything."

"Well, try to describe it."

"Okay. It took a while to get caught up at the station. I'd been off for a week because of the flu. When I finally went out on patrol, I wanted to check on this group of wayward kids I'd seen cutting school.

"Instead, I found John on a park bench in the fetal position.

"I remember thinking, why was he taking a nap? It was freezing out. It was rush hour… noisy.

"He was facing the back of the bench.

"When it's cold, he usually stays home. And the way he faced the back of the bench was weird, too. I don't think I've ever seen him sleep with his back to the world like that.

"When he does pass out somewhere, he keeps his back against a wall and, even asleep, holds pretty tight to his bottle. But I didn't smell any drink, and the team didn't find a bottle.

"I stayed with him until he was loaded into the van and the coroner took him away.

"It's probably nothing, but it still haunts my dreams."

Charles made some more notes, "Okay, is there anything else you remember."

"No, at least not concerning John. But that was just the first part of my shift. Other things seemed strange, like why my symptoms got worse after I took a second dose of cold meds and why my radio stopped working.

"I'm positive I didn't kill anyone, but why can't I remember what happened that night? How will I help with my defense if I can't remember?

"What really bothers me is, if I can't clear my name, even if I'm not charged, no one will trust me again." Jason couldn't sit still, so he got up, "That's what's got me worried. I love being a cop... I'm good at it.

"Bad cops ruin it for the rest of us. There's a smear campaign, and I don't want to be part of keeping the drama going. If I'm charged, it will just throw more fuel on that fire."

Turning to Charles, "I know it's a hard job, especially now, but I love it."

"Most cops I know just try to keep the Gen-Pop safe and hope to go home healthy at the end of each shift. If this keeps up, who will people call when they need help?

"Shit, then someone will sue the city because no one shows up. Well, I don't want to provide the vultures with another smear campaign."

Jason sat down heavily in his seat.

It reminded Charles of when he was a boy and would pout about something he thought was unfair. "Well, at least I can see why you've been messed up.

"But Jason, you've been trying to manage this alone.

"Get this straight, you've never been alone. So, stop feeling like a cad for asking for help.

"Don't forget, your dad was my best friend. We were as close as blood, and I loved him. So, there's no way I'd stay out of it.

"Don't worry, we'll find a way to clear your name. But right now, we need to focus on keeping you out of prison. Then we'll worry about your reputation.

"I'm not happy that the DA hasn't sent over this information. It's part of the disclosure for the case they're building against you. I'm the attorney of record, for Christ's sake! They're required to provide this information to me.

"I'll present this to a judge and ask for an order to compel them to turn it over.

"Tell me what you can remember, and we'll go through it together."

"Right. That whole shift was weird. But I shouldn't have gone to work that day. I was still sick, trying to recover from the worst flu of my life. I'd been off for over a week and was scheduled to go back. And I was chomping at the bit to get back. So was Stryker. I thought a few cold meds might help me through the shift, like it had before.

"But I didn't do it! Even if I'd known Billy had sabotaged Dad's van, I wouldn't have shot him. I would have found a way to put him away for the rest of his life."

Pausing for a drink, "I think I might have been framed. The problem is, I can't figure out how, who, or why anyone would go to that much trouble.

"If someone wanted Billy dead, they could have just ended him. But why go to the trouble of setting me up for his murder? And yet… I have to admit that a setup also makes some sense, especially if you need a scapegoat.

"But how did they even find out where we were?

"Then there's Jack. He was the first on the scene, and he saw the condition I was in. I think he'd verify that I looked drugged. But we've barely talked since the alley. And even then, it was only to find out about Stryker. I was hoping he'd be a character witness, but now I'm not so sure."

"What do you know about him?"

"We met in Afghanistan. Remember the attack when I was escorting that caravan? He was the guy overseeing it. The one right next to me when we were trapped by the Taliban and had to fight our way out."

"Of course. As I remember, it was one hell of a fight."

"It was. But we got lucky. Dash showed up in his bird just in time to help us finish them off, and we made it to Kabul.

"It was a bad day. We lost some good men. I didn't know all of them, but it was still hard to lose them. Dash flew their bodies back to base to make sure they made it home for a proper burial.

"Jack and I didn't keep in touch after I came home. I had no idea that he lived here or that he was a cop until I signed on with the K-9 unit a few years later. We ended up on the same shift and spent a lot of time together training our dogs."

Charles put his hand on Jason's shoulder. "Okay, well, I'll want to talk with him at some point. But for now, give me some time to look into a few things."

When Jason was ready to leave, Charles said, "Just remember to keep your head down. The only thing that can imprison you is the cell you create in your own mind. Try to relax a little. You might remember something that will split this whole thing wide open.

"And make sure you keep me in the loop. I'm on your side."

That night, Jason slept fitfully. His dreams jumbled together like a collage. Images and colors melded one into the other and then jumped around.

Shrunken to the size of a child standing in front of a tall wooden judge's bench, like in a cartoon, the angry judge leaned over the top of the bench, stretching like he was made of elastic until he was right in Jason's face.

With a loud crack, the gavel struck the bench. The judge shook it at Jason and roared, "Guilty!"

The scene changed, and Jason was running from a masked stranger.

Snot dripped like a leaky hose bib from his nose.

The scene shifted between fragments of fog and shadow.

With blurry vision, he stumbled from one dark alley into another and got trapped in the enclosed alcove.

Then, in a swirl of chiaroscuro, it began. The nightmare—the one that had plagued him intermittently since the hospital.

It always started the same: struggling to get out of bed, sick but determined. Each step as he remembered it until he found John.

Like an ugly mosaic, the scene scrambled into a mess of injustices. It was as if something, maybe his subconscious, was trying to point something out to him like it knew something his conscious mind couldn't grasp.

But without a smooth transition, scenes took on a strobe effect, similar to an old movie, where movements appear jerky and detached.

In the past, whenever he got close to uncovering something, he'd wake up in his room alone and disoriented.

After waking in a sweat several times, Jason decided to find a way to stay in the dream. As uncomfortable as it was, he needed to see what happened.

The flu had left his body weak. He could feel the weakness descend over him again as he relived the experience.

The cold meds had probably compromised his ability to think. But there was more that he needed to remember.

Then, he was next to John, trying to wake him. The picture froze in the evening chill, and a blink later, he was at the station, staring at the report he struggled to complete.

It startled him a little when the scene jumped to his locker. He'd decided to complete his shift and wanted the meds to help get him through. Between finding John and talking to Jack, he'd been distracted.

He was too intent on completing his shift to notice that the lock wasn't fully engaged.

The scene froze again.

At first glance, the lock looked engaged, hanging there. The pin lined up with the keyhole, but then he noticed that it wasn't inserted.

It was a small detail, but one that was important.

Did I enter the combination?

In three-quarter time, the scene continued.

Staring at the lock, he shrugged. *I must have forgotten to close it. Maybe I opened it without thinking about it?*

When did he start feeling woozy? How long did he start feeling strange after leaving the substation?

Something was pushing him to remember. At the same time, his mind was insisting he wake up.

In that half-awake state, it felt like he had to claw his way back into the dream.

He wanted to see more, to watch as a conscious participant, much like a spectator in ethereal form might observe a room full of people yet remain unseen.

He'd heard of lucid dreaming but had never experienced it before and wondered if he was truly experiencing it now.

Captured by a whirl of color, he was lifted and dropped at the gas station in time to watch as he and Stryker moved in on the men struggling with the weapons crate.

The meds that had helped with his symptoms earlier now fatigued him. He could feel his energy slowly drain out of his body. But before he could grasp what was happening, the dream shifted again.

His heart beat against the interior of his chest. His body shivering with fever while his thigh and calf muscles spasmed.

Sweat dripped into his eyes – burning and running down his over-heated face. His lips were cracked from panting hot air from burning lungs, and a raw throat.

Even though it was Spring, winter hadn't quite given up its hold. With intermittent blasts of rain and light snowfall, winter displayed its strength by being unwilling to give in to the sweet-smelling warm breath of spring.

In a flash, he drew his gun—and moved blindly down the alley corridor.

Barks echoed like miniature explosions in the confined space, increasing the pressure of a headache brewing.

At the alcove. A quick peek.

Billy cowered on the dumpster behind the metal lid. Stryker is jumping and snapping.

Dark shadows hovered in every corner like demons waiting to pounce—the dim light above the doorway—too weak to expose them.

Then Stryker was beside him.

The echoes of his barks still reverberated in Jason's skull.

Jason turned his head to call for help, but then — it happened.

Footsteps?

Then, he felt it. The sharp sting of a projectile hit his neck with a searing pain, throwing him off balance.

His gun tumbled from his hand when he instinctively reached up to protect his neck.

He hadn't remembered the crack of the flashlight lens when it hit the ground or the twirling beam spinning away across the ground.

Fear of death seeped into his awareness and increased his adrenalin. But like a match snuffed out by a drop of water, the rush that coursed through his system evaporated in a heartbeat as paralysis took over.

He fought it—the enemy invasion, willing his body to remain standing even as his vision blurred. His head flopped, his neck too weak to hold it upright.

Air whooshed from his lungs as if he'd been punched in the gut.

Fighting dizziness and confusion.

His legs quivered convulsively.

He watched through slitted eyelids as Stryker turned to look behind them.

He dropped—fell with a plop. Like a ragdoll collapsing in a heap without muscle or bone to hold it up

First, he landed hard on his right shoulder before the back of his head bounced off the ground. The trajectory then twisted him partway on his left side, where the bend in his leg held him.

A growl, a man's curse, a thump, a yelp.

Laying on the icy ground, strange sensations permeated his body as he succumbed to the sensations.

He couldn't see, but he heard voices.

Was that ice-crunching?

The dream had always jumped around, leaving too many holes to understand what was happening before.

The scenes too convoluted to decipher. And when he'd wake, he'd feel the dissipating heat, only to lose the dream.

This time, he refused to wake.

He needed to find out how the gun got back into his hand.

Stubbornly, he clung to the dream.

Another swirl of color.

Then he heard…

"Man, am I glad you showed up? For a minute there, I thought I was toast."

The squeaking sound of the metal lid moving kept Jason from falling into the abyss—from succumbing to the darkness.

That's when he was rolled onto his back. The familiar weight of his gun placed in his hand. He must have lost a glove because the chill of the metal was cold—the weapon heavy, and his hand too weak to hold onto it.

A voice very close to him said, "You have nothing to worry about, Billy. It's all part of the plan. You can get down now."

Two hands held the heavy object in his hand. His fingers pinched together.

A ping of metal followed by a gunshot and a gasp.

A blast of heat warmed his cold hand.

On the edge of consciousness, he felt something roughly pulled, creating a suction, inside of his neck—thwap!

Falling into an abyss.

Then, all was quiet.

CHAPTER SIXTEEN

More Pieces of the Puzzle

Jason woke with a start and jumped out of bed, worried he'd forget what the dream had shown him.

Memories were already vanishing.

Rushing into the front room, he grabbed a notebook and started a list.

• The lock shaft was lined up, but it wasn't closed. I always lock it out of habit. Does someone have access to my locker or know the combination? Did I forget to close it? Check the initials on the back.

• The cold meds helped until they stopped, and I started getting worse. Check to see if forensics tested my cold meds.

• What was wrong with my radio? Was it a problem with my gear, or was it a transmission issue?

• I was hit with something on the right side of my neck. The doctor said it looked like a puncture wound. I fought it—what felt like some type of drug. Get a copy of his notes, the pictures, and the tox screen.

• Someone was there. I didn't see him, but I heard and felt him. He rolled me over and shoved my gun into my hand. I heard a shot and felt the warmth. I need to find out what forensics found. Did they find any voids in the gun residue? Get a copy of the forensic report.

• Before I blacked out, I heard Stryker growl. Did he bite someone? There was a swoosh noise and a thump. Stryker yelped. Did they do a tox screen on Stryker at the kennel? Get a copy of the Vet's notes.

• Billy was talking with someone – something about a plan. But what plan?

• If it was Ponytail, how did he know where to find us, and why take out Billy?

• I think I was framed - but by who and why? Maybe an old arrestee? Check old case files.

• Billy wasn't even a blip on my radar. I didn't see the new report and didn't know about his early release until after the incident.

• Dad's death wasn't an accident - the new report confirmed his van was compromised. But why was Dad targeted?

• They found Billy's prints and DNA on the van's undercarriage. When did Billy have access to Dad's truck? When and where did Dad and Billy cross paths? And who put Billy up to it?

• Are Dad and Billy's murders connected? And why was I made part of it?

Jason understood that things might have been a little different if he hadn't been sick. And yet, if someone had it in for him, they would have found another way to frame him.

Going over the list, he had more questions than answers. But at least his memory was coming back.

Someone was in that alley. He might not be able to say who it was, what their motives were, why he was framed, or have a clue how they pulled it off, but at least he knew that much.

Now, he just needed to find out who it was and figure out how to prove he was framed.

Jason went over his conversation with the doctor during his examination in the emergency room.

"Well, it's pretty red and swollen, all right. Do you remember what hit you?

"No. I just kind of woke up on the ground with it throbbing."

"Hmm, well, you have a pretty decent size knot here. I've seen this kind of injury before – when a baseball…"

He pulled glasses from his pocket, "… only it looks like you were hit with something… sharp… I almost didn't see it. The swelling masked what appears to be a… puncture wound.

Distracted, the doctor's voice softened to almost a whisper. "A strange size, though. Maybe… a fourteen or fifteen gauge?"

Even with the bed elevated at thirty degrees to reduce the pressure on his head and propped up on pillows, Jason couldn't help but flinch at the additional pain the doctor's examination caused.

"Hey doc, I know you need to examine me, but take it easy, okay?"

"Oh, right, sorry – I'll stop pressing on it, but it is a bit puzzling.

"There's the swelling, of course. But I noticed a… well, there's a circular indentation around what looks like a puncture wound… an injection of sorts.

"The swelling nearly hid it.

"I was trying to confirm… because an injection on your neck… under these circumstances…."

Turning to his assistant, he said, "Kelly, please go get the camera and the tape measure. I'd like to get a good shot of that puncture wound and measure it. See what you can get … zoom in tight. As you can see, bruising is already coming to the surface… try to get that too.

"Oh, and call downstairs and get him into radiology and the lab. I want a CT and a full blood panel."

As the nurse rushed away, Jason asked, "Hey doc, can you give me something to stop the dizziness? Maybe something to get rid of this headache? It feels like my skull might crack open.

"My stomach's sick, too. I'm not sure what's left in there, but it's rumbling again."

Grabbing an emesis basin, Dr. Gates handed it to Jason, "Here. Use this if you need to vomit.

"Right now, you're talking and breathing normally. That's a good sign. But head and neck injuries are a serious business. Until we know what we're dealing with, I can't risk giving you something that might complicate things.

"I've ordered some tests, which should tell us more. Just hang in there; this will all be over soon."

Not nearly soon enough, as far as Jason was concerned.

The nurse took pictures and helped Jason change into a gown before quickly transporting him to radiology.

He had just found a comfortable place on the pillow for his head when Smothers showed up.

More photos, more swabs, more pain.

It took three weeks of watching the side of his neck turn colors blackish-blue to purple and finally an ugly yellow before the knot had dwindled to a tolerable size and discomfort.

After rereading what he remembered, Jason took a snapshot to text to Billings. He'd promised to let Billings know if he remembered anything, and he had.

Adding to the text, 'Hey, Boss, I'm texting this because I remembered a few things. This list is what I've remembered so far. If I remember anything else, I'll be in touch.'

After grabbing some breakfast and another strong cup of coffee, he headed to the desk to attack the bank boxes.

The bulky yellow envelope he'd found taped to the back of his dad's filing cabinet was in the box closest to him.

When he picked it up, he realized that there were more than old papers inside. He unlatched the metal fastener and tipped it upside down on the desk, surprised by the contents that spilled out.

Two thin journals and five miniature audio tapes littered the top of the desk, one of which fell to the floor. "What the hell?"

Picking up the tape from the floor, he looked at the writing. Each audiotape was labeled chronologically in his father's handwriting. However, without a miniature recorder, he put them aside to listen to later, stacking them in order at the back of the desk.

When he picked up the journal, he noticed Matt's name stamped on the lower right edge of the soft leather.

Inside the front cover in his mother's cursive, Jason read, 'My dearest Matt, journaling is one of the truest forms of release.

'I hope you will use this small gift to organize your thoughts, make plans for our future, note any romantic ideas (hint, hint), and document that little rascal inside of you.

'You have so many wonderful qualities, and I love every one of them. Yours Forever, Sofia.'

Tears burned his eyes, and as he rubbed them, he thought about how the loss of his father had left a hole in their lives that might never be filled.

Matt was not only a hardworking man of honor and integrity but also an amazing husband, father, businessman, and friend.

Jason wondered how many men could master the complexities of life and love while remaining humble and playful, the way his father had.

Matt's character was beyond reproach, and yet, somehow, he was mixed up with Billy. And maybe worse, Jason was holding yet another part of his father he didn't know.

A side that Matt had kept secret.

Although it seemed out of character, Jason wondered if his father had kept secrets from his mother, too.

Seeing the neat print, similar to his own, Jason relaxed and began reading the journal.

Matt touched on his initial concerns and shared them with Sofia. He thought she'd want him to pass on the job, and he wasn't ready to do that.

His notes read, I had to draw the blueprints from memory; the owner refused to give me a set. I thought it was weird, but the prints were off from what I saw during the walk-through anyway.

He'd like to start next week, although I haven't even given him the bid yet, and I have some concerns about doing this job.

When I was leaving, I saw a sentry with an AK47. That's pretty extreme, even for a wealthy eccentric. Still, it's hard to pass up the kind of money that will let me take some time off to spend with Sofia. She's been so patient, and we both deserve an amazing vacation.

The rest of the page was taken up by a blueprint of the house. He could see lines that had been erased, as if Matt had realized an error and corrected it.

While the clock ticked the minutes and then the hours away. Jason made notes and used Post-it flags to mark areas he wanted to refer back to.

The next entry read, *October twenty-eighth, 2020. We started on the fifth, and things were going pretty smoothly. But today, I'm a little worried.*

I heard something totally unexpected. At first, I thought I'd heard it wrong. It made my skin crawl. I hoped I was wrong about this place, but I can't deny what I've gotten myself into. If I'm right, I need to be very careful from here on out.

I was in the basement, sending a snake camera through the pipes, when I heard the owner talking.

It went something like this: the owner said, "Did the shipment go through okay?" *the other male voice said*, "Yeah, but we have a problem."

The owner asks, "What problem?" *The voice says,* "Just as MT finishes the transfer, I notice a small tear in one of the bricks, so I do a double take. Because it was a big shipment, I didn't want the buyer to find out and think we'd ripped him off. So I point it out and offer a discount in case there's a shortage. The buyer was happy that I noticed, especially after I handed over some of the cash.

I didn't have a chance to ask MT about the shortage because he took off while I was resolving the issue. Since then, I've been asking around. And get this: MT has been skimming off every shipment. Seems he's been selling on the side, building himself a little business."

Then I hear the owner say, "Family or not, I won't have this. I want you to take him out! You figure out how and where. But I want it done. And make sure word gets out that I won't tolerate disloyalty."

At that point, I considered walking away from the job but worried they'd suspect something. I didn't want to put Sofia or Jason in harm's way.

Jason set the journal down to work through the wave of emotion that had hit him. Leaning against the counter with a refreshed cup of coffee in hand, he was somewhat comforted that Matt was exactly who Jason believed him to be.

Lost in thought, Jason didn't hear Stryker until a paw landed on his leg. Setting the mug aside, he crouched down to stroke his friend. "Hey buddy, how did you know I could use a friend right now?"

After several minutes of ear scratches and rubs, Jason gave Stryker a chewy, then picked up his father's journal to continue where he'd left off.

October twenty-ninth: I have an appointment with the DEA. I can only hope they'll know what to do.

The journal was filled with drawings along with Matt's notes.

On one page was a portrait of an angry-looking, morbidly obese man. The top of his head cone-shaped narrow alongside the eyes. The hair shaved close to his scalp.

The eyes themselves were dark, sunken into the folds of flesh that surrounded them. The cheeks bulged, making deep crevices along the rounded nose. Thick, full lips, a nub of chin, and a thick turkey waddle.

The moniker read *Mr. Morales, aka: the Fat Man.*

Jason stared at the drawing for a long time, wondering if this was the man who ordered the hit on his father and Billy.

The word 'shipment' was enough to infer that Morales might be a drug supplier - even a kingpin. And since Billy was a dealer, it made sense that Morales and Billy would know each other.

Matt was doing a job for Morales, and that was the link between them.

Jason knew that he'd found the connection between his dad and Billy and added those tidbits to his notes.

• The link between Dad and Billy is a man named Morales who may be a supplier.

• Dad overhead a threat and contacted the DEA. He must have believed that it was drug-related.

Halloween 2020... I came home early to help Sofia decorate. Halloween is one of her favorite holidays. She goes all out for the kids and delights in seeing the little ones in their costumes.

I know she misses when Jason was that age.

November 2020: I met with DEA agent Clay Thomas. He had my service record and knew I'd been trained *in covert operations.*

He asked for my help, but I wasn't sure I could do what he asked. I've been retired from the service for years, and I'm not getting any younger. But after he told me about Morales, I found it difficult to say no.

They believe he's following in his father's footsteps. Morales isn't even his real name. It's the name he adopted after his mother died.

His real name is Francisco Magluta. He is the son of Sal Magluta, the drug kingpin who built a cocaine empire with Willy Falcon out of Florida. Sal is doing his time in ADX Florence, Colorado, while his son built a compound just a few hours away.

The DEA has been trying to build a case and arrest Morales but hasn't been able to catch him red-handed.

Agent Thomas said they believe he's ordered multiple hits, but they've never been able to trace the murders back to him. Even when they catch the person carrying out the orders, they haven't been able to break any of them.

Clay figures their families are well cared for, or maybe they receive a bonus for staying quiet. In any case, no one has given even a hint about the operation.

I may not be a soldier anymore, but I'm still a patriot, and I believe in doing what's right. So, I agreed to help them collect evidence.

I'll complete the job as a civilian and place their recording devices. But I'll have to be careful. Morales is just paranoid enough to have a bug detector. Plus, Henry the butler is always watching me.

Once I pull the tapes, I'll make copies and arrange a drop-off for Agent Thomas. The copies are insurance in case any get lost. Who knows where Morales has moles?

November 9, 2020: I have to be careful contacting Agent Thomas. I'm worried about blowing my cover. I just hope it'll be enough to help take Morales down and stop him from polluting our community. I hate keeping this from Sofia, but I can't tell her and keep her safe.

November 12, 2020: Good news! The recordings provide information about a gathering being planned at the compound. I'm told it's a big deal! It could be what blows this thing wide open, so I can't stop just yet.

November 13, 2020: Today was a close one. I was in the hall bathroom, hiding another recorder, when I turned to find Henry behind me. For a minute, I thought he might have seen what I was doing. Luckily, my back blocked his view, but it sure made my heart jump into overdrive.

Every day that I go to the compound, I risk being discovered. But the things I've heard are enough to keep me on it. The man is repulsive.

Today, he was on the phone complaining about one of the blackjack dealers. He wanted her fired because he didn't like how she dealt his cards. Then, he changed his mind and told one of his goons to "take care of her."

I feared for the girl's life, so I sent a text to Clay. It's shit like that reminds me that I'm doing the right thing. I just need to get enough evidence to put that SOB away.

The following pages showed the same layout but with plumbing, electrical, and alarm systems drawn with different colored pencils.

Already on his fourth cup of coffee, Jason was enthralled with his father's journals. It gave him insight into a side of his father he didn't know.

In the second journal, there were additional drawings of pipes indicating the locations of the recorders.

There was also a layout of where the cameras were inside the house, a partial plat map of the compound grounds, and a detailed map of the cabins.

November 14... Today, I overheard another conversation about a shipment in Denver. It sounded like a large shipment, but the voices were too soft in places to make out what was said. I'm hoping Clay can fix it with his high-tech equipment.

I'll get this to him ASAP, but I need to be careful. If Morales or one of his goons sees me... well, it won't be good.

The job is almost done. I'm afraid it won't take me as long as we need. The summit is set for the weekend after Thanksgiving. But at this rate, we'll be done in a few days. I don't think I can drag it out much longer than the twentieth. He's planning a big feast for his guests. Agent Thomas hoped I'd hear names, but I haven't heard anything yet about who will attend.

Jason took another sip of his coffee, trying to wash away the tightness in his throat.

Matt had been killed that same Friday, the twentieth. Instead of having a big gathering to express thanks, Sofia and Jason had been forced to plan a funeral.

Jason stood up and walked around in an effort to distract himself from the grief that attacked in waves. Afraid that, once he accepted Matt's death and allowed himself to mourn, he'd fall apart and lose his objectivity.

After all this time, he might have a lead on what happened to his father. He needed to stay the course. There would be plenty of time later, when the craziness was over, to give in to his grief.

He was working a case, plain and simple. It was important that he didn't let emotion influence his objectivity.

He had to stay strong.

November sixteenth... When I entered the devil's den this time, additional sentries were walking the parameter. All with AK-47s. They're securing the compound and getting ready for the conference. Armed sentries are positioned at the front and back of the mansion.

I've tried, but I can't stall any longer. Henry keeps asking when we'll be done. He told me that they are expecting company and everything must be in working order for their guests. I agreed to make the Twentieth my last.

I'm glad that I sent JD and the rest of the crew out on other jobs once the cabins were done.

Jason put his fingers to his eyes and pressed, rubbing the sore orbs in an effort to relax the tense muscles behind them.

Even though the journals were only a quarter-inch thick, his father had managed to fill them with both drawings and notes. It was funny, but Jason never thought of his father as a spy.

Seeing another portrait by Matt marked Henry and several of the unnamed guards provided insight into his father's thoughts.

November eighteenth... The job is done, but then it has been. I'm just playing a part now. Henry has been noisier than usual, but it's our last chance, so I have to keep him happy.

November nineteenth, I'm discouraged. Morales was talking to a man he called the Doctor. He was supposed to have a designer drug ready for the gathering. Morales was beside himself, yelling that the Doctor promised it would be ready. The Doctor said that he'd had a setback, and it might take another year.

After screaming his head off, he made several calls canceling the weekend. I'll have to contact Clay and tell him about the change in plans. He'll be disappointed after all the work that went into the preparations.

I promised I'd be done tomorrow, so I'll stick with it. Before I leave, I'll pull the recorders and close everything up. I just hope Clay hears more about what's going on when he listens to the new tapes.

The last sketch, drawn in red pencil, depicted different parts of the house. It showed the new positions of a few of the cameras and where the sentries had been stationed. It also included a detailed map of two roads that led to the compound.

That was Matt's last entry.

His father's obituary came to mind: On November 20, 2020, Matthew Braxton Colt, aka Mac to his friends, expired in an automobile accident. He leaves behind his loving wife, Sofia Isabella Colt, and son, Jason Maxwell; his father, Gordon Matthew Colt; and extended family members Charles and Desiree Adams and their son, Dean.

The memorial service has been postponed until after the holidays. The family will send out notifications when a service has been scheduled.'

A shiver went up Jason's back, knowing how Billy got access to Matt's truck and that Morales was the one who ordered Billy to sabotage his father's truck.

Putting down the journal, Jason wondered how Morales found out that his father was working with the DEA.

CHAPTER SEVENTEEN

Connecting the Dots

Decked out in her newest grey and black tracksuit, the newest purchase for her granny disguise, Becca made her usual rounds at the casinos. It was Saturday. On Saturday, she started at the Ameristar casino five-cent slots.

When she first began following the target, she often wasted the night in the wrong place. On other nights, she'd lose him in the crowd. But now, just a few months later, she thought she had his pattern pretty well down.

Sometimes, he came in with a new woman, but most of the time, he arrived alone.

Once she'd made him, she wandered over to a slot machine as close to him as possible, trying to overhear his conversation.

Not once had he bothered to look at her.

No matter which casino he started in, he always made his way to the Fat Man, who spent most of his time at the high-stakes blackjack tables.

Becca wanted to know who the man was and why Mark sought him out. He was obviously older than Mark and seemed to be calling the shots.

She was sure that Mark had killed Joss. And it seemed likely that the Fat Man had provided the drugs.

She was determined to find out one way or another by focusing on uncovering who the Fat Man was.

The slot machine was at the perfect angle to see the man's lips move. Unfortunately, she couldn't get close enough to hear what was said.

She was so focused on their lips that she almost missed it.

Mark looked up and made eye contact – catching her in the act.

At the same time, her heart dropped into her stomach. Mark placed his hand on the Fat Man's shoulder and tipped his head in her direction.

As he began walking toward her, Becca didn't move. She couldn't let on that she'd noticed he'd seen her, which was not an easy task with her heart rate escalating with each step he took.

As he got closer, the hair stood on end all over her body. Her breathing was coming way too fast.

He'd be on her in seconds. She needed to control her breathing and think.

She had to maintain her focus as if she hadn't noticed Mark moving toward her. She needed to come up with a viable reason for looking in that direction.

Then it hit her.

After a quick scan around the room, she went back to playing the machine she was sitting at mere seconds before he reached her.

His voice was soft when he said, "Hello, how are you doing this evening?"

Acting distracted, she turned toward him and somehow managed to keep her throat from closing. "Not very well at all. This machine is being stubborn. I was just wondering if maybe I should pick another one."

As she talked, she purposely looked at a machine directly behind the Fat Man. She wanted to provide a reason for looking in that direction, "I was thinking… I'd try that White Orchid machine over there. But that man has been on it for a while now. I was hoping he'd leave before it hit."

Realizing she needed to acknowledge him in some way. "Oh, I'm sorry. Did you want this machine? I'm just sitting here dabbling with it while I wait for him to leave. I'll move if you want to play. But like I said, this one is stubborn."

As he followed her line of sight, she saw his shoulders relax. "Oh, no, mam, I thought you were looking at me and needed something; I'm sorry to have troubled you."

As he walked away, Becca feared she might fall out of her chair. She could barely believe he bought it. Her heart was beating so hard she thought he might have heard it.

From her periphery, she could see that he stopped to watch her. To eliminate any further suspicion, she played another round on the machine.

She feigned frustration when the play didn't hit.

***

As he observed the old woman, he thought there was something eerily familiar about her.

Her movements were fluid as she took her time, unlike those around her rushing from one play to another.

Finally shaking his head, he chided himself, *I don't know any old women... what am I doing?*

***

Chomping at the bit to share what he'd found, Jason looked at his watch for maybe the tenth time in as many minutes.

He'd messaged Dash to pick up a miniature tape recorder on his way to the cabin. Jason wanted to listen to the tapes.

His dad wouldn't hide them unless they were important.

He'd been waiting most of the day, and Dash was due to arrive any minute. The steaks were seasoned and ready to place on the grill.

Jason was jacked up on caffeine and dying to share what he'd learned. He hoped that Dash tracked down Freddie and learned something, too.

After a half hour passed with no word, Jason was ready to jump in his Jeep and look for him when Stryker's ears perked up.

A low timbre began in his throat, and Jason immediately grabbed his leash and attached it to Stryker's collar. "Hey, settle down, boy. It's just Dash, we're okay."

It had been three days since the escape from the kennel, and Stryker hadn't shown one sign of aggression. Even when they were play-wrestling. Jason had tried to instigate a reaction, but Stryker wasn't triggered. It wasn't uncommon to be bitten when training, but Stryker hadn't even growled at him. In fact, this was the first time Stryker had shown any sign of aggression.

Dash stopped in his tracks, surprised that Stryker was on his lead. "What's up with him?"

"He got triggered when he heard you drive up, is all." Come say hello. Just take it slow. He's been great with just the two of us, but he hasn't seen anyone else, and I don't want him to get aggressive again."

Dean slowly moved toward Stryker, talking as he walked up to him. "Hey, boy, you remember me, don't you?"

At that, Stryker sat on his hind quarters and panted happily, giving Dean the green light to pet him. Once they were reacquainted, Jason put the leash away and gave Dean their usual brotherly hug.

"Hey, dude, am I glad to see you! I have so much to tell you!"

"Yeah, me too! But hey, give me a minute. I really need a cup of coffee. I've been up for the last twenty-four, and I'm wrecked."

Dean smiled slyly as he got coffee. "You are not going to believe what I found out. I'm not sure I believe it."

"Hold that thought for a minute. Let me put these ribeye's on the grill. It won't take but a few minutes. And I have a lot to tell you, too. I hope you're hungry."

"Hungry doesn't cover it."

"Good. I got some spuds, some corn, a pasta salad, and the steaks. That should be enough to fill us up. We can talk while we eat.

Filling their plates, Jason asked, "So, you found Freddie?"

Dean chuckled, "You could say that. And it's a story, let me tell you! I'm just not sure that we can prove what I got."

"So, it took a minute, but I found your guy.

"He took exception to me walkin' up on him. Said it wasn't right me trackin' him down, not knowing me from Adam, as he put it.

"Started posturing and crap.

"But when I played your message, he relaxed a bit—still, made a last effort to play me, wanting money upfront like I'm new to the game. But after I shot that down by stuffing the bills back in my pocket, he got real talkative.

"Said this small Hispanic guy came around asking questions about you."

Jason put his fork down. "Me? What guy? What did he want?"

"I can't say, but he acted like he knew you. Freddie gave me a description, sounded just like the guy you chased with the tail that night.

"Freddie got the impression that he was fishin'. He wanted information on where you were like he was keeping tabs or something.

"Anyway, our boy plays dumb. He said there was something off about the guy and wanted no part of whatever he was selling. No way was he going to let on that he even knew you.

"I asked if the guy talked to anyone else, and get this, he tells the guy he doesn't know you and walks off.

"Only he decides to stay close, just out of sight and within earshot.

"Heard the guy say that he's looking for someone to replace Billy. He wanted to know if anyone was interested in taking Billy's place.

"But this dude must have been way off 'cause no one was buying what he was sellin'.

"When no one steps up, he asks if Billy said anything. Then he starts hinting about a gig that could make someone some cash.

"Then the guy tells Carl that he'll pay him for any info he hears, but Carl has nothing for him and says he's no snitch. As he leaves, he hands Carl a card and says to call if he hears anything.

"Once he's gone, Freddie hears Carl talking to his brother, Ross, about how Billy asked him about a month ago to hold something for him. Carl can't say no, on account he owes Billy for some stash. Billy hands him a box with one of those small locks on it.

"Carl says that Billy bragged that he worked for some hot-shot drug lord up in Central City. He said he's some kind of badass, so Carl didn't have to be told that they'd kill him if he opened it. So he hides the thing and tries to forget about it.

"Then, what does he do? Once Carl hears Billy's dead, the idiot breaks into the kit, thinking it's dope, and finds twenty grand along with a notebook. Now he's freakin' out even more because he knows once they find out he has their cash, he's a dead man. He figures the dude Billy worked for is the same dude that killed him.

"Then, a few days later, that little dude comes around asking questions. But get this, when I ask Carl about what he's holdin', he says, 'You can have it, man, I want no part of any of that shit.'

"I tell him that he can keep the money; I only want the notebook. But he says no way, I have to take the whole package.

"You ever hear of a junkie not wanting cash?"

With full bellies, they grabbed their beers and made themselves comfortable on the couch.

"No, can't say that's been my experience."

"There's somethin' serious going on when a junkie passes up cash. I have to say, he wasn't acting either. The guy was scared.

"Only I think there's more to it than he's sharing. I think he knows somethin' about what happened to you. Just my gut talking, but still."

Jason smiled, "You got a good gut."

"Yeah, well, I just hope there's something in it to clear your name. I haven't had a chance yet to read it, but it's definitely Billy's notebook. His name's all over it.

"The lab should be able to get fingerprints off it. I just need to figure out how to send it in without a case number. But we can figure that out later. Just make sure to wear gloves until we get it sorted out, okay?"

"Right." Jason's eyebrows drew together as he thought about what Dean had told him about Carl. "You know, you're right about Carl giving up that cash. I think we need to talk with him again.

"Get him away from the noise of the neighborhood. Give the guy a day or two to relax. Maybe fill his gut with some good food and drink—maybe buy him some clothes. I haven't seen him for a while—how'd he look?"

Dean scratched his scruff, "Not too bad, really. But he was stressed. Jumpy. But it wasn't like he was on somethin', but he reeks fear for sure."

"I can see that. Probably a bit paranoid, too, considering what happened to Billy."

"Yeah. That would do it all right."

"You said it seemed like he knew more. Maybe he knows about what happened to me that night?"

"Yeah."

"So I'm thinking that if we can get him someplace quiet, someplace away from the city where he can feel safe. He might just share whatever it is. What do you think?"

"Well, he's definitely anxious about something. He might go for it. But where?"

They were both quiet for several minutes until Jason jumped topics. "Right, well… let's chew on that a minute. I still have a few things I need to share. And it's big—like tell Charles big."

"Okay. So spill it."

"I think I know how Dad crossed paths with Billy. But that's not even the best part." Jason gulped the last of his coffee. "Dad was working with the DEA."

"What?! You have got to be kidding me."

"Nope. Not even a little."

Jason spent the next half hour bringing Dean up to speed about his dream and finding Matt's journals. "You can read the journals yourself later. You might pick up on something I missed. You're good at that. Only I have to share what I found."

Then, grabbing the journals off the desk, they went through each flagged section as Jason informed him about what he'd learned.

Then, without missing a beat, he shared what he discovered in the new forensics report.

When Dean finally looked up, his thick eyebrows, one higher than the other somewhat questioningly, and his large, almost translucent green eyes nearly glowing from their moist depths, stopped Jason cold.

Jason knew that look, having grown up watching his friend's emotions reflected in his eyes.

"Dammit, Dean, don't go there. I can't… not now. I tell you… I can't." Getting up quickly, he gathered the papers and journals. "Besides, this is good news. It's what I've been searching for, remember?"

"Yeah, okay, brother. But someday, all of this will catch up to you. And when it does, I sure hope I'm around to catch you before you fall."

Changing the subject, Jason asked, "Hey, any chance you picked up that recorder? I'm dying to hear what's on those tapes."

"Yeah, got it here." Dean pulled a mini recorder out of his jacket pocket and handed it to Jason. "I got one that has the cue marker indexing feature so we can mark important segments."

They spent the next few hours listening, relistening, and marking the tapes even though they were unsure how the tapes might help them.

They didn't recognize the voices on the tapes, and there were difficult-to-understand accents. Many of the conversations were also challenging to interpret without context.

Parts were garbled or missing altogether, and in some cases, the background noise made the voices hard to hear.

After a few voices were heard a few times, it became clear which speaker was the boss. He had a slight accent that was more noticeable when he was upset and a strange, almost formal way of speaking.

Dean made notes on things he wanted to check out. “This could be big, Jason! I’m not entirely sure what you’ve fallen into, but it sounds like Matt got mixed up with a cartel.

“Honestly, I don’t see how we can handle this alone — we’re not trained DEA agents or even detectives, man!”

Jason shook his head. “I know. But what can we do? The only other people I’d even think to trust might be Kade or maybe Jack. But I can’t see draggin’ more guys into it. It’s bad enough I’m putting you at risk.”

“That part’s not up for discussion.”

“...Besides, I’ve been thinking—for the future, I mean. If I’m reinstated, how long do I want to stay with K-9/SWAT?

“They won’t let Stryker work forever; there’s no way he could even if they did. And I’m not sure I’d want to work with another dog.”

“You’ve been thinking of becoming a detective?”

“It’s crossed my mind once or twice. I figure if I can work this kind of crazy out, I might actually be good at it.

“Anyway, that’s all just a big IF. And only after Stryker has been retired from DPD.”

“Yeah, well, an up-an-comin’ detective to figure all the ins and outs of this mess may not be enough.”

Before Jason could object, Dean continued, waving him off. “...okay, okay. Well, even with what you’ve remembered about that night, how do you find the evidence to prove it?

“No court is going to accept your dream as evidence, and we’re no Sherlock Holmes and Watson, man.

“Look. It was bad enough when we thought Matt died in some accident. That was unbelievable enough. Then we find out that it wasn’t an accident, that he was murdered.

“Murder is a hard thing to understand, right? I mean, the senselessness of it alone could keep a person up at night.

“But who would want to murder Matt? Like you said, Billy didn’t have the guts, let alone a motive.”

Jason looked up at his friend, his brow furrowed, "Yeah. Murder. Both Dad and Billy... and what happened in the alley.

"Even if my theory proves out, it seems to me like we need a whole lot of evidence to connect these things. But that's where... it gets... kind of crazy. Almost seems impossible."

"I can see that. But let's not get it twisted. When you look at the full picture possibility, it's a lot. But if we keep making connections like you been doing, we might get some answers."

"Maybe. I guess I'm just frustrated. I don't see how we tie these things together, let alone find the evidence to prove it. And we have to prove it to have any chance of clearing me or Stryker.

"And Dean, nothing short of clearing us is enough."

"I'm thinkin', and I'm sure you are too, that Matt working with the DEA put a target on his back. But then we're back to needing proof.

"I think the bit about linking Matt to the Fat Man and Billy is key—at least it's a good place to start.

"Billy's boss is the key here. If we can prove Billy is connected to this Morales guy, and Matt did a job for him, that could give us probable cause on who ordered the hit on Matt.

"What we do know is that you didn't know of Billy's connection to Matt's accident that night. And that you thought Billy was still doing his time.

"The question is how do we prove it? How do you prove something doesn't exist before it does? And how do we prove you didn't know Billy was released?

"Hey... I think the time/date stamp on the email substantiates that claim. So, there's that."

"That's right! I totally forgot about that. We need to make a list of what we do have and our theories and get it over to Charles. He might be able to use it to keep my arrest at bay."

Dean frowned, "Dad will do his best, you know that."

"Still, what we don't know could fill a book."

"Yeah, but at least what we do have will create doubt about your guilt. And my dad will know how to use it.

"Still, there's Billy's murder, which circles back to you. That's the part that has me stumped. But how did you get looped in?

"You didn't know what Matt was up to, so how do you fit into it, and who'd want to set you up? There's got to be a connection between everything that's happened that we're just not seeing yet."

Jason nodded."Yeah, and I've been working every angle I can think of, but I'm still not sure if what I have is right.

"The closest I can figure is someone is sending me a message. Nothing happened before I started asking questions. Maybe my looking into it made someone blink. And when evidence was found proving Dad's accident was premeditated murder, they set me up to divert attention.

"But here's what doesn't fit; if Billy was told to kill Dad, why did he become a target? If they needed a stooge, wouldn't they just let him burn for it? Why kill Billy and set me up? Seems like a lot of extra trouble."

"Right. But it does make sense if you were getting too close, and they thought Billy would talk. They just killed two birds with one stone," Dean offered.

"Okay, yeah, I can see that," Jason agreed.

Dean took a swig of his drink, "Then we have Carl, who had Billy's notebook and cash.

"It takes a lot for a pusher who dabbles to pass up cash. So, Billy must have impressed on him how he was mixed up in some pretty scary shit. Put the fear of God into him."

"Yeah. Looks like we've circled, huh? We need to see if old Carl can clear up a few things. Maybe lead us to some evidence to take the guesswork out of it.

"If he knows more than what he's said so far, he could be in danger too. We need that information, but I won't have anyone else dying either."

Jason pulled out some cash and tried to give it to Dean. "Here, take this, and let's start making plans."

"Keep it. I'm not worried about money right now. There are too many other things to worry about, like that guy giving the orders on the tape. We got his name. So, I'm thinking, let me see if I can do some checking. I'd bet real dollars he's got a record."

"That makes sense. But since the tapes were still in Dad's possession, I wonder if the DEA got what they needed. I mean, are these copies, or should we contact the DEA?

"With all that talk about shipments, pickups, and deliveries, it seems like it could only help their case. Has to be drugs, right? Why else would Dad take a chance like that?"

"Yeah. But the thing that's messing with my head is why he got involved. His notes say that he had a bad feeling about the job. He already had a reason to stay away. So why take the chance of working with the DEA and recording the guy?"

"That's bugging me too. He was a plumber, not a cop. But seriously, if he needed help... suspected something... why didn't he come to me? I thought we were close… you know?"

Seeing the hurt cross over Jason's face and hearing the catch in his voice, Dean said, "Yeah, I get you, but it won't help to speculate. Everyone knows you guys were close. No one would question that, and you shouldn't either.

"Knowing Matt, I'm sure he just wanted to protect you. It was his gig, and he probably thought he had it under control. After all, he had the DEA, so why would he want to pull you into it?"

Seeing Jason lower his head and look at the floor, Dean put his large hand on Jason's shoulder. "Hey man, I know you miss him, hell I miss him too. Lines get blurred when it comes to our Dads. He always acted like he was my dad, too." Swallowing hard, Dean continued, "But hey, he was also badass.

"I mean, shit, you know our dads completed their tours: Marine's, both of them. I'm not all that surprised Matt would help the DEA. He was all about doing what's right. The man was pretty hardcore. And Jason, as bad as it hurts, you have to know the man was doing what he thought was right.

"And I'm damn sure he didn't plan on dying."

They were both quiet for a while. Each lost in his memories.

This time, it was Dean who broke the silence. "Don't worry, Bro. I know it seems crazy right now, but I think we'll figure it out. We have more now than we did even a few days ago.

"For one thing, Billy was connected to a drug lord in Central City. Matt was working a plumbing job and was recruited by the DEA. I think it's a safe bet that's where we'll get more answers.

"But first, I think we need to talk to that DEA agent and find a way to take down this Morales guy. We're trained. We can finish what he started. And in the process, we just might be able to solve both Matt's and Billy's murders. If we're lucky, we might even exonerate you.

"Like my dad says, we might not have a lot, but we have a good start because we have each other."

Jason nodded. "And that really is a blessing.

"There's just one thing nagging me. If Dad was working with the DEA, with that Agent Thomas, where the hell have they been all this time?

"Doesn't it seem odd that they've never said boo to me or my mom? Wouldn't they send condolences or something? Maybe even let us know that Dad was helping them? Why keep it a secret now?

"They had to know I'm a cop; why wouldn't they debrief me, especially right after he was killed?"

Dean's eyes widened. "Damn! You are so right! I didn't even think about that. How do they just check out like that? Matt was doing them a solid, and they just abandoned him? His family? Man, that is so messed up!"

"Yeah, that's what I was thinking. There's no point in going to see them if they haven't bothered to contact us. They obviously don't want anyone to know they're involved.

"I think if we ask them, they'll just pretend they have no idea what we're talking about. And that's just another dead-end I don't want to deal with."

Scratching the new growth on his chin again, Dean said, "Here's what I think we need to do. I'll follow the trail in Central City and see if I can get a line on Morales. Maybe if we can find some dirt on the guy, the feds will agree to help us."

"I'm curious about that compound, too. Matt left us a map, but I say we should wait to move on that until we know more."

"Okay. You go when you can. But do me a favor and keep your head down. Don't do anything that might put you in jeopardy... okay?

"Stop fussing, I'm careful.

"But if I get the chance, I'll scan the area in my bird and maybe get an aerial shot or two.

"Let's use burners to keep in touch and meet up back here in a few days to go over things. See what the next move should be."

"I'm real curious about what information Carl might have up his sleeve, too."

"Me too. I have some ideas, but maybe we need to think on that a bit more."

CHAPTER EIGHTEEN

In the Shadows

After cleaning up, they called it a night.

Jason lay in bed staring at the ceiling, his mind a whirlwind trying to organize his thoughts and balance the good with the bad.

The good: He wasn't alone in trying to figure things out. The bad: If someone were really out to get him, he'd just put Dash in danger.

The good: He'd finally found a viable connection between Matt and Billy and a solid reason why his father was killed. Painful as it was, knowing the truth was comforting. The bad: They didn't have any physical evidence besides the journals and tapes, and that didn't prove Morales ordered the hit on Matt. Only monikers were used, and that could easily be explained away.

The good: They had a location and possible suspect to vet out. The bad: even though they suspected he was set up to kill Billy to stop his investigation into Matt's death, how would they prove it? It was too convoluted, and there were too many unanswered questions.

For one thing, how did they interfere with his radio? How did they find them in the alley? And how did they knock him out?

Unable to stop his racing thoughts, Jason took Stryker for a walk.

With the full moon lighting their way, Jason watched Stryker run happily down the trail, around the trees and brush, only stopping briefly to sniff something.

Just watching the joy expressed in Stryker's exuberance was enough to validate that he'd made the right decision.

Jason finally relaxed by sitting on the dock, watching the moon's reflection on the smooth surface of the water.

They'd reopened his father's case, changed the initial findings, and gave it to homicide.

He wondered if Montgomery would be assigned the case since he had first-hand knowledge.

When Jason had approached him, Montgomery hadn't actually been assigned Matt's case.

Still, he was supportive and understood why Jason wanted to investigate his father's death. He agreed to collaborate with Jason and provide insight when possible, and they were on friendly terms.

But that was before the alley and his suspension, and he doubted Montgomery would want to be involved now.

Still, whoever got the case might gain some insight talking with him. In fact, the detectives working on his case would learn more about him if they spoke with Montgomery.

Jason felt better knowing that the detectives would create a Murder Book for his dad and Billy.

The Murder Book contained all case-related materials in a three-ring binder. The lists in front documented, in chronological order, and with detectives' names and badge numbers, everything uncovered and collected on the case.

The rest of the book was divided into sections for case notes, interviews, photos, videos, diagrams, suspect lists, warrants, and various reports, from the medical examiner's reports, each division in the crime lab, and arrest reports.

It was important information, not easily found anywhere else. And it was all in one place.

Unfortunately, as a suspect, Jason wouldn't be given access.

Stryker laid down on the dock next to Jason's Adirondack chair and looked up at his favorite human, with eyes shining brightly, dripping water from his muzzle after a drink, and panting from his recent exertion.

Patting him on the head, he talked to Stryker like he would to any good friend: "Now, how are we going to get a look at those Murder Books, huh, Bud?"

Jason needed to fill in the blanks on both cases, "You know, that information would sure be helpful. Whatever they've got in there would save us some guesswork, if nothing else."

Jason knew that the books were centrally located in the unit, but he also knew that the detectives were very protective of them.

He was restricted from the unit and didn't know anyone who trusted him who had access.

And even though Dean might have access, he'd need a legitimate reason to enter the homicide unit. Even then, the place was a beehive of activity, so it was unlikely he'd be able to get a peek.

Since Dean was a fly-boy, he rarely got involved in murder cases unless they were chasing a suspect. Air support usually worked in aerial surveillance for police operations.

But since Dean had access, he'd be able to go into headquarters.

"Dash might get away with asking questions about how the case was going since he knew Matt. But it's a risk. The detectives are naturally suspicious. And if he asks too many questions or if he's caught taking photos, he could get into trouble.

"You know, Charles might be able to get access, too. I'll have to ask Dean what he thinks first thing in the morning.

"If not, we'll be chasing down evidence on what little we know ourselves."

While Dean did what he could, Jason planned on finding the compound drawn in Matt's journals.

That's when another issue smacked him.

If whoever ordered the hit on Matt got wind of the inquiry… Dean would be next, and that wasn't an option.

Jason hadn't gotten much sleep since rescuing Stryker. He was mentally and physically drained. As Jason focused on the moonlight in the water, he began to drift.

Catching himself, he realized that a good night's sleep was what he needed.

Overall, an evening of eating barbeque, drinking beer, and brainstorming with Dash had been very productive.

They'd edged closer to the truth and had several good theories. All they needed now was solid evidence.

Dropping into bed at one-thirty in the morning, just before turning out the bedside lamp, he made a mental note to talk with Dean when Stryker walked up.

"Hey, bud." Stryker nuzzled Jason's hand and rested his chin on top of the covers to receive a scratch behind the ears. "I hope you're up for what's next. It might be dangerous, so I'll need you to stay alert.

"We'll start training in the morning, okay?"

Stryker simply panted happily.

***

The truck was decked out in low-rider fashion with narrow, low-profile tires meant to accentuate chrome rims.

When the black Toyota Tundra's driver's side door opened, the vertically challenged driver leaped out while the rims continued to spin.

At first, Jason was surprised when he recognized the driver. Then, amused since the undercarriage sat only inches from the ground, effectively reducing a perfectly good truck into a superfluous and frivolous toy.

He couldn't help but chuckle behind his binoculars.

The driver was dressed all in black, from his silver-studded Stetson down to his polished cowboy boots. His unbuttoned jacket and western shirt were elaborately embroidered in scrollwork.

The man's face was hard to see, but the long, greasy ponytail gave him away.

It was the perp from the gas station.

Jason pulled his ball cap down over his eyes and used his phone to take a few pictures of the man and his truck.

He watched the driver head to the casino and noticed, at the top of the steps, that Ponytail gave a slight nod to the two men standing like sentries on each side of the entrance.

Both men were large but were a strange antitheses to each other.

The white guy was tall with a thick neck. His bleached blond hair gelled in spikes around the crown of his head. The slim-style black suit jacket was tailored to expose the breadth of his chest and large biceps.

Although several inches shorter, the black man to his left was casually dressed in a tight T-shirt and jeans that advertised his muscular build.

Although they stood feet apart and didn't speak to one another, Jason could tell they were a team. And hired muscle like that didn't come cheap.

But he'd arrived too late. The Fat Man was already inside.

He'd gone to the casino the first time, hoping to make some inquiries about the area, when he'd noticed the hired muscle the first time. Since then, he'd come up empty until now.

It seemed like too much of a coincidence that both Morales and Ponytail would decide to come to the same casino on the same night, which made Jason wonder if there wasn't a connection.

Because of the casino's security cameras, Jason couldn't risk following Ponytail into the casino. But it did present an opportunity.

The men would most likely spend the evening enjoying their gaming, which he hoped would give him time to scope out the property.

He could always double back to the casino later for a little game of follow the leader.

Following the hidden dirt road off Nevadaville Road and County Road 1-S listed on his map, Jason parked behind a large pine away from prying eyes.

After double-checking the map against Matt's drawings, he grabbed his gear from the back while Stryker sniffed around the alpine and shrubs.

Since the compound was off Bald Mountain Lane, they'd need to hike in. His backpack had everything they needed. They could even stay overnight in the brush if necessary.

Stryker was back to his old self. He was playful as a puppy.

Free to run through the rugged terrain chasing small mammals and birds while following Jason at a distance appeared to be the only medicine he needed.

After hiking for about a mile, Jason checked his GPS and marked his surroundings. According to the map, they were on the southwest end of the compound. Dash said it was the best entrance point, as most of the sentries were positioned near the front of the property at the northeast entrance.

Figuring they had to be close, he hurried his steps. He wanted to find a good perch to surveil and take a few pictures before sunset. That was if he found a good place before having to depend on his PVS-14 goggles.

After seeing Morales's personal guards at the Casino, Jason felt confident that time was still on his side.

After spending the last week surveilling the casinos in Black Hawk, Jason knew once Morales was comfortably tucked into a game, he'd be there for the night.

It stood to reason that if there were more guards at the compound, with Morales away, they'd probably be more relaxed.

***

So far, Dean hadn't made it to headquarters, and there was only so much information he could pull up on the department computers without raising suspicion.

That meant he had to do some old-fashioned sleuthing and delve into the stacks of public records at the Gilpin Country Recorders Office on his days off.

The maps Matt had drawn were limited to areas immediately around the main structure and substructures, probably because Matt hadn't been allowed to walk around the compound.

What they really needed was a complete plat map showing the compound layout and the structures.

Concerned that one of the county employees might report inquiries back to Morales, Dean made up a cover story about being interested in panning for gold.

He'd read that in the 1860's, Central City was considered the "richest square mile on earth," so it was the perfect cover story.

The county building was large, but the building department was small. So, unlike most city building departments, he didn't have as many hurdles to worry about.

Once the clerk left to take care of other responsibilities, Dean was free to search through the permits, blueprints, and plat maps in the archive section of the dirty and rarely-used county basement.

Dean found it interesting that the Central City Government building was just miles north of the compound. Whatever was happening in the compound was being done right under the local government's nose.

***

Located on the Front Range of the Rocky Mountains, the terrain was filled with ankle twisters, as Charles liked to call them. The hills and valleys interspersed with bristlecone pine, blue spruce, Rocky Mountain juniper, and rabbitbrush.

Jason figured that he had to be close.

At the top of a rise, he pulled out his binoculars and could just make out a line of what looked like a fence about a quarter mile ahead.

His heartbeat increased with each step.

There was nothing he wanted more than to find those responsible for his father's death. But he was also conflicted.

Getting the answers he desperately wanted, and arresting those responsible for his father's murder, would force him to close the book on his father's life and face the reality that the man he'd looked up to his whole life was really dead.

At the top of the next rise, he took cover behind a lodgepole pine and noticed the green slats interweaved in the links, making the fence less noticeable from a distance while obstructing the view inside the compound.

From where he stood, it looked like the fence surrounded the entire property. He'd have to walk the perimeter at nightfall with his night gear on to look for an entry point.

But he had that covered. To move around more easily at night, he'd brought his PVS-14 goggles.

Stryker had abandoned him to chase something into the brush, so Jason used what light was left of the day to take a few pictures and compare the grounds to his father's maps.

His father's journals focused primarily on the layout of the main house, with similar layouts of the cabins and a few diagrams of the grounds around them.

To the southwest, a roofline rose several feet above the fence line about the size of a large warehouse in downtown Denver. To the southeast was another warehouse about half the size.

Those structures weren't notated anywhere in the journals, which meant that Matt hadn't been in those locations.

Just then, the sound of vehicles close by interrupted the voice of the temperamental wind.

An easy mark at six foot three inches, even decked out in camo, Jason crouched down to blend into the shadows of the lodgepole pines. While he waited for the threat to pass, he added the tall pole lights to Matt's drawings.

At twilight, the pole lights came on, illuminating the interior of the complex.

The light made it easy for him to watch them.

But those under the tall lamps would find it difficult to see him, even if they bothered to look into the darkness.

The difficulty was the night blindness that occurred for those in the light, but it provided excellent cover for Jason in the dark.

Smiling at his luck, Jason was focused on the activity when a rustling nearby got his attention.

He pulled his weapon in time to watch Stryker emerge through the foliage. He trotted up to Jason and dropped down beside him, panting happily. Several minutes later, he was on his side, with outstretched legs, and fast asleep.

As Jason watched the activity, he considered all the reasons a residential property might need a warehouse, especially one of that size. And with such a large warehouse, what would they need the smaller one for?

If they were making meth, they were producing much more product than they'd originally thought.

After completing his additions to Matt's drawings, he put the journal in his pack and absently stroked Stryker's black and tan plush coat.

If his suspicions were correct, they wouldn't find any outbuildings on the approved plat map Dean would find at the county.

CHAPTER NINETEEN

The Miscalculation

Thinking fast, Becca quickly pulled her ocean blue Chevy Silverado into a parking lot, threw it in park, turned it off, and slid down under the steering wheel, trying to melt into the floorboard.

She'd been following Mark most of the day and doing an excellent job of keeping her distance until that moment.

Upset with herself for not waking up early enough to put on a better disguise, Becca tried to compact herself, but her long legs were uncooperative in her struggle.

Feeling compromised, she forced them into a most uncomfortable position bent and twisted with her feet on the center console cup holder.

She didn't have a choice. If he saw her, he'd see Joss.

Or rather her ghost.

As an identical twin, the cap and sunglasses wouldn't disguise her enough to hide her identity from a man who'd known her sister intimately.

If Mark caught a glimpse of her, the jig would be up. There was no way she'd be able to hide after that. He'd know she was Joss's twin and would probably figure out that she'd been stalking him.

Even the briefest glimpse would end her clandestine operation and put her life at risk.

So she stayed in that painful position for more than fifteen minutes, making a mental list of safety measures before leaving the house on a surveillance mission.

When he'd left the Whole Foods parking lot ahead of her, she figured he'd head home as usual. She'd been secure in the knowledge that she could reacquire him.

And that's when she'd decided to take a few minutes to use the restroom at a nearby Mickey D's.

She rarely ate fast food; it wasn't usually her thing, but she wasn't ready to call it a day. And since she'd skipped breakfast, she needed to eat something, so she stayed and had lunch.

She remembered being surprised to see his truck at a light on the Alameda Parkway, wondering where he'd stopped while she'd been off his tail or if he'd made her and was waiting for her to catch up.

But what almost made her lose her lunch was when he made the U-turn and headed in her direction instead of continuing down the road, which left her little choice but to drop out of sight.

She stayed in that cramped position for several minutes more before slowly rising enough to peek out the windows.

Pins and needles assaulted her limbs as she unfolded herself.

But thankfully, Mark was nowhere in sight.

Cussing at the situation and angry at herself, she mumbled out loud, "Fuck, fuck, fuck! I almost blew the whole thing. What was I thinking?

"It serves me right for taking shortcuts. I'm getting way too comfortable — too complacent. If I'm not more careful, I'll never vindicate Joss, and I just might get myself killed in the process."

The day was blown. She was too emotionally exhausted to do anything more.

Back home, she fell onto the sofa, thoroughly discouraged and having a whirlwind of emotion. She needed to think.

When the boys rushed up to greet her but stopped in front of her, she knew that they sensed her mood.

Feeling terrible, she cooed, "It's okay, boys. I'm not mad. Well, not at you anyway."

That's when Slinky, the tiny black & white kitten she'd rescued from the middle of a two-lane back road the month before, made his appearance on the back of the couch and began nuzzling her neck.

Giggling, she petted and cuddled each one of them.

Petting their soft fur and seeing their sweet expressions always made her feel better.

After giving the boys a treat, she left the kitten on the windowsill to sun himself and headed to the safe room.

The room now held five wigs on Styrofoam wig heads. Two held black hair; one short, the other long. The granny wig that she used when she went to the casino and the shoulder-length curly wig that she'd worn when trying to look like a yuppy.

For the first time, Becca had to acknowledge that she wasn't getting anywhere for all her hard work. What the hell am I doing? I've been doing this for so long that I'm getting careless. This isn't a game. This guy is bad news. I need to get it together.

Going back to her list, Becca made only one check mark. Only one check in the last three weeks was depressing. The check mark was simply a confirmation of the connection between Mark and the Fat Man.

Becca suspected that Mark and the Fat Man worked together, and the older man was the source of the drugs — the supplier, which made Mark the distributor.

The problem was she had no proof and hadn't been able to confirm even that much yet.

Taking out a dry-erase marker, she added 'Confirm identities' and 'Need legal names' to the list on the wall.

So far, she hadn't seen any drugs and didn't know where to look for them. She'd thought of breaking into Mark's house but wanted to see what she could find before taking that big of a risk.

The last time she had gotten close to them, she thought she overheard something about a shipment. If she could just get a little closer, she might hear something more concrete to confirm her suspicions. She was sure they were working together, but there was more to it. What was odd was that the men seemed closer than just a drug supplier and distributor.

When she overheard Mark say that he would look into it when he got to work, she was stunned. She had no idea that he might have another job.

That's when she decided to follow him to his 'other' job.

She planned to stake out his place early that morning but woke late and had to rush out of the house without her disguise. She messed up and almost got caught.

Discouraged, Becca tried to comfort herself with the knowledge that she'd made more progress in the last year than Myers had in all the years since Joss had died.

She had to believe she was getting close. It hadn't occurred to her just how difficult it was for detectives to get the tiniest bit of information.

Not to mention correlating events and collecting evidence to prove guilt in court. Of course, detectives had more resources, but if their struggles were anything like what hers had been, it was a wonder that crimes ever got solved.

Detective George Myers had been either too lazy or too incompetent to check into the discrepancies around her sister's death. He assumed that Joss Kennedy was just another druggie who had OD'd, and he refused to budge from that assumption.

But Becca knew Joss. And there was no way she used drugs. There was simply more to the story that Becca needed to uncover. And based on what she'd found so far, she'd been right from the start.

When she started her investigation, she thought she would find out what happened, give it to the DA, and see the responsible party brought to justice.

But she needed proof. Evidence that would prove Joss was murdered. Something strong enough to bypass Myers. Proof the DA would use to put Payton away.

Then maybe her sweet sister would rest in peace. Unfortunately, everything was proving much more complicated. Surveillance had become a full-time job, and with a veterinary practice to run, she was quickly burning out.

But even with what she'd discovered, she was torn between avenging her sister and protecting the life she'd created for herself.

Joss had died when Becca was a third-year veterinarian student.

She'd worked hard nearly every day to achieve her dream to allow it to be ripped away.

After completing a bachelor's degree in biochemistry and a minor in physics, she spent two years completing her veterinary program.

Then, there were the externships and internships and getting into a residency program.

But like a thief, the work stole her time, energy, and attention.

Still, she'd managed to finish the program even earlier than expected.

She was a large and small animal veterinarian.

But she almost gave up the dream when she lost her twin and best friend. In fact, the deep depression she fell into might have killed her too—if Myers hadn't dropped the ball.

Unfortunately, the requirements to complete the program left her little time. It wasn't that she'd neglected to investigate what happened to Joss entirely.

It was the time it took to teach herself how to investigate a murder.

No matter how many books she read, trying to become a detective, especially without any training or resources, seemed hopeless.

And yet, she never gave up. She was finally getting close to the truth.

Once she'd bought the property from Dr. Taylor and started to remodel it, she had a lot more time and a better understanding of what to look for to really dig into it.

But what really energized her was finding Mark at Red Rocks Amphitheatre. After that, it didn't take long to lose him somewhere in Lakewood.

They were her first successes. After that, she felt like she was finally getting somewhere.

Relaxing in the comfy orange chair in her office, Becca felt torn between her practice and her investigation. The demands of both were taking a toll on her physically and emotionally, and that was dangerous.

Thought processes and reaction times slowed with fatigue, which increased the chance of making mistakes. What happened that morning following Mark was proof of that.

Something had to change because she couldn't keep working all day and spying all night.

The mission she'd undertaken to vindicate her sister wasn't something to play at, and neither was her practice. She was trying to do everything on her own—she needed help.

After going round and round, she finally decided to close the clinic to all but emergency patients.

With that decision made, she thought, *if I find what I need to prove Mark did this, I can turn the evidence over to the DA and vindicate Joss. Then, I can focus on my practice. I might need to take more risks, but if I'm careful, it will work out. It has to.*

CHAPTER TWENTY

Dog Down

Sitting on the dock over the lake, Jason handed Dean a beer from the cooler as he continued to describe his exploration of the compound. "… it's weird. At night, the back half of the compound lights up like a movie set, and there's so much activity—it looks like an assembly line on steroids.

"Once the lights were on, I was able to see through the slats into the compound. I checked for cameras, and, surprise, there were no cameras on the south side of the property.

"But there were two light poles with cameras about eight to ten feet high. One faces a large warehouse to the west, and the other faces a row of shipping containers along the fence line to the northwest. You may have seen them when you did a flyover."

Dean nodded. "I wondered what they were. I was on borrowed time, so I only got a quick look."

"Several men, not sure if they were guards or just the labor. But they had AKs strapped on their backs, moving wine barrels from a warehouse to those shipping containers. I doubt it's wine; there are no fields of grapes nearby if you get my meaning."

Jason pointed to his map of the area. "Not sure what they're protecting, but these guys are serious. Big guys, big guns, moving big barrels.

"Yeah, and did you see the helipad at the southwest corner, farthest from the main house?" Dean added.

Jason nodded. "I thought that's what it was, but there wasn't much light there and no structures from what I could see, so I kept moving. But I'd bet money that none of that's on the plat map you found."

Dean shook his head. "Nope."

"Didn't think so. Sheesh. Someone's getting paid to stay quiet."

"Must be." Dean agreed.

"Did you notice the small warehouse at the southeast corner?"

When Dean nodded, Jason continued. "No lights there. If not for the moonlight and stars, you can't see much in that corner, and nothing was happening at that end.

"I think that's the best spot to breach the fence. If I can enter undetected, I'd like to see if I can find out what they're doing in there."

Dean pulled a beer out of the cooler and replaced it with his empty, "Yeah, well, that may be difficult.

"When I did my fly-by, I noticed three cabins to the west. Not all that far from there. They're probably bunkhouses for staff.

"There's one cabin that's larger than the others. It's real close to the small warehouse.

"I figure whoever lives there oversees the staff. And as close as it is to that small warehouse, and since we're thinking they're producing product, I'd lay odds whoever lives there is the chemist.

There is cross-fencing between the lab area and the cabins. And another that separates the cabins from the main house. I doubt you could see any of that from the ground. It might be tricky getting past those cabins even if everyone's asleep."

"Damn, you're right. Well, just add it to the list of things we need to figure out."

"Hey, where's our boy? I just noticed he isn't around."

"He's resting. We had a problem last night. Stryker stepped on something that must have hurt like hell. Poor guy was limping and whimpered something fierce. I was worried they'd hear us, so I picked him up and ran. It probably didn't help me jiggling him around; he started crying.

"I thought he might have gotten bit by a rattler—scared the shit out of me. And I only had that small first aid kit with me. But I was shocked when I saw this huge tack. Had to be close to an inch in diameter." Jason demonstrated with his fingers.

"It took a minute to pull it out. Honestly, hearing him squeal like that, I had to hold him down. But once it was out, cleaned, and wrapped, he seemed okay.

"Poor guy. I think that's the first time he's ever hurt like that. At least, it's the first time I ever heard him make that noise.

"But Dash, you should have seen the thing. It looked like one of those big old Clavos nails you see on wine barrels. And it was stuck deep in the pad on the poor guy's foot.

"It had to come off one of those barrels I saw. But it looked ugly—rusted and dirty.

"Which reminds me, I don't have any antibiotics, and I'm worried about his foot getting infected. I need to take him to a vet, but I have to be careful about it. It can't be anyone who knows us. Any ideas on that?"

Dean was quiet so long that Jason turned his whole body to look at him. "Hey, man, you okay? You're being awful quiet, and we both know that's not your norm."

A few more minutes passed in silence, and Jason's muscles began to tense up.

Meanwhile, Dean was staring at the fish making small ripples near the surface of the clear water. He was uneasy about telling Jason what he had to say. Like his father, he always took his time to contemplate the delivery of bad news.

When he found his voice, he said, "I think we have a problem."

"Okay — so tell me what it is already… we'll figure it out, brother."

"Not sure it will be that simple. I'm not even sure how to explain it. It's more like a bad feelin'."

"Jesus Christ, Dean, what the fuck! Just fuckin spill it already. You know I can't stand it when you try to spare my feelings. And right now, you're scaring the shit out of me! What happened? Start at the beginning."

"Okay, okay, man — geez, relax. Drink your beer or something."

While Jason took a swig, Dean moved his camping chair so they could face each other. "Okay, so here's how it played out.

"So I'm at the substation, just shooting the shit with the guys and hoping to get some info about your case when I see Jack is there with Max. So, I'm thinkin' maybe I can ask Jack how Max is doin' and see if he might be willing to help us out."

As Jason opened his mouth, Dean waved him off. "I know. We said we wouldn't bring anyone else into it. Just don't go getting pissed right off. Just hear me out.

“So, like I said, I was thinkin’ we needed a little help. We’re fighting the clock here, bro. We don’t have time to screw around. Sooner or later, they’ll have enough to bring you in.

“So, yeah, I get it. You don’t want to put anyone else at risk, but I think we need to reevaluate that decision.

“Anyway, that’s what I was thinkin’ at the time.

“So, I go up to Jack real subtle like, just feeling him out before I say anything. Only before I can ask or say a word, he gets all accusatory on me.

“Starts talking real loud. Like he wants to make sure everyone hears.

“Says he’s surprised to see me there. Like I don’t belong at HQ or something. It really pissed me off. I mean, for fuck’s sake, I’m a cop too. Fucking bigot.

“Anyway, like I said, I took offense. So, instead of asking for his help, I step up on him and ask what’s his problem.

“So, he lowers his voice like it’s a secret and says, ‘I know you boys took Stryker out of the kennel.’

Then he gets loud again and says, ‘Look, if Colt’s on the run, then he did the deed.’ Then, after a beat says, ‘I won’t stand behind no bad cop.’

“For a minute, I’m just standing there with my dick out… not sure what to say. The fucker totally caught me totally off guard.

“So, I’m thinking this fool needs a good beatdown, but I don’t want a suspension. So I just give him a look.

“Then he gets all soft again, says, ‘Hey, big guy, just messing with you. Says he hopes we did save Stryker and asks how you’re doing.

“He ends it by saying, ‘All this has gotta be tearing Colt up, huh?’

“Asshole.

“Honestly, man, his whole vibe had the hairs standin’ up on the back of my neck. Gave me the heebie-jeebies’ somethin’ awful.

“I swear if I didn’t have my dad’s ways, I would have knocked the boy out. And if he wasn’t a cop, I might have put my hand on my weapon. That’s how bad it hit me.

“It wasn’t right, Jason. I never did like that fool, but seriously, I know you worked with him. I figured you guys were friends. So, I kept my tongue cause I didn’t want to cause somethin’ between us.

“Brother, nothing on this planet could come between us.”

Smiling, Dean continued, "Right. So I keep my cool and kinda laugh it off and tell him I haven't seen you on account I was away on tour with the Guard.

"I can't say if he believed me, but I didn't give a shit.

"I'm telling you, brother, something is off with that guy. Way off."

Jason didn't know what to say.

He trusted Dean's assessment, but he hated to think that Jack was against him after all the time they'd spent together. It wasn't like they were pals, exactly, but he had thought the man had his back.

Dean could see that Jason was torn. "Look, man, I get that you've known the guy since Afghanistan. But the way he acted… I just don't trust him. I think he was trying to get me to say something... maybe cop to taking Stryker from the kennel, or maybe let slip where you're stayin'.

"Anyway, it seemed like he was fishing, but his tactic just put me off."

Jason got up and paced a few times on the deck. "Man. I've worked with Jack since I started with K-9. We never were close, but I thought he was a good guy, a work friend. Someone who had my back. But that does sound off. I wonder what's going on with him."

Whether he wanted it to be true or not, if Jack believed he was a bad cop, he didn't know Jason very well. "Did you happen to check your rearview on the way up? Make sure he wasn't following?"

"Are you kidding?! I was pretty freaked out. After that, I just went home to sort myself out and tried to get some perspective before I came up here. But I just can't shake it off. So I had to say something."

Jason sat down, "Don't sweat it, brother. Let's just keep our heads on a swivel and our ears wide open."

Dean took a deep breath. "Man, am I glad you're okay with what I said about Jack. And I appreciate that you didn't get too freaked that I think it's time to increase our numbers. I'm just not sure who we should approach."

"I get it, and you're right. To be honest, it's been bouncing around in my head too. Kade hangs with us all the time and he was my partner. He's a good guy. I trust him. But I struggle with how to keep him safe. I don't want anyone to get jacked up over this."

As the sky began to blend in shades of purples, pinks, and golds, Jason and Dean discussed a plan for another reconnaissance mission and then walked back to the cabin.

As they walked into the kitchen, they found Stryker on the floor, panting heavily and whining. Jason's heart dropped and he fell to his knees. "You okay, boy? What's wrong?"

As he unwound the bandage on Stryker's paw, he saw how swollen it was moments before a rank scent wafted up.

Looking up at Dean, he said, "Shit, Dean, he needs a vet — now! He's way worse than I thought. Do you know any around here? One that doesn't know me?"

"Well, I haven't met her, but I heard of a lady vet who bought old Doc Taylor's place a while back. She was remodeling it about a year ago. It's not that far from here. Let's just take him there and see if she'll help."

It was only about seven miles from Upper Bear Creek to the clinic outside of Evergreen, but it seemed to take forever.

Jason felt horrible. He'd taken a huge risk to save Stryker, and now the poor guy was in trouble again.

As they pulled up to the gate, Dean jumped out to open it. Jason parked, then gently picked up Stryker and rushed up to the door.

A big CLOSED sign was posted on the window that left both men temporarily speechless.

Dean checked the door… locked.

Jason's voice was rough when he said, "I swear to God, Dean, if someone doesn't come soon, I'm breaking in. Stryker's in a bad way; he needs antibiotics — where the hell is the vet?"

An old-fashioned decorative bronze doorbell sat to the right of the door with a sign that read, Emergencies Only.

Dean pushed the doorbell but couldn't hear anything, so he pushed it several more times just in case.

He hoped that if it wasn't ringing inside the clinic, it was making a hell of a racket at the main house.

Just as Jason was about to use his elbow to break the glass on the door, lights flicked on inside the clinic.

The woman who opened the door looked nothing like what Jason expected a veterinarian to look like. Not only was she younger by at least a decade, but she was more beautiful than he expected. Even in wet clothes and completely disheveled as she was.

Her dark brown curls with auburn highlights had been carelessly pulled into a bun that sat on the top of her head in a style that reminded him of a Geisha.

Her dark brown raised eyebrows accentuated intense bluish-green eyes, which seemed to burn with irritation.

She was dressed in teal leggings that accentuated long legs and a soaked orange crop top that exposed part of a smooth, flat belly. A colorful, nearly sheer, floral cardigan kimono billowed around her as she moved.

He could see her full lips moving, but he couldn't grasp what they were saying. He was too busy taking inventory.

Becca slowly opened the door and stepped aside to let them in when she saw the wounded dog, "What happened? What's wrong with him?"

Jason was so busy staring that he didn't answer right away.

Dean elbowed Jason in the ribs to wake him up and said. "We're sorry to bother you, ma'am, but our dog is in a bad way.

"He stepped on something; we wrapped it up, but he's just getting worse. We know you're closed, but we don't know where else to go around here. Please help our dog."

Becca looked from the dog, who looked sorely in need of help, to the two men. "Okay, bring him in, but please lock the door behind you. I don't need any more unexpected patients; I'm supposed to be on vacation."

Becca led them into a room and gently lifted Stryker's injured paw. "Hm… you said he had a nail in his foot?"

Jason finally found his voice. "Well, it wasn't like a regular nail, not as long but fatter like one of those Clavos nails used to hold the straps around wine barrels.

"I took it out because he seemed to be in pain. Poor guy let me mangle his paw, trying to pull it out. But I could tell it was hurting him pretty bad, so I did what I could to get it out.

"I washed the wound and wrapped it. At first, he seemed better, but a little while ago, he started getting lethargic and whining. It scared me. I think the nail was rusted. It's in the Jeep if you need it."

"That's okay. The injury will tell me what I need to know, and I'll run a few tests to identify the infection. By the way, I'm Dr. Kennedy... Becca. And you are?"

"My name is Jason, and this is Dean."

Focused on the wound, she stroked Stryker, cooing to him, "Aw now lookie there. What a sweet boy you are. Even with your paw hurting, you're being so good. Well, don't you worry; we'll have you feeling better in a jiffy.

"Now you just rest, that's it, just stay still for me, that's a good boy. I'm just going to take this bandage off and take a quick peek. I'll try to be careful, okay?"

Stryker allowed her to unbandage his foot with only a few whimpers.

Then, talking as if to herself as she rubbed Stryker behind the ears, "It's okay, sweet boy. I can see how that hurts. Your paw is infected, and we need to stop the infection before it spreads. You just lie still now… there's a good boy."

Looking up at the men, "I need to give him Novox for pain and prepare a Cefovecin injection. It's a strong antibiotic. He'll also need subcutaneous fluids to avoid dehydration.

"Then we wait to see how he does."

Looking back down, she rubbed Stryker's ears. "I hate to say this, but I'm afraid this might hurt a little. But don't you worry. I'll give you a little something right now to make you feel more comfortable."

Pulling a syringe and a vial from the cabinet behind her, she prepared the syringe and injected Stryker.

"That will take a few minutes to take effect."

As Stryker panted, she looked back at the men. "I'll need to keep an eye on him, but once I release him for home, I'll give you some gabapentin for residual pain.

"For now, just stay with him; I'll be right back."

Before Jason could ask what she meant by keeping an eye on him, she was gone.

"Dean, what did she mean by that? I can't leave him here?"

"You don't have a choice. An infection is bad news, brother — you don't want to mess with that."

Jason felt the stress of the situation tightening his gut. All he could think of was that he'd rescued Stryker from a death sentence only to put him in a different kind of danger.

Becca returned with a metal tray holding syringes, a bottle of saline, and other implements they didn't recognize.

She filled a bowl with saline and said. "You may need to hold him as I flush the wound. The pain medication should sedate him, but just in case, no one needs to be bitten, and I'd rather not muzzle him if we don't have to. Muzzles just tend to scare them more than anything I do to them."

It only took the narcotic a few minutes to sedate him.

Jason laid his hands gently on Stryker's head and shoulder while Dean did the same with the hindquarters.

Becca gave the remaining injections and began flushing the wound.

While she worked, she attempted to let them know what she was doing and why. "This isn't the way I typically work. Normally, we'd take him to the surgery and work in there. But without an assistant, well, I thought it would be easier for everyone concerned to do it this way. He'll be more comfortable with his family close by."

Her actions were fluid and precise. When she picked up a scalpel to open the wound, Jason felt heat rise from his chest to the top of his head.

"I need to open the wound enough to drain the puss that has collected under the subcutaneous layers of tissue.

"It looks like the infection was starting to spread.

"It's a good thing you brought him in when you did."

Watching her tenderness while working on Stryker produced an emotion in Jason that he hadn't expected.

Gratitude certainly, but there was another feeling that he couldn't identify.

After Stryker was all bandaged up, Becca asked Jason to carry him to the back kennels to recuperate.

"I'll have to keep an eye on him for a day or so to make sure that wound drains and begins to close properly.

"We don't want to take the chance of it being reinfected.

"I'll leave it open for now to drain, and sew it up tomorrow evening if everything looks good. Make sure you leave a way to contact you for updates."

Jason was reluctant to leave Stryker. "Couldn't you just wrap him up and give me some antibiotics to take home? He's been through a lot lately, and I hate leaving him like this."

"I wouldn't recommend it. There's no telling what was on that nail or if the infection will continue to spread. The debridement should help the growth of healthy tissue, and the antibiotic should help stop the spreading of infection. But things can change quickly with animals. It would be best if he's under professional care."

"But I thought you were on vacation; who'll look after him if you're not here?"

"Well, it's more like a staycation… besides my vet tech, Alice, comes in daily to check on the animals in the infirmary; she exercises them and cares for the animals being boarded.

"She's highly qualified and knows what to do in an emergency. So there's nothing to worry about, I promise.

"Plus, I'll be close enough that if Stryker takes a turn, I'll be able to get to him. And if I happen to be out of the area, Dr. Hamilton in Golden is my backup. Trust me, you have nothing to worry about. Stryker will be well cared for."

Jason realized he was pouting. Pushing his shoulders back, "Of course, I'm just sorry that we ruined your staycation. But I have to thank you. We were both so scared." Jason looked at Dean and poked him.

Dean smiled and nodded, "Yeah, it was hard to watch the poor guy."

"Of course. It's hard to watch anything suffer, but when it's your pet, it's even harder."

She gestured for them to follow her back to the lobby. "We love our pets. They become family. And because of their dependence on us, they're like our children."

At the front desk, seeing their confused expressions, she continued. "No, really. When something happens, when they get sick or hurt, it can be scary.

"After all, we're all afraid of losing those we love. And that's a good thing because then we take better care of the things we love."

After several minutes passed without a word, she smiled at the worried looks. "But don't worry. Right now, he looks good. And with a little rest, I'm sure he'll be just fine. It's just best not to take any unnecessary risks.

Grabbing a clipboard from behind the reception desk with the forms, she quickly printed out an estimate. "I promise, if his condition changes, I'll call you right away."

Handing it all to Dean, "However, gentlemen, right now, I need to clean up here and finish washing my dogs. Please fill out those health forms, and I'll see you out. I can only guess the mess they've made of the room by now."

Sitting down, Jason mumbled, "Thank you."

Dean shoved the clipboard at Jason and said with a smile, "Yes, doc, thank you so much. My brother and I would be lost without Stryker."

While Jason filled out the paperwork, Becca disinfected the room they'd used and created a file for Stryker. While sitting at the front desk waiting for them to finish the forms, she couldn't help checking out the two men.

Each man was beautiful on his own. But together, they were a compliment in contrasts.

Dean was at least two inches taller than Jason.

He had a much thicker build, broad shoulders, thick arms, and chest, but a gentle and kind face.

His hair was cut close to his scalp, and his smooth, mocha-colored skin complimented the most enchanting light green eyes she'd ever seen. Eyes that seemed to look right through a person—almost ethereal with thick black eyebrows that framed them perfectly.

The smattering of black stubble along his jawline accentuated the shape of his face, as did the perfectly clipped mustache above his luscious full lips.

Jason was more casually dressed in a flannel shirt; the sleeves rolled up on his forearms.

He was much lighter in color than his brother, more bronze than fair. But nearly as broad in the chest.

His thick jet-black hair was cut short in the back and around his ears but feathered along the sides and with a long mop on top. Parted on the side, his bangs often fell into his eyes.

He didn't have a mustache, but he had the same thick black brows that framed mesmerizing dark blue eyes, and she had to force herself to look away when he caught her looking.

After locking the door behind them, Becca watched the Jeep until it turned onto the main road.

On her way back to the house, she thought, *I definitely wouldn't mind seeing those two again.*

CHAPTER TWENTY-ONE

Hide Out

With his index finger pressed against pursed lips, he beckoned her to be silent and gently guided her into the kitchen.

Becca would think about that moment later and wonder why she'd been so angry when she should have been afraid.

He'd caught her off guard, broke into her house, and calmly but insistently pulled her into the kitchen.

Her heartbeat had quickened, whether from his touch or from being startled; she couldn't tell. But for all of that, she'd felt more excited than afraid.

He was too close, nearly touching her with his body, and with each step, he got closer, forcing her to take another step back.

Maybe it was that last step when she backed into the island that had set her off. Or maybe it was his natural smell, musky and masculine.

Looking up, she was captured in the depths of his eyes, which were a stunning shade of cobalt blue.

With their eyes locked, he must not have noticed the island had stopped her steps because he briefly pressed his body against hers before taking a step back.

Feeling foolish, she quipped, "What do you think you're doing? I would have opened the door for you if you'd rang the bell. And why are you shushing me?"

"…Shh — he's on the porch. I think he's up to something."

"What are you talking about?"

"There's a giant on your porch, fair maiden; I caught him watching your place. Men don't just stare at a woman's home unless they're planning something. I think he's stalking you."

Unsure if she was more afraid or offended, she stiffened her back, "What are you, some kind of knight coming to my rescue? Well, don't concern yourself; the dogs will sort him out if he tries to break in."

"I'm not so sure. They're used to all sorts of people coming and going. And they weren't worried about me coming through the back door, so why would they worry about someone coming to your front door?"

Annoyed but reasonable, she smirked, "Okay… that's fair, might even be true. But if someone tried to hurt me, they'd come to my rescue."

Then, realizing her boys were nowhere in sight. "Okay, so you saw him watch the house. That doesn't mean anything. He might have a wounded animal. If you were so concerned, why not just call to tell me someone is watching me? Why did you feel a need to break into my house?"

"I was coming to check on Stryker when I noticed this goon across the road with binoculars watching the place. It was suspicious.

"I parked and started walking up to him, but he ran to his car and took off.

"Then, a few minutes later, I saw him come down the drive to your house. I was at the clinic when I saw him, so I came around through your back door, just in case. By the way, your door was unlocked, so I didn't have to break in."

Becca held up her hand so he'd shut up and let her think for a minute. Her heart seemed to stop for a minute as she realized that she might have been identified.

If Mark had followed her…

No. It couldn't be him. She would have noticed him following her.

She'd been dusting when Jason barged into the front room and corralled her into the kitchen. And even though he hadn't hurt her, she couldn't help but feel a bit irritated that he'd been right about Radar and Scout. They hadn't even barked when he'd come into her house.

But that was a problem she'd have to deal with later.

For a brief moment, Becca allowed herself to inspect the man in front of her. He'd been forceful but gentle while insistently guiding her into the kitchen.

Standing in front of her now provided an opportunity to evaluate the man face to face.

He was tall, probably over six feet, and even more beautiful than she remembered. The real problem was his scent. It was soothing and intoxicating at the same time, distracting her.

Still, she had to admit that she was enjoying herself.

"By the way, how is he? Stryker, I mean?"

It took a minute to process what Jason had whispered in her ear because the heat of his breath felt good against her neck and ear.

But when she looked up and saw his self-satisfied smile, her ire was ignited all over again. Before she had the opportunity to express her displeasure, she heard a noise at the front door that got her attention.

Ignoring the question, she moved quickly past him into the hall just in time to see the doorknob move back and forth.

Seconds later, a cacophony of noise erupted from the back of the house as her boys ran, barking and half-skidding on the hardwood floors all the way to the front door.

Becca thought, finally - better late than never, I guess.

And, with one hand on her hip, she turned to give Jason a satisfied grin.

Through the circular opaque glass insert in the front door, she could see a distorted view of a large man. Thankfully, it was the wrong height, size, and shape, so it couldn't be Mark.

Looking back at Jason, she said firmly, "I think I need to address this head-on. Don't worry, with you here… well, if he tries anything, I should be okay, right? I mean, since you're my knight in shining armor and all?

"Oh, wait, no armor. Oh well. It doesn't matter."

Pushing the hand, he reached out to her away, "I refuse to hide in my own house. I need to know what this man wants and why he's here."

As she reached the door, she gave a firm command, "And you two sit."

She had to admit. Jason was right. The man did look like a giant.

Standing awkwardly on the front porch was a large man with bleached blonde hair styled into spikes with too much mousse.

A hypertrophic scar ran the length of his right cheek into his thick neck. Sunken black eyes, close together, were small in scale compared to his large square head. One ear stood out away from the side of his head and was bigger than the other. A broad hawk-like nose sat at an angle like it had been badly broken and never properly fixed.

All in all, his face was like the misfitted pieces of a Frankenstein monster.

His broad shoulders seemed to fill the doorway, but Becca squared her own and looked up at him. "Can I help you?"

The man seemed stunned at seeing her, as if her presence was unexpected. "Um, is your grandmother home?"

"She's resting. Is there something I can help you with?"

"Um, well… I was driving behind her on my way home and noticed that her front tire seemed low. She drives a white Toyota Corolla, right?"

"Yes and…."

"Anyway, I saw her pull into your driveway. I had to rush home to put my groceries away before something melted, or I would have stopped then. But since I was driving by now, I thought I'd stop and tell her before she gets a flat."

"Oh, I'm sure she'll appreciate that. What did you say your name was again? I'll be glad to tell her and make sure she gets it looked at. But if you'd like to leave your phone number, I'm sure when she wakes, she'll want to call and thank you hers…."

Before she finished, he'd turned around and rushed down the steps, saying over his shoulder. "Um… that's okay. I just wanted to do the right thing. I have to go now, bye."

Becca couldn't fathom why the man would run off like that. He had expected an old lady to answer the door. But since Becca had cleaned up a half hour before Jason had arrived, the old woman's disguise had been put away.

More agitated after two unwelcome strangers intruded on her day, she shut the door a little harder than necessary.

Then, she swung around right into Jason, not realizing he was standing directly behind her. When she looked up to give him a piece of her mind, she smacked her head into his chin. The sharp pain only provoked her more.

Rubbing her head, she scolded, "Do you mind stepping back?" Pushing past him on her way back to the kitchen, she didn't realize that Jason was right behind her.

As she stormed down the hallway, he wanted to apologize, but all he could say was, "I didn't know your grandmother lived with you."

Becca stopped and turned so abruptly that Jason nearly skidded into her. If he'd been any closer, he would knocked them both to the floor.

In a tone that brooked no argument, she said, "And why would you? Why would you know anything about me? That man might have been my boyfriend, for all you knew. Jesus! Who the hell are you?"

Jason's eyes were large, and his mouth was open as if to speak, but words failed him.

Answering herself, "You're a stranger, that's who. A pet parent who brought an injured dog to my clinic. And at one of the most inopportune times, I might add."

Her eyes were blazing, even though she wasn't yelling. The green bits overtaking the blue continued to darken as she spoke, making the aqua color appear more teal.

Realizing that she was more upset than the situation warranted, she took a deep breath. "Look. I'd appreciate it if you'd limit our interactions to the clinic. And even though I shouldn't have to ask. Please don't come into my house without an invitation."

But it took everything he had to keep from laughing at her suppressed rage. Even though he knew it was justified.

Of course, she was pissed. Why wouldn't she be? He'd invaded her space and scared her. But damn, if she wasn't impossibly cute trying to be reasonable while she bit off her words, or maybe it was the way she struggled to keep her voice soft and even.

Shit! Chastising himself, I shouldn't have scared her like that.

Maybe his recent history was making him paranoid. The guy ran away, for Christ's sake. Not the typical behavior of a monster.

Holding up his hands to quiet her, he said, "Okay. You're right. And I'm sorry if I misunderstood the situation. I saw something that looked shady and thought I should warn you. I'll just go back to the clinic and leave you to whatever you were doing before I barged in."

As he turned to go, she couldn't help but admire how quickly he took responsibility for his behavior. No excuses, no false apology to appease her. Just a sincere expression of regret with a tinge of embarrassment.

And if she was honest, it didn't hurt that his jeans hugged his backside in a very flattering way.

Unhappy at herself for letting her temper get the best of her, she reached out an arm and gently touched his. "Hey, wait. I'm sorry. I didn't mean to dump on you.

"But to answer your question, Stryker is doing much better. Of course, the cone of shame to stop his licking is definitely not making him happy.

"I was able to drain the wound and close it. It'll be sore, so he should rest as much as possible and not walk too much on that foot. Give him at least a week. But the more he can rest now, the quicker he'll heal.

"At home, you'll need to make sure that he doesn't reopen the incision by licking it.

"I'd give it a few weeks. And be careful taking him into unknown territory. He's welcome to stay here a few more days so I can make sure the wound knits back together properly. Then just a quiet place to recuperate would be best."

Jason couldn't help it; he was getting lost in those eyes again. He wondered how anyone could look into them and not get lost. Shaking himself out of it, he smiled. "Thanks for telling me, doc. I've been worried about him. He's been through a lot this last year, and… anyway, it's a long story.

"You mentioned that you board animals here, and I think it would be better if I let you keep him. I have to go out of town. I should be back by Friday or Saturday at the latest. I can pay you now or when I pick him up."

His smile unnerved her, and she couldn't understand why. But when he said he was leaving town, she was strangely disappointed.

"Sure. Go on up to the clinic. Sarah should be there, and she can give you the boarding forms to fill out. I'll meet you up there in a few minutes."

As he walked away, she took a few seconds to enjoy the view, then closed the door and went to change out of the frumpy housedress she'd put on after her shower.

She couldn't help but feel frustrated. The man was always arriving when she wasn't dressed for visitors. And something inside of her wanted to look good when he visited.

Unfortunately, his breaking into the house only raised her temper.

***

As Jason surveyed the compound, thoughts of Stryker filled his mind, slowly transitioning into images of Becca.

Each time she came to mind, he couldn't help but smile. He wasn't sure which aspects of her were more attractive to him.

He knew Stryker was in good hands, but he still felt his partner's absence. Admittedly, having Stryker around made life easier to manage, knowing someone always had his back.

As he pulled his gear from the Jeep, Jason listened to the sounds around him in the woods: birds chirping, calling out to one another, squirrels chattering as they scampered through the trees, while the wind made a mournful howl.

Then it got quiet. A little too quiet.

As Jason stood and listened intently, a rush of air brushed the bangs off his face with the gentle touch of a lover.

He'd spent many nights walking the perimeter of the compound and knew all the sounds. At night, the area was usually buzzing with activity. So, the quiet at midday was a little disconcerting.

Visiting the compound during the day seemed reckless. He'd only returned because the night before, he'd almost broken a leg tripping into a hollow that he wanted to see with the light of the day.

As he slung his pack over his shoulder, he stopped to listen, trying to familiarize himself with the unfamiliar sounds around him. Then, he began the short hike to the location he'd saved on his GPS.

His destination was on the east side of the compound, not far from the entrance. If he hadn't almost fallen into it the night before, he might not have found it at all.

As he reached the coordinates, hidden amongst a group of quaking aspen and ponderosa pine, he noticed a dark depression close to the ground.

On closer inspection, it was a small opening.

Taking off his pack, he sat on the ground and looked inside. The interior was much larger than it appeared from the outside, with the opening large enough for him to get inside.

Clearing some brush away from the opening, he crawled through the opening.

Dropping down a few feet, he was pleased to find a three-foot irregular depression cut into the ground, measuring approximately eight feet by ten and standing just shy of six feet from the floor to the apex.

Long branches bent into wide arcs provided a dome over the interior that allowed rainwater runoff. A small channel along the interior perimeter wall would catch any runoff and leave the floor dry.

The walls and roof consisted of a large camo tarp sandwiched between a top and bottom layer of thin branches and twigs woven together and held in place with twine. Thick lashings secured the roof structure to thick boughs embedded deep in the ground.

Much larger than any hunter's blind, the floor area was spacious enough for a man his size to stretch out comfortably. Perfect for a lengthy stakeout.

On the exterior, only three feet of the structure stood above ground level, about the size of a good-size scrub bush.

Cloaked in a patchwork of branches and thickly seeded with leaves, the shelter blended in perfectly with the surroundings, making it the perfect place to surveil the compound without being noticed.

It didn't look that old, so it seemed strange that anyone would go to so much trouble to build it only to abandon it.

It was yards from the fence and far enough away from the main road and guardhouse that it seemed an unlikely location.

Was it possible that those at the compound knew about it?

Would he be taking too big of a risk if he used it?

He contemplated the risks but decided that it was worth the risk to find out.

As a rookie, he witnessed an intruder alert technique a detective used to catch a trespasser.

After multiple calls for assistance, believing a stranger had been in her home, a detective was asked to look into it.

Without the money to purchase surveillance equipment, the detective placed a small piece on the hinge side of each door while the woman agreed to be out of town.

When the suspect opened the door, the little flag fell, alerting the detective that someone had entered. Within days, the detective caught a neighbor who'd gained access by copying her house key.

For more than a year, the neighbor had been stealing small possessions, including some jewelry, and moving her things just enough for her notice.

By the time they caught the guy, he'd gathered a bag of things he needed to rape and kill her.

By a twist of fate, she'd missed her flight and was forced to stay away an extra day. That gave the detective enough time to find the neighbor, who was found on the floor of the woman's walk-in closet, asleep and clutching several pairs of her worn underwear.

By chance, Jason and his training officer arrived at the scene to pick up the suspect.

But Jason never forgot how a small bit of paper saved a life.

A simple technique that would assist him as well.

A few days later, Jason was back with everything he needed.

Leaving his gear inside, he began searching for thumb-sized branches. Then, sitting comfortably on the ground with his back against a tree, he used his knife to make a door that didn't look like a door.

Cutting the branches at varying lengths, he removed unwanted offshoots, leaving just enough to make it look like a bush.

Laying the branches in a row on the ground, he lashed them together with twine into a simple open and close gate big enough to cover the opening.

He braided three circlet hinges and used them to connect the door to a thick vertical branch on the left side of the opening. Then braided two latches and attached them on the opposite side.

By splitting a twig in two, he created latches to hold the door closed. When he checked it, the pin-locking system worked perfectly.

Lastly, he punctured a leaf with the latch.

Once the latch was pulled from the circlet the leaf would fall, notifying him that the hide had been compromised.

Sometimes, a few seconds made all the difference. And even if no one found it, a door might deter animals from dragging his stuff away.

With that chore completed, Jason unpacked.

Placing a tarp on the floor, he unrolled a three-season sleeping bag, pulled off his flannel shirt, laid down, and extended his legs.

He had barely slept in days, and the sleeping bag had a nice bit of loft.

The temperature was comfortably warm under the shadowed bows. A warm breeze blew in through the entrance.

Days in September could be warm, but inside the shelter, the temperature was perfect in a t-shirt and jeans, and Jason soon fell into a deep sleep.

The sound of large trucks rumbling close by awakened him with a start. For a moment, he was perplexed, wondering where he was.

Night had fallen, and it was pitch black inside the structure.

Waking in an unfamiliar place was a bit unsettling, but Jason knew those familiar sounds.

Grabbing his binoculars, he rushed to the opening in time to watch the last truck pass through the gates.

As usual, lights illuminated the compound, but they must have finished filling the barrels and loading them into the shipping containers because the trucks had left the compound.

At some point, he would need to figure out where the trucks were going and what exactly they were carrying. But for now, he needed to meet up with Dash.

They had a lot to talk about, and they could always figure out how they might follow the trucks undetected later.

He left the sleeping bag and tarp behind and secured the door with the leaf, figuring he'd wait a few days before returning to check on it.

If his stuff was left undisturbed, nothing touched or moved, he'd set up a camera and continue his stakeout.

As he made his way back to the Jeep, he wondered how Stryker was doing. And how the beautiful Becca would react to him the next time they met.

She'd been on his mind a lot lately. In fact, he'd been dreaming of her when the sound of the trucks had pulled him out of a very titillating dream.

CHAPTER TWENTY-TWO

Trust Your Instincts

Jason had been watching the compound for days and had memorized the guards' schedules. He'd even given them names based on their appearances and temperaments.

He dubbed a short, stocky guard with a thin black mustache Little Adolf because he not only looked like the Nazi but yelled forcefully when he spoke as if he were in charge.

Bucktooth, Scrawny, and Grumpy were the older guards responsible for the guard house, Ratchet searched the undercarriage of the vehicles, and Columbo walked the fence line poking the bushes and trees with his AK-47, searching for intruders.

He made a note of each guard's description and assigned station. Hoping it might come in handy when he entered the compound.

But one guard troubled him more than the others. A huge Shrek, looking guy, he'd named Ogre.

His upper body was thickly built, and his head was oddly shaped. His wide square face and slightly cone-shaped on top with spiky blond hair on top. One ear stuck out away from his head, while the other was deformed like a boxer who had gone too many rounds with too many blows to the side of his head.

He was the same guy Jason noticed in front of the casino and the same guy who stayed glued to Morales whenever he left the compound.

But what bothered Jason most was that Ogre was the same guy he'd seen watching Becca's place and ran away after Becca asked for his number.

Just like the bizarre connection between Matt and Billy, Jason couldn't fathom how a guard working for Morales in Central City managed to find his way to a veterinarian on the outskirts of Evergreen.

Could it just be a coincidence? Is it possible that Becca knows Morales, or is it just one more improbable connection?

She lived and worked at least thirty minutes from the compound, and as far as Jason could tell, she was clean.

So why was Morales's bodyguard anywhere near her place? Is it some kind of fluke, or is Becca in danger?

Nothing made sense.

After discussing everything with Dean and before adding another unknown complication, they agreed to focus on the reason the guards carried assault weapons – which they believed had to do with the production and transport of controlled substances.

Nothing in Billy's background or his arrest record hinted at his being dangerous, and there was nothing in the journals to indicate that Matt had met Billy or that Billy had any reason to kill Matt. But even if Billy had a vendetta, after all of his drug use, he didn't have the brains to pull off a premeditated murder.

What seemed more likely was that Billy's knowledge as a mechanic was needed after Morales discovered that Matt was working with the DEA.

If Jason could prove Morales manufactured drugs and that Billy was his dealer, they'd have at least one solid connection—one clean fragment in an otherwise distorted picture. And one piece was usually all it took to lead them to another and another.

In time, the connections would bring clarity to an otherwise convoluted puzzle.

But even if he could prove Morales had ordered Billy to do the hit, he questioned if the DEA would commit to helping him find justice for Matt. They seemed to have their own agenda.

Otherwise, if they'd recruited him as the journals suggested, how could they just abandon him?

Even if there was something more significant in the works, Jason was a cop, for Christ's sake; why not bring him in and debrief him on what they knew? And why not help him solve the case?

But because that was only one piece of the puzzle, Jason had to consider all possibilities—and there were still too many missing pieces, like why go to so much trouble setting him up for killing Billy and where Becca came into it.

That's when he decided that before he considered bringing in another law enforcement agency to take Morales down, he wanted the whole story.

Later that evening, Jason watched the men transfer the barrels from the warehouse area to the shipping containers during his nighttime inspections walking the boundary.

As he hiked back toward the shelter, he stopped at the gate he discovered the night he'd nearly fallen into the dugout.

It wasn't shown in any of the journals, but it was located on the east side of the compound, directly in line with the staff cabins.

A partially concealed dirt road driveway led up to a gate. The dense trees and foliage concealed the winding road.

He'd considered following a car in. But that seemed too risky.

Through the slats, he'd been able to make out three cabins that housed the workers.

They were set apart from a larger cabin that sat between the smaller warehouse at the southeast corner and the second gate. That cabin likely housed a gatekeeper or someone else of importance.

Cross-fencing between the cabins and the main property provided privacy, while the gates provided necessary access to the other areas of the property.

After reviewing the journal, Jason decided that the best point of entry wasn't through a gate where he might be detected but from behind the smaller warehouse.

Even with the cabins nearby, it remained farthest from light and security.

Jason trusted his instincts; his mother had taught him to do so from a young age. He was sure that whatever was inside the compound would provide the answers he needed.

Typically, the sentries rotated every six hours during the day, with an increase in activity from sunset until well after midnight. That left him only a small window for moving around once he breached the fence line.

He figured that he'd use the sounds of activity for cover to breach the fence and then lie low until the workers went to bed.

Once all was quiet, he'd check the smaller warehouse, then take the route behind the cabins to the big warehouse and shipping area while keeping to the shadows and away from the cameras and the main house where security might catch him.

With a camera attached to his helmet to keep his hands free he could record his movements and the evidence without having to stop for any length of time.

And he hoped to grab a few samples from the barrels.

As Jason scanned the area, he noticed that old Grumpy was alone in the security booth, but the front of the property had more muscle than usual.

He thought, *Why increase security now? Are you expecting company? What's changed in the few days I was away?*

After he and Dean had talked about needing more help, the only person who came to mind was Kade. Jason had known him since the academy and after training and gaining experience walking a beat, they were partnered and worked patrol together.

Kade's parents moved to the States from Japan when Kade was only a few months old.

Kade wasn't his birth name, but even as a child, Kade said he knew that it was meant to be his name. He couldn't remember where the name came from, but after multiple arguments with his father growing up, he was finally allowed to change his name legally, as long as he kept his surname.

Jason didn't want to implicate Kade, but he didn't know who else he could trust, especially after what happened when Dash approached Jax, and he was running out of time.

Sooner or later, the department would have to indict him. He needed something to help prove his innocence or create doubt about his guilt. Without it, he wouldn't be able to avoid arrest or prosecution.

He had to believe that Kade valued their friendship as much as he did. And he hoped Kade knew him well enough to know that he wouldn't intentionally kill anyone.

Fearing the worst, Jason grabbed the box of evidence he'd collected and made his way to Griffis Cheesman Park apartments.

Kade lived very comfortably in a large apartment on the fifth floor that overlooked the Denver Botanic Gardens.

The twenty-three-acre park, right in the middle of downtown Denver, boasts a wonderland of flora and fauna in the five distinctive gardens, dining, a library, artwork to inspire, a conservatory, and a sunken amphitheater that regularly hosts concerts.

One of the things Kade liked best about the location was listening to the concerts while sitting on his balcony or when entertaining friends.

The first time Jason was invited to the apartment, Kade told him that he'd moved into the complex because it provided a front-row seat to both beauty and entertainment.

Kade's father had made a fortune in the stock market and, with a knack for business, had done very well for himself as an investment banker. And even though he didn't follow in his father's footsteps, Kade got a degree in finance and worked with his father a few times a year, walking away with a good amount of extra cash.

It was a risk going to see Kade. The guy could easily arrest him. Jason hoped that the evidence he'd brought might help convince Kade to help.

Jason rang the bell with trepidation, but when Kade Tanaka answered the door, his face lit up at seeing Jason.

Jason nearly dropped to the floor with relief, and his fears that Kade might turn on him melted away.

Kade looked genuinely happy to see him. "Oh, my God, Colt! Geez, man, I heard about the shooting. That had to be so messed up.

"But hey, man, I didn't believe for a minute that you did it. No way would you shoot someone unless he drew down on you first. But damn, Colt, where have you been?"

Then realizing they were standing in the hall, he said, "Oh shit, come on in."

Jason could barely talk; his emotions were too close to the surface for several seconds. "Thanks… Kade. You have no idea how much that means to me."

Jason picked up the box at his feet and walked into the apartment. "I should have contacted you sooner, but I've been trying to gather evidence to prove I'm innocent. So much has happened, and it's all so complex.

"I recently discovered that there are people that I have trusted that might not be trustworthy. Cops…friends. I know it sounds crazy, but I've had to be careful. I didn't know who to trust. And those I did trust, I didn't want to jack up.

"I know I can trust you, Kade, so don't look at me like that. I was just afraid to implicate you in the shit show that's become my life."

Kade put his arm around Colt and led him to the balcony where he'd been enjoying the symphony playing in the park while dabbling in the stock market.

"Don't worry about it. Take a load off. The concert's almost over, and after that, we can go inside to have more privacy. You want a beer?"

"Sure. Thanks." As Jason waited for Kade, he began to relax, listening to Rachmaninov's Symphony No. 2.

"Look, Jason, I get it. But I have to admit, at the time, I was pretty pissed that you didn't bother to call. It was like you dropped out—nothing but radio silence, leaving me with nothing but the BS rumors flying around.

"I thought we were friends, and when I didn't hear from you, I hate to say that I questioned that."

Jason knew his friend well enough to tell that he was hurt at being left out. Even with his emotionless expression, "We are friends, Kade!"

"Okay. So, what's going on then? And what's so bad that you can't return a call? I left a message, but you never called back."

"I know. I'm an ass. I'm sorry. The truth is I didn't want to bring my hell down on you. And trust me, it's bad.

"I might even mess you up just by being here."

Kade didn't look convinced.

"To be honest, I really didn't want anyone involved. But the more I try to do things on my own, the more fucked up things got. Which is why I'm here now.

"It's gone on too long, and I'm running out of time. So, I have little choice but to ask for help and risk putting the people I care about in jeopardy."

"Okay, I get that. I even respect it. But what was so troubling that you couldn't call?"

"Didn't you hear? The guy killed in the alley was Billy Gordon."

"No shit?"

"Yeah, you remember him? A small dude… about the size of a twelve-year-old…. red hair. We first saw him that first year we rode together."

With the final notes fading from the concert, Kade nodded toward the apartment to indicate they should move inside, "God, who could forget that scumbag. Your friendly neighborhood pusher was one twisted mother. I hated that guy. Fucker was selling to kids.

"Didn't I tell you that I caught him selling to a ten-year-old? I couldn't believe it! Scared the kid nine ways of Sunday and beat the shit out of Billy myself.

"Didn't even arrest the scum bag, just warned him hard with a beat-down. Then, I told him straight up that if I ever heard he was selling to underage again, he'd see me up close and personal-like.

"But hey, don't repeat that."

"Who me? I didn't hear a word."

"You know, I don't generally come unglued like that. But that little fucker was giving his shit out free. You know my code: I never hit anyone who doesn't strike first…."

"Ooh-rah."

"But he'd been put back on the streets twice, and I wasn't about to sit back while he got a young kid hooked. I thought the fear of losing some teeth might make him think twice.

"Those gummies looked a lot like candy, but they weren't just infused with THC – a few were laced with PCP. I had them tested. They come in different colors like gummies, and each one has a taste of X, meth, coke... whatever, just like flavors of candy.

"They call the most potent one Dragonfly."

"That's some pretty scary shit Kade. But I've never heard of Dragonfly. That's a new one on me."

"What gets me is that even when we stop the dealers before they can get the kids hooked, if parents have them around, kids go after them because they look like candy. What kind of sick fuck thinks up this shit?"

Jason understood Kade's frustration all too well. But he also knew that Kade was a good man and a great cop—usually easygoing and even-tempered.

It would take a lot to send him off.

He always reminded Jason of Kimball Cho, the character on The Mentalist.

Only Kade was more genial.

If Kade lashed out at someone, it reflected more on a flawed judicial system than on Kade's character.

Selling drugs to kids was a crime against humanity—against the future.

Jason shook his head, "Yeah, I know. I caught Billy selling to a kid once. Man, I was pissed. I'm surprised you got the beatdown on him. He just disappeared on me. Thinking back, that was probably a good thing because I'm not sure how I would have handled it.

"It's really messed up though. When I was still on the job, I heard at least a dozen horror stories about small kids dying from getting into their parent's stash."

Kade took a pull on his beer and said, "Yeah, and the gen-pop just doesn't get it. One thing's for sure: the drug situation is out of control. But until the cartels are taken out, I'm not sure we can stop what's coming."

"Well then, I doubt you'll like this. I just found out that they're looking to replace Billy in the neighborhood. Some guy apparently came around looking for volunteers to take his place. Can't imagine what the next guy might be willing to do."

"Unfortunately, I can. We just can't keep the creeps off the streets. And like you, I'm not sure we can win on that score. Gets worse every year.

"It's up to those in charge, and they have their own agenda."

"You got that right!"

Jason was quiet for a minute, then said, "But hey, I have to own up about my own shit. I think I messed up that night."

"What are you talking about?"

"I didn't recognize him—Billy, I mean—at least not that night.

"I was told later at the debriefing, and it totally blindsided me. I thought he was still doing time, but he must have gotten an early release or something. But it made sense… the red hair. I realized it was him the second they mentioned his name.

"That night, I was sick, and the alley was so dark.

"I know, no excuses. But that night, I could barely see... but I did get a peek at his red hair. I'd forgotten about it. And I couldn't tell you why Billy didn't come to mind the minute I saw it."

It felt good to confess his deficiencies to his old friend. Kade had always been a great listener.

"But hey, enough of that crap. I heard you made detective. Congratulations! I can't think of anyone who would do a better job."

"Yeah, lucky me, I'm a rookie again. But yeah, it's good. Thanks. But if I'm honest, I've always wanted to be a detective."

"I can believe that. But you never said."

"Well, you know how it is. I wanted to pass the test before I said anything. Then, I wanted to see if I was picked… I don't know."

"Well, I'm surprised you'd worry about it.

"But when did you know you wanted to be a detective? I mean, you've always had an uncanny way of figuring things out. You see details others either don't see or brush off as unimportant. Why do you think I'm here." Jason teased.

"Huh, I thought I told you about how I helped the cops nab some creeps when I was around ten?"

"Nah, I don't remember that."

"Well, I was with a friend. We were riding bikes around an apartment complex in the neighborhood—just doing stupid kid stuff.

"Only as I ride past this first-floor apartment window, the curtains are open. So, I get curious and take a peek.

"These two guys are inside, and there's a bunch of stuff on a coffee table. The taller guy is pulling a TV out of one of those TV cabinets while the other one is unplugging stuff from the back of it— only for some reason it feels all wrong.

"I ride off, but then go around the building and come back for another look. Only this time, the curtains are closed.

"I'm a kid, right? So, I blow it off, and we ride for a while. Only it keeps bugging me. So, I head back to that apartment and wait.

"When they came out, their arms are weighed down with stereo components and the TV, but they're not going to a moving van or anything.

"So, now it makes sense. What the tingly feeling in my gut was saying: these guys are bad news.

Afraid they'll see me, I head in the opposite direction, and once they turn the corner, I follow them. They're walking on the sidewalk in front of the complex, and I'm riding down the section between apartments, keeping them in sight but at a good distance.

"I admit it was stupid, but I was excited.

"At the time, it didn't occur to me to be afraid or that if they figured out what I was up to, they could really hurt me. Nope. The whole time, I'm wondering where they're going with all that stuff.

"My friend was smarter. He hung way back in the center of the complex, watching me.

"But that's what I mean about kids. They have no idea what they're getting into.

"Anyway, it was strange... the guys were on foot. If they'd had a car, they would have left me in the dust.

"On that street were two churches at the end of the block across the street from each other.

"Anyway, I reach the end of the complex on the apartment side of the fence between the church parking lot and the complex.

"I ride up and down real casual like, just watching them through the slatted fence.

"For a minute, I was a little disappointed because I thought they might be taking the stuff to the Lutheran church for some event. But after a minute of looking around, the guys crossed the street to the Protestant church.

"Anyway, they hide the stuff behind these big bushes on the side of the church, and then they just take off.

"Man, was I confused. Why take something and just leave it in the bushes where no one will find it for a long time?

"So after they leave, I ride over and take a look, and sure enough, the stuff's just sitting there behind the bushes.

"Thinking they were thieves like on TV, I want to tell the cops. Only I'm scared.

"Everyone was at work, so I went to the apartment manager and told him what I saw, and because my friend lived there and backed up my story, the manager called the cops.

"When they roll up, I take them to the loot. I can't say too much about what happened next cause no one said, but at some point, the cops caught them, probably when they came back to get the stuff.

"But a while later, I got a five-dollar reward from the renter because he was getting his stuff back.

"It was a big deal at the time. A lot of money for a kid who didn't need it, but it validated me. Here I was, just a dumb kid a whole five months before I turned eleven, and I helped catch two bad guys.

"I was really into Batman at the time, NYPD Blue, NCIS—I was so into all those cop shows.

"Most of the time, my parents didn't like me to watch… but I always managed to find a way.

"It's just what kids do, I guess.

"But that's when I knew that I wanted to be a cop. And over the years, that feeling has only gotten stronger.

"And because of that gut feeling, I know when something's off, even when I'm not exactly sure what it is. I know the DA doesn't like it when we talk about a gut feeling, but it tunes me into whatever's going on. And I think it will make me a good detective one day.

"I'm excited about the new position and hope I have the chance to show off a little.

"The downside is that I'm also a rookie again, so it may take a while to make an impression.

"A long story, I know. But you asked. It was nice of you to acknowledge the promotion.

"But hey, you're here for more than an old story. So spill it; what's up?"

"Yeah, you're right.

"The truth is I need help, but the problem is, it's a big ask. Dean's been a big help, but even he says we can't do it alone.

"You're a good friend and one of the few people I trust, so I'm here with hat in hand, hoping you'll be willing to help.

"But you need to know, this whole thing is really complicated, and I'm no detective.

“I could really use your gift. I’m over my head here, which is exactly what I believe someone is trying to do. The more convoluted the more impossible it will be to untangle.

“Buy hey, no matter what, I don’t want to jam you up; even talking to me could be enough to cause you a problem, so please tell me if you’re not okay with it, and I won’t mention it again.

“But here’s the deal, Kade, it’s not enough that I didn’t kill Billy. Maybe not even enough to uncover the truth. I need to clear my name. If I can’t do that, I’ll lose my job. Even if they never have enough to arrest me, I still lose if everyone believes I’m a bad cop.”

“I love my job, and I want my life back. But that can’t happen until I fill in all the holes in my story. And trust me, there are many. I’ve gathered a lot of information, but it’s not enough to clear me. I hope that you can help me find the proof I need to clear my name. Otherwise, we’re just wasting time and putting you at risk for nothing.”

Kade nodded. “Sure, I get it. Since the shooting, you’ve been trying to make sense of it. I see that. And you know, friend or not, I’d arrest you in a second if I thought you were guilty. No way I’d ask you into my home, okay?

“I appreciate you wanting to protect me, but I wouldn’t be sitting with you if I thought for a minute you did it. I’m a big boy, so just tell me, what you’ve got so far?”

“Fair enough. But I don’t know who I can trust, so we need to keep this just between us… well, the three of us.”

“First thing, and maybe the biggest thing you should know, is that it wasn’t an accident, Kade. My dad was murdered!”

Snarling, he continued, “And I think a cop helped to cover it up.

“It was all too convenient.

“This cop was outside his jurisdiction but just happened to be the first on the scene. How often do we see that? And to add to that question mark, his report didn’t add up right, either. It was missing information.

“The Cap inquired on my behalf and ended up taking over the investigation.

“And it wasn’t until they took a second look that they found Billy’s DNA and fingerprints on the undercarriage. They think it proves he was the one who fucked with Dad’s van and why I had motive to kill him.

"But then, there's a lot of holes in my theories, too, like proving Morales ordered Billy to sabotage Dad's truck.

"Kade, I think I was set up because I reopened Dad's case, and to add kooky to this crazy mess, I believe his death might be connected to Billy's.

"I have a lot of theories like that, but little proof.

"Carl said Billy was pushing drugs for a guy out of Central City, and my Dad was working in that location for a guy named Morales.

"I believe that's how Dad and Billy crossed paths. And it's not that big a stretch to link Billy to Morales.

"If Morales ordered the hit on Dad and wanted to stop me from looking into it, and if he was cleaning up loose ends—meaning Billy. And if I can connect the dots somehow, I just might be able to prove my innocence."

"Damn, Colt, I see what you mean. That's a whole lot of ifs. You have some great theories, but too much supposition that could prove super challenging to prove.

"What I don't get is why this Morales character would want to kill Matt. Did Matt witness something?"

"That's one of the missing pieces. We just don't know yet.

"But I found out that he was doing recon for the DEA, working with an Agent Thomas.

"The way I see it, Morales somehow finds out that Dad was working with the DEA and paid Billy to mess with his van.

"Then he finds out I'm looking into the accident. So, maybe he wants to clean up some loose ends. Orders the hit on Billy to ensure he stays quiet. Maybe thinks, hey, why not kill two birds with one stone... so he sets me up for Billy's murder and gets rid of both loose ends in one move."

Nodding his head, Kade agreed, "Man, that makes a lot of sense. It's a sound theory, but proving it won't be easy."

They spent the rest of the day and evening going through Matt's tapes and journals, along with the evidence, notes, and pictures Jason and Dean had collected.

"Man. I had no idea what you were dealing with. But this is amazing work, friend. Obviously, way more is going on than the investigation team is aware of. Have you considered sharing this stuff with them?"

"I would, but there's… um… well... some.

"Shit, I guess I should just confess everything."

CHAPTER TWENTY-THREE

Learning to Trust

Jason took a deep breath. "Well, I feel bad about it, but I'm the one who let the dogs loose at the kennel and tagged the wall. I took Stryker out of the DPD kennel.

"I know what you're going to say, bad move. But I had to save Stryker after the brass decided to put him down. I just couldn't let that injustice happen.

"It was one of the toughest decisions I've made as a cop. But I couldn't let them kill him. He's been a good dog and a good partner. And since his escape, I swear he hasn't been aggressive at all.

Kade nodded, "Dude, I get it. I know what he means to you."

"It was just so unfair. He'd just been through hell, and then he wasn't allowed to so much as see me. It was cruel from the get-go.

"I know why he bit that rookie, but I can't explain why he was aggressive with Jax. But since he's been with me, he's been his old self.

"Even after he was injured — no aggression. I'm boarding him with a vet now, and he hasn't been the least bit aggressive with her. Not once."

"Okay, but why not share the info?"

"Here's how I see it: if I turn myself in for breaking Stryker out. They'll have good reason to lock me up. Then they'll just finish the job on Stryker.

"I just can't let that happen, Kade. Stryker doesn't deserve a death sentence.

"Okay. You don't have to convince me. I know Stryker's a good dog… and I agree that you didn't have a choice… okay, and…."

"…if I just turn over what I have, that's it. No way that they'll let me be part of the investigation. And I can't just sit back and do nothing.

"Right now, what I have isn't enough to clear me. It might create reasonable doubt and get me off, but it doesn't clear my name. Plus, they already have some of it from when they cleaned out my office.

"Besides, Kade, what if it goes missing? Like I said before, I don't know who to trust.

"What if Morales has someone on the payroll in the department and my Dad's tapes and journals just suddenly disappear? I might sound paranoid, but it's not unheard of. And if someone got access to my locker, they might have access to whatever the detectives find, too.

"Someone was in your locker? How… I mean, how could you tell?"

"When I was at the substation after I found John, I barely noticed at the time. But I recently remembered that the lock wasn't engaged. It wasn't locked. And I always lock it... it's a habit.

"I was upset after I found John. Plus, I was sick… I wasn't paying enough attention and just shrugged it off, figuring that I'd forgotten to close it all the way.

"An easy oversight, that would mean nothing if I didn't have all the rest happen.

"That's what I mean about not knowing who I can trust. If someone had access to my locker, they probably have access to other areas in the department.

"I just can't take the chance that what evidence we do have will get lost."

"Jesus Jason, this is way more complicated isn't it?"

"Yeah. But I'm starting to remember stuff, so that's been helpful. The problem is it's slow going. I remember little things like the lock and my cold meds not working right…"

"What?"

"Oh yeah, instead of drying me out, they stopped working, and then I got weak… groggy.

"I think my cold meds were messed with. Just one more thing that put me down that night.

"I'll say. But honestly, I can't see how we prove sabotage of your meds if the lab didn't uncover it."

"Which is just another reason why I've been keeping everything so close to my chest.

“I’m hoping to clear my name, so that maybe they’ll let me stay on with the department. I might get written up for the breaking-in to save Stryker, but I can live with that.

“And if I can show that Stryker isn’t dangerous. They might want to retire him, but I can live with that as long I can have custody.

“But I need a little more time and a lot more help to prove I was set up. Okay, now I’m rambling.

“Do you think you might be able to help? I mean without putting yourself in jeopardy.”

Kade grabbed them another beer and opened it while he contemplated what Jason had told him.

“Man, this is intense. And at the moment I’m not sure how much I’ll be able to help. But let’s break it down.

“So far, there’s no APB out on you. We can’t count on that to last. If or when that happens, you’ll have to turn yourself in. And it won’t be pretty if they figure out that you have Stryker before they arrest you. You need to be ready just in case that comes up.”

“I know. Charles will take care of it… he’s an attorney.”

Smiling, Kade agreed, “Yeah, I’d bet when most people see him coming, they get out of the way. No one would ever expect a guy that big to be so kind and gentle. “

“Well, that’s part of his charm. But don’t let that fool you. The man is good at what he does. He’s truly extraordinary, and I know he’ll have my back if it comes to an arrest.

“Until then, I just need to gather every bit of evidence I can find, including a get-out-of-jail-free card if we can find one.

“Let’s walk through that stuff again. Try it from a different angle. Maybe I’ll notice something you didn’t, or you might see something you missed before.

“When consumed with the intensity of a problem, the picture right in front of you can become distorted. In order to see the picture clearly, you might need to look at it from multiple viewpoints.”

They spent the next few hours discussing Matt’s journals and then added Jason’s notes while Kade made a list with bullet points: “Wow, this is good.”

"We know Matt was working for Morales on a plumbing job. But the question that came up for me was, what made him decide to go to the DEA instead of Homicide?

"I mean, if Matt overheard Morales order a hit, why assume drugs were involved? Why automatically go to the DEA? Drugs had to be involved to do that, right?

"Yet, there wasn't anything in his notes about drugs before meeting up with Clay. And I heard references on the tapes, but nothing specifically about drugs or the hit he overheard.

"If he'd gone to Homicide instead of the DEA, the case would be on file. That would have changed how the department investigated the situation in the alley because the incidents happened so close together.

"But since he went to the DEA and Thomas didn't bother to share with DPD, there wasn't a trail for Homicide to follow for your case."

"Man, I never thought of that."

"There's no doubt Matt was targeted; we can see it was premeditated on the new forensic report. But then I have to ask, why didn't forensics do a better job with the first pass of the scene? Who processed it? And how was Morales able to find out you'd pushed for another inquest?

"It was outside DPD's jurisdiction the first time, so maybe Morales has a mole in Central City PD."

"What was that officer's name? The one that arrived first on the scene?"

"Kipling Roberts. Another strange piece in the puzzle.

"He's State Patrol, but out of his jurisdiction. He didn't call for Gilpin County. It didn't make sense to me, especially if he was off duty, as Roberts claimed.

"I could understand if he just came on it driving by, but why start the investigation without calling it in?

"That might be something to follow up on. But I was never clear on whether it was an anonymous caller or if the Trooper called it in. He said it was a 911 call, but his report didn't mention it.

"Sounds like you're thinking that maybe Roberts influenced that first report… maybe left out some important details on purpose?" Kade asked.

"I don't know, it's just another thing that seems off to me. How often does a fatal accident get investigated twice? Most accidents like that are investigated thoroughly the first time, so they don't need to follow up.

"Why would a case be closed if there's any question about what happened?"

"I hear you. But since it was a one-car accident, the Trooper might not have thought it more than an accident.

"Still, I see where your train of thought is headed. If you were pushing for answers or asking to reopen the case, who better to inform Morales?"

"Yeah, that's pretty much what I've been wondering."

"You're thinking he might have been paid off?"

Shaking his head, Jason took a minute to answer. "I'm not sure. When I talked with him, he seemed legit, and I don't want to discredit the guy by making accusations if he was just trying to help out."

"I get that. I'm just thinking out loud. We don't have proof, and there's no point in making accusations without it anyway. But it would explain how Morales found out you were investigating Matt's death."

"Damn, you really are good at this." Jason said, "But what about Billy?"

"Hmm… well, it's not a stretch to say it would be over his head to plan a job like that on his own. He was never that bright to begin with, and he probably tested the product he sold, which only made it worse. But I don't think he was a killer."

"Agreed. And even if he was a killer and he did figure out dad was onto him selling, the thing that gets me is, what was his motive to kill him? Dad wasn't after Billy. As far as I can figure it, Morales was the only one who had any motive here."

"Okay. So, if Morales wanted Matt dead but didn't want to get his hands dirty, it makes sense that he would pay Billy to do it.

"Billy would know how to disable the brakes and the steering. And on that road, Matt wouldn't have a chance. That had to be one hell of an e-ticket ride."

When he looked up from the document he was holding, Kade noticed the look on Jason's face and immediately felt like a tool. "Shit, man, that was a totally fucked up thing to say. I'm really sorry, Jason.

"Going over all of this has to hurt like hell, and what I said was insensitive."

"Yeah, but it's nothing I haven't thought of myself... as fucked up as it is to talk about, you were right. It had to scare the shit out of him. No one should have to die like that. But trust me, I'm under no illusion about it. I've seen enough accidents to have a good idea what his last moments were like.

"Besides, what other choice do I have if there's any hope of figuring this out? So, don't sweat it.

"No matter how it might hurt, we need to go over everything and check out every possibility."

"Right. Well, at least we have a connection between Morales, Billy, and Matt — well, almost. But how did Morales find out about Matt spying on him, huh?

"Morales spoke freely on the tapes. Wouldn't that indicate that he didn't know he was being taped?

"And then there's Billy.

"Was Morales cleaning up loose ends like you said, or was there more to it?

"Might be a thread to pull.

"We need proof -- a connection between Billy and Morales. Theories don't cut it. But where I think it gets complicated is where you come into it, Jason."

Kade took a minute, "So, you should be the focus. Whatever happened in that alley is where things got twisted. Don't get me wrong, what happened to Matt was calculated. But everything that happened in that alley took way more planning.

"You're the one in the pressure cooker here. I think we need to go back to the beginning of that shift and move forward slowly. Take each incident apart until it makes sense. Or connect the dots enough to get to the truth.

"I'd like to make copies of what you've collected here. That way, I can go over elements of the case without risking contact.

"As a detective, I'll have access to your case, and I'll be able to keep on top of whatever evidence the unit uncovers.

"Once we can clear you and, of course, Stryker, we can go back and fill in the missing pieces on what happened to Matt. Hell, if we figure out your case, we might clear up his, too."

The idea sounded good. "Great idea. Let's do it. That way, if anything happens to the originals, we'll still have something."

They went into Kade's office to take pictures of Matt's journal and make copies of the maps and documents Jason and Dean had collected.

The tapes took a little longer because they had to listen to them again so Kade could record them on his phone.

With that out of the way, they returned to the sofa and began reminiscing about the old days.

Between car chases, protecting crime scenes, and making arrests, they were taking care of the general population in other ways.

Like the time they helped a woman in the middle of the street find her way home. She'd wandered away while her husband was asleep and had been missing for twelve hours. Her whole family was out looking for her.

One day on patrol, they witnessed a little boy fall off his bike. After driving him home, his grateful mother rewarded them with the best batch of chocolate chip cookies warm from the oven they'd ever eaten.

Kade said, "Man, those were some damn good cookies. You might not believe me, but I still think about those damn cookies sometimes."

"You know, I do too. They were big and gooey but not too sweet. And that homemade vanilla ice cream on top was the game changer."

"Yeah, I'd have to say that was one of our better shifts."

That's when one of their worst days on the job came to mind.

They'd only been on patrol for a few shifts when they got a call about a suspicious car cruising back and forth on the same street.

Colt and Kade had arrived on the scene just as a black tricked-out low-rider turned the corner and headed toward a greenhouse in the center of the block.

The Lincoln Continental, with suicide doors and smoked glass windows, was lowered nearly to the road.

The tinted glass hid the individuals inside the vehicle, but Colt caught a glimpse of two shadowed heads in the back seat when light filtered through a side window that was slowly rolling down.

A young boy was playing basketball in the driveway of the house. He was small, a bit skinny, around ten or eleven years old, and very focused on his game. A little young for the hoop and backboard attached to the garage, he struggled to shoot the ball high enough to go through the hoop.

Kade had parked the cruiser a few houses down, "I have a bad feeling about this."

They monitored the black car for a few minutes, trying to see if the people might be looking for an address. But the car just continued moving slowly toward the intersection at the end of the block.

After seeing the car at the intersection, they got out of the patrol car and started walking toward the boy. About two houses away from the kid, the car suddenly sped up and made a fast U-turn, heading back in their direction.

That's when they saw the window was all the way down, and the long muzzle of a semi-automatic was sticking out of it.

Almost simultaneously, both Colt and Kade pulled their guns and jumped into action. It seemed likely that the boy was the target.

Colt and Kade had started shooting at the car just as the first ring of bullets ripped through the neighborhood from that semi-automatic weapon.

Before they could reach the car, or shelter the kid, there was an explosion of powder followed by rapid popping like firecrackers going off in succession.

They watched as the ball dropped through the hoop at the same time the boy hit the ground. The onslaught of bullets ripped the small body apart.

Emptying their guns into the car, they managed to kill the driver, who slammed head-on into a telephone pole.

The guy in the passenger seat was thrown through the windshield partway onto the hood of the car.

One guy in the backseat tried to jump out and make a run for it but ended up tripping out of the suicide door. Kade took off after him and was able to tackle him before the guy made it to the fender.

The other passenger from the back seat opened the door and fell from the Lincoln to the ground. He crawled a few feet, bleeding from a chest wound, gasping for breath. He wasn't going anywhere.

While Kade kept control of the prisoner and called for an ambulance, Colt ran to the small boy, hoping to save him, but it was too late. His spirit had already left his mangled body.

Two gangsters were dead, and two were seriously injured, along with one innocent child who'd had a lifetime of experiences stolen from him for no reason at all.

A travesty of justice, to be sure. Not to mention some harsh lessons for a couple of wet-behind-the-ear cops.

It wasn't until later that they found out the shooting was part of a gang initiation – a complete and unnecessary waste.

The memory still haunted both of them.

During the trial, the gang's lawyer had found a loophole. A minor technicality that freed the two living gang members to repeat a similar nightmare in another neighborhood only months later.

Although justice hadn't been found in the courtroom, justice was provided by a vigilante.

The father of the small boy had managed to find the gang's hangout and killed the two men responsible for his son's death, along with eight of their compadres.

The boy's father had made an impassioned statement in open court during his trial, "I protected this country—three tours in Iraq. Why did I bother to fight and kill over there if we're not willing to do the same here?

"The only difference is that their home-grown-terrorists!"

"My boy was gunned down in front of our home for nothing more than some kind of sadistic initiation ritual. And then, those depraved animals get off on a technicality. They were allowed to go back to their evil ways to hunt down a child… because of a technicality.

"And why? Because they have rights.

"What about my son's rights, huh? What right did he have to play without the fear of being gunned down?

"He was nine years old. Not even big enough to sink the ball through the net. But he was trying that day—real hard." He choked up for a minute. Tears filled his eyes, "He just wanted to show me that he was a big boy and could do it."

Wiping his eyes, anger filled his words, "What kind of country did I sacrifice my life for, that filth like that can run free amongst decent people and be allowed to kill a child?

"And now you want to judge me? I should get a medal for cleaning up the streets of that kind of scum!

"Until this country wipes the sociopaths who procreate like cockroaches off the face of this planet, no one will ever be safe.

"But you go ahead—do your worst. Condemn me for getting justice for my son. For doing what I was trained to eliminate overseas. What should have been done long ago to the terrorists that continue to run free in this country."

"I almost broke down in court that day," Kade said.

Jason nodded, "Me too. I'm glad we took the time to see him. I think it gave him some comfort to know that his son had a brief moment of joy, sinking that ball before he… passed. I think it helped to know his son got his wish."

Jason remembered a poem he'd read and recited it for Kade.

"Under Heaven, I saw you there
Gun in hand, arm in the air
A swarm of bullets ravage the night
With a blast of light to extinguish life
Blood stains concrete where innocence is lost
To make us witnesses to the cost
Colors of madness flash through the streets
As a gang screams victoriously at a boy's defeat
Had I not seen with my own eyes
The fall of the boy and his demise
I wouldn't understand what I do now
That under Heaven we witness Hell"

Kade shook his head. "Man, that's…wow."

A shiver made its way up Jason's back. He'd lived it and would never forget the swish of the ball as it went through the hoop, the brief surprise and joy on the young face. Or seconds later, seeing the small, mangled body lying on the blood-soaked driveway.

The concert had ended hours before, so they sat in companionable silence, lost in their troubled thoughts, until Kade broke the silence, "That was a terrible night, but we need to stay strong and not let this shit get to us. It comes with the territory.

"Unlike the gen-pop, we have to put our lives on the line, deal with the dregs of society, live with the horrors we witness without complaint, and tolerate those who judge us for how we do the job.

"I know it's fucked up, but that's the job.

"I can't speak for all cops, but I feel like we try to make a difference."

Jason gulped down the rest of his beer. "I do, too. Why else put ourselves through it? I don't know many people who'd be willing to do our job.

"But even though I hate what happened to that boy, when someone I arrest is convicted— I mean actually put away— it feels good to know that I stopped one of the bad guys from harming or corrupting another citizen.

"It makes me proud to be part of a brotherhood dedicated to defending those who can't defend themselves.

"Only, since the alley, it… it feels like *my* life has been corrupted—stolen. At least the parts of that had real meaning. It's pretty devastating.

"Which reminds me, we need a copy of my hospital records. There was a large lump on my neck. The doc thought it was a puncture wound of some kind. He took pictures.

"To be honest, it hurt like a mother. It felt like I'd been shot… but a bullet would have caused more damage—it would have killed me.

"I haven't received the results of the tox screen or the pictures the nurse took either. I think there's a possibility I was injected with something or that something was added to my cold meds. If we can get access to those records, we might find a clue as to why I blacked out and couldn't remember anything. I'd think the puncture wound alone should make them question my culpability.

"Maybe Jacobs or Chambers have found enough to make them question their quick-to-judge theory.."

After an afternoon of sleuthing and theorizing, Kade knew what he was about to tell his friend was going to freak him out. But he needed to be honest. To explain. "Jason, I need to tell you something you might not like. I don't think it's that big of a deal, but I think you deserve to know that..."

Jason inhaled deeply. "It's okay, Kade. I understand if all of this is a bit much. Just say it."

"...um, well, you may not believe me, but I just heard this morning that I'm going to be assigned to the team… that's investigating your case."

Jason's mouth fell open. "What? I thought you were going to help me. Why didn't you say something before? What kind of game are you playing at?"

Jumping off the dark grey sectional, Jason started shoving his things back into the box and headed for the door.

CHAPTER TWENTY-FOUR

Friends First

Kade rushed to block Jason on his way to the front door, “Please stop for a minute.” Raising his voice, he ordered, “Colt, stop! Just listen for a minute!”

When Jason stopped to look at Kade, he continued, “Look. I get it. You’re past your breaking point, and you don’t feel like you can trust anyone. And that may be true of most, but not me.

“I swear, I didn’t know about it until early this morning. And trust me, I wasn’t happy about it either. But as a rookie, I don’t get to pick my assignments. You know that!

“It’s no secret that we came up together. Maybe they thought it would be a good way to test me… I really don’t know.

“But think about it. You know how it is with rookies. They’ll probably have me doing grunt work or worse. And even as part of the team, how much muscle do you really think I’ll have?

“I don’t even start until Monday. Talk about timing, huh?

“I didn’t say anything at first because I was happy to see you. Then, it was really good reminiscing, and honestly, I didn’t want to scare you off.

“Think about it. You know me. If I thought you were a bad cop, do you really think we’d still be talking? If there was a bolo out, wouldn’t I call it in? Arrest you?”

Jason saw the sincerity in his friend’s eyes and heard the truth in his words. But he was angry and unsure. Too much had happened, and his anger had been boiling up for too long without release.

Setting the box on the floor, he took a step toward his friend, “I don’t think so. But how do I know for sure?

"For all I know, you could be trying to make points… waiting for a confession—good thing I don't have anything to confess… besides breaking into the kennel, that is.

"But that wouldn't be a big enough fish for you, would it?"

Kade took inventory of his friend.

Jason had squared off his stance, was barely blinking, his jaw clenched, his brow furrowed, his eyes slightly squinted, his fists clenched, and he'd gotten close enough to strike.

Kade was trained in martial arts. He and Jason had spared during training, but they'd never battled. Kade was sure that if they ever did, one or both would end up seriously injured.

Instead of backing away, Kade stood firm, resigning himself to take the hit to prove his loyalty. He just hoped it wouldn't escalate after that.

"You're pissed. I get it. I would be, too. I could have handled the situation better, and I'm sorry. But Jason, I swear, I wouldn't do anything to hurt you.

"Jesus. I haven't seen you since that night at the bar before you got sick. And after what you'd been through – well, I didn't want to add to it, so I was trying to figure out how to tell you.

"Come on, Jason. How could I know they'd put me on your case or that you'd show up today and need my help?"

Jason relaxed slightly. He didn't have many options.

Kade was a good man – a good friend. And although he was primed for a fight, lashing out at Kade to dispel his anger wasn't going to solve anything.

"Okay, I hear you. This whole thing has been pretty fucked up. Even guys who I thought knew me and thought were my friends are looking at me sideways.

"I've got too much to lose to take chances, and I took a big one coming here. I only did that because I know you're a standup guy and because we've been friends for so long."

Feeling awkward in the silence that followed, Kade said, "Just know I'm on your side.

"Look, I actually think this could be beneficial for both of us. I'll stay in the shadows while I work on the case.

"Maybe I prove myself, maybe not. But maybe, together, we find the truth, which is what I really think you want."

Jason didn't say anything.

"That's what I believe detective work should be, you know—a desire to find the truth.

"No preconceived opinions or notions of guilt, seeking whatever evidence can lead to the truth. Jason, with me on the unit, the good news is I'll be in a position to do just that.

"I'll have access to all the evidence… on both sides. And if things stall, I'll work your theories in until they play out."

Without waiting, Kade turned and walked into the kitchen, "I don't believe you're guilty. And we both believe the truth is essential.

"It'll be on me if I get caught helping you. But I don't think anything will come of it.

"You asked for help while I was off duty and in between positions. Besides, they know we're old friends and that we were partners. No bolo is out for you, so it's not like I've done wrong. If asked, I'll say that we've been looking for the truth.

"Hopefully, we'll find something before then, but if things go sideways, well, then I'll have to arrest you."

He turned to Jason, who had followed him into the kitchen, "Fair enough?"

Jason nodded. He had to admit that Kade made a good case, "I'm not sure you'll escape getting sanctioned even if you don't do anything outside department policies.

"I was worried about bringing you into it. I didn't want to ruin your career in case everything went to shit. But if you believe I'm innocent and you're willing to help, I could really use it."

"I do. I'm actually excited that we'll be working together again. And think about it – how often does a detective get to work both sides of a case like that?

Most of the time, we follow a few leads and try to build a case. If we're lucky, we stumble on more leads. A lot of time is spent questioning witnesses and suspects. We might make an arrest or two, but it can take months to get anywhere, and leads dry up fast.

"And even when you have the whole story, you need evidence to prove it in court. So, the way I see it, we're ahead of the game!

"I know your story, your theories, and we have some leads and the evidence you've collected.

"Come on, Jason, this will be fun. Take a risk and work with me!"

Jason was so relieved that he reached over and hugged his friend and said, "Thank you for believing in me, Kade. I really appreciate it."

Blushing slightly, unused to that type of expression of affection, "It's all good. Now let's grab a beer, and I'll make us something to eat."

As Kade put dinner together, Jason felt foolish for distrusting his friend and for getting so emotional.

The truth was it really didn't matter. If someone had to arrest him, he preferred someone trustworthy, even if the person was a friend.

***

Jason was still considering what he and Kade had talked about several days later.

Stryker sat quietly, his eyes and ears alert. His muscles tensed with anticipation, primed and ready for his next command. It was good to have his partner next to him.

Jason appreciated the eerie green glow of his PVS-14 binoculars, which made the darkest of night as clear as day.

Three more goons were added last week, doubling the security detail at the front of the compound.

It was relatively quiet on the west side, where there was usually activity at this time of night.

Since he'd been away, things had calmed down in that area.

Still, with all the security, it looked like something big was about to go down, and Jason wanted to record it.

He'd brought Stryker even though Becca had warned him that Stryker needed a little longer to heal completely.

But Jason knew that neither one of them would be happy if he left Stryker alone at the cabin. To ensure Stryker's paws were protected, he'd purchased heavy-duty Ruff Wear Grip Trex dog boots.

Stryker wasn't a fan, but his paws were protected.

As he scanned the area, Jason was distracted. His mind kept drifting back to Becca when he'd gone to pick up Stryker the night before.

He found her in the dog run with Stryker, Radar, and Scout, throwing a ball for them. When Stryker brought the ball to her, she checked his paw and ruffled his fur, praising him.

Jason had left Stryker with Becca much longer than planned because he'd been working on gathering evidence with Dean and Kade.

When she noticed him watching her, she called the dogs into the clinic to meet him and thumbed toward the clinic for him to join them.

Stryker ran to Jason, wagging his tail enthusiastically, and Jason kneeled to give him a big hug. "Hey, boy, I'm happy to see you too! Looks like you're doing a lot better."

Meeting Becca's glance, "And I'd bet real money you've been well cared for, too."

When Radar and Scout came over, he petted them as well. "Sure looks like you boys are having fun."

She used her annoyance to push aside the attraction she felt seeing him with the dogs. It was hard not to like the guy when he was being so sweet with them. Still, he hadn't bothered to call or check on Stryker, and she wasn't ready to let the irritation go just yet. "Well, I guess you finally remembered that you'd left your dog here. For the last few days, we wondered if he'd be a permanent resident."

His smile unnerved her and increased her pique. "I've got to say that I'm not used to patching up pets and having their owners abandon them. Didn't you receive any of our messages? Would you care to explain, or should I just get your extensive bill ready and send you on your way?"

He was still smiling, that seductive yet boyish grin that made her heart pick up speed.

Taking a calming breath, she wondered what it was about the man that irritated her so much. Anger wasn't a normal go-to emotion for her. Yet, with him, she was always set on simmer.

He hadn't said a word, which was only making her more uncomfortable. "Look, I'm sorry if I seem irritated, but I am. I think it stems from having too many of my boundaries crossed.

"Since we've met, you've interrupted my vacation, broke into my house, and left your dog in my care for an extended period without any explanation or contact.

"I'm not accustomed to owners abandoning their pets or behaving like… well… so inconsiderate. I find it troubling. So, before I release this poor creature back into your care, I think it would help to know what's going on."

She stood in front of him, hands on her hips, shoulders squared, her chin tilted up slightly in defiance, looking into his eyes.

Her hair was in a long French braid that ran down the middle of her back. Highlights shimmered in variations of browns and whisps of auburn every time she moved.

Her long, shapely legs were accented by hand-painted leggings, while a low-cut purple knit top wrapped around and tied with a bow at her waist clung, accentuating her breasts.

As she waited for a response, her eyes seemed to glow like fiery emeralds. He'd forgotten how beautiful she was.

Beauty, strength, and passion in one tight little package. If only he had more time.

When he finally shifted his stance to take a step toward her, he wasn't sure what to say, "I know you're right. I'm sorry. But it's a long story and difficult to explain. I wouldn't want to bore you."

"You've said that before."

"Yeah, okay. Well, at least I'm consistent." The goofy smile that usually worked wasn't working on her.

Changing tact, "Look, I do appreciate your taking care of Stryker. I wouldn't have been able to do what I needed to otherwise. I planned to check on him and would have if I wasn't out of range.

"Just tell me what I owe you, and I'll get out of your hair."

As he was talking, Becca noticed that he was holding his side. As he backed away, she saw that his shirt was darker in that area, as if wet.

A bit alarmed, she could tell that it was blood. She moved in to shorten the distance between them and lifted his shirt to inspect the injury.

A blood-saturated square of gauze was taped to his side. It was pulling away from the skin.

It was apparent he was sweating.

In a voice just above a whisper, she said, "What the hell?" Looking up at him with a deeply furrowed brow from a bent position, she asked, "What happened? Should I call the police?"

He pulled away to let his shirt fall back into place. He struggled with a response. He knew the wound had started bleeding again but had forgotten about it while watching Becca play with the dogs.

She was still waiting for an answer. Only now, with a hand on her hip and one eyebrow raised in question.

"Um…no, I don't need police. I just need answers, and they're proving harder to find than I realized."

Becca didn't understand what he was talking about, so she just waited, watching him pace back and forth like a caged animal.

"When I started this, I didn't know how convoluted it would be. Honestly, it's a long story."

Becca softened a little at seeing his distress.

The man was hurt, he needed help, and he was obviously in some kind of trouble. All she had to do was decide if she should help him. "Look, I'm not a medical doctor, but I can take a look and see if I can clean that up. While I'm doing that, you can tell me what's going on. A good story will help to distract us both."

He walked to the window and looked out. No one had followed him, and he really didn't want to leave. He was drawn to her.

Turning toward her, he resumed eye contact, "Okay. If you're willing, so am I."

With a smile that made his heart quicken, she said, "Just follow me."

They walked to her surgery, and she began gathering what she needed. She stopped in mid-stride when she turned around, her voice catching in her throat.

He had pulled off the soiled black and grey plaid flannel shirt, and for the briefest of moments, she could speak.

His chest was covered in black curly hair that trailed down a flat stomach under his waistband into intimate regions. He was a beautiful man.

Pulling her eyes away, "Please lay down on your side, injured side up."

As he got settled on the metal table, she reorganized the supplies to keep herself from staring.

"Like this?" He grimaced as he moved into position.

"That should be fine." The bandage was soaked. When she removed it to clean the wound, she looked up. "Jesus! This is a bullet wound!"

"It's okay, don't get excited, it just grazed me."

"That's not the point. Who shot at you? What the hell are you into?"

"It's not that big of a deal… really."

"You know, I'm supposed to report this."

"I know, but please don't. Just let me explain. But remember, it's a long story."

He stayed quiet for a moment until she gave him a short nod.

Swallowing hard, he blurted out, "My father died in an accident last November. Only it wasn't an accident. Not too long ago, I found out that he was murdered."

"Murdered! Oh, my God, I'm so sorry."

"Yeah. I've missed him a lot. He was an exceptional dad, and we were close, real close.

"But it's been even harder on my mom. She can barely leave the house. They had a marriage that most people only dream of.

"Anyway, she's never really said, but I think when she's doing things alone, things that they used to do together... it forces her to accept that he's not coming back.

"It must make her day seem empty… lonely." His voice softened, "It breaks my heart to see her like that. That's just not who she is."

For a moment, the memory of Sofia's bruised face came to mind.

"I pushed for his case to be reopened and long story short, they found evidence that his truck was tampered with.

"Then, in April, someone set me up for killing the guy who murdered my dad. And it's only gotten crazier from there. The beginning of some weird domino effect."

Becca stopped what she was doing to look at him.

"Look, I know what you're thinking. But if you want a cop, you're stitching one up on your table.

"Stryker and I work for Denver PD SWAT/K-9. That is, we did until that night in April. We've been in limbo ever since. I'm not sure where either of us stands now, but the department planned to put Stryker down, and I broke the law to prevent that."

"But why would they want to do that?"

"Like I said, a long story. I'm just giving you the key points."

"Okay, go ahead."

"Anyway, I'm trying to prove I didn't do it. You'd think it should be easy to prove your innocence, but it's not. And... well, that's my story in a nutshell."

Returning to her work without comment, he continued. "I've been reluctant to bring anyone into this. But the more I try to keep people out of it, the more they end up getting involved..."

"What I didn't know until recently was that my dad was working on his own investigation with the DEA. I found that tidbit in his notebook. It gave us our first real lead, and I'm grateful that he did that."

Finished with cleaning and prepping the wound, Becca grabbed a syringe and a suture kit. "Well, that is one hell of a story. So, your dad was a cop, too?"

"No, he was a plumber."

"Huh? A plumber?"

"Yeah. That's just one small segment that makes it all so convoluted. But it made more sense after I found his journals and tapes."

"Journals and tapes? Okay, obviously, there's a lot more to this story. Just don't forget to explain the part about how you got shot — grazed or not.

"I knew you didn't believe me when I said it was a long story. I'm trying to give you an abbreviated version."

The iodine made him grit his teeth against the sting. "Okay. Well, just keep talking. I'm going to numb the area — you'll feel a quick pinch or two, and then I can start sewing this up."

Using local anesthesia, she injected around the wound to numb the area. "I think a few stitches will help this heal faster."

Focusing back on his story, he continued, "I was at this compound in Central City, that's near Black Hawk, when..."

Becca froze. Every hair on her body stood up on end as a wave of dizzying fear rushed from the tips of her toes to the top of her head.

Was it possible that he knew that she frequented the area? She didn't believe in coincidences, and yet he'd been in the same location.

Could he be looking for the same people?

He was still talking, but she'd missed part of what he'd said. Pulling her focus back, she tried to concentrate on what he was saying.

"...I've been trying to find out what's going on inside the place. I might get some answers inside the compound.

"We believe it's a drug trafficking ring... a cartel right here in Colorado."

With the words drug trafficking and cartel, a loud crash interrupted him as the metal tray she was holding clattered to the floor.

She didn't realize she'd been shaking, or that her breathing had increased, or that she had begun to hyperventilate. For just a second, she stared at him in stunned silence, then, seeing the confused expression on his face, waved him to continue as she bent to pick up what had fallen.

"Hey, are you all right?" For just a moment, she'd looked pale, shaken, like something he'd said had knocked the wind from her.

When he started to sit up, she placed her hand on his shoulder to subdue him. "Everything's fine. I just had the tray too close to the edge. Sit still while I get this cleaned up and get a sterile kit so I can finish."

She could feel him watching her.

"But go on — finish your story, don't mind me."

She bent again, giving herself a few moments to gather her wits and calm her shaking hands before reaching for the syringe that had rolled under the table.

At the sink and while keeping her back to him so he couldn't see how shaken she was, she spoke over her shoulder, "A drug ring, huh? Sounds so dramatic, doesn't it? Where did you say this... uh, compound is?

"Central City near the border with Black Hawk. You know, near the casinos up there."

Becca fought the dizziness by holding onto the edge of the stainless-steel sink. Her blood seemed to run cold for a brief second as anxiety began its escalation.

Refusing to give in to the intensity overtaking her, she steeled herself against it. Only a tiny bit of sweat above her lip exposed the unpleasant sensations she was feeling.

Brushing the sweat away with the back of her hand, her back ramrod straight, she washed her hands and put fresh gloves on. Then, with a sterile kit, she returned to his side and settled herself. "Oh, that's right, you said that. Is that where you got shot? At the compound, I mean."

He hesitated for a moment, watching her. Something had changed, but he couldn't figure out what. He stubbornly countered, "I wasn't shot. A bullet just took some skin."

And feeling defensive added. "Look, the only reason I told you any of this was because you saw me bleeding, and I didn't want you to report it. I thought if I explained the seriousness of the situation, you might give me a break."

She realized that if she wanted to hear more of his story, she had to put him at ease. Make him relax so he'd share what he knew. And she desperately wanted to know what he knew.

So far, he hadn't indicated any knowledge of her connection to Black Hawk. If she could keep it that way, she just might gain some information without giving herself away. "Look, I'm not going to call anyone. From what you've said so far, it sounds like you've really been put through hell. I'm not obligated to call the police.

"But let's get real about this, okay? Whatever you'd like to call it — you were shot. Now, stop being so defensive. Sit still and let me finish while you tell me what happened."

He had to smile at her tone. And yet, he felt like something had changed. She hadn't made eye contact since returning to his side.

Watching her, he couldn't imagine what he'd said that might offend her, but he could sense she'd pulled away. Was she just trying to stay focused so she could work?

Jesus, why the hell were women so complicated?

Not wanting to make things worse, he picked up where he'd left off, "Okay. So, I made a mistake. A miscalculation is probably more accurate. I got too close to the compound.

"Usually, I keep my distance during the day. But today, I got too close because I saw that the warehouse was open and I wanted to see what they were doing.

"One of the guards saw me. He yelled at me, but I pretended like I didn't understand. I yelled back that I got turned around and needed to find the casino where my car was parked. That's when he swung his gun off his shoulder and took a shot at me.

"I don't think he meant to hit me, or I'd be dead. He probably just wanted to scare me off because he could have easily killed me if that's what he wanted.

"I ran but caught the heat from the bullet. I didn't realize that it caught some skin until later.

"I'm just hoping he didn't get a good look at me. I'll just have to be more careful from now on. I definitely can't afford any more mistakes."

Jason rubbed at the tension forming in his shoulders and neck from the weird position he was in.

He was getting antsy. Time was moving even while he was still, and he couldn't afford to waste it.

I need to regroup, check in, and see if there's any news. And yet....

Becca interrupted his thoughts, "Well, it sounds like you might want to stay away for a few days just to be sure they forget you."

She finished knotting off the last stitch and bandaged him up. "Okay, all done. You should be as good as new in a week or so. The sutures are designed to be absorbed as you heal, so you don't have to worry about having them removed. Still, you better keep a sterile bandage over the wound to avoid infection."

Wanting to know more, she offered, "I'm not sure if you have plans, but if you're interested, I was just thinking it's almost time for dinner. It might do you some good to relax and heal for a little bit.

"I was thinking pizza, and maybe you can tell me the rest of your story. It's intriguing. Mind you, the pizza is nothing special; it's just frozen, so I'd understand if you want to take a pass."

Her invitation quickly dispelled his worries about wasting valuable time. And when those big blue-green eyes looked up at him, his mind screamed, *accept already!* "That sounds great! I'm starving! Thanks."

At the house, the dogs took up valuable real estate on the kitchen floor, making it difficult for Becca to make dinner. After a few missteps, Becca snapped her fingers, pointed, and gave a one-word command. "Bed."

That was all it took to get Scout and Radar from underfoot. As they left the kitchen, Stryker followed.

"Impressive."

"Huh?"

"I was just admiring how well-trained your dogs are. You must spend a lot of time training them."

As she put the pizza in the oven and started making a salad, she replied, "It was easy to train them. They're smart, and the best thing about dogs is that they only want to please.

"Radar is a Goldendoodle mix. I got him from a shelter almost five years ago.

"Scout is a red merle Aussie. Purebred. I lucked into him a few years ago.

"Animal Control had discovered this horrible puppy mill just outside of Golden. They shut it down, but there were about thirty dogs on the premises. A few were dead, and several had to be put down.

"Scout was only a few weeks old and had been left in a filthy cage with his dead mother. Poor thing kept trying to nurse, but… well, anyway, he was starving."

"What a horrible way to come into the world."

"Yes, and unfortunately, it happens a lot with unregistered breeders who are only in it for the money. They have no conscience. They don't care what happens to the animals or the suffering they cause them. When they can't sell them as pups, they over-breed them, stuff them into small cages, and don't allow them to socialize or play… it's just horrible, completely inhumane.

"My friend, Charlie, works at Animal Control and contacted me to help out caring for some of the newborns.

"It's a monumental task caring for newborns if there isn't a dam available to nurse the pups. They need to be bottle-fed every two to four hours. It's a lot of work and requires commitment. Especially if you have more than one. When pups are that small, they're vulnerable to illness. And most people can't manage it. They just don't have the time to devote to that kind of care.

"I could only take five pups myself and one Golden mother. Her babies were stillborn because she was so malnourished.

"It worked out, though. After a week or so of eating well and moving around more, she regained some strength. It was encouraging. Especially after we realized that her body was still producing milk. We introduced the puppies, and she took over feeding them. She adopted the pups and took over their care. She was such a trooper. I named her Ellis – the benevolent one.

"Anyway, I was allowed my pick of the pups, and I kept Scout. He's been a true joy—one of the best dogs I've ever had, actually.

"The others grew up healthy and happy in the clinic until they were old enough to adopt out.

"My neighbor adopted Ellis. She's been very happy over there with his older dog, Sampson. They oversee and care for his other animals.

"She still visits from time to time, and Scout goes over to see her."

He couldn't help but watch her as she made the salad and set the table. Her movements seemed so fluid—graceful, like watching a choreographed dance.

While she described Scout and his adopted mother, he could make out the side view of a soft smile.

But when she looked at him, a glow of joy seemed to radiate from her eyes. "Dinner's about ready. Why don't you go clean up down the hall? Then you can tell me more of your adventures at the compound while we eat."

He found it difficult to speak, lost in the beauty of those kaleidoscope orbs.

CHAPTER TWENTY-FIVE

Running Out of Time

"Doctor, you still haven't said when your creation will be ready to reveal, and the committee will be here in only a few weeks.

"Your last discovery was over ten years ago. But our customers require something new to play with. This was to be our latest and greatest. You failed to have it ready last year, and I do not want a repeat of that humiliation. The time is here. I need to know it'll be ready this time.

"I cannot delay the gathering again. I want to surprise our friends at the feast—a little surprise to ensure their continued support and allegiance.

"So, tell me, Doctor, what's the hold-up?"

The Doctor knew that he wouldn't be able to stall any longer. To embarrass Morales for a second time in front of the committee would mean death.

Morales might find another chemist, but the Doctor wouldn't escape with his life if the Fat Man found someone with even half of his talent. Even if he somehow escaped, Morales would have him tracked down and slaughtered. Even worse, they would likely torture him first.

As the Fat Man droned on, the Doctor went to the window and looked down into the manicured garden, walking the pebbled paths with his eyes.

Each path was edged in rows of knock-out rose bushes.

The thick-thorned beauties were placed to deter wanderers from entering the lush, landscaped berms full of beautiful columbines, red-twig dogwood, hollyhocks, oakleaf hydrangea, coleus, purple smoke bushes, salvia, Japanese maples, and lavender.

The paths undulated through the garden to a large fountain at its center.

However, the true meaning of the garden's design could only be seen from that vantage point, and few understood the symbolism.

All paths seemed to lead to the fountain. The fountain represented the head of the monster: the undulating paths, the cephalopod arms of an octopus. Only with four arms instead of eight.

A subtle allegory of Francisco's four business interests: drug cartel, human trafficking, money laundering, and investments.

His favorite was his secret partnership with the casinos, where he could enjoy his favorite pastime, launder his money, and make a profit doing both.

While the Fat Man complained, the Doctor contemplated how he might plant his employer amongst the thorny treasures.

Visualizing that expansive mass thrashed and sliced with gaping wounds, with his eyes bulging from their sockets, forever in shock at the brilliant but shocking attack by his subordinate.

The doctor envisioned his employer's bloody and bruised body. Eviscerated -- his organs bulging from his immense gut to become nothing but a juicy banquet for beast and fowl, worms and beetles, larvae and spiders.

Even as the leaves from the dogwood trees fell with the touch of the fall wind, the flower's petals withered each day by the touch of winter's breath to build a discolored plush carpet amongst the leaves.

The Doctor only wished to add the Fat Man to the pile of rot.

The man's pontificating was becoming unbearable. He'd done his part, and it wasn't his fault that the drug wasn't ready. He needed another subject to test it, but he'd been denied what he needed once again.

How can I be expected to produce a product if I'm not provided with the tools necessary to complete the job? I need to ensure the product's viability, don't I? If this blowhard wants the product, he needs to provide more test subjects. It's as simple as that.

The Doctor had heard enough. His employer was under the misconception that what he did was a simple matter of mixing chemicals. But research and testing were just as important.

It was time to set his arrogant employer straight.

He resigned himself to the notion that if this was the end of the road, then so be it.

The wizard may have just cast his last spell, but his legacy would live on.

Turning to Morales, he simply lifted his hand to stop Morales from continuing with his diatribe. He rarely called his employer by his first name, but he had nothing left to lose. "Please, Francisco, allow me to correct a few misconceptions."

The Fat Man's eyes narrowed. The Doctor had never spoken to him in that tone or with that superior attitude, and he didn't like it.

Seeing the prize just out of reach was unbearable. He needed the man, at least for the time being. No matter what else came from this meeting, he needed that product in time for the summit.

Sitting back heavily on the springs of his executive chair, he picked up his glass of wine to cool his temper and spoke over the lip of his glass, "I'm listening."

"Three years ago, I came to you wanting to create a product that anyone could use without fearing detection. I needed capital, and you agreed to invest. I researched and spent months researching, then years, to make a perfect drug. But unfortunately, like anything worth all that trouble, it has taken longer than planned. I hoped to create a drug that would give the euphoric effects our customers desire without detection by regulated drug screenings.

"In other words, a brand new and perfect drug.

"Any chemist knows the ins and outs of the chemicals used to comprise a drug. But few can create a new drug. That takes more than a chemist; it takes a wizard!

"I'm a hair's breadth away from success. But here's the problem—you. You continue to undermine me. By refusing to supply my toys even though we'd agreed that this was part of my compensation, you have impeded my ability to finish my work. And by doing so, you have effectively obstructed the completion of my greatest creation.

"The very product you insist must be ready for the summit.

"You forget that my toys are not just for my pleasure. They are also the test subjects we require to ensure the product's viability.

"You know this, yet you rant at me as if I'm not doing my job.

"I've honored our agreement, and I believe that it's time for you to do the same. I can't understand why you would hold me back like this on this crucial step when we are so close.

"You know I can't complete my tests without subjects to test the product on, so why are you tying my hands?

"I fear that you are setting me up to fail, which doesn't make sense. But what would you have me do? Unveil an unsafe product? One that hasn't been tested and could prove deadly?

"Tell me, what is your recommended dosage?

"If customers start dropping like flies, your colleagues will lose business. If enough people die, the authorities might even trace it back to them, and that'll lead them straight to us. And even if it doesn't, do you think they'll be happy? I don't. I think they'll want to kill us. Are you willing to take such a risk so that you have something to show off at the gathering?

"I'm committed to the success of this product, but at this point, I have to ask—are you?

"Please tell me how you'd like to proceed. I'm at your mercy, and I can't go any further without testing the product.

And as you've just spent the last several minutes pointing out, we're running out of time."

***

Dean took Carl out for an excursion, as he called it.

It wasn't the typical meet-up with a street snitch, but Dean knew that if he could get Carl out of the city, he wouldn't be so twitchy or so influenced by his crew.

Dean hoped to learn something that could help them.

Carl might be a dealer, maybe even used sometimes, but there was a hurt, scared little boy hiding somewhere inside of him who just needed someone to listen to his story.

Dean took Carl to buy some clothes and insisted that Carl get a new coat. Since they were going to a lake Carl picked up a pair of swimming trunks with sharks on them and smiled. "Man. I can't even remember the last time I went swimmin'.

"When we was kids, we spent most of the summer at the apartment pool. Our uncle would act like a whale sometimes, give us rides on his back. Damn, them's was some good times."

The weather had cooled with the season, but Carl's boyish excitement and the goofy look on his face made Dean laugh. "Okay, dude, go ahead and get um. But mark my words, you're going to freeze your nuts off."

They picked up Kade, and within a half hour, they were fishing sitting comfortably next to the water.

After a few hours the early morning chill faded away and was replaced by a comfortable warm wind.

After his forth beer and second fish, Carl pulled off his hoodie and kicked back in his camp chair. With his new rod in the holder and a beer in hand, he was completely relaxed.

Dean looked over at Kade on the other side of Carl and signaled him that it was just about time.

While they relaxed on the bank with their lines in the water and beers in hand, Carl just talked about whatever came into his head.

As if a history was required, Carl started with a personal narrative, beginning with what got him into the life and how he wished he'd never tried ecstasy—one of the products he sold. "You know, I forget how it can be — clean, I mean. It's been a while since I had a day like this. I's got's to thank you guys."

And once he started talking, it was like the floodgates opened.

Dean and Kade sat back and let him talk, completely unaware and unprepared for what they were about to hear.

After a short pause, Carl seemed to go into a trance. His eyes became fixed on the horizon, and his face went slack. As he spoke, his whole body tensed like he was reliving the story he was telling.

At first, Dean and Kade didn't understand what he was talking about. He was rambling about his brother, where he lived, and how he'd gotten to be a dealer.

But when he mentioned something happening behind the gas station, both men sat up and paid closer attention.

He spoke slowly at first, like he couldn't find the right words. "So... it's like this. I'm just walkin' to my brother's to hang when I sees a cop. I hang back ‘cause, hell man, I don’t need no trouble, ya know? But then I sees it’s ol’ Colt.

Everyone down here knows him. One of the few cops treats us like humans, even when he slaps them there cuffs on, ya know.

“Uh... besides you guys, I mean.

“He’s checkin’ the door on that station and starts walkin’ down the side. Has his dog with him, too. He stops short when he sees these two guys doin’ somethin’ in the back. Has to be illegal cause Colt turns to his radio thingy, pulls his gun… and starts walking up to um.

“Now I know what’s about to go down, but I’m curious.

“Then I hears him yell at them to drop it. I couldn’t see what it was, but in a few minutes, it’s like all hell is breakin’ loose. One guy takes off, and ol’ Stryker goes after him.

“Then that other dude, he charges ol’ Colt and knocks him down. I’m thinkin’, oh no, you didn’t.

“But ba-bam…” Carl slaps his thigh, “…as soon as Colt hits the ground, he bounces up and haul’s ass after that little dude.

“First, I wondered, why’s Colt chasin’ the guy? He’s just a kid. But it ain’t no kid. ‘Twas that same small freak that came by asking after Billy.

“That’s the one with a greasy ponytail. The one I told you about.

“Geez, that dude is one sick mo-fo. You can almost smell it on him. Small but nasty-lookin’ with that long, greasy black ponytail. Shee-it! That guy gives me the willies.”

Swallowing the rest of his beer, he grabs another from the cooler, “Anyway, so they’re runnin’ right past, so I finds me a hidin’ spot cause I ain’t gettin’ in the middle of that shit. But I’m curious, so I kinda follow.

“It didn’t take long for the little dude to disappear. I tell ya, man, that little dude is a freak of nature! Just disappears into thin air.” Snap.

“Colt’s lookin’ everywhere, so I just heads for my bro’s place.

“It ain’t a few blocks, I hears a dog barkin’. Seems far off, but here comes ol’ Colt runnin’ like the devil’s on his heels right for me.

“I take off ‘cause, like I say, I don’t need no trouble.

“Now, mind. I run fast, but I don’t slow up till I’m far ahead.

“When I slow my roll, I light up to calm my poor nerves. My brother is waitin’, so I start his way about the time the dog barks again.

"And just a few blocks later, I'll be damned if I don't seem to be goin' the way Colt's headin'. Only now I'm scared, wonderin' what the fuck is goin' on. Like, is he after me or what?

"So, I's keeps to the dark and stay quiet. Dog barks, and soon I hears footsteps.

"Has to be Colt, right? But I'm downtown surrounded by all those big buildin', and I's has to hide, cause somethin' real bad has to be goin' down.

"Sun's down… streetlights ain't workin' so good… can't find no good place to hide. So I go behind this big ol' column lookin' thing. Figure I'll just wait till Colt passes and go another way to my brother's.

"I'm just about ready to come out of my hidey-hole when I hears ol' Colt runnin' down the street. But when I's sees him, I tell ya… I was like, what the?

"That boy didn't look good… can't say why exactly, but I ain't never seen him look like that. His eyes half closed, and his face… all red and sweaty.

"That's about when I see this other cop drivin' way behind goin' real slow like. So I stays put. I mean, he was movin' slow. I'm thinkin' maybe he's looking for me. Only I can't figure it… I ain't done nothin'."

Dean and Kade look at each other as Carl stops talking long enough to gulp down the rest of his beer. This was the first they'd heard of a third person -- and it was a cop.

Carl starts breathing fast, like he's scared, so Dean reaches into the cooler and pulls out a cold one. "Here, buddy, have another."

"Yeah, okay, thanks."

He takes a minute to guzzle more than half and says, "So, I'm thinkin', why ain't that cop picking up Colt? Givin' him a ride cause of all that runnin', he's got to be tired.

"I know he sees the boy, but no, he's just like pacin' him from way back.

"So, I'm like curious, ya know… like, what's this guy doin'?

"Takes a minute, but I wait till they pass. Then I follow, um. Only now, I'm way back.

"Colt slows way down and looks around. But before he turns around, the other cop parks real quick and kills the lights.

"I was goin' to stay put, but that ol' curious has me follow, um. And damn, if that curiosity shit didn't nearly get me caught. Only that cop has eyes on Colt, and I get by him.

"I stay in the shadows, but I keep watchin' that cop. I had to backtrack after I hears the dog someplace behind me. I finds me a place and I sees down that alley okay.

"That's about when Ol' Colt pulls his gun and starts movin' into the dark part of the alley.

"But then, it's like my eyes deceive me or somethin' cause I see that other cop pull this fancy-lookin' gun out of a case in his trunk. Let me tell you, it was one mother of a gun, too. Like nothin', I've never seen before. I'm thinkin', when did cops get guns like that?

"He starts runnin' toward that dark alley, and I'm thinkin', okay, it's goin' down. The cop must be goin' to help Colt with whatever's happenin'. I'm gettin' all kinds of excited. I can't help myself 'cause it's like I'm in the middle of a real-life TV cop show.

"I was creepin' out a bit keepin' to the shadows, trying to get a peek. And 'bout the time I try to cross the street, I see that cop standin' there. Fucker's hidin' in the shadows, but my eye caught him move. So, I back up before he notices, and I hide close enough so I can watch.

"But hell, you won't believe it. I sure didn't. But that cop raised his arm. I'm struggling with what I'm seein'. I can't be right, but I know he's gonna shoot Colt.

"I wait for a boom, but there ain't none. Barely a whistle… then this sick thunk sound. But whatever ammo it was, I sees poor ol' Colt falls off to the side like he'd been hit with a sledgehammer.

"I swear it took all his will—stopped that boy from droppin' straight to the ground, but he somehow keeps his feet.

"I had to cover my mouth with both hands so I don't make no noise. I move closer behind this cement thing.

"Poor Colt grabs for his neck, wobbly like… all unsteady like he's drunk. When he falls, he smacks his head but good on the ground. Cr-runch! God! A fuckin' awful sound and to see it bounce like that. Made me want to spew.

"When he stops movin', that cop walks up to him. Mind you, now, I can only see Colt's head and shoulders. The rest of him's behind that buildin', and that bad cop's blockin' whatever the fucker's doin'. But no doubt Colt's down."

Carl swigs the rest of the beer and doesn't notice when he misses the cup holder and the empty falls to the dirt.

"He's lying there, ice from the last storm still ain't melted, so I knows it's gotta be freezin' him cause I'm freezing my balls off and I ain't layin' on the ground.

"That bad cop walks over to Colt, but that ol' Stryker gets vicious and lunges. Then the bad cop yells and points that weird shooter, and poor Stryker falls down where I can't sees him no more neither.

"Now I'm thinkin' they both must be dead.

"The cop looks at somethin' in that hole I can't see. He's squatin' down next to Colt. Hear talkin', but I can't... can't make out what they're saying. Can't tell if maybe he's checkin' for a pulse or somethin' and talkin' to hisself.

"Looks like he's on Colt, only I can't tell what he's doin' to 'im 'cause he's bendin' forward like.

"Hand to God, I'm so freaked I can't move. I have no idea what to do.

"All a sudden, this other guy is hiding in the shadows, just appears out of nowhere. Only saw him 'cause he moved— saw im' out the corner of my eye. And I'll be a son-of-a-bitch if it ain't that little dude, and somethin's in his hand.

"I stay put. Watch that dude 'cause I don't know what else to do. Can't call the cops, 'cause they's already here.

"All I know is I can't feel my toes, and I could swear my balls have frozen right off. Worse, I feel like I need to pee, only I can't move so I stay put.

"And that cop, he's leanin' more where I can't see, and the next thing, BAM. It… was so loud...."

Carl's slurring his words, and his speech has slowed.

Kade and Dean stay quiet and wait.

"Made me drop flat.

"I'm shakin' so bad... scared that devil cop be comin' for me next.

"... I get ready to fly. Try to peek out. Only I hear footsteps, so I short-up, like real quick.

"I keep real still, and wait till it gets all quiet.

"When I peek again. Colt's on the ground, but the cop's gone. His car, too. That's when I take off for real. Only I stay in the shadows and go another way. And let me tell you, I don't think I've ever run so fast in all my days and..."

Carl stops for a minute shaking his head.

"... next day I learn it's ol' Billy got hisself dead. Was him… killed by that boom, in that alley hole.

"I thought that cop did ol' Colt too…made him dead.

"But then a few days later, I hear ol' Colt's alive. But that cop killed ol' Billy. It's sad ya know? No one cares. Not about no street scum.

"Still, I was happy Colt lived, but….

"Hey, I know y'all think I'm a junkie, but honest Abe, I just dabble sometimes. Never the big H. I ain't totally stupid.

"But ol' Billy messed me up real good givin' me that shit I gave you; ya know? I bet that's what got him dead...

"That's the reasons… I didn't want that shit I give you… coulda used that cheddar too.

"But no. No, thank you. I want no part of that shit. My life may be hard… okay. But after what happened to ol' Billy... that stuff comes with a... death sentence… I still want to be here… ya know?

His words came slower as his head tilted slightly to the side. "Might... be… it's time… to go straight, ya know?

"No, sir. I don't... be needin'... me none... of that shit."

After reaching for a beer that wasn't in the cup holder, "Sh-it yeah... okay... heard ol' Colt made it... Stryker too.

He paused for a minute, shook his head, "Man... gotta be like… some kind-a-fuckin'-miracle."

It was apparent that Carl was ready for a nap.

Before he could fall off, Kade jumped in. "Geez, Carl, that must have been rough, man… watching all that.

"Do you remember what the cop looked like? The one with the fancy gun? Like maybe his height or hair color, or maybe a tat?"

Carl thought for a minute with his eyes almost closed. "Ya know, there was somethin' kind of familiar bout that boy... a white boy for sure…

wearin' one of those…um…greenish… ya know… suit. That's 'bout all I remember."

Carl's eyes closed.

But just when he seemed to be asleep, they popped back open. "Hey, ya know, I think that bad cop? He had him a dog too… in his car… heard it whining when his door opened, and he got out."

As Carl dozed, Kade showed Dean the recorder on his iPhone.

He'd managed to record Carl's eyewitness account of the night in the alley.

The problem they faced now was that the truth required taking down a cop.

Hard enough to go to IA with concrete proof.

But especially difficult when it was a cop they couldn't identify.

CHAPTER TWENTY-SIX

The Warning

At the Denver PD Air Support Unit, under the large umbrella-like structures just outside Centennial Airport, Kade watched Dean and another pilot talking at the coffee kiosk.

Kade needed to talk with Dean alone. But even as early as it was, there was way too much activity. Kade wasn't part of the unit and had no excuse for being there, so he kept to the shadows to avoid being stopped.

After a few minutes, the other pilot put a lid on his cup of coffee and headed out toward the parked copters.

Dean was obviously in no hurry, which only intensified Kade's frustration.

Finally, after answering his cell and gathering his belongings, he headed out toward his rig. Kade positioned himself behind a wide girder, and as Dean walked by, Kade pulled him behind it.

Dean turned, ready to fight, until he saw Kade. "What the fuck are you doing, man?"

"Look, is there somewhere we can talk privately? I mean, no eyes or ears."

"What's going on, Kade?"

"We can't be seen together. Is there a place?"

"Yeah, mechanics aren't here yet; we can go into the hangar."

They moved to the back of the repair port, staying in the shadows. The aviation crew wouldn't be in for another hour, but Dean was scheduled to fly over Denver and give a report before then.

"Okay, so what's up? I've got to get goin' soon."

"Dean, I need you to get a message to Jason. I haven't been able to contact him. The detectives working on his case are looking for him. They have questions.

"They were working a big case that distracted them for a while, but now they want to talk with him, and they can't find him. He's not returning calls, and they're thinking he may have left the state.

"He said he was staying at your cabin. And I don't think they've clued into the connection, but if I'm right, he should probably move to another location for a while.

"Can you reach him? He must be out of range, or maybe his phones dead. I just wanted to give him a heads-up. They'll be putting out an APB on him if he doesn't make contact soon. And they're not the only ones. Billings has been asking a lot of questions."

Dean pulled the cap from his head and wiped his brow. "Why's Billings in it? He's not part of that unit. Is he working with the detectives to take Jason down? Do they have enough to arrest him?"

"Not that I can tell. I think they just need to ask some questions about things that aren't lining up, but they couldn't reach him. And with Billing's pushing like he is... well, I just don't think it's wise to wait until they put an APB out.

"They think the worst first and then react."

"Yeah, I know the type -- hot heads.

"Not sure what's Billing's beef is though. I thought he liked Jason. Doesn't make sense he'd sic the dogs on him.

"Okay. Thanks, Kade, I appreciate you telling me. I'll go find him after my shift."

Dean looked down at his shoes, unsure if he should ask. Then, making up his mind, he asked, "By the way Kade, I was wondering if you'd check something out for me."

"I can try, what's up?

Dean looked out of the hangar into the bright morning and sighed. "I'm not sure, that's it's a problem. And it might piss Jason off me askin', but you've met Jack Hanson? Goes by Jax?

"He's on K-9/SWAT with Jason. You might remember Jason saying that we met him overseas."

For a minute, Dean just looked out of the hangar, trying to figure out how to say what he wanted.

"Yeah, and... come on, Dean, what's up?"

"Okay. I'm just going to say it. I think something's up with that guy. Jason works with him, but I have a bad feeling about the guy. I just can't pin it down yet. Has he talked to you at all? I mean, asked questions about Jason's case or anything?"

Kade took a second to think about it until the hairs began to rise on the back of his neck, remembering the conversation he'd had with Jax the week he started on Homicide. "Son-of-a-bitch! I wondered why he sought me out. I thought he just came to congratulate me on my promotion. Son-of-a-bitch!"

Kade began pacing back and forth as he talked. "He took me out to lunch, celebratory, like. But while we ate, he asked about Jason. If they'd found anything new to exonerate him, questions like that. That SOB pumped me for information. I can't believe it! I should have followed my gut.

"I disregarded the feeling I had... but figured he was just concerned about our friend. Trying to be supportive, like maybe seeing if there was anything he could do.

"Damn, I felt something was off, but shit, man, he's a cop! And I thought he was Jason's friend! Who suspects a cop, right?

"I was thinkin' that the more people we had to work on clearing Jason, the better. Geez, I let my guard down with the dude. For fuck's sake, just tell me how big of a chump was I?" Kade asked.

"Don't stress on it, Kade; Jax has always been different, detached. He's not like us. But he's supposed to be one of us, right?"

"I had the same experience. But I just blew off how I felt because he was a cop and a friend of Jason's.

"Jason said that they weren't all that close, but they did train together. So, I thought there had to be a bond there. I didn't want to cause friction and say anything against the guy.

"The problem is I can't pin it down. It's not anything specific. Well, maybe that's not entirely true. It's like he's not really who he seems to be. I don't know how else to explain it. That's why I thought you might want to look into him. I don't really have much.

"Except... maybe... I saw him while I was at headquarters, and we started talking. Only he said some stuff that made me question what he was playing at. He changed his tune pretty quick… said he was kidding, but it sure didn't seem that way. I was really put off by it."

"Yeah, okay. And after my lunch with him, I'd have to say your feelings are justified. I'll do some research on my end and see what I dig up.

"I'll have to be careful; they monitor my computer, especially with personnel files, so I'll have to try another way."

"Look, here's my burner phone number. If you have any problems, don't hesitate—just call."

***

The night couldn't have been more perfect for what Jason had in mind. The sky was clear, the air crisp, and a hunter's moon lit the sky, giving off just enough light to make it easy to move through the brush without his night gear.

Fall, in all its glory had painted the landscape in red, orange, purple, and gold.

Stryker's little vacation with Becca had done him a world of good. He was his old, playful self, and at his last post-op, Becca declared his paw healed.

Stryker still needed shoes to protect his feet, but Jason no longer had to worry that the wound would reopen or get infected.

Dean had secured all of the evidence in the Adams gun safe, which made them all feel more secure.

Charles thought it best that Jason continue to stay at the cabin but keep the evidence with him. Attorney-client privilege protected everything Jason shared, including the evidence they'd collected.

Charles had spoken with Ron Tomas, the chief of the Denver Police Department. He explained that some new evidence had come to light that might exonerate Jason. He asked the chief for a little more time while they tracked down someone they thought might be a witness to what happened that night.

Billings had received the information Colt had sent him and supported giving them a little more time.

The detectives' investigation had taken longer than expected, and they still didn't have enough evidence to charge him.

The chief agreed that Jason could remain on administrative leave for the time being as long as he stayed in contact with the detectives.

Since Jason was in constant contact with Charles, Desiree kept Sofia informed so she wouldn't worry about Jason's absence, while Charles kept a protective eye on everyone.

They were all feeling the pressure of time slipping through their fingers.

It was up to Jason to find the evidence. And fast.

CHAPTER TWENTY-SEVEN

The Catch

Jason sat in the dugout waiting for nightfall, listening to the light rain that made hollow plopping noises on the thick-leafed roof of his little dwelling.

The drizzle had been intermittent throughout the day, saturating the ground. But Jason had remained warm and dry inside the little foxhole.

Stryker napped comfortably, even outfitted in his tactical lift harness. They'd practiced the drill several times, and Jason felt confident that Stryker would be ready when the time came.

Jason checked his gear for the third time, making sure he had everything he needed: ropes, carabiners, a folding grappling hook, a headlamp, two flashlights, the satellite phone Kade gave him, a walkie-talkie, the lock picks his father gave him, the plat maps Dean found, and Knipex bolt cutters to cut the chain link fence.

To keep his hands free, he wore a tactical helmet that supported his PVS-14 and a GoPro camera. The camera was linked to his iCloud account, which saved the real-time images.

That would let Dean and Kade see what was happening too. As long as they could get a signal.

For protection, he had a small arsenal: his Ka-Bar knife attached to his belt, a Sig Sauer P-226 strapped to his right ankle, a Glock 19s similar to the one issued by the department strapped on his thigh, and an M&P 9mm Luger Smith and Wesson in his rucksack.

Satisfied that he had everything he'd need, he went over the plan once more in his head.

Tonight was the night. They'd thought of every possible contingency. The plan was good. He'd run operations like this when in the military.

Dash had signed on for an overtime shift and would be in the air most of the night. If anything happened, Dash could be at the compound in less than ten minutes. It would feel like a lifetime, but the copter would provide backup and a quick escape.

Watching the compound for hours on end was boring. It was hard to stop his mind from wandering. It kind of bugged him that it had been five months since the night in the alley and just over ten since he lost his father.

Reflecting back, Jason realized how much he'd been given in his life.

He'd never considered how lucky he was until it was all taken from him. Losing his father, his mom's assault, almost losing Stryker, and now facing the possibility of losing the job he loved and possibly his freedom had woke him up to acknowledge his good fortune.

Recognizing how ungrateful he'd been was a bitter pill to swallow and he felt contrite for his arrogance, and for how he'd taken the people in his life and the opportunities he'd been given for granted.

Life is precious, if not all too short.

He finally got that. He finally understood that the love of his family and friends were life's gifts. And the moments of joy experienced with those gifts, were a bonus not to be taken for granted.

The losses he'd suffered were painful, but thankfully, he'd gotten the message and was all the more grateful.

It was time to accept that things would work out when and how they were meant to. He had no control over any of it, but he hoped that something would release him from the nightmare that kept him frozen in limbo.

But even with his name cleared, nothing would bring Matt back.

The honorable man who'd taught him what being a man truly meant, was gone.

And since that day, Jason hadn't had time to grieve.

It was impossible to accept that his dad would never again walk into the kitchen and playfully chase his mother around the island, take Dean and Kade with them to a Broncos game, teach them how to fix their trucks, or take them water rafting, dirt biking, or fishing.

And what about their family gatherings with the Adams? They were all so close. Jason had never realized how sheltered he'd been inside that little group. The barbeques, the summers at the cabin, the celebrations, the vacations, and all the swim parties growing up.

All the fantastic times they'd had together.

Since Matt's death, there'd been a lot fewer get-togethers and no celebrations. More loss that seemed to swallow him whole when he thought about it.

Feeling inadequate. Knowing all he could do to honor his father's memory was to be the man he'd been taught to be, didn't seem near enough.

He had to find the person who ordered his father's murder.

Jason mentally shook himself. It was almost time for the switch. Jason closed his pack and pulled out his gear from the hideaway. Crouching down, he waited for the guard change that would keep them busy while he made his way into the compound.

He checked his watch, making his way toward the southeast corner of the property.

Five more minutes.

***

She'd been working at her desk since he arrived.

Her attention was riveted on whatever she was doing. Only a single desk lamp and the glow from the laptop illuminated her soft features as the sun blanketed everything around them in darkness.

He'd managed to disable the automatic lights before dusk when they could be activated by motion.

The dogs had eaten the tranquilized meat and were sound asleep in the large cages that had been provided to him in the training yard.

With those chores completed, he had plenty of time to study her.

Her focus was so intense on what she was doing that she didn't seem to sense his presence.

Standing hidden behind the large pine that stood just outside of the dog run, he had a good view of her in the office. He wondered if she realized that she was on display sitting in front of the large picture window at her desk.

The light inside the house would make it hard for her to see him coming out of the darkness.

For a moment, she sat back in her chair and looked directly at him.

In that fleeting moment, he saw a ghost.

Ice ran down his spine, making the hairs stand on his neck, head, and arms.

Impossible!

He was stunned, shocked, really. *A twin? A duplicate?*

Joss had never mentioned a sister, let alone a twin.

He hadn't seen her face until that moment. Didn't even have her name. The truck was registered to a business. He had come because he needed to find out who she was, what she was after... what she knew.

Then he'd simply make her disappear.

He watched her expression change as she appeared to struggle with something she was working on. Lines had furrowed her brow, and she was pursing her lips.

He was quickly reminded of Joss. And was quickly reminded of the fun they'd had until she'd stumbled onto his stash. The day he'd been forced to manage the situation.

Just like he would do with her twin now.

Still, she'd been one of his favorites. A beauty and one of the few women he'd had in a long time that could satisfy him in bed.

It made him wonder if her twin would be as good.

Then, the double in the window stretched as if on cue. Stretching her arms high over her head, arching her back, lifting her breasts high enough for him to admire the hard peaks pushing against her top.

The pose was all the more seductive because the show was just for him.

A longing began in his groin, rubbing the bulge; he thought if she stretched any longer, he'd have to satisfy himself right there.

But since she immediately resumed her work, he instead considered the ways he might enjoy her before killing her.

***

After the day's events, Becca tried to focus on the clinic's books, but it was proving difficult since her thoughts kept going back to her discovery.

Although she'd easily entered the weeks' timecards into the payroll system, she kept getting stuck on the quarterly business taxes. No matter how hard she tried, she just couldn't focus. Finally, giving up, she decided that it was time to hire a bookkeeper.

Ugh! Throwing her pen on the desk, she rolled back from the desk and half-reclined, crossing her ankles on top of it. When she looked out the window, she was surprised to see that night had fallen.

Staring into the darkness, she thought about what she'd uncovered. No wonder she couldn't concentrate. She'd just discovered that a cop had killed her sister.

But how would she be able to prove it.

It had been hard enough to find evidence when he was just - some guy. But now that she knew he was a cop, it seemed impossible. Hopeless.

That afternoon, when she'd followed Mark, he'd driven to an out-of-the-way building in downtown Denver by way of the side streets.

He parked near a one-story building hidden from the street in the back corner of a parking lot behind a high-rise. It didn't look official. In fact, there was nothing special about it. It was dark brown and unmarked. No address or business name that identified it.

The front of the building was hidden mainly by an overgrown brush. The front door was concealed in dark shadow made by a trellised overhang.

Out front and to the side of the entrance were oversized truck tires angled against, and slightly on top of each other in front of a chain link fence.

If it weren't for the four DPD patrol vehicles parked nearby, its purpose might have remained mysterious.

She watched him go through an unmarked door into an unmarked building. Later, coming out in a jumpsuit uniform with a large dog, he walked to an empty lot at the far end of the parking lot.

It took a minute to register that she'd stumbled onto a police substation and that Mark was a cop.

It was a revelation that made her head spin.

Since she was in disguise, she thought it was a good time for a face-to-face meeting. So, quickly grabbing her cane, she wrote an address she knew nearby on a piece of paper and began to meander around the parking lot, trying to look lost.

Once he began walking back toward the building, she made sure to wander into his path.

As he saw her, he gave the dog a command. When the dog sat, she said, "Excuse me, young man, but can you please help me? I have an appointment, and I'm late. I've gotten myself all discombobulated."

He replied, "Sure. Do you know the address?"

She gave him the paper, and as he was preoccupied with it, she read the name on his jumpsuit: J. Hanson. *What the hell?*

While preoccupied with giving her directions, she did her best to note his features. It was Mark, all right, only the name on his jumpsuit wasn't Payton as he'd told Joss. It was Hanson.

So, who the hell are you, she wondered.

Pointing to the north, he said, "You just turned in a little too soon. You want to go another block, and it should be on your right."

"Well, thank you so much. I was getting myself all mixed up. By the way, I see the name on that tag says: J. Hanson. If you don't mind me asking, what is the J for?"

He chuckled. "Oh, yeah. We use our last names while on duty." Reaching his arm out to shake her hand. "I'm K-9 Officer Jack Hanson… happy to help, mam."

Gently touching his hand as an old woman might, she said, "Well, aren't you polite? And you can call me Lily. I'd like to think I'm too young to be called mam though."

With a shy smile, she turned away before he could see through her disguise and said, "Well, I best be going before I forget the directions you gave me. You take care now."

Using her cane, she made her way to an older model Prius in the middle of the parking lot. Far enough away that he wouldn't spot exactly which car she'd gone to.

At the driver's door, she fiddled in her purse as if looking for a key. Keeping her head down, she watched him walk back under the shadowed overhang.

After a few minutes, she closed her purse and walked to her truck, whispering in a biting tone, "Okay, Jack Hanson, aka Mark Peyton, aka Mr. Policeman, what's your game? Because one way or another, I'm going to figure it out, and I'm going to take you down."

***

The surprise mixed with fear that flashed across her face when she realized he was standing in her hallway was exhilarating enough to make him hard in an instant.

But when the color drained from her face, his excitement was replaced by discomfort.

He'd seen that look before. It was the same look Joss had in those last few moments before she died. Trepidation, sure, but also something more condemning — disgust.

When fear settled over her features like a black cloud, it was time to take control. He tried to smile one of his boyish grins, but the hunger of desire still burned in his eyes.

Her response told him that he appeared more evil than attractive.

Becca immediately realized the huge mistake she'd made taking her truck when the Toyota wouldn't start. In fact, if that look was any indication, it might have been her last mistake.

The man was obviously disturbed.

As she searched the room for a weapon, the 3D crystal paperweight sitting just out of reach on her desk caught her eye. A photo taken during their last family vacation the summer before Arianna died was laser-etched into the crystal.

A remembrance of a happy family moment - frozen in time.

Becca's heart sank at the thought of desecrating that beautiful, intimate moment—until she looked up and noticed the bulge in his jeans.

He wanted to wipe the hateful expression from her face. It was totally out of place, like a tear on a clown, it just didn't belong.

Then he saw it, a shift in her demeanor and attitude.

She squared her shoulders and lifted her chin as if preparing to go into battle. Her tone was gruff when she said, "How did you get into my house, and what do you want?"

His smirk was infuriating.

The transformation from damsel in distress to warrior woman was comical. *Who did she think she was anyway?*

She had to accept that she was at a distinct disadvantage.

Then, in a more worried tone, "What have you done to Radar and Scout? Where are they?"

He saw the fear return to her eyes as she realized that her dogs hadn't come in from their little tête-à-tête playing in the yard.

He replied with a boyish grin. "There's nothing to worry about; they're just taking a little nap and will wake soon. But we'll be gone by then."

He watched as her face quickly changed from concern for the dogs to anger. Her raised brow furrowed. Her jaw tightened, and one side of her lip curled up.

But it was the intensity of her eyes that was most disarming. As her eyes squinted, the colors darkened, and the kaleidoscope patterns shifted.

If looks could kill, he thought, *I'd surely be dead.*

"I'm not going anywhere with you. Why are you here? Why are you doing this?"

He could see her eyes search the room and knew she was seeking a weapon or maybe a way she might escape.

He could even smell it... the desperation. But that only excited him more.

Before she did something stupid to ruin his plan, he changed tactics. Smiling, he walked over to an overstuffed chair conveniently placed in a small nook at the entrance to her office and sat down.

He was amused by how the colorful chair hugged the corner, placed perfectly so that his long legs would easily block her exit. Thus, the simple placement of a chair had sealed her fate.

Resting his booted ankle on his knee, he said, "I wonder if you understand how impolite it is to spy on people—illegal even. And by the look on your face, you understand your mistake.

"I have to admit that your disguise was impressive. I would never have suspected an old lady. I rarely even look at them.

"An excellent job with the makeup, by the way. Even though we were within arm's reach on two occasions, I didn't see the cracks in the disguise. And I'm trained to look for deception.

"Yes, very impressive."

He stretched out his legs.

"It was a risk approaching me at the substation. A big mistake I'm afraid. I'm surprised you took the chance.

"Well, actually, you made two mistakes. The first was believing that I wouldn't recognize the old woman I'd recently encountered at the casino. The second was giving me an opportunity to watch you drive away."

She was very expressive, and her look of surprise made him chuckle. "I know. You thought I didn't recognize you. You thought I'd gone inside, didn't you?

"I have to admit it took a minute to place where I'd seen you. If you hadn't looked familiar, I might not have given the encounter a second thought.

"But you were familiar, and that's why I observed you from the shadows.

"That old lady act almost got me—almost.

"The part where you hobbled around on that cane was a decent depiction. You acted the part perfectly so I must applaud the effort.

"But seriously... spying on a cop? Don't you realize the dangerous game you've been playing?

"It's okay, you don't have to answer."

He smiled and shook his head as he jeered. "Oh, and when you tried to throw me off by searching in your purse by that sedan… like you owned it. Okay, now that looked pretty legit. In fact, at that point, I was almost convinced that seeing you again might just be a coincidence.

"So, it was a good thing I waited, huh? Because minutes later, after you assumed I'd gone inside, the old lady was transformed and no longer required the cane for support!

"Man, that was some transformation.

"I witnessed a miracle!

"I'm sure every woman over fifty would love to have that trick.

"Still, what really sealed your fate was watching the way you jumped into the truck. That's where you blew it… wouldn't you say?

He didn't wait for an answer.

"It's a shame that you didn't get into that sedan. I would have never figured it out."

Shaking his head, "A monumental mistake. After I saw that, it was just a matter of running your license plate and wallah - here we are."

Apparently, he liked to hear himself talk. So, while he prattled on, Becca worked on coming up with a plan.

"At first I was surprised. I mean, it was kind of odd. I'm a man - but not just a man - a cop. It never occurred to me that a woman would stalk me. It would just be too... ridiculous.

"I could see maybe some sicko I arrested, but a woman? No. Women aren't good at that kind of strategy. And really, what possible motive would a woman have?"

I could think of a few. Becca thought.

"I had my theories, mind you. All the way here, I wondered if you might be a PI or an old lover. I even considered whether my uncle was having someone check up on me.

"It wasn't until I saw your face in that window that I began to understand that your game is basic.

"Vengeance, pure and sweet.

"For your sister's murder, I presume.

"I can understand that. Just recently, I was able to mete out some vengeance of my own. And revenge did taste sweet.

"When I first saw you, it was a bit of a shock, like seeing a ghost, really. I just couldn't believe my own eyes until it registered that you're Joss's identical twin.

"Although it might make you sad to know that she never bothered to mention you. I guess you weren't that close."

The insult was meant to slap her into submission, but it only made Becca angrier.

"But the initial shock soon passed since the last time I saw Joss... well, she was dead."

But that remark, even though it validated that he was Joss's killer, made her want to vomit.

When she glared at him with eyes narrowed and her mouth set in a firm line, he knew he'd hit a nerve. Now, he just needed to get what he came for.

Laughing outright, he continued, "It's only fair. I mean, now that I've figured out your reasons, you need to share the rest—winner takes all, as they say. And you must play fair. I've obviously won our little cat-and-mouse game. It's time to concede. Becca, is it?

“What the hell do you want?”

“It’s pretty simple, really. I want to know what you’ve been up to. You know, the details.

“What you’ve been able to uncover about me and my uncle. Oh, and the names of anyone you might have told.

“I swear, if you just tell me the truth, I’ll make it easier for you. Quicker even.”

“Make what quicker?”

“Oh, I’m sorry. Isn’t that obvious?”

CHAPTER TWENTY-EIGHT

A Change of Plans

While the guards were busy with their shift change, Jason signaled Stryker to follow him through the brush toward the southeast corner to cut the chain link.

But as they moved down the fence line, he saw headlights enter the narrow dirt road leading to the staff gate.

Jason signaled Stryker to get down and squatted low beside him.

Thinking it was one of the staff returning home from a night out, he waited to see if he might take advantage of the situation.

There was the possibility that he might be able to follow behind the vehicle. Regardless, there was no point in rushing. Once inside, he'd have to wait for the driver to get settled into the cabin before he entered the compound.

Moving through the brush to get closer to the gate, Jason managed to duck out of sight just as a truck drove past them.

Jason's heart dropped, then quickly accelerated.

The jacked-up black Ford F-150 crew cab with chrome accents was too familiar. Momentarily stunned, he tried to comprehend why that truck would be entering the compound and how the driver would know about the staff gate.

The truck stopped at a control panel, and a man's bare arm reached out of the driver's side window. The rolled shirt sleeve revealed a familiar tattoo on the forearm, removing any doubt about the identity of the driver.

The eagle, globe, and anchor – was an unmistakable insignia.

However, Jason had only seen that symbol, with that much detail, in red and blue colored ink, tattooed on one person.

He could picture it, in its entirety. With the eagle's wings spread protectively over the globe. In its mouth, a ribbon undulated in the wind with the words 'semper fidelis' emblazoned across it. Along with a large anchor loosely wrapped in rope clutched in the eagle's claws.

Under it all, in large, sharply pointed barbed text that speared the lower part of the trailing ribbon was written, USMC est. 1775. The year the Marine Corps was founded.

Jason had seen it so many times during training that he could draw it from memory.

It wasn't uncommon for a soldier to have a tattoo representing his service. But there was just no mistaking the detail on that tat.

There was only one like it, and it was tattooed on Jack Hanson.

Jason felt his body break out in a cold sweat.

Dean had been right about Jax all along. The question was, how big a part did he play?

Jason swallowed hard. *How did Jack get involved in this shit? He's a cop for fucks sake! If Jack is involved with this compound and its producing drugs, then....*

It hit him like a punch in the gut. ... *then, could Jack be part of the hell we've all been put through? Could he be involved with what happened to Dad?*

Feeling sick, *Oh my God—could he be the one who ordered the hit on my Dad?*

Lost in thought and having a very unpleasant physical response while connecting Jack, Morales, and Matt to his own nightmare, Jason almost missed the opportunity to follow the truck in through the gate.

***

Stryker's deep-throated growl pulled Jason back to the present. The hard realization that Jax was associated with Morales had temporarily dazed him.

But now he was even more determined to get answers. To know what Jax was up to and why.

The truck moved slowly through the gate as if the driver wanted to keep things as quiet as possible. Jason signaled for Stryker to follow him closely through the brush, staying low and away from the mirrors so Jax wouldn't see them.

At the gate, Jason signaled Stryker to sit while he made sure it was safe to enter the compound. Once he cleared it, he signaled Stryker to follow him just as the gate began to close.

The truck turned southwest, moving through the interior gate to the small warehouse.

Something was wrong.

When they were kids, Jason and Dean called it spidey-sense, just like one of their favorite comic book characters.

While Jason's mom insisted that it was his natural intuition.

All the cabins were dark. Most of the glaring lights that turned on at dusk to light up the transport section of the compound had been extinguished.

Only one bright post light at the far corner of the shipping containers remained on.

The absence of activity and noise was even more eerie when combined with discovering Jack's involvement.

Staying in the shadows, ducked down low, Jason scanned the area as he and Stryker followed the truck.

Cross-fencing separated the cabins from the warehouse area. A thick line of pine trees on the warehouse side obscured the cabin's view, which made it easier to stay out of sight once they'd passed through the entrance.

Using the pine closest to the gate as cover, Jason watched as the truck stopped in front of the side door.

When Jax exited the truck and walked around the back to open the passenger-side door, Stryker growled.

Jason had a good idea why Stryker didn't like Jack but wondered how long Stryker knew what had been going on. *Too bad dogs can't talk.*

For a minute, Jack seemed to struggle with something inside the truck.

He lifted something long over his shoulder. When Jason saw what it was, it stole his breath.

Stryker's growl was deep. Although the sound was a good barometer of Jason's rage, he knew the stakes were too high and quickly signaled Stryker to be silent.

With a tight throat, he patted Stryker on the head and forced down the emotions that had started to percolate. For the first time in his life, he understood how quickly the desire to kill could replace a reasonable thought.

In that moment, he was compelled to pull his gun and kill the bastard. The problem was that he didn't have a silencer, and without one, the sound would wake the residents.

Plus, he might accidentally hit Becca.

Still, it took every bit of self-control he possessed to stay in check.

Looking around for an answer, the situation seemed impossible.

Seeing Becca slumped over Jack's shoulder in a fireman's carry, her hair covering her face, and her arms limp and hanging down Jack's backside, Jason struggled with the primal urge to kill.

Even if he could sneak up and take Jack out, he would never take the risk of Becca getting hurt.

Jax punched a code into the keypad next to the side door and went into the building.

Before the door could close, Jason ran, managing to pull off his glove and catch the door just before it closed.

The glove prevented the bolt from sliding into the striker plate and locking him out by stopping the bolt from engaging the lock.

He was trying his damndest to stay calm. He needed to think, so he didn't put Becca in more danger.

He held his breath and counted off the minutes.

Before entering the building with Jax, he needed to think things through and let the others know what was happening.

Staying between the building and the truck, he opened his pack to grab the walkie-talkie.

As he clicked the button to speak, it hit him.

The scene of the alley filled his vision, and before he knew it, he was reliving that night.

Running—trying to call for help.

Lost in the dark.

Reaching for his mic.

Pffft—he's shot.

Spinning.

On the ground—shivering.

Stryker's down.

Voices—boom—footsteps.

Frozen in time, precious minutes pass.

Fear attempting to keep him captive.

It didn't help that it was dark in the compound or that he was on the ground.

He had to break the spell. Shake it off.

Remembering. Taking deep breaths… *in... and... out... in... and... out... in... and... out... okay, that's better.*

There was no more denying it. He'd suffered a trauma, and that was the PTSD flashback the therapist had warned him about.

The flashback really does take over the mind. But fuck, I don't want to go through that again. One way or another, I'm getting rid of this shit, even if I have to go back into therapy.

Regaining control, he sat up and grabbed the walkie-talkie from the discarded rucksack and turned down the volume.

It wasn't just his life he had to worry about. He had to save Becca from whatever Jack had planned for her.

How could Becca possibly know Jack? Jesus, did he kidnap her? It doesn't make sense. Why jeopardize everything? Kidnapping?

She was obviously out cold. For fuck's sake, what is Jax thinking? And why Becca? Did he follow me to her place? Has he done this before? If he's lost it, I'm not sure we'll get through this.

This new dilemma had changed everything, or rather, Jax had changed Jason's plans by going after Becca.

She had to be his immediate concern now.

Afraid to make any noise, he used Morse code to send messages to Kade and Dash and waited for the two-key response that indicated that his message had been received.

Minutes passed.

Painfully slow, feeling more like hours.

He fought the growing apprehension.

But finally, he decided that if they didn't respond soon, he might have another flashback, which would delay his ability to help Becca.

Unable to wait any longer, Jason slowly opened the door just enough to look inside. The pitch-black interior made it risky to enter, but he stepped blindly through the door into a small glassed-in vestibule with Stryker on his heels and turned on his PVS-14.

He was in an antechamber separated from a larger room beyond by a glass wall.

The area appeared sterile.

A bench ran the length of the wall, three lab coats hung on hooks, shoe covers, and nitrile gloves in boxes on a shelf, and a self-closing hazardous waste can; nothing else was in that small space.

The glass wall held a sliding glass door that allowed entrance from the vestibule into the main area.

Opening the slider, Jason moved into the main chamber with his gun drawn. The expansive room was a fully equipped research laboratory.

He'd never seen anything like it. It could even compete with the crime lab at DPD.

The place was more than big enough to hold all the microscopes, centrifuges, glassware, burners, hot plates, stirrers, incubators, and ovens, along with a refrigerator and countertop machines with space to spare.

As he walked further into the lab, a glow of light caught his attention from the main entrance to his left, which had a similar vestibule setup to the side entrance.

He made a mental note two exits were always better than one.

A door stood slightly open just off to the right in front of him. A light could be seen through the opening.

It was too quiet behind the door. It unnerved him.

Where's Jax? Does he know I'm here? How many rooms are in this place? Where's Becca? Is she okay? Is this a trap?

Jason signaled Stryker to hide.

It was a new game they'd been playing for the last few weeks. Jason would call Stryker only if he needed him, and until then, Stryker knew to wait.

As he pushed the door open enough to view the entirety of the room, he saw Becca duct-taped to one of the chairs. The back of the chair was against the desk, and she was facing him, but her eyes were closed.

Her hands were secured with duct tape to the arms of the chair. Her ankles were taped to the legs. Her knees were bent outward in a very unladylike position that would have exposed her femininity if she hadn't been wearing leggings.

She was out, slumped awkwardly in the chair so that her head rested on the back. Her face tilted to the side.

She looked horribly uncomfortable.

Jason felt the heat of anger burn up his neck into his face when he saw the red, swollen area under her left eye, and just to the side of that was a half-moon cut on her cheekbone.

Taking deep breaths to swallow his anger, he told himself that the red swelling would subside and turn into an ugly bruise, and the cut would heal hopefully without leaving a scar.

She was breathing, and that was all that mattered.

He turned off the night vision but left the video running, set the helmet on his pack, and kneeled next to Becca.

He didn't know where Jax was. He couldn't hear him moving around, but he knew he would return soon.

That meant Jason had to get Becca out fast.

He shook her shoulder, whispering, "Becca, wake up. We need to get you out of here."

Grabbing his knife, he began cutting her bindings, doing his best to be careful not to cut her tender skin tightly pressed into the tape. Working to cut her hands free first.

He could see her effort, but the drug was heavy on her, and she slipped back into unconsciousness.

He whispered, "Come on, open your eyes; come on now, Becca, you can do it."

When he bent down to release her feet, she started moaning softly, and he looked up and said softly, "It's all right. I'm here. You just wake up.

Not deterred, he resumed working on the bindings around her ankles. They were even tighter than the ones on her wrists, which made them even more difficult to cut away without cutting her.

Once he released her, he wasn't sure how he'd fight his way out of the compound while having to carry her, but he was determined to find a way.

While focused on cutting through the tape without hurting her, Jason didn't hear Jax creep up behind him.

The minute he sensed someone near and began to turn, Jax hit him in the head with the butt of his gun.

After that, Jason only knew darkness.

CHAPTER TWENTY-NINE

The Gathering

Francisco sat comfortably near the fire in his library, feeling very princely. The extra-wide, high-back, tufted green velvet wingback chair with nail-head trim was more of a throne than a chair.

His father had always told him that he was a prince, the son of a king. Well, okay, the son of a kingpin in the drug cartel, a gangster, but still a king. Francisco chuckled to himself as he reminisced of his fondest memories of his childhood in Cuba.

He wanted his guests to have the image of a prince, a man in charge, seared in their minds.

He looked through the golden liquid in the Champagne flute held in one hand. Then, at the fancy bacon-wrapped shrimp topped with Beluga caviar canapé in the other.

The joy that bubbled up from his chest at both seeing the tiny creation and knowing the depth of flavor he'd experience from popping it into his mouth made him giddy.

As he popped the delicacy into his mouth, he closed his eyes to savor the perfect blend of flavors, which sent his salivary glands into overdrive, just as they had been since the first time his tastebuds were activated by a culinary experience.

As he swallowed the last tiny morsel of that first treat, he looked to all the others artfully displayed on the highest quality, fine porcelain china. His Regency Turquoise Royal Crown Derby oval platter rested on the Theodore Alexander with swirled burlwood table.

He'd only recently acquired the treasures, but each piece complemented the other.

As he reached for the next dainty delight, the anticipation of its taste filled his mouth with saliva.

Eyeing the platter, he mentally cataloged each elegantly designed canapé: duck bacon-wrapped scallops; deviled quail eggs with porcini and parmesan; French ham and pear crostini with truffle honey; smoked salmon, caviar and crème fraîche on mini toast; oysters with bacon, cream and truffled breadcrumbs in the shell; and for their eye-catching beauty, the foie gras jewels with wine gelées.

Treasures made explicitly for a prince -- for him.

Each, a perfect concoction made to catch the eye and tempt the palate.

He was savoring the moment and enjoying himself while he waited for Henry to settle his guests into their rooms. This was the first gathering they'd had in more than ten years.

Traditionally, they would only agree to assemble if there was a good reason, usually requiring putting more money in their pockets. Otherwise, communication was done on the phone or through Zoom.

It had been a very trying few weeks, but after providing the Doctor with several junkies to finish his research, even though that hadn't been his preference, the product was finally ready to unveil.

Since his father couldn't attend the unveiling, he had hoped that Willie might make an appearance. Unfortunately, Willie had some health issues and had to decline. Francisco swallowed his disappointment and focused on the delicious canapés.

One of his favorite games was matching people with food.

While he waited, he enjoyed each of the treats and imagined the canapé that each guest might favor.

Francisco had planned on having a group of six for this gathering, but after Willie declined, he quickly adjusted. He would just pick two favorites for himself.

Kenny would enjoy the smoked salmon, Yulan the oysters, and Julio the deviled quail eggs. But he thought Guillermo and Jesús would prefer the French ham and pear crostini.

Willie would have preferred the duck bacon.

Once settled in their rooms, they would join him in the library just as they'd done at the last gathering more than ten years previously.

They would start at the banquet table, which was decorated to display the appetizers artfully. Next to the appetizers was a large crystal fountain cascading the best Champagne from his collection.

Everything was elegantly set so they could enjoy the culinary treats while getting reacquainted.

Several chairs had been arranged in a semicircle around the fireplace. Francisco's chair faced them all and was the center of attention, as was his want.

He would see if his predictions regarding the canapés were correct once his guests were settled with their plates.

It was just after lunch, which meant dinner wouldn't be ready for a few hours. They had plenty of time to reconnect and rest from their travels before then.

Francisco wanted nothing but the best for his guests. They needed to be relaxed, comfortable, and unguarded before they would be forced to bow to him.

But that was the end goal.

Francisco had always hoped to play the long-con, like in the movie The Sting. He could still remember the first time he'd seen it.

He'd spent the whole day with his father, which was rare. They'd Stopped first at his father's work. Although he was too young to understand exactly what his father did, he still remembered the enormity of the operation along with his father's words as they walked through the rows of packaged bricks of cocaine, "One day, son, this will all be yours. I will teach you how to be a leader, my little kingpin, a lord amongst men."

While waiting for his father to complete his business, Francisco replayed the little endearment and decided he liked being called kingpin.

After the warehouse, they'd gone to lunch and to the movies to see the newly released movie with Robert Redford. He was only five years old then, but The Sting had made a strong impression on him.

Only the con he'd devised would prove even more profitable.

His long-con was a just another game.

One of strategy that required a higher intellect to play. His unsuspecting rivals were the players.

He would lure them to play with a promise of unimaginable wealth that required only a minor investment.

The Doctor had assured him that the substance couldn't be replicated, at least not for years. He had no intention of providing them with the formula.

They could attempt to imitate it, but without the formula, they would lose customers to his dealers, which would increase the demand for the product. The product only he provided.

Once he discovered their disloyalty, he would increase their contribution. They would beg for his mercy and pay his price, bowing to his superior intelligence.

But he would only play the game until he was bored of it. Then he'd stop supplying them altogether. At that point, they'd kneel to him or have their organizations dispatched.

And tomorrow was the beginning of his big day. The day his con – a con with a distinctive flair, would begin. One so ingenious that it would go down in history.

The day was planned down to the last detail. First, they'd have a most satisfying breakfast. After which the drug would be introduced.

Allowing time for negotiations and discussions between drinks and meals, a tour of the new facilities to show off the efficiency of his operation would be provided.

He felt that making them wait would keep their attention. But more than anything, he wanted to show off his ingenuity.

Unlike the fools strung out on a fantasy, his colleagues were savvy enough not to be lured by a freebie. He would have to make it interesting, even a little challenging for the men coming to his little party. But before the end of the summit, he planned to offer them a limited supply, for a small investment.

He had always been great at visualizing. His mother had called it daydreaming.

But to Francisco, his mind was a playground and he loved to play out each scenario of his new production and predict how each guest might respond to ensure the best possible outcome.

It was almost too easy. But the prospect of success was exciting.

He would anticipate their requests and manipulate the negotiations. Then, he would provide preconceived plans for introducing the product into the market.

Without a clue of his intentions, they would do all the work while paying him for the privilege of mainstreaming his vision.

Yes. This game will be my greatest triumph.

***

Dash struggled to understand the message.

It didn't make sense. He rarely used Morse code, even when he was in the service, and translating it was even more difficult while flying.

He thought he got the gist, but he called Kade to confirm.

Kade had been stationed at the Grand Z Casino to surveil the suspect and signal when he was returning to the compound.

If Morales was at the casino, security would be more relaxed, and Jason would have more time to search the compound.

Only, Kade hadn't seen the man. Which meant that he needed to join Jason at the compound in case he needed backup.

With his ear pods in, it looked like Kade was listening to music, but the pods were connected to the walkie-talkie in his jacket pocket.

He was surprised that Jason had used Morse code. Obviously, something was going down.

When he deciphered the SOS part, he started walking toward the parking lot. Just as he started his car, he got a call from Dash on the burner.

"Hey, Dash, I'm making my way to the hollow now. Did you get the SOS? I had some interference on my end… but I got the SOS. Did you understand it?"

"Yeah. But for fuck's sake, I haven't used Morse since boot camp; why's he using that instead of just calling on the walkie? Something's up. I thought it was an SOS."

"Yeah. But there was more. Something about a woman and Jax. But if it was… I mean, Jax always has a lady. But why the SOS, then? And how does Jax figure into it? What's he doing at the compound?"

"Yeah, that threw me off too, which is why I'm calling. I figured I might have missed something.

"But I doubt Colt would use Morse unless he had to."

"Yeah, that's pretty much what I thought. I'm heading there now. I'll let you know what I find."

Kade parked just a few yards from Colt's Jeep on the other side of some brush.

After pulling his gear out of the trunk, he couldn't help but admire the copper color of his Lexus in the moonlight before covering it with a camouflage blanket.

Worried about his friend, Kade wondered where Colt was and if he'd made it into the compound; *I really hope you left me a clue to follow, buddy.*

Dean's call interrupted Kade's thoughts. "Hey, it's almost time for my break. I'll get to you as fast as I can. I'll drop down at the clearing south of that small cluster of trees and follow the dirt road east. That should take me close to the dugout. I'll meet you there.

"In the meantime, see what you can find out about our boy and the SOS he sent out."

Kade looked at his watch. "Okay. It's zero two-twenty-two hours now. I'll expect you around what? Zero three hundred?"

"Yeah, probably before that."

"Okay. I'll wait at the dugout until I hear from you. Well, unless something pops and I need to split."

After they hung up, Dash called DPD Air Support Dispatch and told them he was taking his break. After that, he turned off the onboard RC radio and hauled ass toward Central City.

Kade had the GPS coordinates Colt had given them. But the dugout blended so entirely with shadows, and with the trees blocking the moon, for a moment, he worried that he wouldn't find it.

He was wasting time trying to see the dome, so he moved directly to the spot indicated on his phone and was finally able to make out a dark mound in the landscape.

He hadn't realized how close he was to the entry until his foot slipped into an opening.

Pulling back, he bent down to a pitch-dark hole.

Colt said he kept the door closed when he wasn't there, and Kade wondered why it was open.

Figuring his friend must be inside, Kade poked his head in, but before he could say a word, he was grabbed by his vest and pulled into the shelter.

At first, Kade thought it was Colt, but when he was grabbed around his neck from behind, he began to fight back.

Ju-jitsu wasn't much use in a confined space, in the dark, and with his back pressed against the guy who was holding him in a chokehold.

A disembodied voice whispered, "Please relax and stay quiet."

A whoosh filled his ears, as the blood rushed to his head.

Kade felt his heartbeat increase, pushing adrenaline through his system to activate muscles into action. But instead of fighting, he intentionally forced his body to relax. He would wait for an opening to present itself.

The voice continued, "I won't hurt you. Just take a breath and relax. Who told you about this foxhole?"

Kade knew if he stayed calm and played along, he might learn what was going on and where Colt was. "Uh... a friend found it."

"Who is your friend?"

"You wouldn't know him."

"Try me."

"You know anyone named Jason?"

The arm slowly released him. "Yes. Please tell me. How is my son?"

Once released, Kade kicked away from the man and was surprised to find that there was more room inside the dugout than he thought.

Jumping onto his feet he took a fighting stance, finding plenty of room to defend himself.

His eyes adjusted to the darkness, but it wasn't easy to make out anything but the silhouette of the man in front of him. "What did you say?"

There was a soft glow under the man's thigh. His head was bent, and he was fiddling with something. "I asked how my son is. It's been months since I saw him, and I've missed him very much."

"Who are you?"

"My name is Matthew Colt. I'm Jason's father. You know me, Kade, as I know you."

Kade felt the blood that had just rushed to his head fall to his feet.

Getting angry, which helped push away the dizziness, he countered, "You're a liar; Matt was murdered in an auto accident last November on his way home from this compound."

The man was quiet for several minutes as he continued working on something Kade couldn't see.

"I recognize your voice, Kade. Don't you recognize mine? How are your parents, Hiroshi and Emi?"

Fear prickled Kade's skin as ice water seemed to run down his spine, forcing him to sit.

His instinct screamed at him to grab his flashlight to see who was in the shelter. Instead, he rested his hand on the butt of his gun.

"You don't need your gun; I'm not going to hurt you. That should be obvious by now. I know you think I'm dead. We had to let you think that I died in that accident. It was necessary. But there's way more going on than you know, Kade, so please relax. I am who I say I am."

Kade's mouth was open, ready to object, but he couldn't. He knew that voice.

That voice was there when he and Jason had graduated from the academy, at the barbecues, fishing trips, and get-togethers.

That voice had comforted him when his mother was diagnosed with cancer and at the party to celebrate her recovery, too.

Kade felt an intensity of emotion that he hadn't felt since his grandfather died. As he crossed his legs, tears welled up in his eyes, and his voice cracked a little as he said, "Matt, is it really you?"

A click and a flashlight illuminated the face in front of him. "Oh, my God, Matt!" Tears filled his eyes before he could wipe them away. "We've been trying to find out who ordered the hit on you!"

Kade wasn't used to displays of affection, even having spent the last few years around the Colt and Adams families, where hugs seemed to be commonplace.

It had always felt good to be around people who were kind and loving and had no problem showing it.

As his distrust disappeared, Matt reached over and rubbed his back. "It's okay, son. It's a lot to digest. I'll explain everything a little later. But right now, Kade, I need you to fill me in on what's going on with Jason."

"Shit! Jason! I almost forgot."

While Kade filled Matt in on why they were there, he gave a quick rundown of what happened to Jason in the alley, what led him to the dugout, and why Jason had been surveilling the compound and Morales.

Then he explained the SOS… "We don't know why he sent it. We made out something about Jax and a woman. That's why I'm here. Dean's on his way."

"Okay. Well, it sounds like my boy needs some help."

While they'd been talking, Matt had macraméd a rope ladder with loop footholds spaced about a foot apart. "Here, try this out. Not the best job, but it should work well enough to get us inside if we need it."

As Kade placed his foot in a loop and tested its strength, the crunching of leaves and twigs on the forest floor reached them.

Matt placed his hand on Kade's shoulder.

With no way to identify who it was, they needed to stay quiet.

CHAPTER THIRTY

The Report

Becca woke with a tremendous headache. It took several minutes before she could bear to open her eyes to the bright fluorescents in the room.

Each time she tried, her eyes watered, and the brightness intensified the headache.

When she finally managed to peek at her surroundings, terror washed over her like a cold shower. She wasn't at home.

Lifting her head was difficult. Why was it so impossibly heavy? Her neck was sore with a kink, and she blinked to clear her blurry vision. When she tried to move, her body refused to cooperate, and she couldn't readily figure out why.

Then, like a slap in the face, she remembered that Jack was in her house. She didn't remember what happened or where he'd taken her. But she needed to clear her head… and fast.

Closing her eyes against the pain-inducing light, she tried to remember what happened.

The last thing she remembered was seeing Jack standing in the hall.

The horrible look on his face. It was almost obscene in its suggestion, and it made her skin crawl.

Her heart had dropped to her stomach.

He'd been so brazen the way he walked into her office and plopped down on one of her favorite chairs.

It hadn't been easy finding the right size for that spot or the fabric to cover it at any furniture store. Most stores didn't offer custom furniture anymore.

To get exactly what she wanted, she found an old chair at a garage sale and had it reupholstered with fabric she'd purchased online.

Having it overstuffed had been a good call, too. Not only was it better quality furniture and more affordable, but it was so comfortable that she often fell asleep in it while working on her laptop.

The Eddo arched floor lamp highlighted the beautiful rusts, reds, oranges, and golds in the raised velvet floral pattern.

She'd been so proud of how well it had turned out.

But the idea that the monster who murdered her sister had touched it made her want to vomit.

She tried to strategize. Find a way to call for help, run to her safe room, or hit him with something.

Cornered, she couldn't move past him, couldn't win a fight even with her proficiency rating in her self-defense classes. He outweighed her, and he was a cop, for Christ's sake. He had more training. That, along with his height and strength, made a fight risky.

And what was the law against hitting a cop even if he was a bad guy threatening you?

He had the advantage.

She glanced at the bookcase behind her, but it was hopeless. He was way too close. He'd catch her before she could reach the door to the room.

She became agitated, unable to stand the suspense of what he planned and not knowing what he'd done to her boys.

Jumping from her seat, she yelled, "Where are my dogs? What did you do to them? I need to know they're okay."

But as she moved toward the doorway, he jumped up and grabbed her, turning her quickly he forced her backside against him.

She was a strong woman, but he'd trapped her arms, and before she could stomp on his foot… well, that was the last thing she remembered.

The clearer her mind became, the more her body complained. But that was just the tip of the current issue.

Her neck was sore, and one spot was throbbing.

As she reached toward her neck with heavy arms, she realized that they wouldn't move.

Blinking to clear her vision, she looked down.

Her wrists were taped to a chair.

On closer inspection, the tape had been cut, and more tape had been applied. She wondered how many times she'd been in and out of the chair and for what reason before she woke up.

She pulled and tugged, but the bindings barely moved. In fact, the movement increased the pressure of the tape around her ankles.

Unable to move, an overwhelming sense of panic rose to take possession of her.

Stomach contents flowed into her esophagus and reached toward her mouth to make her gag.

Her heart raced fiercely. Thumping against her chest cavity, thundering like pounding hooves on a racetrack.

A weight on her chest made it hard to catch her breath.

Getting dizzy, she remembered her training. By controlling the breath, it was possible to reduce panic.

She'd used that skill many times to de-escalate anxious pet owners.

My breath is coming too fast. I have to slow it down, or I'll hyperventilate. And I don't want to pass out again.

Tears filled her eyes, and sweat broke out all over her body.

Closing her eyes, she tried to focus on her breathing.

First, she held her breath to slow it down. Then, she intentionally inhaled slowly and deeply.

I need to think clearly if I have any hope of living through this.

A few minutes later, the tension held in her contracted muscles began to release. Her breathing and heartbeat slowed, which eased the pressure on her chest.

With her breathing back to normal, she was able to focus on the situation.

Opening her eyes, she looked around the room. When she looked over her right shoulder, she received another shock.

Jason was taped to a chair just behind her.

His chin rested to the side, almost to his chest, and his shoulders were hunched forward. At that angle, she could see that his hair was caked with blood, and he was out cold.

Rotating her head to take in her surroundings, she was relieved that Jack wasn't in the room.

Holding her breath, she listened for any sound that might indicate his return or that might indicate that someone else was nearby.

Whispering, she called to him, "Jason! Jason, wake up. Please wake up. We're in trouble."

Seeing that he wasn't waking, she used a sashay movement with her hips to scoot her chair a bit closer to him. "Jason, seriously, wake up!"

With no movement, she scooted until her chair was against his. Then used her head to push on his shoulder. "Jason, please wake up!" Without the ability to move her hands or feet, head-butting him was her only option.

Fearing Jack would return any minute, she kept at it until he finally moved.

Pushing herself up higher in the chair and leaning over as much as possible, she put her mouth as close to his ear as possible. Then, using her stomach muscles in a loud whisper, she spat, "Jason, you need to wake up. He's crazy, and we need to get out of here. I'm scared, and I need your help. We need to work together."

Jason heard his name and tried to push through the darkness. As he did, his nerves began to wake up, too.

Not good, since they seemed to be on fire.

His skull felt like it had been smashed in with a hammer that created a throbbing that beat in tempo with his heart.

The pressure in his ears made it difficult to make out what was being whispered, and something kept hitting him.

His shoulder, arm, and the side of his chest were tender in spots where blows continued to thump him.

It didn't feel like a fist, and the blows weren't hard enough to cause injury. Still, he was getting sore.

His eyelids were incredibly heavy, and he left them closed while he tried to concentrate on what was being said.

"Please wake up… please!"

As if he'd been hit with cold water, that voice pulled Jason into consciousness. He remembered where he was and who he'd been trying to rescue.

The thumping continued, so biting back the pain, he groaned, "I'm awake. Please stop hitting me."

"Jason! Oh, thank God! Where are we? I'm not sure how you got here, but we have to leave before Mark... I mean... Jack, comes back."

Trying to push the fog away, he mumbled, "The compound. I know why I'm here… but why are you here, Becca? How are you connected to Morales?"

As he slowly opened his light-sensitive eyes, he could see that she was staring at the doorway. Pressing his eyes closed, he pushed the fog away.

When he opened them again, he noticed the tears wetting her cheek and her bottom lip was trembling.

She looked back at him. "It's a long story, and we don't have time right now. Mark... damn it. I mean, Jack… fuck whatever, he'll come back soon.

"He's crazy, Jason! We have to get out of here before he comes back. I don't know how long he's been gone, and...."

Jason was struggling to stay awake. He interrupted, "Give me a minute. I've been drugged. I need to clear my head. Just keep talking; it's helping me stay conscious."

She closed her eyes and bent her head toward him, trying to be patient. "Okay. Fine. I'm here because Jack murdered my sister. I found out and started following him, trying to get proof.

"He found out, and now he wants to kill me, too.

"But I have no idea why you're here. Were you following me?"

Before Jason could answer, a slow clapping began from the other side of the room forcing them to look in that direction.

Jack stood in the doorway with a cocky smile on his face and his shoulder casually leaning against the frame.

He took a few steps into the room, "Well said, sweetheart—a great synopsis, if not totally accurate.

"Still, is this a pretty sight or what? The two of you cuddled up as if you actually know each other.

"Now, how did that happen, I wonder? Well, you'll just have to tell me all about it."

"The sun will rise shortly to a beautiful day. A special day.

He set the duct tape roll he'd been holding along with a bag on the desk. "But there is still plenty of time to play a few games. Then again, I have a lot to do, so we can't play just yet.

"Hmm… maybe there's time enough for you both to answer some questions.

"But no. That's not much fun.

"Oh, I know… we can play 'til death you will part.

"Yes, yes… I like that, and we don't want to drag this out too long, do we?"

His amusement was interrupted by a loud tone on his cell. Pulling it from his jeans pocket, he read the screen and turned down the volume.

"Unfortunately, we have way too much going on today for my favorite games. Especially the ones I had planned for you, Becca.

"Do you know that when I was a kid, having a tasty treat before breakfast was a punishable offense."

He snickered, "But now that I'm a man,…" He rubbed himself, "Um, correct that… very well-endowed man. I find that it's a craving that must be indulged before I can start the day."

The distaste that had pinched Becca's face quickly turned to an expression of fear. And that only intensified Jason's anger.

"Oh, that's perfect! You should see your face, Colt! You actually look like you would kill me if you weren't restrained in that chair. I always wondered what it would be like to kick your ass."

"Well, cut these bindings, and let's give it a go. I'm at a disadvantage since you clobbered and drugged me. You might actually win."

"Well, damn Colt. I must admit I'm torn.

"But, after waiting all this time, I'd rather take you down when..." Another tone, although softer, interrupted him.

His face turned red with exasperation as he read the text.

While Jack was distracted, Jason worked his wrists and hands back and forth to loosen the bindings, nodding to Becca to do the same.

"Damn. It looks like our little party will have to wait.

"Henry needs my assistance. You see, my uncle and I have waited for this day for too long to let anything get in the way. Our plans are finally in full swing now.

"You two will just have to wait until later this evening for our fun and games.

"What the hell, Jax? Why are you doing this? I thought we were friends. And you're a cop, for Christ's sake!

"So how is it that you're working with Morales? Does he have something on you?"

Putting his phone back in his pocket, Jack laughed, mocking Jason as he continued, "Did he what?" He laughed in earnest, "Oh man, you really don't get it."

Moving closer, spittle sprayed from his mouth as he said. "Look at our golden boy now, huh? Rushing in to save the day. But I bet you never thought you'd be the one who needed rescuing.

"Ha! A hero, my ass! Just a moral fanatic who doesn't care how his ideals inflict pain on those around him."

"What are you talking about?"

"Really? Are you really that ignorant? Was I that good of an actor that you never suspected? How is it possible that after all this time, you can be so dense? So out of touch?"

As he moved closer to them, his nose wrinkled like he smelled something putrid. Then, waving his hand, he turned on his heel, "It doesn't matter. Just know that both good and bad actions have consequences, Colt!"

"Jax, for God's sake, what are you talking about? I've known you a long time, and I've always treated you as a friend. I've never done anything to you."

As he turned back to them, his eyebrows were pinched together, his lips pulled back from his teeth in a sneer, "Did you ever wonder what happened to that Private First Class?

"The one you turned in who was packing a crate at the distribution center?

"Think hard now. It was the same day we were ambushed in the desert?"

"I…" The memory hit Colt hard. When he filed that report on the contraband, he had no idea who the guy was at the time—and it had never occurred to him that the person might be Jack.

The ambush and surviving it had erased everything that happened in the hours leading up to it.

He'd actually forgotten that he'd made a report.

They hadn't known each other before that gunfight but had stayed alive by fighting back-to-back to save each other.

Jason had thought that theirs had been a friendship born in battle. Which probably explained why he'd overlooked so many of Jack's questionable actions.

But to hold onto a grudge after all this time and never say a word or try to resolve what happened was just childish.

Lowering his voice, Jason said, "Why didn't you say something? I was just doing my job. I honestly didn't think anything would come of it because I couldn't identify the guy. I never saw your face.

"I was doing my duty even though I didn't have much to put in my report, so I don't know how they figured it was you."

"Well, after our little gunfight, do you remember how we were treated?

"The guys in Kabul were thrilled we brought their supplies and the guys back at base… well, you remember the party the night we returned?

"We were treated like heroes! Me and you and that fly-junkie boyfriend of yours, Dash.

"Well, that hero's welcome ended for me just weeks later when they caught me adding to the supplies.

"That never would have happened if it wasn't for you, Mr. Boy Scout.

"I had a good thing going, and your report put them on notice.

"Only by then you'd finished your tour and went stateside.

"You left the military a hero, while I was put through hell and marked as a criminal.

"All because you had to stick your nose into my business."

"I never knew what happened."

"Of course not. You and Dash shipped out before the news got out.

"So let me tell you… I was pushed out. Told I was lucky to get an other than, instead of a dishonorable discharge, which they thought I deserved.

"I only got out slightly better because my Corporal backed me, and my uncle called in some favors. But even after all of that, I got an other-than-honorable discharge.

"Somehow, it didn't show up when I applied to DPD. But then I think my uncle fixed that, too.

"He needed someone in the department, and I was the best fit.

"But because of you, I lost everything!

"The perfect cover I'd developed for our overseas operation, millions in product and even more in cash. It nearly ruined me.

"Do you really think we could be friends after that?

"When you came to my unit, I thought it was the perfect opportunity to return the favor someday. Maybe catch you doing something sketchy and take you down… maybe even find a legit reason to kill you.

"But I never got the opportunity.

"That is until your dad stuck his big nose into my uncle's operation. That gave me the break I needed. His failure to take us down was my opportunity to pay you back.

"Did you know it was me? Did it ever occur to you that I was involved or that it was me in the alley that night?

"No? Well, it was. I shot you and Stryker with a fucking dart gun. Can you believe it?

"I've always possessed superior skill with weapons, but the power of that thing was intense. And there was a moment or two when I thought I miscalculated.

"You should have seen it. When the dart hit you, it pushed your whole body... must have been a few feet at least. For a minute, I thought I'd broken your neck—killed you. Not that I cared either way.

"But then you roused yourself just in time to take the blame for Billy.

"They knew you got hurt, but since there was no proof, they figured you'd done it to yourself.

"And the best part... the best part was that I got to watch you suffer.

"I knew you'd be the prime suspect for killing Billy. Especially when it came out that Billy did your dad. And you even helped when you had the accident reinvestigated.

"Of course, they'd think that you knew about Billy.

"Man. You made it so damn easy for us."

Jason couldn't believe what he was hearing.

"I helped my uncle produce a fantastic show, and man, did it feel good to see you fall. So fucking sweet!

"Payback never tasted as good as it did that night. It was fucking spectacular!"

A cell phone tone distracted Jack long enough to look at it.

For Jason, it was difficult to accept that his training partner, a brother in blue and a man he thought was a friend, could take such joy in causing so much pain.

"But the look on Jack's face replaced any doubts about his true nature.

With a slight lift of his head, the overhead light accentuated his delight in the unfocused, far-away look of his eyes.

"It was all planned perfectly, and it came off better than any play. You might even say it was choreographed to perfection."

As he spoke, his eyes bulged, his brow furrowed, his nostrils flared, and his lips pulled away from his teeth into a sickly wicked grin.

Jack turned his focus back to them, "It's a shame that no one else will ever get to see how it all played out. It was epic!"

Then, placing a hand on his puffed-out chest, "I, of course, played the lead in our little production." Sweeping his arm through the air and bending in an exaggerated bow as if his captives had just applauded him, he continued, "And, of course, I was brilliant."

As he slowly straightened, "Although the plan was executed masterfully, I only wanted to ensure your defeat. And I did!

"Because of me, you lost your dad, that homeless bum, the job you love, and to top it off, Stryker.

"I made sure that those closest to you suffered—even your mom!"

In a muffled voice while looking at his feet, "Damn I almost forgot about her."

Jason was stunned. He'd been so distracted since John's death. He'd ignored his intuition that something was off about it and made it a low priority.

He interrupted Jack's insane rant long enough to ask, "You killed John? But Why? He had nothing to do with my investigation."

"Because he was a worthless piece of shit, and I knew it would fuck you up. I was playing the odds and figured that his death would keep you off your game. Figured it would throw you off even more for the big event.

"But that wasn't all I did. Who do you think doctored your cold meds?"

He was so caught up in his depraved delight while describing his perverted plot that he hadn't noticed the disgust mixed with contempt etched on the faces of his spectators.

When he finally noticed them, his face melted into something altogether foreign.

The demonic smile transforming into a pinched sneer that turned his lip up, while his eyes narrowed to slits that thickened his brow, and he looked from Jason to Becca.

Their repulsion at his horrifying disclosure was unmistakable.

Suddenly feeling self-conscious, Jack began pacing, trying to regain his composure.

When he stopped in front of them again, he pointed at Jason, "But you're the idiot here. You're the one who couldn't figure it out, could you? Ha!

"I took everything from you. Me!

"Some lawman you are."

A perplexed look crossed Jack's face briefly before he changed subjects, "Don't think you're fooling anyone, Colt. I know you helped Stryker escape. I tried to point the finger at you, but some punk tagged the wall and was blamed instead.

"But hey, don't worry, once we find him, I'll make sure he's put down. I might even put a bullet in his head myself.

"If you hadn't joined our little party uninvited, I was looking forward to seeing you locked up. I thought I'd let you suffer for maybe a year, or until I was bored and put the word out that you're a cop to let someone else do the job for me.

"But you've ruined my plans now that you're here.

"Not that they'd believe anything you would tell them about our time together, especially if they find you whacked out on H.

"Then again, it might be more satisfying to kill you myself — only slowly.

"I'm still deciding.

"I have all day to make up my mind what to do with you, and it's more fun to let you sweat while I take my time."

The same tone from his cell interrupted Jack, making him frown. Only this time, he ignored it.

"It's a busy day for us and …" The tone sounded again.

Pulling his phone roughly from of his pocket, he quickly punched in a reply text, and screamed at it, "Fucking give me a minute!"

Then, shoving the phone back in his pocket, he turned to them, "But before the fun begins, I'm needed elsewhere. It's a very important day that I really can't miss.

"But don't worry. There's plenty of time to play."

Then, turning to leave, he stopped with his back to them and said, "Until I return, I recommend that you keep quiet. You don't want to force me to give you that little cocktail.

"Trust me, you'll enjoy it until your last breath."

CHAPTER THIRTY-ONE

Thunderstruck

Dash squatted down. His long frame required him to fall to his knees just to see inside the shelter. Whispering, he said, "Kade, I think I have an idea of how we can distract them. There's a propane tank and…"

Struggling to get his long legs through the opening, he scooted into the dark hole.

"Once inside, he took off his pack. "Kade, you in here, man? I can't see anything. It's pitch in here."

Two arms wrapped around him in a firm bear hug.

He pulled away. "Hey… what the…"

Then, as if struck by lightning, he recognized the hug and squeezed back. "Dad, is that you? What are you doin' in here?"

As he was released, a familiar voice, not nearly as deep as his father's, said, "Hello, son, it's been way too long. I've missed you and your dad."

Leaning away, Dean's skin crawled like ants making a freeway up and down his back, arms, and neck.

He wondered if he was losing it talking to a ghost. "Mmmatt?"

Kade said, "Yeah, Dean. It's Matt. He's not dead."

Dean couldn't speak. It was as if someone had turned off his vocal cords.

Stunned, a feeling like he was falling overtook him, and for that brief moment, he thought he might pass out.

Then Matt started speaking again. "I know it's hard to believe, but I didn't die in that accident.

"Like I told Kade, I'll explain everything later. But right now, we need to work fast.

A team is coming, and we need to find Jason before they get here and all hell breaks loose.

It'll be easier to look for him with the guards distracted. But it will be harder for the guards to see us if we enter while it's still dark.

"I'm worried about Jason. Kade said he sent an SOS, and he hasn't heard anything since.

"I don't think he'd send for help unless something had gone wrong.

"Dean, when you came in, you said something about a propane tank. Do you think we could use that as a distraction?"

Dean laid a plat map out in front of them. "If the drawings are right, there are two propane tanks on this property. The largest is a five hundred gallon on the east side to the right of the main entrance.

"I think that one's way too big.

"But there's another smaller tank to the right of the staff gate. I'd guess that one feeds the cabins. But it's the better choice for a diversion."

"But what's the best way to use it? Can we set it on fire?"

"We can over pressurize it. That will cause the tank to BLEVE.

"The problem is that we can't predict how long it will take or what the blast radius will be because we have no idea how full the tank is.

"We'll need to move as far away as fast as possible after setting it up."

The three men crawled out of the shelter and moved as one through the brush to the smaller propane tank.

They'd agreed that Kade would place the heating element under the propane tank and set it to one hundred-and-twenty degrees. As the heat caused pressure to build, it would increase the pounds per inch in the confined space until the pressure BLEVE'd the tank.

Most of the sentries were stationed around the main house, so the area was vacant.

It was still a risk.

Using Matt's rope ladder, Kade quickly scaled the fence.

As dawn began its slow climb, an eerie glow was cast in a line along the horizon. And by the time Kade had made it back to them, the sun was peeking over the mountains.

It was time to find Jason.

***

Colt and Becca were quiet for several minutes after Jack left them.

Just after hearing a door close, there was a very distinct whistle, followed by padded feet coming from the darkened corridor into the room.

Amazed, Becca watched as Stryker padded out of the darkened lab into the room.

Jason called softly, “Good boy, Stryker. You did great. Bite here.”

He wiggled his fingers and moved his wrist as much as the bindings would allow.

He looked at Becca. “You did good, too, by the way.”

“What do you mean?”

“Well let’s just say, it’s a good thing that you didn’t say anything about taking care of Stryker, or we’d be sunk.”

It took several minutes of coaxing before Stryker grasped enough of what Jason wanted him to do repeating his praise, encouraging Stryker even after being bitten a few times, “Good, boy, bite! That’s right, good boy!”

Stryker ripped the tape, going after it in earnest until he freed Jason’s hand.

Jason pointed to the tape on the chair near his ankles. “Here, buddy. Bite here.”

While Stryker began tearing at the tape on the chair leg, Jason worked to release his other hand. Once his hands were free, he reached over and started working on Becca’s bindings.

Becca was impressed. “I knew he was a good dog, but now I see that he’s amazing! How does he know what you want him to do?”

As he worked to release her, Jason explained, “I’ve spent hours playing different games with him, training him in various scenarios.

“Although I have to admit that it never occurred to me to train him for this something like this.

“I’ve taught him a lot of whistles and hand signals, too, a type of sign language.

“And… this might sound crazy, but he is very intuitive. It’s hard to explain, even harder to believe, but he’s been easy to train because of his intuition.”

Thinking it would distract her while they worked to get free, he told her a story. "He once saved my life when he was young and still in training.

"Most of the department was out looking for a dangerous escapee from lockup when we got the call.

"Jack, Max, me, and Stryker joined the hunt.

"The two-time offender was armed after taking a gun off a guard he'd half beaten to death when he escaped.

"Jax and Max had taken the lead while we followed.

"The dogs are trained to pick up on what's called a fear scent. It's typically secreted in the sweat when attempting to evade capture. No matter what maneuvers or tricks are used, the dogs follow the scent.

"Anyway, Stryker picked up on that scent the minute we entered Skyline Park and took off like a shot. Jack had already split off, and by the time I caught up to Stryker, he was running in circles around a bench.

"I thought he lost the scent.

"I didn't notice that the escapee was hiding in a tree behind a cluster of leaves or that he had his gun sighted on me.

"Stryker must have heard something because, without warning, he jumps on the bench, kicks off, and knocks me down just as the escapee pulls the trigger.

"Luckily, the bullet missed and ricocheted off the concrete under the bench.

"I knew if I didn't move, we were dead. And it turned out that I barely had enough time to roll, turn, and return fire. Because just as I fired, a bullet whizzed by my head.

"I only got off two rounds. The first missed, but the second bullet caught the guy in the head.

"He fell hard right next to me.

"But I wouldn't have made it that day if it wasn't for Stryker.

"How Stryker learned that maneuver was beyond anyone's understanding and is still a mystery. He had never been trained to push his handler out of the way, and yet, he knew exactly what to do.

"Everyone was baffled. So, we tried to replicate it. But Stryker didn't worry about Jack in the tree. He barked at him, but he never reacted. He never pushed me out of the way, like he'd done with the convict.

"It was like he sensed what to do in the moment and then just forgot about it.

"By now, you get that Jack is a K-9 cop, too."

"Yeah, from all the talk, I kinda figured you worked together somehow."

"Well, even though we trained our dogs together, we were never what you'd call good friends.

"I actually met him while on a mission in Afghanistan – as he pointed out, I guess I saw him before I met him. I really had no idea about any of that."

With her arms and feet finally freed, she jumped from the chair and rubbed her wrists. "All I know is that we need to get out of here before he comes back.

"I don't know what he gave me to knock me out, but I don't want to find out.

"There's a sore spot on my neck. Probably an injection site. And I don't want any more crap put into my body.

"I say we get the hell out of here and catch up later."

Jason figured that it would be better if they left from the lab's front entrance since Jack's truck might still be parked at the side entrance.

He also realized that the tools inside his pack and his weapon would give them a better chance to escape. But as he searched the office, Becca was nearing the doorway.

Changing tactics, he quickly caught up, "Hey, slow up. We can't charge out of here. We don't know what's out there. We could be walking into a trap, so stay close, okay?"

The lab was dark except for a small beam of soft sunlight filtering through the glass doors at an angle.

Reaching for Becca's hand, he whispered, "We need to stay alert. It looks like we've lost the cover of darkness. The sun's already coming up, so it's going to be hard to hide.

"As soon as we pass through the front door, we'll rush around the building to the right and jump the fence. Remember, go right.

"You go over the fence first. I'll take care of Stryker and hand him down to you.

"Just stay low and remember we have to keep quiet.

"If we're caught, I'll cause a distraction, but don't wait for us. Just run. Get the hell out of here any way you can. Jump that fence and go for help. Dean and my friend Kade should be out there somewhere. They'll protect you.

"But, hold onto me however you can until we get to safety. I don't want us to get separated, okay?"

After she nodded her affirmation, she grabbed his shirt tail, which made him smile and nod.

Letting go of her hand; he gently positioned her between the wall and his body.

Although he moved cautiously, he also moved quickly. His muscles tense, ready for an attack.

With each step, he searched the shadows and looked for his gear.

Halfway through the lab, they almost tripped over his pack. Releasing a deep sigh, he gave her a big smile and lifted it for her to see.

Jason wondered where Jax had gone as he strapped on his helmet, turned on the camera, and threw the pack over his shoulder and onto his back.

As they made it to the front door, Jason signaled for them to stop while he searched the area before leaving the building.

As they rounded the building, they saw three shadowy forms on the other side between the fence slats.

Jason signaled for Becca and Stryker to stop while he scrutinized the situation.

He used a birdcall that he and Dean had learned at camp when they were kids. "Coo, Coo!"

In a low whisper, Dean said, "I'm here, Jason. You okay?"

"Will be. I have a civilian with me that we need to extricate. Who is with you? I saw three outlines but can't make you all out."

"Hey brother, let's just get you out of there. We can make introductions later. Where'd you cut the fence?"

"I didn't have to. I followed Jax in. But let me cut it now… we can use it again later to come back.

"By the way, I got some good intel I need to tell you what happened."

"Yeah. Well, you'll never believe what we found."

After cutting a three-foot-high length of chain link fabric, he pulled the fence back and signaled for Becca to go through, then signaled for Stryker to follow her.

Once he was through, he turned back to the fence to hook the links back in place, to make it harder for the breach to be noticed.

It wasn't until he turned back to the group that he was nearly driven to his knees.

CHAPTER THIRTY-TWO

Pleasure Meets Purpose

Francisco woke to the delectable smells of breakfast: freshly brewed coffee, cinnamon buns, and bacon, and thought, what a delightful way to start the day.

The evening was great fun.

Francisco was pleased with his guests' responses to the fantastic array of gourmet dishes that began with crab and bacon stuffed mushrooms.

Each course had been presented with one of his most sought-after wines from his massive collection.

Each dish excited the taste buds while it satisfied the body.

From the grilled coconut shrimp with shishito peppers, parmesan herb roasted potatoes, porchetta with bacon and brioche, Caprese salad, Italian beef braciole served on a small bed of orecchiette pasta in a rich marinara sauce, roasted Brussels sprouts with bacon, and finishing with crème Brulé and baked Alaska for dessert.

A few of my favorite dishes are placed in an enticing array.

Throughout the two-hour affair, his guests complimented the cooks and the wine. They had even applauded Francisco for the tantalizing menu.

The highest compliment came from Kenny, who said that he'd never been so happy to gorge himself.

Francisco considered this the most flattering compliment he could have received.

Lying in bed, he replayed the evening.

Everyone had gotten along splendidly. They played billiards, smoked his favorite Cuban cigars, drank his best spirits, and caught up on the changes in their lives, bragging about new additions to families and business acquisitions.

And as the evening waned, they complained about their aging bodies.

Although the evening had been a complete success, it was nothing in comparison to what the day would bring.

That is, after I satiate all of their gastric desires at breakfast.

Today was his day, and there was nothing that could spoil it.

The cooks had been up since before the sun, creating a smorgasbord of his breakfast favorites to serve to his guests.

Soon, the smells would call them all to the dining room.

As he pushed the plush covers aside, he made his way into the bathroom, discarded his silk pajamas on the floor, and stepped into the expansive shower.

Sitting comfortably on the shower seat, he allowed the hot water to run over his rolls of flesh. *There are approximately twenty-two million people in the world addicted to drugs. That may be enough for the ordinary drug lord making millions. Addicts are simply a necessary commodity to keep a man in business.*

I, on the other hand, am extraordinary and I deserve more. Wealth is easy and doesn't compare to status.

The heat and power spray sensitized his scalp and his nipples.

With images of his upcoming triumph and with the water flowing over his body. Like a gentle tickle it sensitized the glans of his penis exciting him to full erection.

As he stroked, he thought, *after so many years of the mundane status quo, I'll finally launch my legacy and fulfill my destiny as a god amongst my peers.*

His product would be in high demand. So addictive that once tried made it impossible to live without it.

He would not only be rich beyond measure, but he'd control every human on the planet and never again feel the sting of judgment or the pain of a woman dismissing him with disgust.

No! To get the drug they crave, they will bow to my will. Pleasure me in any way I ask.

I will be their king, their savior!

His excitement grew with these thoughts, and he convulsed briefly as he expelled his seed into the streams of water.

His morning routine finished, he quickly washed with a soaped loofah and got dressed.

It was time for breakfast, and more importantly, it was time to dazzle his associates.

***

"Dad?"

Tears filled Jason's eyes as he stood with eyes wide and his mouth open. He was finding it impossible to believe that the man who'd been lost to him for almost a year was standing right in front of him.

Grief. Relief. Pain. Fear.

It hit him all at once, leaving his body weak and his mind confused.

Struggling to keep his voice low, "B-but how? I mean… fuck. I don't know what I mean."

He wrapped his arms around his father and held on, fearing the mirage would fade.

For a brief moment, time stopped, giving Jason a few precious moments to relish being in his father's arms.

"All I care about is that you're alive, Dad."

As Matt slowly pulled Jason back at arm's length to look at him, he smiled, "I'm really happy to see you too, son."

With tears still wet on his face, Jason asked softly, "Jesus, Dad, how? I mean, how is this possible? We thought you were dead. The van. The fire. How did you survive that? They found your body? How? Where have you been all this time?

"You have no idea what we've been through… how much we've missed you?"

He wiped another tear, "Oh shit. Mom! She is going to be so pissed at you."

And with that, they both burst out laughing, which was enough to break the tension.

Whispering, Matt said, "Hey guys, let's move a little farther from the compound and regroup before someone hears us."

Patting his son on the back, then with his arm over Jason's shoulder as they retreated, Matt responded, "It's okay, son. We'll work it out. Your mother is an amazing woman.

"She'll get mad, cuss a blue streak at me, then forgive me.

As they grouped again, Jason said, "Becca, I'd like to introduce you to my dad, Matthew Colt—the man who rose from the dead. Unless I'm seeing a ghost."

Smiling, Becca said, "It's nice to meet you, sir."

With a wink at Jason, she added, "You may be the best-looking specter I've ever seen."

Dean added, "I think we can agree that we'd gladly talk to Matt's apparition if he could help us figure things out.

"But right now, Matt, you said you had a team on the way. I think we need to hear more about that."

Patting Jason on his back, Matt grabbed a stick and drew in the dirt, "They've been trying to take Morales down for years but couldn't get enough to put him away. When they heard about the summit on the tapes, they got lucky.

"Having all the main players in one place gives them a definite advantage. Not only to take the players down but to dismantle each syndicate in one synchronized sting.

"The summit was supposed to happen last year, the weekend after my accident, actually, but something went wrong. It was canceled.

"When no one showed, the DEA regrouped and decided to hold off until they had more intel.

"It was a major disappointment for all of us—even if for different reasons.

"Once I was released from the hospital, I couldn't go home without exposing the DEA's cover-up and exposing my family to danger since Morales wanted me dead.

"It was important to the mission and my family to maintain the game, so I agreed." Turning to Jason, Matt said, "I know it's been hard for you and your mother. For everyone we know, I guess.

"But what we're doing here could potentially save thousands of lives… maybe more. They've been keeping tabs on all of the players ever since the plan fell apart last year.

"Over time, I became an honorary agent using my past military training to help out where I could.

"After months of planning, they discovered a few months ago that the summit was only postponed. It's taken weeks to put every part of the plan in place.

"Recently, they suspected that something was in the works when they noticed an increase in activity. And their suspicions were confirmed when the players started taking flights out yesterday.

"We knew that Jason was getting too close, especially after I'd discovered that he had found my dugout. That's when we realized he needed to be stopped before he alerted Morales or his cronies to an invasion.

"I volunteered to stop Jason from unintentionally ruining their plan, while I get in place to enter the compound before the fences drop.

"The compounds have been synchronized to be hit simultaneously. The idea is to surprise the residents and prevent anyone from being alerted ahead of time.

"They believe this bust will interrupt the flow of drug trafficking, long enough to take down even more organizations. There are way too many spread across America.

"The good news is that not all of them are as big as these. These are the granddaddies, two from New York, one from California, and two from South Texas. Each owns a compound just like this one.

This is the first time in over ten years that they've gathered in one place. They're calling it the Six-Headed-Snake take-down.

"Magluta and his group, being the sixth head, of course.

"In essence, cutting off the heads before the others have time to grow a new one. Right now, teams are setting the charges on tactical explosives to drop the fences simultaneously.

"The closer I get to the house before the fences drop, the better chance I'll have of getting to the evidence.

Once the guards are busy fighting, I'll enter the house and start saving evidence.

"How can we help?" Dean asked sincerely.

"I'm glad you asked, Dean.

"If you choose to help, you need to know that we're on our own and that it's a risky mission."

Dean's half smile said it all, but he replied anyway, "I'm not even a little worried about that, Matt. And there's no way I'd let you go in there alone." Looking over at Kade and Jason, he continued, "Doesn't look like they're too worried either."

Kade was nodding as Jason pipped up, "Yeah, Dad. No way, we'd let you do this alone. We're a team, and we want to help."

"Okay then. We need to put a strategy together before that propane tank goes.

"After it does, we need to hit it… hard.

"We won't have much time to get inside the house and look for evidence before Morales torches it. And he will torch it.

"I think the best strategy is to split up. Hit the house from different sides and collect what we can.

"Based on the tapes, Morales is planning a big release of a new drug that could increase the number of addicts by more than ten times the current epidemic.

"Look for any documentation on shipments, bank accounts, and any lists with names. And make sure you grab any electronics: phones, hard drives, laptops. If they can pull prints, they can get into anything, so keep your gloves on.

"Let the DEA handle the arrests and stay out of sight as much as possible.

"I'm hoping we can breach where Jason cut the fence. Maybe we'll be able to get across the compound before the tank blows. Once it does, we need to find cover.

Looking over at the only female in the group, Matt said, "Before we head out, we need to get Becca safe."

"Excuse me?" They all looked at Becca, who had her arms crossed over her chest. "I'm not some damsel in distress. I've worked hard to get close to that son-of-a-bitch murderer and I'll be damned if I'm giving up now. I want to help."

"Damn, that girl's feisty." Kade guffawed.

Becca questioned, "What about my sister? Does the DEA know about what Jack did to Joss?"

"They know enough, my dear. They spotted you at the casino several months ago." He raised his hand. "Please, Becca, we all understand why you did it. You don't need to defend yourself.

"We know about George Myers, the cop working on your sister's case. He's been a roadblock Morales paid to make you go away.

"Trust me, we've sent documentation to the DA's office already. He'll be part of the roundup along with Jack Hanson. And if we find any more information, anyone else connected to your sister's death will pay.

"Believe me, you're not alone. We've got your back."

Becca couldn't believe it. Just like that, like a flash in a pan, her sister's name would be cleared, and the person who killed her would pay.

The weight she'd carried for so long, the grief she'd held at bay in order to stay strong, wasn't necessary anymore.

A wonderful yet strange and painful feeling hit her all at the same time. All she could do was nod as tears ran down her face. "Thank you."

Jason put his arms around her and let her cry on his chest, patting her back. "It's okay, Becca, it's okay. We're here for you."

He looked over his shoulder at the men who'd been by his side even though they'd had every reason to mistrust him. Pulling slightly away but keeping his arm around her, he said, "There's so much I want to say to you guys, but I'll save it for when we have more time.

"But before we go in there, I have to tell you what Jax said when he captured us.

"He was there! In the alley. He used a dart gun to incapacitate me and Stryker so he could set me up for killing Billy!

"Jack killed Billy.

"And dad, he killed John Marshall too. We have to tell Charles and make sure that they reopen John's case. And with Becca's sister, that's three. And I'm afraid there could be many more that we haven't connected to him yet.

"I think we need evidence on him too. Proof that he is the killer or that he's behind the killings."

Everyone nodded their heads, and Matt checked his watch. "Okay, people, it's showtime. We've only got minutes now.

Matt smiled and said. "Becca, I promise to do everything I can to bring Jack to justice.

"Dean, Kade, and Jason are trained officers. They're experienced in battle. I know it's hard to hear, and I'm really sorry to be the one to say it, but you're just not trained for something like this."

He held up his hand when she opened her mouth to argue, "Please, Becca, let me finish and try to understand. We can't take you in there.

"What's about to happen is just too dangerous. There's no guarantee we'll even make it."

He could tell that his words had affected her, but he needed to make sure she didn't do anything. "Look, Becca, I know that you wouldn't want any of us to get hurt trying to protect you. So I have to ask you to stay behind for our sake.

"Can you do that for me, Becca — can you wait for us, please."

Becca looked at the men surrounding her and realized that she was out of her depth.

They were primed to go to war. And regardless of how well she'd been trained, she wasn't at their level.

Assenting, she said, "Okay, Matt. But please look for anything I can use to vindicate my sister. Oh, and one last thing: You make sure they get Jack for me, okay?"

"I'll do my best." Matt agreed. "I'm glad I got the opportunity to meet you, Becca. You are a very brave soul, and I'm grateful for this short time we've had together.

Looking to the men huddled around him, "You boys will never know how good it is to be with you again. Everything in life is so much easier when you have support, and you guys are the best a man could ask for."

Then, looking at Jason, he said, "It's definitely not the reunion I'd hoped to have with you, son, but we'll do it right once this is over. Right now, we have to get moving."

"Take Becca to the dugout. Leave Stryker and a gun with her just in case she's found.

"Becca, do you know how to use a gun?"

Becca nodded. "Yeah, I took classes shortly after Joss died."

"In case anyone approaches you, the safe word is apricot. Remember it. If anyone other than the men here comes to you, they need to say the safe word. If they don't, shoot first and ask questions later, okay?

She nodded.

Jason said, "Stryker is well trained and will protect you, but otherwise, you're on your own. Just keep your head down, and you'll be fine.

"I'm leaving my helmet with you so I can get around a little easier."

Looking at Stryker, "Stryker schutzen… Becca." Stryker immediately moved to stand next to Becca.

Helicopter blades overhead could be heard getting closer.

Jason nodded to his Dad. "I'll take her to the dugout and meet you guys inside."

After Jason saw that Becca and Stryker were safe in the dugout, he ran to catch up with the others.

CHAPTER THIRTY-THREE

The Breach

Francisco felt that he was exactly where he was born to be, seated comfortably at the head of the table amongst men of supremacy—leaders.

But today, he would show them all that he had risen above them. He was more ambitious, resourceful, intelligent, and competent.

By introducing his new product, the men who were enjoying his food would no longer be able to compete. They'd be stuck supplying common goods like meth, coke, and heroin.

Drugs completely inferior to what he was about to release.

He would change the face of addiction. And without joining in his vision, his competitors organizations would falter and disintegrate into nothing.

He looked over at the Doctor, who was smiling and chatting with Julio, who was seated next to him.

Francisco didn't like how friendly they seemed.

Julio had once tried to steal the Doctor from Francisco, which continued to be a source of irritation.

The Doctor belonged to Francisco. And what was Francisco's would always be his.

Well, at least until I decide that I don't want it anymore.

Julio had insulted Francisco then, and Francisco had forgiven him.

But now he was being disrespectful in Francisco's house, at his table, and in front of his guests.

This will not stand.

He remembered his father's words, "Those who try to take what is yours are a threat. And a threat needs to be eliminated."

But not today. He reminded himself.

Francisco made a mental note to bankrupt Julio before he put out a contract on him.

It was time the man learned some manners.

Taking out Julio would resolve two problems. First, it would stop Julio from trying to acquire the Doctor. Second, his very public assassination would send a warning to the others that they should think twice before attempting to be disloyal.

After that, no one would disrespect him again.

He'd only invited the Doctor to explain that the chemical composition was designed to be nearly undetectable while maintaining the quality of the high.

While his ire grew, he looked around the table. Smiling at his guests as they enjoyed themselves.

I won't need Julio to negotiate distribution from Mexico or Cuba while he increases his percentage every year.

Once we have proof of concept, I won't have to negotiate with anyone. I'll be set for life.

And I won't need the Doctor either.

I know. I'll hire another chemist to act as his assistant. Work beside the Doctor until he learns the authentic recipe and can duplicate the product exactly.

Then, the Doctor will have outlived his usefulness.

So, what more will I need from either of them?

I will be untouchable by then and will have no qualms about taking them both out.

Feeling satisfied with his decisions, he pushed the annoyance away and went over the main points in the presentation he would give while they relaxed after breakfast.

The Doctor would answer any questions about side effects, and then Francisco would present the financial advantages.

He'd been rehearsing his speech for almost a year, and he knew it by heart, "The best thing about this product is that your customers won't have to worry about hangovers or drug tests because the substance is undetectable. They'll never have to worry about getting a DUI, spending a night in jail, or losing their jobs.

"It's the perfect commodity because it guarantees lifelong customers, and the low-cost buy-in ensures that you won't lose money while assessing all of its many benefits.

"You don't have to decide now. Relax and enjoy the food and spirits that have been made available to you, and take the day to think about it.

We've prepared a dossier for your consideration that you will find in your rooms."

What he wouldn't be sharing is that his drug would make all other drugs, including those that were their current bread and butter—obsolete. Or that once the product was in demand, he would raise the price again and again until they begged for his mercy.

Yes. This day was destined to be one of the greatest in my life.

A day that begins a new era. One that will ensure that I become a lord of lords.

The food caught his attention once again, quickly changing the direction of his thoughts.

The scents were enticing, and he was excited that soon, the men would get lost in the food. He enjoyed watching people fill their bellies almost as much as he enjoyed filling his own.

His eyes lighted on the beautifully arranged banquet of French toast, stuffed waffles, omelets, pancakes, bacon, sausage, various pastries, muffins, toast, and fresh fruit plated on his most expensive china, which seemed to make everything look even more delicious.

Next to the buffet was a fountain of mimosas, pots of coffee, and a variety of juices.

The garland made with the various plants and flowers from his garden pulled the eye to the display.

Elegance in presentation, just as he required it.

He couldn't help but salivate as his stomach rumbled. "Gentlemen, it looks as if our food is ready. Please help yourselves."

Once his guests were enjoying their food, Francisco happily dug into the mound on his own plate, he observed his guests and mentally noted their preferences, feeling more pleased that he'd been right about his food predictions.

As he savored his creation—a breakfast burrito-stuffed waffle with crispy bacon, sausage, onion, egg, salsa, cheese, sour cream, guacamole, and hashbrowns—Francisco couldn't have felt more content.

Then, all hell broke loose.

***

Jason met up with Matt, Dean, and Kade, who were checking their gear behind the lab.

Matt patted Jason on the back as he joined them and said, "Now that we're all here, we need to know where to go once inside the house."

Matt pulled out his map as the group circled around him.

"Once the DEA breaches the compound, they'll move toward the main house. The fight will keep the guards busy. They'll try to keep the team back, which will give us the time we need to get into the house.

"As they make the arrests, they'll haul witnesses offsite and secure them on a bus about a quarter mile from here.

"If you notice people getting away, don't engage or try to assist.

"Even though I've notified the crew about all of you, in the chaos, you could easily get hauled off.

"So, just keep to the assignment.

"The DEA believes that Morales is dealing in drugs and human trafficking. While you're in the house, you may stumble upon prisoners.

Jason interjected. "I know a little about their drug trafficking. I caught Jack smuggling when we were in Afghanistan."

Matt nodded and smiled. "I'm sure they'll want to know all about that to share with Interpol.

"Again, don't engage. Remember the cell phones will be down in this area, so just use that extra satphone I gave you Kade. It's the only way we'll be able to stay in touch."

"The main house is our target, but it'll be protected like a fortress by several highly trained men protecting Magluta and his cronies.

"Stay clear of them if possible.

"Leave the fighting to the agents. Don't engage in a gunfight unless you have to. If you end up in a fight, shoot to injure, not kill. We need them alive to interrogate.

"There are four areas in the main house we need to focus on: the main library, where Magluta spends most of his time, and his bedroom suite, located on the first floor.

"There's a smaller library in the open loft on the second floor between two wings. Check for a safe behind artwork, in the floor, or in a piece of furniture, and text me if you find one.

"I've already pinged you that information from the DEA's unique iCloud account. Remember, your phones won't work because of the jammer, so download the link I sent to your cells now. It's hit or miss if it'll work, but it's a life-line just in case.

"Dean, Kade, I'd like you two to take the upstairs. It's probably the most dangerous assignment due to the exposure you'll have while ascending that long staircase."

Dean and Kade looked at each other and shrugged, "Anything specific you want us to do?

"Check the upstairs library and bedroom suites. Collect evidence and check for safes. Look for laptops or cell phones since that's where a lot of the evidence will be extracted. But mostly, I just want you to stay safe—so just cover each other.

"Jason, you take the main library on the east flank. Look for sensitive documents and a safe. It's probably hidden.

"Once he panics, he'll want to destroy the evidence and head to his office there. And keep your heads on a swivel; he won't be alone.

"I'll do the master suite.

"Whoever gets done first needs to act as backup for others. But if you need to, just get the hell out of there.

"We'll meet back up at the dugout.

"Jason, you and I will take separate paths. You go east to enter the library from the veranda… here.

"I'm heading south to enter through the basement.

"Dean and Kade, you enter through the kitchen here. That'll give you a shorter path to the stairs.

"Once they hear the explosions, most of the house staff will be hiding or running from the house.

"Until we get close enough, we'll need to cover each other. We can split up in the garden.

"Any questions?"

They all shook their heads.

"All right, secure whatever you find in your packs. And for God's sake, be safe. I'm hoping we find what we need and get out fast."

As they started around the lab, the propane tank exploded. "Okay, boys, Semper Fi!"

Men inside the compound rushed from the cabins to put out the small fires around the ruined tank, shouting at one another as they worked to contain the fires.

Hiding in the pines along the cross-fencing, Matt said, "One last thing. If stopped by a DEA agent, give them my name and the code discharge. Don't forget… Colt and discharge. Otherwise, they'll think you're one of the guards and take you in with the rest of the group.

"Now, let's move fast before those guards checking on the propane tank return to the house."

Surprisingly, they made it to the garden without running into a patrol.

Matt pointed to the thorny rose bushes and shook his head.

Staying low, they went to the shadowed end of the garden, where Matt used a closed-fist signal to stop.

A sentry with a cigarette hanging from his mouth was on the veranda. Once the guard moved around the corner of the house, Matt nodded, and they split up and headed in different directions.

The voices coming from the dining room didn't sound concerned about the propane tank explosions. The sounds of utensils against plates, laughter, and conversation let Dean and Kade know that the residents were still enjoying their breakfast.

Obviously, they'd been advised that the situation with the propane tank was under control.

Kade and Dean moved quickly past the dining room to the foyer, holding double-shot tasers at the ready.

As they were ascending the staircase, loud, successive popping could be heard all around them.

Within seconds, screeches of metal, followed by thumps, could be heard as large sections of fence dropped to the ground, revealing an army of agents that swarmed into the compound from all sides.

Within seconds, a whiplash of rapid gunfire erupted.

In the loft, Dean and Kade heard the smashing of glass, the squeaky-grating sound of chairs being pushed across the floor, along with thuds, and crashes, and followed by a thunderous stampede of panic that rose up from the first floor.

They felt the pressure increase just as the bata-bata-bata slapping sound of helicopter blades moved in so close that the thing could have been roosting on the roof.

A gritty voice commanded, "This is the DEA. Drop your weapons and lay face down on the ground, hands clasped behind your head."

The sentries engaged the DEA agents to stop them from gaining ground. However, there were more agents than guards, and they were surrounded.

They just didn't know it yet.

Jason made his way across the compound, keeping to the shadows to avoid contact with a gunman or an agent.

Barely jumping clear before a section of fence landed heavily behind him.

As he reached the steps to the veranda, a guard came around the side of the house with his weapon drawn. He pointed the gun at Jason and smiled just as a bullet caught him in the head.

Without waiting to find out where the shot came from, Jason ran up the steps to the library door.

It was unlocked.

Entering, he scanned the room as he rushed to the open interior door to check the hall before quietly closing it just shy of the latch catching.

In the top drawer of the oversized desk, he discovered a small pocket pistol. After pulling the slide back to check for ammo, he quickly secured it in his waistband.

As he tossed the remaining drawers, he was somewhat disappointed with the haul. A calendar, cell phone, and some files took up little room in his pack.

Stopping to scan the room, he leaned on a statue bust sitting on a pedestal, surprised when it moved. At the same time a panel slid open on the wall, exposing a hidden room.

No wonder the desk had so little of value in it.

As he entered the small room, he found a row of labeled filing cabinets, an oversized chair, and a table with a lamp.

Opening the top drawer of the first cabinet, he was amazed at the sheer number of files. It seemed perverse, but a cartel was a business like any other; records were necessary to keep things running smoothly.

Still, there was no way he could take it all, even if only a third proved significant.

Faced with a monumental task, he had to prioritize.

As he searched for evidence related to the cartel business, he realized that the files were methodically organized and indexed with sections and subsections.

Taking off his pack, he got to work.

As he searched through the files, he found everything they'd need to put Magluta away for years. While pulling the files out of the drawer, a black file dropped onto the floor.

Inside were lists with dates, the names of officials, the payoff amounts, and the reason. Jason couldn't believe his luck as he stuffed the file into his pack.

After that, he found documents related to a legal partnership with two Black Hawk Casinos. He thought they might prove important at some point, but at the moment didn't seem relevant to his assignment.

That's when he uncovered detailed files on human trafficking. Each one held a dossier and photographs of a young woman being sold off like livestock.

There were far too many to take, his pack was nearly full, and time was slipping away.

Grabbing a handful of files, he hoped the team would find the rest still intact when they breached the room. With his pack bulging with evidence related to the cartel and human trafficking he turned his attention to matters that hit closer to home.

The file on John was thin, Billy's not much thicker, but without opening either, Jason stuffed them in with the others.

Fearing he was taking too much time, Jason looked in the K-L drawer and grabbed the file marked Kennedy.

His heart sank into his stomach when he made the mistake of opening it.

Photographs of Becca displayed provocatively amongst a heap of garbage, her skin tinted a greyish-blue, and her beautiful kaleidoscope eyes—empty.

Logically, he knew it was Joss, but the twins looked so much alike.

Shoving the file into his pack, he swallowed hard and changed gears.

He was surprised by the amount of private information Morales had on Charles, Dean, and Kade. Personal records including military, employment, medical, financial, and tax documents.

It was obvious that Morales and Jack had planned to cause the maximum injury to those Jason cared most about. It was impossible to fathom that they planned to do even more damage.

Although Kade's file was similar to Dean's, the information on his family only included Hiroshi's financial information and business dealings.

The noise of the gunfight was getting closer to the house, telling Jason that he was quickly running out of time.

Pulling open the drawer marked C-D, Jason pulled the files on the Colt family, which had multiple photographs and complete dossiers on both Matt and Jason.

Like the previous files, Matt's documents contained his military and business records. However, they also provided an answer to his question about how they knew he was working with the DEA. The documents included a series of pictures showing Matt emerging from the DEA complex.

One close-up had a black X drawn across it.

The last set of photos showed Matt's van engulfed in flames in the gully, with unrecognizable debris surrounding it, all captured from a distance.

The file on Sofia had several long-shot photos; At the sink, gazing out the window with a bemused smile on her face, the day she went grocery shopping, and one of her in the hospital bed with her face banged up.

Quickly shuffling through them, he was surprised to find several of his parents together shopping, dressed up, holding hands at a restaurant, washing the cars, and doing yard work.

In those pictures, they were smiling or laughing while throwing leaves at one another. Precious moments, locked in time forever.

The two last pictures stopped Jason cold.

The first was of his mother dressed in black, her face drenched with tears, sitting in the front row at his father's service. Jason's arm around her shoulders, and his head bowed.

A complete invasion of their privacy while they were most vulnerable.

But as depraved as that was, the last photo was even worse.

It was Sofia, standing alone at the kitchen window, with tear-filled eyes raised to the clouds. Holding a pot in one hand and a box of pasta in the other. Elbows against her sides, her hands out in a questioning gesture, as if she was asking his father what he wanted for dinner.

The photo sent a chill through Jason and angered him.

He'd never seen his mother so sad. But what was worse was the sticky note near the bottom that read; use her for leverage as needed.

Swallowing hard, Jason forced the zipper closed on his overstuffed pack and shoved those personal files under his vest, behind the gun, and into the waistband of his jeans. Then readjusted his belt to secure it in place.

He'd just have to remember to tell the agents about the room and let them sort through the rest of it.

Throwing the heavy pack over his shoulder and onto his back, Jason pushed the drawer closed and hurried from the room.

Once back in the library, he stopped in mid-stride.

Standing directly in his path was the Fat Man wrapped in a black silk robe embellished with gold trim, ascot scarf, and slacks looking every bit a pompous ass.

Two guards flanked him, pointing their AK-47s directly at Jason.

Ogre, the man who had gone to Becca's house, took a step closer. He would be hard, if not impossible, to take down, especially with the weight Jason had on his back. Not to mention, the man obviously outweighed him.

Ogre's counterpart was about Jason's height but was built like The Rock Dwayne Johnson, only with dark chocolate coloring.

Between the two, there was no way Jason was getting out alive. Realizing that he was outmanned and outgunned, Jason just smiled.

"How nice of you to come for a visit, Mr. Colt. It's a shame that you didn't wait for a proper invitation. I would have gotten to you eventually. But it seems you couldn't wait, and now that you and those agents have spoiled a beautiful banquet, upset my guests, and ruined the unveiling of my new treasure – well that was very rude, don't you think?"

Jason knew he was trapped. Thinking fast, he managed, "I hadn't intended on disturbing your little gathering, but since you had no trouble hurting my family, it seemed only fair that I return the favor. I'm sure you understand."

"Well, congratulations. You have put yourself at the top of my list.

"Before I have you killed, let's see if you can make this easier on me."

"And why would I do that?"

The Fat Man's lips curled into one of the ugliest smiles Jason had ever seen. "Pity. Sometimes, it's better to cooperate. Now I'm afraid you'll have to remain a guest with us permanently!

His voice bellowed the last words that reverberated around the room. "Take him!"

The two guards quickly grabbed him and held his arms in what felt like vice grips. Although it pinched, he didn't put up a struggle. There wasn't any point. Instead, he played along, hoping he'd find an opening to slip through.

Even with his compound in a gun battle, Morales acted like he was in control. "Take him to the Doctor. He should be at his cabin by now. Tell him I want answers within the hour!"

As they moved toward the door, Jason said, "You're going to prison, Fat Man! Let's see how you like prison food, huh?"

A hard blow to his gut made him bend over, but the vest and the files prevented him from receiving any serious injury.

But the blow to the back of his head nearly knocked him out.

With his head throbbing, he fought to remain conscious, but his knees buckled, forcing the men to drag him from the house.

As they made their way through a maelstrom of gunfire toward the Doctor's cabin located on the other side of the garden, Jason said, "Hey guys, we're gonna get killed if we stay out in the open. Maybe find some cover, huh?"

Saying nothing, the men dragged him along what remained of the fence line, occasionally stopping to add to the barrage of bullets as they went.

CHAPTER THIRTY-FOUR

The Doctor

Once at the Doctor's cabin, Jason was dragged inside and thrown down the basement stairs.

Between the pack and his Kevlar vest, his body was saved from the onslaught of injuries the tumble down the steps would have otherwise delivered. Even though his arms and legs weren't spared the full impact of the sharp-edged treads.

With his head still throbbing, he bracketed the sides of his head from impact with his arms, hoping to avoid a concussion.

The men watched him tumble down the steps.

At the bottom, they picked him up off the ground, tore off his pack, threw it under the stairs, and dragged him to the other side of the room.

With blood dripping into his eyes from a cut on his forehead, Jason saw an oversized metal chair bolted to the floor moments before, the guards carried him over and shoved him down onto the hard seat. Then enclosed his wrists in the iron manacles attached to the arms.

Jason looked around the dank and poorly lit room. The décor reminded him of something out of a medieval TV series or maybe the set from a horror film.

Dark, discolored walls, a rusted metal cage that hung from the ceiling in a corner. A medieval rack was pushed against the back wall and looked like it would easily pull a person apart.

The shackles on his wrists had dark stains. On closer inspection, he was able to make out splatters. Tiny drops that he assumed was someone else's blood.

Medieval weapons were hung within reach on the walls: a battle ax, crossbow with arrows, whip, mace, club, polearm spear, along with multiple knives, and swords.

All prominently displayed with gallery lighting like works of art.

Obviously, the Doctor was a collector of medieval armor and torture devices, but did he use those weapons to torture, or did he just use them for effect?

Jason hoped that the man just liked to frighten his guests and didn't actually use his collectables.

The Doctor took his time walking down the steps.

Even in the dull lighting, Jason recognized him right away. "I know you; you're the guy behind the gas station."

Ponytail took his time to walk up and stand in front of Jason. The without warning, he swung.

"That's to let you know who's in charge here."

Jason was stunned. The slap had taken him by surprise. Not the slap itself exactly, but the power behind the strike.

The man was obviously much stronger than he appeared, which explained how he knocked Jason down that night at the station.

"You will call me Doctor for as long as I keep you alive. You will answer my questions the easy way or the hard way." He waved his hand in dismissal, "It doesn't matter to me. I will enjoy it more should you resist."

At this range, Jason was able to obtain an accurate description.

Even though he looked like a child from a distance, up close, I'd say he's probably closer to forty. No taller than five foot six, maybe 145 pounds. Based on his darker skin tone, jet-black hair, bone structure and slight accent, ethnicity is most likely Mexican.

The Doctor moved away.

Overhead, the rat-a-tat of gunfire seemed more sporadic. Less fighting meant Jason had hope of being found in time.

But the Doctor didn't seem at all concerned.

His movements were precise and unhurried as he put on a black rubber apron and began collecting items from a shelf.

At a nearby table, close enough for Jason to see, The Doctor unfolded a velvet cloth pouch and pulled out a large, intricately designed brass-trimmed syringe.

Then, he connected a needle to the syringe.

His voice echoed in the room when he said, "It's a shame that we don't have time to play. Even as the battle rages around us, the tempo of gunfire is dwindling. And I refuse to be interrupted when I'm in the game. So, I'm afraid we'll have to hurry things along."

From another specially designed pouch, the Doctor unveiled a row of labeled vials. Cutouts in the leather exposed labels, but Jason couldn't read them from where he was.

The Doctor picked up one of the vials and turned to Jason with a smirk as he stuck the needle into the soft top of the vial and pulled back the plunger, slowly filling the barrel with the drug.

Jason kept his tone friendly and light when he said, "Look… um, I give. I'm not sure what you want, but it looks like you're serious. So,… hey, no need for that… stuff. I give up. Just tell me what you want to know."

The cocky smile left the Doctor's face. "Oh, so now you'll cooperate. A soldier giving up without so much as a struggle. How noble."

Setting the prepared syringe gently on the velvet, the Doctor replied, "Okay, if that's how you want to play it. But be advised any hesitation, and I won't be deterred again.

"Tell me how you found this compound. Who told you about this place, and what evidence does the DEA have?

"If you answer quickly, I promise I won't make you suffer. I'll make your death – quick." He snapped.

Outside, the gunfire was getting more intermittent.

Jason estimated that the agents were probably at the main house. He hoped they would soon storm the cabin.

Hopefully, while I'm still breathing.

Thinking fast, Jason said, "Look, I really don't know much. But this is how I got here.

"I followed a lead to the casino where I saw you. I remembered you from the gas station and followed you here. And that's how I discovered the compound."

He needed his hands free if he had any hope of fighting his way out of the dungeon. "But seriously, Doc, do I really need to be shackled with these goons here?

"It sounds like the gunfire is around the main house, so we have a little time. I'm being cooperative, and if you're going to kill me anyway…." Jason shrugged.

The Doctor looked at his hands and smiled. "I'm sure they are very tight... I would think—painful even. They weren't made to hold a man, although they are a tad adjustable.

"So far, you've answered truthfully. Still, I think it would be best to give you a little shot to ensure this continues. Just a little something to relax you and ensure you remain cooperative. We don't want to take a chance that you have something up your sleeve."

"No… really, that isn't necessary. I'd rather live my last minutes without being drugged."

Smiling, the Doctor picked up the needle and flicked the syringe. "You mean this sweet little drug? You misunderstand. This is but a light sedative to keep you manageable until we're done here.

"It alters cerebella function and inhibits transmission to the central nervous system, which decreases motor activity. Some believe it's a truth serum. But that's debatable.

"I like it because it inhibits the brain from reasoning, and if you can't think, well, it's harder to lie. We don't have time for lies, so this will ensure that your answers are truthful.

"It's true name is sodium pentothal. Not used much in the US anymore. But I find it useful, so I keep it in stock.

"It'll definitely disinhibit you, much like having a few too many drinks, and you may experience confusion, grogginess, or a dream-like state.

"But don't worry, these effects wear off, unlike the other chemicals we could try.

"I'm sure you would appreciate my newest creation. I call that masterpiece… Obsession. It would be a most pleasant way to die, but unfortunately for you, that's just not my style."

Jason saw saliva building up on the Doctor's lips as he spoke, revealing his more sadistic tendencies.

A predator enjoying his conquest. And right now, unfortunately, Jason was the prey.

Resigning himself to the situation, Jason quickly thought of a plausible story. A half-truth that he might remember and which might buy him more time and increase the man's confidence enough to release his hands.

Cradling the syringe, the Doctor stepped closer and, grinning, said, “This isn’t as fancy as the drug I gave you in the alley. That sweet little concoction was my very own brew.

“Another old favorite of mine was mixed in with your cold medicine.

“Only enough to change the chemical composition. I was actually surprised at how well you were moving by the time you got to the alley.”

His ears heard it, but he was confused. “Wait. You were in the alley? But how? I mean, you were running in the opposite direction. I didn’t see you. And Jack said he was the one who shot me.”

“Oh, he shot you; that’s true. But who do you think prepared the syringe in that dart?

“You can’t possibly believe that Jack is smart enough to calculate dosages? He’s not even bright enough to understand a simple physics equation for distance. The idiot nearly killed you when he refused to listen to my instructions and got too close.

“An inch closer would have impaled you. It might have even gone straight through your neck. Either way, you would be a dead man.”

To keep him talking, Jason asked, “I’m curious, how did you get away from me? I looked everywhere.”

Having stroked his ego, the Doctor was more than willing to share his prowess. “Yes, I’m sure that little trick stumped you. It was merely an illusion. A simple sleight of hand. A misdirection designed to separate perception from reality in order to fool the mind into believing that a misconception is truth.

“I’m a master of illusion and more ingenious in my craft than a magician. I am a wizard.

“But, in truth, it just comes down to the brain’s need to fill in the gaps.

“You need to understand. There was nothing you could have done to change the outcome of that night. You were way too physically compromised, in addition to being illiterate in the ways of the occult.

“There was no way you could have predicted our plan, even if you suspected something wasn’t right.

“It was a brilliant plan… brilliant!

"A play of puppets, and I was the master puppeteer. And the best part is that I can relive our perfect drama anytime I choose."

As if slapped, Jason was momentarily stunned. A sensation swept over him as he asked. "But why go through all of that? If you wanted Billy dead, why not just kill him?"

"You still don't understand. You brought this on yourself by persisting with your investigation. You left Francisco no choice. He couldn't risk you uncovering his operation or ruining our plans.

"It was either ruin your reputation or kill you outright. He thought killing you would just provoke a more extensive investigation.

"And Billy... well, he brought it on himself too. His biggest mistake was when he confided in his so-called friends.

"So, we choreographed events to take you both out at the same time, one dead, one in jail. The plan ensured nothing would land back on our doorstep."

Jason was listening when it hit him, "Wait, what did you mean when you said you can relive it anytime?"

"Well, since you'll soon be dead and dead men tell no tales… I think it can be our little secret.

"I'm quite proud of it, actually… I recorded the whole thing for my collection."

Jason nearly choked on his saliva. "You recorded it? All of it? Can I see it?"

Perturbed to realize that he was running out of time and getting impatient that the man had managed to keep him talking so long, the Doctor raised his voice, "No!"

Pointing to the shorter guard. "You. Open his sleeve and leave us. Keep everyone out. I'm not quite done here. If I need you, I'll call."

The paid muscle had the strangest look on his face. For a minute, Jason wondered if the guy might actually be on his side.

Adio hated working for the little man. He didn't like the Doctor's tricks and illusions, but he despised being forced into his games of torture that reminded him of the mambo priestess back home in Jamaica.

Because of his size, thick muscled, and stocky, he'd worked most of his life as a bouncer.

But, in truth, Adio had no stomach for violence.

Adio might seem more threatening due to his size, but in reality, the Doctor was the truly dangerous one.

Adio attempted to do what was asked, but he couldn't steady his hand, and while using his hunting knife to slit open Jason's sleeve, the blade nicked the skin underneath the shirt before Adio realized it.

When the Doctor noticed the thin trail of blood slowly bubble up, he yelled, "Fool! You've cut him!"

Then, he retracted the statement with a flick of his wrist. "Oh, never mind. Since we will be dispatching him soon, we don't have to worry about infection.

"You can go."

Jason hadn't felt the sharp bite of the blade, but that didn't hold true for the pinch of the needle, the sting of the liquid, or the burning sensation that was pumped through his veins with each heartbeat.

As the muscle took their cue and left quickly, the Doctor smiled down at Jason. "That should just about do it. Let's give it a few minutes. It doesn't take long for the drug to work its way through your system."

The Doctor turned his back to Jason while he looked for something on shelves under the stairs. "I must say I'm a bit disappointed. I was really looking forward to a struggle; I had hoped we had enough time to play a little."

Gunfire erupted close to the cabin above them. "Aw, yes. We are quickly running out of time. I'm afraid your friends will soon find us."

When the drug hit Jason, it was like he'd plunged off a cliff into deep waters.

Falling, he naturally tried to grab onto something to prevent the fall, but the shackles cut into his wrists and stopped his hands from moving more than a few inches.

At the same time, the sensation triggered a replay of the alley.

The disorientation, drowning in mud, the thunderous migraine that threatened to rip open his skull.

And just as painful, watching his partner suffer the same fate.

He fought the drug, feeling dizzy and disoriented. As a fog infiltrated his brain, compromising his vision with blurry waves. A wavy darkness began closing in from his peripheral vision and his head involuntarily flopped to the side.

"No, no, no, you can't go to sleep yet!" The Doctor cried. "They will come soon!"

Grabbing a fistful of hair, the Doctor lifted Jason's head, to check his pupils with a penlight, and took his pulse. "Yes, I think you're just about ready. But we must get some answers before we finish you."

Jason peeked up at the Doctor, tried to raise his hands as much as the shackles allowed, and tried to speak through a thickened tongue. "My wrists-s hu-urts!"

Frustrated, the Doctor roughly removed the shackles and returned to the table to finish preparing the lethal dose.

Picking up a vial, he admired the liquid inside. "This beauty is my latest masterpiece."

"If I didn't have to kill you, I could watch you suffer for years. One dose of this, and you wouldn't be able to live without it.

"You would be at my mercy. Do anything I ask. Break any law, anything, and would be a totally willing participant. All for the hope of another dose.

"That's what Francisco has planned once we verify the effectiveness of the product."

Jason whispered, "Evil promising salvation through profound exaggeration or intentional misrepresenting. Using a drug to monopolize every weakness until it takes complete possession and destroys it's host -- like a parasite.

"Who said, beware of those who speak with a forked tongue?"

Looking briefly over his shoulder, he smiled at Jason's blubbering. "It's time to tell me what I want to know.

"I've prepared my special brew at the maximum dose. It will kill you quickly; however, at this dosage, the intensity of the drug may prove excruciatingly painful.

"So there's still time for a little fun for me before I take my leave."

With his eyes on the filled syringe, he licked his lips, turned, and took a step, "Yes, just enough time for a little fun before you die, huh?"

Even in the dim light, Jason saw the deranged gleam in the man's eyes.

The explosion rang in Jason's ears a nanosecond before blood splattered the front of the Doctor's apron.

Jason looked down—the small gun from the desk was in his hand.

He clutched the weapon like a drowning person might to a life vest and awkwardly pulled the trigger a second time just before the Doctor fell to the ground.

The sodium pentothal had thrown off his balance the first time. He could only hope that the second shot had hit the mark if the first hadn't.

Trying to stand, he swayed and stumbled. Feeling like he was walking in quicksand.

Stumbling across the room toward the stairs, he tripped over the Doctor's leg. His chin nearly hit the cement before his hands flew out to stop the fall.

Resting for a moment on his stomach, he noticed his pack under the stairs. Moving onto his hands and knees, he grabbed the strap to drag the pack behind him as he crawled up the staircase.

Determined to find the video the Doctor mentioned, he figured that it was somewhere in the cabin's main living quarters.

Before he reached the top landing, the heavy pack got stuck when he pulled on it, causing him to lose his balance and tumble down several steps before he caught himself again.

Finally, at the top landing, he stopped and slowly opened the door.

The bodyguards were gone. They either ran away, got arrested, or were fighting with the others.

Leaning against the threshold, Jason struggled to focus. His eyelids were heavy, and his limbs were like rubber and his body kept pressing him to be still and sleep, but he refused.

As he pushed the basement door open enough to take a step, he fell face-first into the main room.

When he finally opened his eyes, shadows were climbing the walls like phantoms.

A production of shadow and light projected through the picture window and cast upon the walls in distorted moving images.

He fought the lethargy and tried to remember the layout he'd seen while being dragged to the basement.

He hadn't seen a TV or DVD player.

The sound of rapid gunfire was too close, transporting him in a blink to the desert, firing his weapon at the Taliban. He could smell the sulfur and feel the concussion of the explosions. They needed air support. They were running out of ammunition.

A couch.

He'd seen it when they entered.

His weapon dissolved in his hand, and the scenery changed into a living room.

Near the window.

Jason turned his head and saw a giant television mounted on the wall.

A large console under it.

He crab-walked, dragging the pack over to the console. Falling on his butt in front of it, in lieu of falling on his face.

Two long drawers ran along the bottom.

The first held DVDs. *Fuck, nothing but movies.*

The second drawer had rows of cases labeled with names and dates. All seemed to be women's names, and none referred to him or that night in the alley.

Time wasn't his friend, but he couldn't leave without the video.

Jason tried to stand, but the movement threw off his equilibrium, and he fell—hard.

On the way down, his arm hit the edge of a tray sitting on an ottoman, flipping the various items into the air and in every direction with a crash.

Lying on the floor, his eyes heavy, he thought maybe the Doctor gave me too much of the drug.

He began to fall into a void until a sensation that felt like he was leaving his body jolted him awake. "No, Goddamn it!" Jason yelled.

The fear of dying, like a plunge into ice-cold water, made him jump onto his hands and knees and shake his head to clear it.

When he put his arm on the ottoman to pull himself up, he noticed a case on the floor, half under the ottoman. He reached for it and saw his name.

But when he opened the case, it was empty.

There was only one other place it could be.

Moving as fast as possible on hands and knees, Jason opened the DVD player and laughed out loud when he saw that the disk inside had his name on it.

After putting the disk in the case, he stuffed it in between the file folders under his vest and belt. Then grabbed the pack and staggered to the front door.

Holding onto the doorjamb, he took a minute to watch a group of DEA agents walk a group of men in the direction of the staff gate. He was surprised to see the Jamaican man amongst them with a smile on his face.

Some agents wore black hoods, others just helmets, but they were all dressed in black combat gear with DEA in bright yellow on their backs.

The fog was slowly clearing, so he kept moving toward the opening in the fence as quickly as the dizziness allowed, hoping to find his team gathered there.

It was also the safest route, with agents still engaged in intermittent fighting and making arrests.

Despite his best efforts to rid his system of the drug, it continued to distort his vision. The ground appeared to undulate, making it difficult to run without stumbling.

Once at the fence, he didn't bother to look back. He just shouldered the pack onto his back and reached for the opening in the fence.

Just as he put his foot outside the boundary, he was grabbed from behind and thrown to the ground. "Where do you think you're going, asshole?"

Jason looked up in time to roll out of the way, avoiding a kick to the face, then jumped to his feet, swaying slightly, moving far enough out of reach to plant his feet.

As Jack came at him, Jason pulled the trigger on the small gun he'd pulled from his waistband.

The bullet hit Jack in the leg, cutting it out from under him. But as he fell, he grabbed Jason's jacket, pulling him down with him.

Struggling to maintain his balance under the added weight, Jason kicked off before he could be pulled to the ground. Altering their trajectory and propelling Jack backward through the fence. Jack landed hard on his back, momentarily knocking the wind out of him.

Jason purposely drove his elbow into Jack's midriff to ensure Jack would be out of commission for a few minutes.

The combined weight of Jason and the pack temporarily paralyzed Jack's diaphragm, making it spasm while he gasped like a fish for breath.

Jason wrestled with the weight of the pack to pick himself off Jack. Then he lifted himself enough to knee Jack in the groin, pressing down with all his weight as he pushed off.

As Jason slid completely off of him, he was unaware that Jack had pulled a knife from a sheath on his belt. Jack threw his arm at Jason.

Believing his pack would stop the blade Jason raised up on his elbow and punched Jack in the face.

Crunch.

Jason was weakened. He needed a minute to regain some of his strength. If he had to, he would fight to the death, but until his head cleared more and his strength returned, he needed a break.

Jack was still down.

Still too dizzy to stand, Jason implemented a commando crawl, and after several yards, he used a tree to stand.

When he looked back, Jack was on his hands and knees.

Not stopping, Jason kept moving, trying to put as much distance between them as possible.

After a few more yards, Jason saw Jack in his peripheral vision, dragging his leg – advancing.

Jack's focus was intense on Jason, holding his KA-BAR knife in reverse grip, his eyes squinted, lips tight, obviously determined to kill.

Jason realized that if he kept moving, he'd lead Jack to the shelter, putting Becca and Stryker in danger.

He needed to stand his ground and fight Jack where he stood.

Considering his options, even with Jack's injured leg, as long as the fog compromised Jason's thoughts, Jack had the advantage.

The drug was dissipating, but not quickly enough. To survive another attack, he needed to save his strength and prepare for the assault.

Turning onto his back, he readjusted the pack to support his upper body in a half-sitting position.

When Jack got close enough to lunge, Jason was ready.

There was a blur—and Jack hit the ground – hard.

Jason figured the drug was still influencing his perception. It took a minute to comprehend that Stryker had jumped on Jack, knocking him away.

What he didn't know was that the impact had caused Jack to lose his knife.

"Watch out boy, he has a knife!"

But Stryker wasn't done. He viciously bit down, shaking his head, tearing and ripping Jack's flesh.

Stryker deserved some retribution after the hell that Jack put him through. Seeing that Stryker was managing the situation. Jason got to his feet and stumbled away into a group of trees to rest.

Without a knife, Jack had only his fists, but before he landed a strong enough blow, Stryker bit down on where Jack had been shot.

Jack screamed and tried to hit Stryker, but the dog held on until he ripped away both cloth and meat from Jack's leg.

As the drug finally dissipated enough that he could get his bearings, Jason headed toward the shelter and after hearing several screams whistled for Stryker.

Seeing his best friend run up to him, panting happily with blood covering his muzzle, was surprisingly gratifying.

Rubbing Stryker's head, he said, "You are such a good boy. I'm so proud of you, partner. I hope you know how much you mean to me. Come on, let's go find Becca."

After a few yards, a sharp pain broke through the adrenaline. Jack had managed to stab him -- at least once, and with enough force to penetrate his vest.

Pressing down as hard as he could to stop the bleeding and unsure of how much blood he'd lost, he quickened his pace. If I can reach the dugout, Becca will help stop the bleeding.

A few yards later, his energy seemed to seep out with the blood.

Stumbling, he leaned against a tree, lost his balance, and hit the ground.

A small group of trees acted like a basket for some thick brush. Unable to carry it any longer, he shrugged off the heavy pack and hid it there in the thicket.

Holding his side, he pushed himself up against the tree.

A few more steps.

Don't give up. Just keep moving.

Even without the pack, he could feel his energy draining.

You can do it!

He'd never felt so weak.

The thwomping of helicopter blades hovering overhead bored into his brain.

Pain is weakness leaving the body.

Bravery is being the only one who knows you're afraid.

Time seemed to stand still.

There was a rushing sound in his ears that seemed to wrap over the top of his head.

He hit the ground.

Stryker nudged him.

Tugging and pulling on Jason's flak jacket, but he only managed to move Jason a few feet.

Licking Jason's face and pawing at his arm did nothing to rouse him.

Unable to wake him, Stryker took off to the hideout.

Hearing Stryker running back and forth, barking at the entrance, Becca said, "Stryker? Where have you been? What is it? What's wrong? Is it Jason?"

Becca shoved the gun down into the back of her waistband and did her best to follow Stryker.

He was obviously stressed, running out of sight and then back to her as if to say hurry up.

Finally, she saw Jason on the ground. Rushing to his side, she dropped to her knees beside him, "Jason, can you hear me!"

Performing a sternal rub, hoping to rouse him, she released a sigh when he responded.

Still a bit out of it, Jason said, "Hey, Becca… Jack cut me. Pretty good... I guess I… must have... passed out for a minute. We have to keep moving. Stryker stopped him, but Jack's still out there, and he wants blood. Mine apparently."

Jason's clothing was saturated with blood, and she couldn't tell if he was still bleeding. She could only hope it had stopped on its own. "Yeah, well, I need to take a look at the damage."

His breathing increased slightly. "I had to leave my pack. It's not far—by a big tree—a grouping.

"You have to find it, Becca. We can't let Jack get to it. It has evidence… important evidence. Do you still have that gun?"

"Yes. But first, we need to take care of that wound. Then we can worry about your pack."

"No. Please. We can't leave it."

Through the paint smeared on his face, Becca could see that he was pale. "I promise I'll come back for it. But first, let's get you to the shelter where we're not sitting ducks out in the open."

"I'm not sure I can make it to the shelter."

She knew that she'd run for at least a quarter mile before she found him, but she wasn't about to tell him that. "It's not that far. We'll do it together, okay? Just lean on me and stay awake, okay?"

"...yeah, okay, but no matter what, Becca, you go for that pack."

Helping him to his feet, "I promise to go back for it in a minute. Let's just focus on getting to the shelter for now."

He was heavier than she realized, and she was thankful that working with livestock had kept her muscles strong.

As they began moving, Stryker circled them in slow, wide circles.

Becca figured he was ensuring that no one was following them.

After a few hundred yards, Becca felt her strength fading. But tenacious, she pushed on.

When they finally reached the shelter, she set Jason down and rolled her shoulders.

"I'll be right back. See if you can't get yourself inside while I'm gone."

As she turned to leave, Stryker grabbed Becca's hand with his mouth. "It's okay, boy. I'll be right back. You stay here. You take care of Jason."

Rushing past where she'd found him, she looked for the grouping of trees. Smoke had filled the area and it was making her eyes water.

The pack was only a few yards from where she'd found Jason.

Grabbing the pack, she considered asking for help from one of the team in the compound.

She knew that teams of DEA agents and firefighters were on the scene, but they were all busy putting out fires and rounding up suspects.

As she squinted through the smoke, she saw the outline of a man limping in her direction and realized that it had to be Jack.

She ran to the hideout and dove inside.

Jason was keeled over in front of the opening, obviously unconscious again.

Using her legs against the wall of the hideout, she grabbed onto his vest and pulled him inside.

In a firm, low whisper, she ordered, “Stryker, you need to back me up. Stryker you stay out there. Go hide. Protect Jason, okay? Go.”

She was shaking but knew what she had to do.

She didn’t want to sacrifice Stryker, but she was quickly running out of choices.

With tears in her eyes, she pointed away and added more softly, “So go okay. Go.”

The smoke surrounded them, hovering like a cloud just above the ground, burning her eyes.

Rolling Jason further back into the dugout, she heard the rustle of leaves and snapping of twigs and knew their time was up.

The smoke had thickened, choking her. It was hard to see.

Her heart boomed loudly in her ears, making it hard to hear.

Covering her nose and mouth with the edge of her shirt, she rubbed her eyes and strained them to search through the smoke.

A silhouette of a man moved slowly through the bushes, limping in their direction. She knew it was Jack, but it took a minute to make out his face.

The man—the monster who had killed Joss, kidnapped and drugged her and Jason was coming and she needed to stop him.

She reached for the gun at her back, but it was gone.

As fear washed over her, sweat broke out over her body.

Putting her body in front of the door to block Jason, she prayed that Stryker could stop the man from killing them.

He stopped less that fifty yards away. Swaying for several minutes.

Becca was sure he could see her.

The pungent odor of sweat mixed with the remnants of smoke made her gag, but she swallowed hard and awaited her fate.

Maybe he was sizing up his prey.

Weakened, his arm shook as he raised a weapon and lined up the barrel, yelling, "Where's Colt? I know he's in there. Move aside bitch."

"No."

Even in the dwindling smoke, he saw the determination on her face. Joss's face. "I didn't know there were two of you. She never said she had a twin.

"I didn't want to kill her. She was my favorite. But she was too clever. She found the drugs. And she was so mad about it. She said she didn't know that I was that kind of person. She threatened to report me! I didn't have a choice!

He stepped closer, "That kind of person. Like I was trash to her. Well, she's the one that ended up in the trash – huh?

"You're just like her. Fuck!" He shook his head.

"But I didn't want to do it! And now I have to kill you, too. Kill her, my beautiful Joss, all over again.

"Why couldn't you just leave it alone?"

As he hobbled a few more steps, Becca thought she recognized the gun she lost.

Pushing her shoulders back, she pushed her chin forward and closed her eyes, "My sister was an amazing woman. She was gifted and strong, and smart, and loving.

"She was a beautiful human being who was worthy of life!"

Moving to fill the entrance with her torso, she lowered her head slightly, tightened her lips, furrowed her brow, and looked up at him through blazing hate-filled eyes and spat, "Unlike you, who offers nothing but perversion and corruption!

"You soil this planet with your very existence!

"You're the one who should be dead. This world doesn't need or want the likes of you.

"But you'll have to crawl over my dead body before I'll let you take out another beautiful soul!"

Using his other hand to help lift the weapon, he pointed it directly at her head, "That won't be a problem."

A loud crack followed by a thud made her whole body jump.

Stunned, it took a minute to reopen her watery eyes.

When she did, Jack was lying on the ground just inches away. A dark patch of blood-soaked hair stared back at her.

A tall man in a black balaclava stood just feet away.

He looked straight at her and, without saying a word, shook his head, lifted Jack into a fireman's carry, and walked away.

A few yards away, as a breeze cleared the remaining smoke, Becca noticed Stryker sitting calmly, panting with what looked like a smile.

CHAPTER THIRTY-FIVE

The Getaway

Becca checked on Jason.

He was still out cold, and his shirt was saturated on the right side.

She didn't have a medical kit or sterile pads, and the light wasn't as bright inside the shelter to be able to do much anyway.

Among the supplies in the dugout, Becca found a bandana. Although she doubted it was sanitary, she thought she could use it to stop the bleeding.

The sunlight was filtered through the tree canopy and the leaf-covered shelter.

Not knowing what lay ahead or what trauma he'd suffered, she decided to do a quick exam, stop the bleeding, and provide medical care until she could get Jason to a hospital.

Instead of undressing him, she loosened the Velcro on the side of the vest enough to take a peek, knowing the vasoconstriction helped to reduce his blood loss.

She used her fingers to search for the injury and was surprised when she touched what felt like thick paper.

Hoping it was helping to staunch the blood flow, she left the unknown untouched and moved her fingers until she felt the laceration.

It was in the upper abdominal region and longer than expected.

Working quickly, she packed the laceration with the bandana.

Taking Jason's vitals, she considered their next move. Afraid that since Jack had found them other's might as well.

The biggest problem was figuring out where she was. She knew the compound was in Central City next to Black Hawk, but she had no idea where Jason's Jeep was or who to trust to ask for help.

And she hadn't seen Matt, Dean or Kade since they headed out.

It seemed like forever since daybreak when they'd left the warehouse. Without knowing how extensive Jason's injuries were, they couldn't just wait it out and hope their team would get to them in time.

Time just wasn't on their side.

Becca called out softly to Stryker, "Stryker, come here, boy!" Her voice was just above a whisper.

Opening her mouth to call out one more time, Stryker poked his head out from a bush near the front of the shelter.

Becca half-smiled as she reached out and patted him on the head. "Good boy. For just a minute there, I thought you took off on us."

Nudging Jason until he woke, Becca said, "I think it's safe to go. You need a hospital – Jack took a pretty good slice out of you."

Jason sounded loopy. "No! No hospital! I'll be okay."

"Says you, but I'm not so sure.

"We don't have time to argue right now. We need to get out of here. Where did you leave your Jeep?"

"It's just over a small ridge to the south. It's a bit of a hike, and I'm not in the best shape.

"Do you know how far it is?"

He took a minute to answer. "I usually park about a klick away. Hey, at least my head feels a bit clearer.

"I don't know what a klick is, but I'm glad you're feeling better. Can you walk?"

"I'll do my best."

"Okay, just lean on me, and I'll let you lead the way."

Jason managed to crawl out of the shelter. "We just go south, then turn west at the crooked tree."

Once they got him on his feet, Becca put the heavy pack on, "Damn, whatever you got in here, I sure hope it's worth it. This thing weighs a ton."

"Trust me, it's worth it."

"Well, let's get moving."

Seeing that he was still unsteady, Becca wrapped an arm around Jason's waist so that his injured side would be protected against her body and held onto his belt, "Better?"

"I'm always better when I'm next to you."

"Okay, Casanova, but why don't we save our strength to stay upright, okay?

She was reminded of the way she helped her mother. And the importance of using her legs instead of her back.

Holding his weight as they meandered around brush and trees was proving to be much more taxing than when she helped her mother.

Stryker stayed close as she continued to pull and tug Jason along, stopping for breaks now and then to give them both time to catch their breath.

When Becca stopped to rest, she watched a cloud darken as it moved across the sky.

I hope we make it to the Jeep before it starts to rain.

As they pushed on, Jason knew his short-lived energy burst was nearing the end, and at the crooked tree, his legs finally gave out.

Becca helped him to the ground and then sat down next to him.

"I hate to say it, but I can't go any further. My head may be clearer, but my legs are rubber. Check my pack. My two-way radio should be in it."

"Well, shit! Why didn't you tell me that before we moved you?"

"Because we were too close to the compound. The DEA jammed the frequencies as soon as they blew the fences so no one could call out. But we may be far enough away now."

Pulling the walkie out of the pack, she handed it to him.

"Damn, still no signal. Look, Becca, just leave me here. The Jeep should be just on the other side of those rocks up ahead. Take it and go. Find Dean, he'll help."

"Fat chance I'm leaving you like this. You're weak from blood loss. Too many things could happen while I'm gone.

"Besides, I might get lost, and that would put us both in jeopardy. I only have a vague idea of where I am.

"So it looks like I need you as much as you need me. So buckle up, buddy. You're stuck with me. I'll drag you the rest of the way if I have to."

"Buckle up, buddy?" He laughed, "Really?"

She couldn't help it. She busted up laughing, too. "Okay, so sue me. I couldn't think of anything better to say.

Smiling up at her, he said, "You are really something, you know that? You really swept this guy off of his feet – literally."

At that, they both chuckled.

Whether it was because of the stress that had been building for hours or that they were still in trouble, neither one knew.

"Ow! Stop! Please. It hurts." Jason was holding his side.

"Oh, God. I'm sorry. I really don't know why this is so funny."

"I know. But it hurts to laugh. So now, what do we do?"

She stopped laughing and was suddenly serious. "We move. So move your ass, soldier, or I'll move it for you. I think a storm's moving in, and we're already at a disadvantage. We definitely don't need to add more to an already difficult situation."

Her concern was genuine, so he didn't argue. Not that there was anything he could say that would wipe that stubborn look off her face.

"You're right about that."

This time, when she got him up, he was heavier—shuffling his feet along the ground and stumbling every few yards.

But what really got to Becca was the noises both Jason and Stryker were making. Every time Jason moaned, Stryker whimpered.

It was so touching that unshed tears burned at the back of her eyes. "Would you two quit? You guys are killing me."

At the Jeep, Jason had just enough strength to climb in and lay down on the backseat, with Stryker on the floorboard beside his legs.

"Okay, now tell me how we get out of here."

The road was rough, and with each bounce or jostle, Jason either grimaced or groaned.

Finally, they were on I-70 and Becca knew her way.

It didn't take long after that for Jason to lose consciousness.

As they neared I-65, Becca reached back and jostled Jason's shoulder, "Jason, I really think you need a hospital. I'm a vet, not a doctor. You were drugged – stabbed, and God only knows what else. And to be honest, I don't want to lose you, or for that matter, my license."

Jason tried to change her mind. "Look, I promise I won't tell anyone that you helped me. I'd never do anything that might get you in trouble. Especially not after everything you've done for me today.

"But I can't go to the hospital. Not yet.

"We don't know who Morales has on the take. I trusted Jack, for God's sake! And if I can't trust a cop, who can I trust? If I go to the hospital now, I… I could lose everything, Becca.

"Please. Just stay with me a little longer. I need to see this through. I'm so close to ending this nightmare.

"You fixed me up once, and I know you can do it again—at least enough until I can finish this. Then I promise I'll do whatever you want. Please, Becca, I swear I wouldn't ask you to do this if I was worried."

Watching pain wash over his face in the review while he attempted to sit up almost made her refuse. But when he lightly touched her, she didn't have the heart to say no. "Okay, but I sure hope neither of us lives to regret this."

He gave her that crooked smile as they made eye contact in the mirror, then fell back on the seat and into a dreamless sleep.

On the drive, she considered the best course of action to care for Jason's injuries.

The clinic couldn't accommodate someone his size, but the large animal surgery was sterile, more than large enough, and had everything she needed.

Since the renovation, she'd only used that surgery a handful of times. Remembering her last surgery put a smile on her face. She could still see the beautiful black and white paint horse named Checkers.

Checkers belonged to a pretty little, long-haired girl named Trina. Trina's mother, Kate, had rushed the horse in when he'd been injured after jumping an old wooden fence.

One of the cross braces on a three-rail fence was broken, pointing up when Checkers jumped it and that piece of wood impaled his breast like a stake, creating a penetrating thoracic injury at the sixth rib.

Becca recalled the young girl. The flow of her beautiful brown hair with natural golden highlights that rippled in waves of gold as they walked Checkers from the horse trailer into the barn.

When they handed the reins to Alice to prep the horse for surgery, Trina's beautiful almond-shaped brown eyes were spilling rivulets of tears down her sweet face.

Becca would never forget that sweet child who, months after his recovery on the farm, sent pictures of Checkers along with thank-you notes addressed to Becca and her staff.

Becca told herself that treating Jason wouldn't be that different from treating a large animal. Only instead of removing a sharp piece of fence from a horse's chest, she'd be closing the wound on a human abdomen.

She decided to use the sevoflurane gas for sedation because it didn't require intubation and would allow him to revive quickly once she turned it off.

And once the sedation wore off, he'd be able to ambulate to the house, where she'd have a place for him to rest while he recovered.

As soon as she stopped the Jeep, having made up her mind how to manage the situation, she opened the gate and ran inside the barn to get things ready.

Everything in the surgery was kept sanitary, but Becca gave it a quick scrub just to be sure.

Then, helping Jason from the Jeep into the barn, she asked him one last time, "Are you sure you want me to do this?"

"Absolutely! I trust you."

Stryker followed, but he couldn't be in the surgery. "Stryker, you stay. I promise to take good care of Jason."

Jason turned slightly and patted Stryker on the head. "You be a good boy for Becca. Sitzen, bleiben."

In the holding area, she helped Jason up on a rollaway, "Okay, Jason, you go ahead and undress and put your gear on this counter. Just leave your clothes there. I'll pick them up later.

"But do me a favor, before I come for you, cover yourself with this drape. It's probably too big; we use it for the ponies, but it'll work. I'll let you know when I'm ready."

While Jason undressed, Becca got the machines ready and went through her human anatomy book, marking each page she might need with post-it flags.

She'd had the book since her mother got sick. At the time, it had helped her feel more connected to her mother.

Once she got Jason settled on the padded surgery table, Becca administered the sevoflurane gas, checking the MAC score to make sure it stayed at the correct dose. After an aggressive sternal rub to make sure he was unconscious, she went to work.

His blood pressure was low, and he had a slight temperature, but thankfully, he was strong and healthy.

Once she checked the laceration and saw that the bleeding had stopped, she soaked a sterile cloth in a saline solution and began bathing him.

She thoroughly debrided his head wound, washing away dirt and debris so that she could check his injuries.

Under the smeared face paint and grime were minor scrapes and bruises in various stages of healing.

Making a mental list, she triaged each one.

He had a nice-sized laceration on his forehead, a large gash at the back of his head, a minor cut on his left forearm, and multiple superficial abrasions, along with some discoloration over his arms and legs that she believed would soon turn into some ugly-looking bruises. The vest had protected his upper torso, so his chest had minor damage.

The area she'd stitched up the week before looked inflamed. Without having enough time to heal before the day's assault and was now caked with dirt. She made a mental note that infection was a distinct possibility.

All in all, the stab wound in the upper right abdomen and the head injuries were the worst of it—the minor abrasions and lacerations notwithstanding.

The blood-soaked bandana that she'd used to stop the bleeding was stuck to his skin with dried blood and would need to be removed carefully so as not to rip the skin.

She washed around the wound, removing some of the clotted blood. Saturated the bandana and then washed his arms and legs.

After bathing him from head to toe, she removed the soiled drape and re-draped him.

Then, she went to the sink to scrub all over again while she considered what to do next.

She was worried about the head injuries. Her equipment was for animals, and she didn't know what to look for when looking at human scans. There was no way to tell if he had a concussion or bleeding on the brain.

To rule out anything serious, he needed a CT. All she could do was sew up his head. But if he took a turn for the worse, she would take him to a hospital whether he liked it or not.

Although she didn't like the situation, she was committed to treating him and was determined to do her best.

Putting on surgical gloves, she moved to his side to focus on the stab wound.

After flushing the area around the knife wound, she removed the wet and sticky saturated bandana using gauze pads to soak up the fresh blood. Then washed his abdomen in betadine and draped the surgical area.

To clearly see the damage, she was forced to excise the wound, making a midline incision in the abdominal wall and dissecting it down to the fascia with electrocautery.

She packed the abdomen with lap pads in all four quadrants to control the bleeding and cleared the view so she could identify the source.

After removing the pads, she inspected each quadrant and identified a three-centimeter laceration in the lower right lobe of the liver. After suturing the laceration, she examined the other three quadrants.

With no other signs of organ injury, she looked for injuries to the surrounding organs but found them intact.

Taking an extra heartbeat or two to ensure there were no leaks, she irrigated the area and suctioned until the effluent ran clear.

After one final inspection, she noted good hemostasis.

Once satisfied that his organs had been addressed, she checked his vitals and closed the fascia and then the skin.

Moving to care for his head lacerations, she stopped long enough to look at his beautiful face.

Even unconscious and damaged, the man was easy on the eyes. With a big sigh she moved on.

The laceration on his forehead wasn't too bad; it only needed surgical glue and a couple of butterfly bandages.

However, the gash on the back of his head was another story. It required stitches.

Pulling off her gloves, she grabbed a wedge support to comfortably lift his shoulders and brace his neck while she cleaned and stitched the wound.

Without an assistant, she was glad she had the equine sling. It was used to lift livestock onto the hydraulic table, but it would safely lift Jason while she got him into position.

Once he was appropriately positioned, she scrubbed once again and put on a new set of gloves. Then, cut and shaved the hair around the wound and debrided it.

It was a relief to find that the wound wasn't nearly as deep as she feared. It hadn't cracked the skull, and only a few sutures were required.

After checking his vitals, she was encouraged to see that his blood pressure had stabilized and that he wasn't clammy or feverish anymore.

With her job completed, Becca slowly rolled her head, stretched her neck from side to side, and rolled her shoulders. She hadn't realized how long she'd been bent over him.

Her whole body felt stiff, her muscles sore.

Standing up to stretch, she looked through the clerestory windows in the surgical suite and noticed a blanket of dusk was slowly overtaking the brightness of the day.

A very long and trying day.

Looking up at the clock, she realized just how very long and unpleasant the day had been, and she was glad it was nearly over.

Since the table was big enough to fit a horse, Becca didn't worry that Jason would roll off of it.

While waiting for the gas to wear off, she gathered up his clothes. Along with the gear and folders he left on the counter and noticed that the files were stuck together as if glued with his blood.

She wrapped the files in a small drape, picked up Jason's clothes, and headed to the house to prepare a recovery area.

Once inside, she set the wrapped folders on the counter beside the washing machine and threw his clothes into the washer.

In the kitchen, she rewashed her hands while watching the sunset through the large kitchen window.

That's when it hit her. They were alone.

Jason had just gone through surgery and needed time to recover, and they had no idea if anyone had slipped by the agents.

They needed protection.

Rushing to her bedroom, she grabbed her Smith and Wesson 9mm luger out of the bedside table, hoping she wouldn't need it and shoved it into her waistband.

Then, she went to her storage shed to get her mother's wheelchair and her dad's old camping cot that she hoped would make a makeshift recovery bed.

As the sun was setting, the temperature was dropping. So Becca decided to build a fire.

She loved the old dark-rust cast iron wood stove inset in an alcove between the kitchen and dining room. It kept the whole back of the house warm and would provide a comfortable room for Jason to recover in.

And because it was part of the original build, it had been grandfathered in during the renovation.

During the day the large kitchen window over the sink let in natural sunlight, which spilled across the kitchen and into the dining room.

Looking at the room, she admired the large Drexel Heritage dining table, which had been her grandmother's, and was still one of her favorite possessions.

Becca had refinished the old table and chairs herself—sanding and staining the maple in a rich mahogany.

She taught herself how to reupholster the cushioned chairs and purchased a large floral pattern fabric in maroon, green, pink, gold, and blue that she knew her grandmother would have loved.

Seeing it always brought back some of her happiest childhood memories of their large family gatherings at her grandparents' house. They would stuff themselves with her grandmother's excellent cooking and play board games until all hours.

Mentally shaking herself, *memories can wait. Right now, I need a recovery room.*

After closing the drapes on the large dining room window, she moved most of the chairs against one wall and pushed the table close to the matching sideboard buffet to make room for the old camping cot.

After she set up the cot a few feet from the wood stove, she folded a few thick quilts to create a softer bedding on top of the rigid canvas and metal frame. Then, encased it all with a sheet, another quilt, and a pillow.

Grabbing an armload of firewood from the porch, she carefully placed the kindling crisscross inside the stove and lit a fire, knowing it wouldn't take long before a comforting wood heat would fill the back of the house.

Stepping back, she looked at the makeshift recovery room and said, "There. We have a clean, warm place to recover."

Back at the barn, she checked Jason's vitals and sat with him until he woke up.

Still groggy but feeling no pain, he smiled at her. "Hey, gorgeous, where have you been?"

She figured he must have woken at some point while she was gone, "Getting things ready for you. Now, how about you help me get you into this wheelchair? Do you think you can do that?"

"Maybe."

"Well, just take it nice and slow."

She wrapped a clean drape around him and helped him into the chair. Getting him to the house was a little bumpy, but it would prove to be the easy part.

Stopping at the front steps, she looked at Jason. He still looked pale in the porchlight. "Okay. Now, here's the hard part. We have to climb up these stairs. How're you feeling? Is your head clearing up? Are you in pain?"

Shrugging, "Um… I'm okay, just a bit loopy, but I think I can make it up there."

"I know it's a lot to ask after surgery. But I can't carry you, and I don't have a better way to get you into the house where I can keep an eye on you.

"So, here's the plan. We'll go up the steps together. You can lean on me, but I need you to watch your feet. There can be no missteps. We can't take the chance of you falling down the steps and busting yourself open… okay?"

He smiled up at her from the chair and gave her a thumbs-up.

"Good. Now, once we get to the porch, I'll sit you down on that rocker while I bring up the wheelchair.

"After we get you back in the wheelchair, you won't have to walk anymore, okay?"

"S-u-r-e!"

Worried that he still seemed too loopy, she took a minute to consider an alternative. But it was getting colder by the minute, and she was out of options.

"Alrighty-then." Locking the wheels on the chair, she helped him up.

Holding Jason with one arm and the railing with the other, they swayed up each of the four treads looking, she was sure, like a couple of drunks.

But even breathing hard while she pulled, realigned, and steered their way up the steps, Becca managed to keep them both upright without either of them taking a nose dive.

Once he was situated in the wheelchair, getting him inside took little effort.

The final struggle came when she tried to get him onto the cot.

As she helped him from the wheelchair, they both fell onto the cot. Luckily, Jason fell on top of her, which cushioned his fall. But she was surprised that their combined weight didn't break the old cot or open his stitches.

With eyes half-closed and a goofy smile on his face, Jason mumbled, "Hmm, this is an interesting turn of events. A soft landing even."

She couldn't help but smile. "Is that right? For now, it might be best if you had a little rest… what do you say?"

His eyes were nearly closed already as he slurred. "I think that's a marvelous idea."

Damn. This man will be the death of me. Cute doesn't begin to cover it.

As Becca untangled herself and positioned him on the cot, with a smile still on his face, he quickly fell back to sleep.

Stryker had followed them into the house and commandeered a place in front of the hearth, enjoying the warmth of the fire.

Watching him brought Scout and Radar to mind.

Rushing from the room, she thought, Oh, my God! I almost forgot. They were drugged, and God knows what else! I have to find them!

Running outside, she called for them.

Worried that they hadn't come to the car when she pulled up, she dreaded to think what Jack had done to them.

As she ran down the driveway, she didn't hear anything until she was near the boarding yard.

Hearing their cries, she opened the gate and found them locked in the boarding cages without food or water.

"You poor babies, I bet you're so thirsty.

"Come here and let me look at you… are you hurt?"

She examined both of them and then filled the kennel bowls with water. While they gulped their fill, she said, "I'll be right back. I still have work to do, then I'll get you some dinner."

In the barn, she checked on Carmela and Henry, the Boer goats boarding with her, and stopped to give them a treat.

She spent the next forty-five minutes sanitizing the surgery. Then gathered the rest of Jason's gear, which included his dirty boots. After depositing them on the back porch, she fed the dogs.

Going back to her patient, she almost laughed when she saw his feet hanging off the end of the cot. Yet even though he looked like a giant in a too small bed, he also looked terribly vulnerable.

It was hard to believe that he'd just survived a brutal assault as well as surgery.

And he wasn't out of the woods yet.

Still, she was seeing an improvement in his vitals.

Seated next to him, she reached down to move a few delinquent strands of dark hair out of his eyes. Then gently traced his thick dark eyebrows and the stubble along his jaw and cheek.

It was difficult not to stare. And she couldn't help but take her time readjusting his covers.

The definition of muscle tone on his chest and stomach meant he most likely worked out, which made sense considering his profession.

The sensuality of the smattering of hair that accented his chest and trailed down under the sheet made her body tingle in response.

From his thick dark lashes lightly touching his cheeks to broad shoulders, defined biceps, thick thighs, and round solid calves, she was drawn to every part of him.

But it was that damn trail of downy black hair that she knew continued under the drape to the bulge of his manhood that made her wet.

Since they'd met, he'd incited a desire in her that she'd never experienced before.

She was so aware of him, it felt like every nerve in her body was on alert when he was around. His scent, his voice. The virility of his very presence seemed to affect her even as he lay fast asleep.

Even the ugly abrasions, stitches, and bandages that covered his olive-complected skin weren't enough to detract from his beauty.

He was simply a striking specimen of manhood.

Closing her eyes, she breathed in his scent and covered him with a quilt. Then, to prevent him from rolling off the cot, she placed a few chairs around it.

Stryker had settled between her boys, positioning part of his body on each of their beds. And like Jason, he was out, his legs twitching as if he were running.

Becca gazed out the kitchen window. The night was clear and even welcoming, but something had changed, shifted for her.

Men had broken into her house like they owned the place. She was drugged. Kidnapped.

Her life had been threatened— more than once.

She put her license on the line to save a man she barely knew.

Jesus, what's wrong with me?

The time she'd spent seeking justice for Joss—was a blur.

It was all too much to process.

On nights like this, with the cast of light sitting stubbornly on the horizon, Becca would grab a cup of cocoa and relax in her favorite lounger in the backyard with a blanket over her legs to ward off the chill, and her boys lying beside her.

She loved to watch the sunset and if she didn't fall asleep, she'd try to find the constellations in the darkened sky.

Sometimes, she'd just let her imagination wander across the galaxy along with a shooting star.

The coffee maker chimed, and with a cup of coffee in hand, Becca headed for a shower.

Her body felt wrecked, with every muscle screaming for relief.

Setting the gun on the counter next to her half-finished cup of coffee, she allowed her clothes to drop to the floor so she could step into the steaming hot shower.

Standing under the hot spray of the massage showerhead, she hoped the water beating on her neck and shoulders would release some of the lactic acids that had been building up in her overused muscles.

Changing positions, she let the hot water pound the tension away while her mind replayed everything from the moment she'd seen Jack in her hallway.

Although her emotions were in turmoil, incongruent with her thoughts she was relieved that Jack would finally pay for killing Joss and trying to ruin her good name.

Arrested with the rest of the criminals at the compound, she was thrilled to think he might experience some measure of the pain he caused her sister.

The pain he caused her family.

Suddenly the intensity of emotion she'd been stuffing down for years, racked her body. Sobs, pure and overwhelming, while she relived the years of pain without her twin.

Until she was finally exhausted and her muscles released some of the tension they'd held since hearing her twin was dead.

The perfume of her shampoo and conditioner, sandalwood and lavender, was comforting. The scents not only helped her relax but also removed the stench of smoke, sweat, and blood from her nostrils and pores.

When she stepped out of the shower more than a half hour later, she felt like a new person.

With a towel wrapped around her head, she put on her favorite floral terrycloth robe and went to the kitchen to put her coffee cup away and check on her charge before collapsing into bed.

Walking into the kitchen, she rinsed the cup and put it in the dishwasher.

She was opening the fridge to consider something to eat when a strange sensation washed over her.

A tingling ran down her back and at the same time the hairs stood up on her arms.

Fully aware that all she wore was a robe and the towel around her head, she was struck with the knowledge that she'd left her gun upstairs on the bathroom counter.

Before turning around she searched for a weapon and quietly pulled a knife from the block on the counter.

Then, inhaling deeply to steady her nerves, she turned to find a man sitting next to Jason.

CHAPTER THIRTY-SIX

The Visitor

At first, she felt a little faint seeing a hooded man sitting on one of her grandmother's chairs. The one she'd only a short time before had placed to prevent Jason from falling.

He was petting Stryker, but his focus was on Jason.

Becca thought it was probably the same man she'd seen carry Jack away.

But she was angry that yet another man had thought he had the right to break into her house.

How did he get in? I'm sure I locked up immediately after getting Jason settled.

And why is Stryker letting the man pet him? Where are Radar and Scout? Their beds are empty.

Who is this guy, and why did he follow us?

Even though she'd forgotten the gun upstairs and had little strength left to fight or run, Becca's anger overwhelmed her fatigue and made her feel stronger than she actually was.

The knife would have to do as her last attempt to protect her home because she refused to go down without a fight.

She didn't move; instead, she chose to stay behind the island while holding the knife tightly. Finally, she took a deep breath and said, "Who are you? How did you get into my house?"

The hooded man had been so focused on Jason that he hadn't registered her presence. But he was now forced to acknowledge her.

With one last pat on Stryker's head, he said, "Oh, yeah, sorry."

As he slowly removed the knit hood, Becca's knees buckled slightly. But she held onto the island counter while she released the breath she'd been holding.

Although Matt's hair was a mess, and a little longer than Jason's, with bits of white at the temples, and although there were a few extra lines around his eyes and on his forehead, the likeness between the two was remarkable.

He even had the same quirk in the way he brushed the hair out of his dark blue eyes. Jason's eyes.

When he looked up, she noticed the unshed tears swimming in their depths.

He didn't attempt to leave the chair. Instead, he gave her a sad smile and, in a soft voice, said, "I don't know how to thank you, Becca. It looks like you had a big job here."

"Yeah, well, he refused to go to a hospital. I couldn't just do nothing. He'd bleed out, so I did my best to sew him up.

"Mind you, I still think he needs to see a doctor and get a CT maybe, and an MRI to rule out anything serious. I just hope it doesn't come back to bite me."

Matt wiped the emotion from his eyes. "I doubt you missed a thing. You're too conscientious. Besides, he's been through worse. But why did he refuse the hospital?"

"He said something about clearing his name before… well, before he stands in judgment, I suppose. He passed out before he really said.

"Look, I'm a vet. I may be great at healing animals, but humans are a breed I haven't worked on before. At least not surgically."

"But you didn't answer my question."

Matt looked back to Becca and smiled. "I'm sorry that I broke in, but when no one answered the door, I had to make sure you both were okay.

"That's when I found him.

"You did a great job taking care of him, but seeing him like this… it broke my heart. He looks just like when he was a boy.

"I can't tell you how hard it's been staying away all this time. We were so close… and letting him believe I was dead… well, I just hope he can forgive me and that we can be close again once everything is cleared up."

She walked over to Jason and took his vitals. "He's doing better than I expected. His vitals are good anyway.

"I'm not sure what Jason knows or what he's told you, but you deserve the truth.

"And, to be honest, I haven't been able to share this nightmare with anyone in all this time. So, if it's okay with you, I'd like to get it off my chest."

Becca sat down in a chair next to him. "Jason told me about the accident and that he was investigating it. He really believed you were dead. But not just dead. Murdered."

"Yeah, well, that's just a small part of it.

"This whole mess started when I decided to take a job I shouldn't have.

"This whole thing is really my fault. I had a bad feeling about taking the job with Morales, but it would have never occurred to me that it might put my family in danger.

"The truth is I got greedy. The job felt all kinds of wrong, but I knew it would put us over the top for the year and give us a well-deserved vacation.

"A vacation I'd put off for years, and, well, I was hell-bent on keeping my promise to take Sofia to Hawaii.

"I let the money, instead of common sense, decide for me.

"I don't even have words to describe how that feels.

"Anyway, I had barely started the job when I overheard Morales order an execution. At first, I thought that I must have heard it wrong. But no, it was real.

"The hit was on one of the drug traffickers hired by Morales. Apparently, the guy was skimming product and cash to start his own business.

"Anyway, I reported it to the DEA, but since I didn't have proof, not even the name, they couldn't do anything—no way to protect someone without a name, a date, time or location.

"When I went to meet up with Clay, he had my military record and because I was in covert ops, he recruited me.

"See, they'd been watching Morales for years, but they couldn't pin enough on him to send him away. There was always someone willing to take the fall for him.

"I agreed to set up a voice-activated recorder while working on the pipes so they could get more information.

"I'm not sure when it happened, but somehow Morales got wise to what I was doing. We figure that's when he ordered the hit on me. Only we never heard anything about it on the tapes.

"Man. That last day was intense. When I think about it now, I can remember the look Morales gave me just before I left - sinister bastard. But at the time, I was just so relieved to be done with the place that I wasn't paying enough attention.

"That is until I lost the brakes on my van.

He had Becca's undivided attention. Not only because she was able to envision the intensity of what he was telling her but because his eyes were just as expressive as Jason's.

"I should have been more on guard… more aware of the changes in the van. When I think back, it started shortly after I left the compound."

"Man. I can't remember ever being that scared before. The van kept picking up speed, and there was no way to slow down after the brakes failed.

"It wasn't too long after that when I noticed the steering was loose. I swear, at times it felt like I held the road by sheer will.

"At that point, I figured that I only had maybe mere minutes before cresting a slight rise. I hoped it might slow the van before it picked up speed again on the other side. If not, I knew it would go over the side at the sharp curve.

"I only had seconds to make up my mind. Seconds to figure out what I could do to save my life.

"First, I tossed out my toolbox - I'd put everything from the surveillance inside, and to preserve it, I threw it out the window.

"Probably one of my better decisions because those tapes gave the DEA what they needed to breach the compound today.

"Even if it was postponed almost a year."

"Wow, that's a long time to be away from family." Becca said softly.

"Yeah, especially when you're within a few miles, and you're forced to let them believe you're dead.

"I'd have to say that it was probably the worst year of my life."

Matt was quiet for a minute, shook his head, and continued, "Anyway, I know the van will pick up speed after it crests the top, taking away any hope of jumping clear before it flies off the mountain.

"So, as the van slowed going up the rise, I opened my door and jumped. It was my last hope of surviving.

"But that's when it got weird.

"I planned to tuck and roll before I hit the ground. Only as I'm falling, I get a glimpse of my truck flying. Like time went into some kind of slo-mo.

"It just holds air, like it's stuck right there in the sky."

His gaze shifted to the wood stove, and he seemed to be transfixed by the fire. "It's hard to explain. Try to imagine watching a movie in slow motion when someone presses pause just as...."

Becca wondered if he was reliving the experience.

After a minute, Matt shook his head and looked up at Becca. "Anyway, it was probably only seconds if that, and my memory gets a bit sketchy after that.

"When I hit the ground, I get the wind knocked out of me. I'm still conscious, but I'm too busy falling, rolling. And before I can do anything, I'm falling off the edge.

"I remember the sound when the van hit the ground. It was so loud—like a bomb had gone off.

"Rolling down the embankment, I remember seeing these snapshot images of the van. It was rolling, too.

"It must have hit something hard 'cause there was a second explosion—that was even louder.

"The gas tank must have ruptured over the hot manifold because then there was a big whoosh, and I saw flames.

"I'm not sure how far I fell, but it felt like I was rolling and sliding down the ravine for a long time.

"I finally landed hard against a tree, which stopped me cold. I must have hit my head because all I remember after that was waking up in a hospital.

"Clay told me later that a tree branch impaled me. I'm honestly glad that I don't remember that part. But from what I was told, it was a good thing I jumped because if I'd stayed buckled in, I would have died for sure.

"Knowing it was my last day, the DEA followed me with a drone. They suspected Morales might do something if he thought I was a loose end and took precautions.

"When they saw I was in trouble, they sent out a team to pick me up, and when they did a sweep of the area, they found the toolbox.

"They wanted Morales to believe I died in the accident, so they placed a John Doe in the burning truck. It was essential to the operation and to protect me and my family, at least until they could implement their plan to take Morales and his cronies down.

"I was debriefed days after I woke in the hospital.

"But no one expected the mission to take this long.

"At first, they thought it would be just a few days, and since I was in the hospital, it wasn't a big deal to wait.

"The tapes they already had told them about the summit. It was the first gathering in years where the heads of several cartels would all be in one place.

"But it was the tapes recovered from my toolbox that told them the summit was canceled, and they were able to confirm it with flight cancelations.

"Clay asked me to stay and help them finish the sting. And the truth was I had to wait until Morales could be arrested. Staying dead was the only way to keep my family and the operation safe.

"I was sick about it, but the risk was too significant to ignore. So I agreed to stay with them.

"Morales was chomping at the bit to show off his new product, so they thought the next summit would happen sooner rather than later.

"But it took way longer than anyone expected.

"Staying away from my family has been the hardest thing I've ever done. It about killed me when they broke into my house and abused Sofia. I was beside myself, but Clay snuck me into her hospital room.

"Men surrounded the hospital. I had two around me the whole time, but at that time of night, she was asleep.

"God, seeing her like that... I wanted to kill Morales myself. She looked that broken and bruised.

"But damn, if that woman doesn't take my breath away every time I see her – no matter what.

"Clay kept tabs on her after she went home and promised to keep a detail on her.

"But then, Jason took care of his mother and put in a security system.

"I was so proud of him for doing that. It gave me some peace of mind to know he'd be there for her.

"Clay tapped into the cameras; they have the technology. And knowing Sofia was safe made it easier for me to continue the ruse.

"It wasn't until later that they learned Jason was investigating the accident and had become a threat to Morales.

"But no one could have predicted that they'd set Jason up for murder."

Becca interrupted; she was well past sleepy. "Let me get us some coffee; I really want to hear the rest of this, and I'm beginning to fade."

"Well, there's not much more to say."

"It will help warm us up. Would you mind adding a few more logs to the fire?"

When she returned, she handed Matt a steaming cup and took Jason's vitals before she sat down.

"I had no idea that Jason was in real trouble until he was suspended. But I should have anticipated Morales might do something to him after they'd gone after Sofia.

"You should know that Jason is like a dog with a bone when he feels something isn't right. He'll worry it until he figures it out. He's been like that since he was a kid. The boy can't let anything go until he understands the why of a thing.

"Unfortunately, that need to know put a target on his back."

Becca smiled, "Funny, but I really understand that need. I'm a bit like that myself. And what I really need to know at the moment is what happened to Jack. Last I saw, he was carried off by a hooded man.

"I'm guessing that was you, right?"

Matt nodded. "I hit him pretty hard. but he was maybe a second away from shooting you, and I couldn't let that happen."

"But is he dead? And as long as I'm asking questions, what happened to Morales? I mean, did the DEA arrest him? Did they get what they were looking for? What about the others at the summit? Were they able to get the evidence they needed?"

"Whoa there, little lady, let's slow it down.

"That's why I didn't follow you right away. I wanted to make sure we got Jack for you, as I promised.

"Jack has a severe concussion, but nothing that will prevent him from doing time for killing your sister. And yes, they got their man along with enough evidence to put the SOB away for a long time.

Becca's eyes filled with tears, as she softly said, "Thank you."

Matt looked at his son and was quiet for several minutes. Finally, he looked up at her. "I have to tell you, Becca, when I saw you move in front of Jason. When you intentionally put yourself in harm's way to protect him…" The words caught in his throat. "I was beside myself.

"Even in all that smoke, I could see the determination on your face. You were going to save him, come hell or high water, even if it meant losing your own life.

"I just don't know why you would do that. From what I understand, you barely know him. Why would you sacrifice yourself like that?"

Becca turned to look at Jason, "I knew you'd come back eventually. Jason was too hurt to defend himself. Either way, Jack was going to kill me after he caught me investigating him.

"The opening was small, and I thought if I blocked it, Jason might have a chance." Smiling, she said, "Trust me, I'm no hero. That's just what I was thinking at the time."

"Still, Becca, that was very courageous. I'm just glad I hit him before he could get off a shot. You really are an extraordinary woman, Becca."

"Well, caring for others is kind of my job. But please finish your story. I want to hear what happened at the compound."

He could see that Becca had done what she felt was right, but didn't feel comfortable thinking of herself as a hero, so he moved on. "Morales and his comrades were taken in. They were hiding in a safe room located in the basement.

"It took a few hours for the agents to find the false wall. No one expected him to be in the basement. They found them with thermal imaging technology.

"Then, it took more time for their computer expert and mechanical engineer to figure out the electronic lock and get it open. They couldn't blast it and take a chance of killing them.

"But in the end, they got all of them.

"I don't think any of those guys will see the light of day without bars for some time."

Matt took a long drink of his cooling coffee. "They also found a hidden room in his library with a row of filing cabinets. I'm sure they'll have enough evidence in there to put Morales away for several lifetimes.

"For me, watching the Fat Man's interrogation through a one-way mirror was the icing on the cake.

"After a few hours of listening to him complain and make excuses, he finally disclosed the reason for the summit once they promised him a deal.

"Funny enough, it wasn't much of a deal. He wanted… to do his time with his father at the ADX."

"Who is Sal Magluta and what is ADX?"

"Sal and his partner, Willy Falcon, AKA the Cocaine Cowboys, started all of this by building one of the most significant cocaine trafficking organizations in South Florida from the 70s until they were caught and sentenced.

"In 2002, Sal was sentenced to the ADX supermax federal prison in Florence, Colorado. But why Morales wanted to be sent there is anyone's guess. You'd think that guy would want to do his time in one of those cushy federal prisons, but maybe he doesn't realize just what super max means.

"You should have heard him prattle on once he got his wish. It was amazing—beyond arrogant. He bragged about a new drug he planned to release. One that would make him a god.

"It would have been laughable if it wasn't so scary. He wants to control as many people as possible. Make them worship him like a king. Heads of state, Presidents, you name it.

"He even disclosed his plans for putting the drug into our water systems.

"Now that's some kind of madness.

"But what was even scarier was when he boasted that this new drug was nearly impossible to detect and was just as impossible to quit.

"Unlike current substances that people can quit even if the addiction lingers. He claimed that this one basically would make you a junkie for life. More like a zombie that would be completely under his control.

“People would be so hooked they’d do anything to get it and would basically cater to his every command.

“How sick is that?

“I’m happy to say that the DEA has chemists dissecting the drug’s chemical composition as we speak. They’ll make sure there’s a way to detect it and counteract its effects in case it somehow gets out into the general population.

“Now that Morales and his cronies are behind bars, and my stint with the DEA is over, there’s only one thing I want to do… and that’s go home to see my beautiful Sofia.

“She has been so loyal.” He swallowed hard. “I feel traitorous not contacting her. I let her believe, for nearly a year, that I was dead. I can only hope that when I explain why I stayed away, she’ll forgive me.

Bowing his head, his voice cracked as he said, “God, I love that woman. So much. I can’t see a life without her.”

He was pensive for several long minutes, then added, “Although now that I think about it, I might not want to show up at night. The shock might give her a heart attack. I sometimes forget that we’re not spring chickens anymore.

“I’ll ask Jason if he’ll help me gently spring my resurrection on her in the morning.” He shook his head. “Hey, but right now, he needs to rest… and we do too. It’s been a long day.”

He looked exhausted, and Becca could empathize. “Look, you’re welcome to use the spare room upstairs. It has a bath so you can clean up. Or, if you’d rather stay by Jason, there’s an overstuffed chair in the office. You can pull it in here with the ottoman if you want. I’ve fallen asleep in it more times than I can count. Just grab a few blankets from the closet in the hall and make yourself at home.”

Matt looked at Becca and realized she was probably just as tired as he was. “Thank you. I think I’ll take you up on that shower. You go on to bed; I’ll camp out here and keep an eye on my boy. If anything changes, I’ll wake you.”

Becca nodded. “That would be great. If I’m honest, I’m pretty whooped. I’m not used to the workout my body was forced to endure today. I’m just lucky that Jason was awake enough to navigate us to his Jeep.”

Realizing that she was complaining, she stopped and said, "I shouldn't complain. I got myself into all of this, trying to find my sister's killer.

"Let's just say we're all lucky to be alive."

She had to smile at the tender way Matt looked at Jason. "I'm sure your face will be the first thing he'll want to see when he wakes up."

Becca gave him a tired smile, then called her boys and made her way upstairs to bed.

The muscles in her back, shoulders, neck, thighs, and calves were still complaining, even after the ibuprofen and the pressure of a hot shower.

Wiggling under the covers until she found a comfortable spot, and before she could worry too much about it, fatigue won out over discomfort, and she fell into a deep sleep.

After Becca left for bed, Matt moved the chair and ottoman next to Jason and then went to take a shower.

He double-checked that the house was locked up and added a few logs to the fire.

Finally, clean and with nothing more than firelight, he lowered his bruised and battered body into the large chair and watched his son in the dancing firelight. "I've really missed you, son… I'm so sorry for what I've put you through."

As his mind began drifting toward dreams, he yawned and thought, Jason would be wise to hold onto that one. I'll have to mention it.

And with heavy eyelids finally closed, a lone tear ran down his cheek along with the thought; *God, it's good to be back!*

CHAPTER THIRTY-SEVEN

Dreams to Reality

As the morning light made its way through the kitchen window and into the dining room, its brightness fell on Jason's face, penetrating his eyelids to wake him.

He'd dreamt of his father, of family get-togethers with friends, and of the excursions they'd shared over the years, which were filled with fun and connection.

But as his mind struggled between sleep and wakefulness, he feared that hugging his father had been a dream. If true, Matthew Colt was still dead, and the last few days had only been part of a dream.

But hope percolated and pushed at him.

As he readjusted himself, a moan escaped. If nothing else, the pain was definitely real.

That small sound woke Matt, who immediately sat up. Elation mixed with concern for his son.

Taking Jason's hand, Matt said, "Jason, wake up, son… I'm here."

Then, seeing Jason squint tightly from the glare of sunlight, "Just a minute… let me pull down the shade so we can actually look at each other."

The familiar voice poked at his sleepy mind, waking him further. Apprehension mixed with joy as he struggled to open his sensitive eyes against the bright morning to see the man behind the voice.

He'd slept deeply and was still groggy.

After surgery, his limbs were understandably heavy and weak. It wouldn't take much for him to slip back into the comfort of dreams.

"I see you're trying to wake up. How are you feeling?"

"Dad? Am I dreaming?"

"No, son. I'm here. How are you?"

Jason slowly opened his eyes and saw Matt sitting in an overstuffed chair. His hair had grown to his shoulders, and he had more grey at the temples than Jason remembered, but his dad was breathing, sitting right next to him.

Jason forgot about his injuries for a minute and tried to sit up, but the pain stopped him.

Flinching, he said, “For a minute, I was afraid I dreamt the whole thing. That I’d wake and find that you were still dead. I missed you so much, Dad… and Mom. Oh my God! She’s barely left the house, Dad!”

“I know, son. And I’m going to make it up to both of you, I promise.”

Matt quickly moved closer to his son and got on his knees. Careful of Jason’s wounds, Matt pulled him into a hug. It was an awkward embrace, but Jason had never felt so comforted.

His body hurt, but he relished in the familiar embrace.

That was the scene that Becca walked in on that caused tears to immediately fill her eyes, partly due to the sweetness of their reunion and partly due to her relief that Jason was okay.

She stood watching them quietly for several minutes, before saying, “I see our boy is looking much better this morning. Anyone want coffee?”

In unison, both men looked up and said, “Yes, black please.” and laughed like children.

“You two are something else, you know that? But seriously, Jason, you really need to take it easy. You just had major surgery.”

After checking his vitals, she went to make their brew. Taking coffee cups down out of the cabinet, she looked at the faces of Scout and Radar, who were waiting patiently as if to say it was time for breakfast.

Jason looked worried when he asked, “Did Dean and Kade get out okay?”

“Yeah, they did a great job. But I’ll let them tell you about it.”

While waiting for their coffee, they went over some of the highlights from the night before.

As she brought the coffee into the dining area, Matt was helping Jason sit up. They’d been talking in hushed voices when she walked in.

Feeling a little let down that they might be ready to leave when she wasn’t yet ready to say goodbye, she said, “You must be anxious to go home, Matt, after being away so long. Just please promise me that you'll make sure a doctor follows up with Jason. Maybe get a few tests."

It came on all of a sudden, like a dam had burst somewhere deep inside of her. The impact so great that she couldn't stop it. All the tension and emotion she'd held back, released without warning in fits and bursts.

She whispered as she turned away. "But… I still need closure. I need to know the truth… so I can… so I can. Oh God, I don't know what I'll do next."

Tears ran down her face as she set the cups on the table, her emotions getting the best of her.

"It's just that… since Joss died, I've spent so much time trying to prove she was murdered. I wanted to prove that she wasn't just some junkie that overdosed like some lost soul that no one cared about.

"I cared!"

"I still miss her! I still wish she was here!

"It's so unfair. Why couldn't she get a happy ending like you did, Jason?

"Don't get me wrong. I'm really happy for you and Matt. But she was such an amazing person—fun-loving, playful, helpful, creative and kind. She deserves to be here, too!

"Until Jack came into her life, she was doing great! She had found her passion and loved her life.

"Jack killed her because she found his drugs. Did you know that? He told me at the shelter. He stole her life, because she was going to expose him."

When Matt saw Jason struggling to get off the cot, he went to help him. His clean clothes were folded on a chair in front of the cot, and with Becca's back to them, Matt held his son steady while he put on his underwear.

Once steady on his feet, Jason made his way over to her and turned her around. He held her steady as she expelled the depth of her grief against his bare shoulder.

He'd just been given a gift with Matt's return and no longer carried the burden of loss or the depth of grief that had plagued him.

"It was as if the darkness that had surrounded him since his father's accident had been washed away with the light of a new day.

But for Becca, there would be no resurrection, and she'd been dealing with the pain of loss for a lot longer. What was worse, was that she was alone in her grief.

She had stayed strong until she could find justice, but it had taken a toll. He wanted her to know that she wasn't alone anymore. He planned to make sure that she had the support she needed to process her grief—to mourn… finally.

Seeing his cue, Matt left them, grabbed a second cup of coffee, and called the dogs to follow him out to the back porch.

As Jason gently stroked her hair, he said, "It'll be all right, Becca. I promise you that I will get to the bottom of what happened to your sister and we will clear her name.

You don't have to carry that burden alone anymore. I know how hard it is to lose someone you love. Especially when you know it's not what it appears.

"I'm right here, hold onto me."

Her sobs grew at his words and broke his heart.

His kindness opened a door that she'd been able to keep closed until now.

In between tears and sniffles she managed, "It's just that I've been so alone since my mom died. Joss and I were always away at school, but our mother meant the world to us -- we all loved her dearly.

"We were a close family too. We had the best times together. But after our mother died, our dad buried himself in his work.

"My little brother Garrett distracted himself with sports and friends.

"I was off chasing my dream to become a vet, and Joss headed to France to attend Le Cordon Bleu Culinary School. When she completed that, she started at the culinary school in Boulder.

"I guess we all felt alone after Mom died. All stuffing our grief to deal with the pain.

"I didn't think that there was anything that could hurt as much as losing her. But when Joss died, it was like a part of me had been ripped away— literally.

"I can't say it's a twin thing, but we were always in tune with each other. If one of us was sad or hurt, the other would know. And if we were apart too long, we'd get anxious.

"When Joss went to France, I couldn't stand it, so I flew out to stay with her on school break. When we were together we always had a great time.

"But that trip to France was the last time we were alone together before she died. We were supposed to meet up at home for school break, but she didn't make it.

"When she died, I felt like a part of me died too. I could barely function."

Jason held Becca a little tighter, "I'm so sorry, Becca."

"Now, my dad has some health issues but refuses to talk about it. Garrett is off doing his own thing. He's become even more detached from us. Says it's because of his work, but I swear he is just like our dad."

"And Garrett is on a mission to save the world.

"I'm sure it hasn't helped us stay close with me building a veterinary practice, and spending every spare minute searching for her killer.

"Were still a family, but we don't see each other very often.

"Maybe once this is over, we'll all be able to move forward together as a family again. I know that's what my mother would have wanted.

"I'm just not sure where I go from here. I've been trying to uncover what happened to Joss for so long that I'm not sure how to live any other way. Losing her left a big hole in my life. But it's the injustice of the whole thing that keeps me up at night.

"My anger at the injustice that took her is all that has kept me going.

"I guess I really didn't consider who I'd be after she received the justice she deserves.

"Even knowing Jack's in custody, it's hard to believe that it's over. That he'll be made to pay for what he did to Joss."

Jason smiled, "Believe me, I know the feeling."

Feeling much better, she slowly pulled away from his bare chest and realized for the first time that he was in his boxers. To discover that he'd been holding her while half-naked was amusing.

She couldn't help but look up into his eyes with a smile.

That look was all it took.

Even with red and swollen eyes, he couldn't help himself. Before that sweet smile could leave her lips, he bent his head and kissed her. Softly at first, then he allowed the kiss to grow with the depth of his desire.

For a minute, she felt transfixed, *or am I floating?*

Her hands left his chest and traveled into his hair to rest on the back of his neck as the kiss deepened.

A heat started in her groin, blossoming up through her abdomen until it filled her whole body. She pressed her need against his growing erection until it was hard against her pelvis.

Moving her hands from his hair to his chest, she gently pushed away to end the kiss.

It took a few seconds before her eyelids slowly fluttered open, revealing the blazing blue-green of her eyes, the green overtaking the blue with passion still smoldering in the deepest recesses of those shimmering pools.

Breathless, she managed to say, "Um, I think it's time for breakfast, and I need to feed the dogs. Plus, I think we scared your dad away. Why don't you go find him, and I'll make us something to eat."

As he looked at her with heavy-lidded eyes, he slowly moved away and started getting dressed.

Walking into the kitchen, she was surprised at how easily he'd soothed her heart. Even while taking her breath away and awakening her passion.

She couldn't help but touch her swollen lips as she stood at the sink, lost in the moment while remembering the kiss.

Feeling lighter than she had in months, Becca put food in the dogs' bowls and then pulled out what she needed to make breakfast.

When Jason came into the kitchen fully dressed, he was moving more steadily.

Only the grimace he made when he bent down to pet Stryker showed the truth.

Later as Jason sat next to Matt at the kitchenette, he said, "That smells great Becca! I'm famished!"

His eyes were still clouded. Whether from the medication that was still in his system, or the need for food, she wasn't sure.

When she placed full plates on the table, Jason tried to grab a handful of bacon, but Becca slapped his hand and pushed it out of reach, saying, "That's not for you."

"Wait, what? What's a guy have to do to get service around here?" His smile was genuine.

Matt laughed, saying, "Jason, behave yourself. What's happened to your manners?"

Jason looked at his father with a half-smile and winked. "My stomach's in charge now, Dad. You stay out of this."

Becca set a bowl of oatmeal with a sprinkle of brown sugar in front of Jason.

"What's that? I smell bacon and eggs — I don't want that mush!"

Matt couldn't help but laugh at his scowl.

Chuckling, Becca sat down next to him. "With the substances you were given yesterday and what you were on during surgery, a greasy breakfast could make you sick. So take what's offered or go without."

At Jason's frown, Matt said, "Oh, she's a keeper all right. She sounds so much like your mother. I'm telling you, Jason, you better hold onto this one; she's a rare find."

Matt, in his usual jovial manner, had unwittingly hit on exactly what Jason was thinking.

As they looked into each other's eyes, the room seemed to pulsate with the electricity of their attraction.

Unfortunately, the spell was broken by the doorbell.

CHAPTER THIRTY-EIGHT

The Morning After

When Becca opened the door this time, Matt and Jason were right beside her.

With bright smiles, Dean and Kade stood on the porch.

Happy to see them, Jason and Matt moved forward, and Becca was enveloped in the reunion.

After hugs all around, Dash said, "Jesus, Colt! You look awful, dude! What the hell happened to you?"

"It's a long story."

Becca was smiling when she said, "Come on in, join us for breakfast."

"Yeah, come in and have breakfast with us. I want to hear what happened. Dad said you were safe, but I want to hear everything you found. We have a lot to tell you guys, too!"

After a delicious breakfast prepared by Matt, who had taken over the kitchen duties, making pancakes, bacon, and eggs, Jason was able to persuade Becca to let him enjoy the feast.

While they all filled their bellies, they shared their war stories.

Dean and Kade were caught gathering evidence and had to fight their way through the house, and then they had to fight to get out of the compound. "I swear, it was like being in a war zone." Kade finished.

"I'm just glad you boys didn't get hurt," Matt said.

"I'll second that." Jason and Becca said in unison.

When the laughter stopped, Jason asked, "Becca, where did you say you put those documents I had stuffed under my vest?"

"Oh, I almost forgot. There in the laundry room, hold on a minute, and I'll get them. But be prepared; many of them are soaked with blood."

"Did you find a disk?"

Shaking her head. "I didn't see a disk, but hey, I was kind of busy." She winked, "I'll just go get it, and you can see what I mean.

"While I'm doing that, why don't you guys clear the table so we have a place to work? I'll find some gloves and some stuff to clean that stuff up a bit. Then we can all see what you got."

By the time she came back, the table was cleared, and the kitchen was spotless. "Man, you boys are awesome. Wow. Thanks for cleaning up. If this is what I can expect, you guys can come back for dinner."

When Jason unwrapped the files, he saw how bloodied they were. It would take time and patience to pull them apart without ruining them. The dried blood had stuck them together like glue. If pulled apart too fast, the paper would rip.

Taking his time, Jason freed each page cleanly and handed it to Becca to dab with distilled vinegar as she tried to avoid smearing the text.

When she finished, Becca set the document in the center of the table for everyone to read at each document dried.

As Jason pulled apart two file folders, he saw the DVD case was stuck between them. Excited, Jason blurted out, "It's here! I didn't lose it!"

Smiling broadly, as he looked around the group, he realized that they didn't have a clue what he was talking about.

Jason swallowed hard, "Guys, this is a video of that night! The night in the alley! I don't know what's on it, but it could clear me!"

"No way! What the…." Dean said.

"I know… that's exactly what I thought when the Doctor told me about it."

"Who the hell is the Doctor?"

"Remember the guy who freaked out Carl? The same guy behind the gas station… the one I've been calling Ponytail? Well, Morales calls him the Doctor.

"Anyway, I was sent to him to torture for information. I guess Morales thought I had something that could get him off. He was the guy who drugged me."

After a few nods, he continued, "Well, he said that he recorded that night, and this is it!

"I was pretty out of it after he injected me, so I'm surprised I even remembered it while I was stumbling out of there. But I managed to find it before I left. Guys, I think it might clear me! If nothing else, it will explain what happened."

Becca finally understood why Jason had been so adamant when he refused to go to the hospital. If he'd undressed anywhere else, the disk could have been lost.

He was holding onto hope. If there was the slightest chance of it clearing his name, he wouldn't risk losing it.

Jumping up, Becca said, "Well, come on then, let's watch it! I have a DVD player in the living room."

As they all got settled, Jason found the electronic equipment in the mission-style console and grabbed the remote.

For several seconds, the screen was black.

Mottled darkness filled the large screen, and the muffled echoing of footsteps in the distance.

The picture bounced with threads of light.

A brick building slowly came into focus, then transformed into an empty downtown street. The eerie glow of poorly maintained streetlights provided an unsettling atmosphere as a distant figure ran toward the camera.

At first, the figure was blurry and challenging to make out, especially with the lens jumping in and out. With each step, the figure got closer.

Then, the lens zoomed in, and Jason's face filled the screen.

He looked haggard and worn and a little unsteady on his feet.

He slowed his pace and grabbed something on his lapel that was hard to see. He was breathing hard, gasping, as he clicked the mic on his collar and struggling to say, "Denver 1, 102K requests… a 10-78… officer… on foot, moving down… um… I… need assistance. I repeat, Denver 1… requesting assistance… don't you hear me? I keep calling… where are you? I need help…backup… now!" His voice cracked.

When the lens zoomed in for a close-up, his eyelids were drooping; snot dripped from his nose, and sweat trickled down his face.

Jason narrated what they were looking at. "God, I was so sick that day, and I was in no condition to work. I thought the Sudafed would help me finish the shift. But looking at this, it's obvious that I was drugged.

"Jack admitted to doctoring my meds to throw me off, but I look like shit."

Colt looks around the street as if he's being watched, but no one is visible.

Barking from somewhere nearby echoes between the buildings. Colt runs up and falls against the building closest to him.

The low-timbre barks continue in the background.

Colt moves to the edge of the building to look into the darkened cavity just as screams pierce the silence.

Hissing, growling, and yowling of alley cats fade into the distance.

Jason narrates, "Oh yeah, I forgot that part. Scared the shit out of me at the time."

Colt wipes the snot and sweat from his face on the sleeve of his jacket and moves closer to the alley entrance. He glances back and looks around once more.

A deep guttural vibrato replaces the screeching echoes of cats.

Colt pulls his Glock and holds it close to his vest as he moves around the corner of the building, and then into the alley as the dark void swallows him.

Minutes later, another man wearing a PD jumpsuit runs into the frame, holding a strange-looking rifle. He stops briefly to check his weapon—a sleek black metal weapon with a bent stock.

The man moves past the camera, which catches a glimpse of a shadowed profile, too dark to identify.

The cop follows Colt into the mouth of the dark alley.

The camera behind them, changes to night vision and zooms in.

Total darkness fills the screen.

Seconds later, the view transforms.

The unidentified man stays hidden in the shadows near the mouth of the alley against the wall behind Colt.

Colt moves deeper into the alley.

The camera follows, tracking the men.

Colt turns into an open space as the man gains ground behind him and takes a firing stance.

The camera pans, stopping briefly on a hooded light over a backdoor that casts very little light.

The barks are loud. Vicious.

The camera zooms in on another man, mostly hidden behind the lid of a dumpster that he holds like a shield in front of him.

Colt points his flashlight directly at the man on the dumpster.

Bright red hair surrounds part of a ghostly white face, concealed in variations of shadow.

The redhead says, "I give up! I give up!".

The dog's hackles are up. He's growling, barking, and jumping. The dog snaps and tries to bite the man just out of reach.

Colt yells, "Stryker, Aus! … Aus!" the camera pans to him and back to Stryker as the dog slowly moves to Colt's side.

"Just move slowly away from the wall, drop the lid, and get down here!"

"Okay, okay! Just keep that… that crazy thing away from me!"

Jason paused the video and said, "He looked familiar, but at the time, I couldn't place him. Even now, and only because I know it's him, can I make out that it's Billy."

"Kade, you knew Billy. What do you think?"

"I think the situation is really messed up. I don't know if I would have recognized him either. I don't know. Maybe the red hair would have given me a clue.

"I can see how hard it would have been for you. It's really dark, and you were messed up. You look like you're about ready to collapse. Look at your eyes, they're half-closed."

Pressing play again, Jason said, "Yeah, looking at myself, I can see how bad I was. But at the time, I thought it was just the flu."

Stryker briefly looks behind him, then looks back at Jason.

While Colt keeps his gun trained on Billy, he reaches toward the mic.

Jason calls, "This is…."

Swoosh—thunk.

The force of the impact snaps his head and neck in the opposite direction.

He loses his grip on his gun and flashlight.

He loses his balance.

Wobbling, he struggles to keep his footing.

The flashlight rolls away under some trash and disappears from view as Jason reflexively reaches for the injury at his neck.

He looks down at Stryker.

Stryker's looking behind them at the camera.

Colt collapses to the ground.

His head bounces on impact with the frozen ground.

Stryker bares his teeth and threatens with a throttled growl as the shooter walks into the frame and momentarily blocks the camera.

Another deep growl—snap.

"Fuck!" The shooter yells—and points the weapon at Stryker, who has turned to lunge; swoosh—thump, Stryker squeals and falls.

"No wonder Stryker kept attacking Jack," Jason says under his breath.

The sound of crunching ice as the shooter enters into the alcove with his back to the camera.

A slow zoom of the lens as it pans to the dumpster.

It's Billy, and he's smiling. "Man, am I glad you showed up? For a minute, I thought I was toast."

The shooter swings the rifle onto his back and approaches Colt.

He's searching the ground, picks up Colt's gun in his gloved hand, squats down, rolls Colt onto his back, and puts the gun in Colt's limp hand as he says, "You have nothing to worry about, Billy. It's all part of the plan. You can get down now."

The gun slides sideways from Colt's hand. But the shooter catches and repositions it, wraps his hands around both the gun and Colt's hand, and raises the weapon.

Simultaneously, the shooter lines up the shot and pulls the trigger. A loud crack, and Billy drops headfirst off the side of the dumpster as the sound reverberates in the small space.

Half of his body gets suspended upside-down in midair, like a life-size discarded toy.

The close-up confirms that it's Billy's limp, contorted body. Billy's sunken, unseeing eyes stare into the lens until it pans back to the shooter.

The shooter drops Colt's hand, reaches over to pull a dart from his neck, pivots on his heels, pulls another from Stryker's unprotected flank, and appears to take something from his collar.

As the shooter turns from Colt, Jack Hanson's face fills the screen, showing bright eyes and a self-satisfied smirk.

Jason pauses the video, "I see it, but I can hardly believe it. After everything we went through together, it just seems crazy that Jack could be that cold. I mean, just look at his face!"

Hitting play, the scene shows Colt and Stryker, but neither is moving.

Both appear to be dead.

Several minutes pass before Colt shows any sign of life.

His arms jerk.

He gasps as if drowning.

His arms flail. His legs kick.

More time passes as he struggles like a fish out of water for breath.

"God, I remember that. It felt like I was drowning in mud. I couldn't breathe. I thought I would suffocate if I didn't reach the surface. It was terrifying."

Then, a tremor appears to shake his whole body as if he's having a seizure. Several minutes pass before the tremor stops, and he takes gulping breaths.

He's still for several minutes and then slowly turns his head toward the camera. When he opens his eyes, they are dark, and his face is etched in pain.

He closes his eyes and reaches out for Stryker.

Jason says softly, "I thought Stryker was dead. It was such a relief when I felt him breathing."

On the screen, Colt's shaky hand reaches for the dog. His arm falls limply on Stryker's side. He slides his hand under the lip of the vest.

Time passes, and Colt tries to push himself up but quickly falls back down, "Ugh!".

He rolls onto his side and then onto an elbow. Once he's in a sitting position, he scans the area.

Squinting, he focuses on the dumpster. He strains his neck to make out the dark mound on the ground.

Still shaky, he manages to get onto his hands and knees as he crawls over to the dumpster. On his way, he slaps into something wet. He pushes back on his heels and looks back at Stryker, a look of puzzlement on his face and wipes the muck onto his pants.

The head and shoulders of the body are on the ground. The rest of the body is suspended up against the dumpster, twisted. One leg is bent over the head, the toe of an Air Jordan nearly touching it. The other is bent sideways at an angle. One arm is half under the torso while the other is on the ground straight up above the head as if asking a question.

Stryker begins to move and whine.

Colt looks back at his partner but moves closer to the body.

Jack moves out of the shadows and past the camera.

Footsteps rumble and then fade into the night.

Jason checks for a pulse.

Stryker moves slowly onto his stomach while crying out in pain.

Colt backs away from the body, turns, and crawls on hands and knees back to his partner while Stryker whimpers and tries to crawl toward him.

With a catch in his voice, Colt says, "You all right, buddy?" Rubbing Stryker's head and ears, Colt grimaces as he sits on the ground and pulls Stryker onto his lap.

He tries his radio again. "Please! If anyone can hear me. We need help."

A slow zoom shows a disheveled, wet, dirty, and blood-smeared man holding a whimpering dog.

Colt looks up as a single tear runs through the dirt down his face.

The screen goes black.

The room is silent.

CHAPTER THIRTY-NINE

The Homecoming

After Jason turned the TV off, he tried to process what he'd seen.

It was hard to watch.

He knew it was ugly, but seeing it like that was somehow worse.

Watching a man assassinated by his hand, even if not by his own volition, was upsetting.

When he finally turned to the others, their expressions brought tears to his eyes.

Matt and Becca both had wet streaks on their faces.

Kade and Dean looked shaken. They were still gawking at the blank screen.

No one spoke for several minutes.

Finally, Jason couldn't stand it. "Well, that was hard to watch. I lived it, and yet… that was really something.

"But hey guys, it would really help to hear your thoughts."

Dean bit off his words when he said, "I can't believe it. That son-of-a-bitch! If I didn't see it…," Unclenching his fists, he softened his tone, "I mean, shit, it's just so hard to believe.

"Not that I didn't believe you before, Jason, but I just… I had no idea.

"I don't know how you guys feel, but that was… like a scene from right out of some horror flick.

"Jesus, brother, I'm so sorry you went through that. No wonder you couldn't explain it. I just watched it, and I don't… well, who would believe it? It's just so… unreal.

"And what did that little fuck think he was doing recording it? Fucking sick bastard recorded it just for pleasure! Jesus! That's just all kinds of messed up.

“But then again, it’s a good thing he did, huh? Should take that asshole Jax down for sure.

“But hey, I think we definitely need to get copies of it. As sick as that sounds. No way we hand it off to anyone before we have copies.”

Jason smiled; he could always count on Dean to be the first to plan ahead. “I couldn’t agree more. That’s exactly why I refused to go to the hospital. I couldn’t take the chance of losing it.

“When you guys told me what Carl said about there being two other guys in the alley that night, I honestly didn’t get it. I couldn’t remember seeing anyone that night besides Billy, and I didn’t even recognize him.

“Well, as drugged up as they got you, I think that’s pretty understandable,” Kade interjected.

“Man, I wasn’t sure anyone would ever understand.

“The bits I did remember were impossible to explain… I mean, how do you explain something like that? I was so out of it… for the crucial parts… anyway.

“That’s why it meant so much when you guys stood by me even though everything pointed to my guilt. You guys never questioned if I killed Billy.

“I’m not sure what I would have done without you guys. You risked everything… I’ll never forget that!”

Matt patted Becca on the back, wiped his face, and sat forward, “I’ll second that. You boys will never know how grateful I am for your loyalty and friendship and… well… just for everything you did for Jason.

“You guys are the best, and that goes for you, too, Becca. I mean, you really didn’t know Jason. So… for you to help him… was a risk.

Kade shrugged his shoulders. “Well, anyone who knows you would find it hard to believe that you set out to kill anyone.

“We just needed to find the proof, is all.”

Matt nodded. “Still, my son is lucky to have friends like you.

“But hey, there’s something else that you guys don’t know.

“Becca risked her life to protect Jason. She actually put herself directly in the line of fire to prevent Jack from shooting him.

Jason’s mouth fell open, and his eyebrows rose, “Huh?”

“When you were hurt inside the shelter… Jack had found you. Man, I have to tell you. It was pretty amazing, and I was lucky enough to have a front-row seat." With a smile, he patted Becca on the knee and added, "If I were you, I'd hold onto this one, son."

Smiling, Jason said, "Yeah, I might do just that." Smiling at her, he added, "She's been a real lifesaver for both Stryker and me. You should have seen her half carry me to the Jeep she…."

Becca was beginning to feel uncomfortable, so she interrupted, "Okay, now. That's just about enough of all that.

"Let's just leave it as we survived an unthinkable situation. And because of everything you boys accomplished, those bad guys will be behind bars for a long time.

"What I hope is that when all this comes out, both Joss and Jason's reputations will be restored."

Jason added, "And don't forget Stryker's!"

Becca laughed, "Who could forget Stryker?" After a few chuckles, attention turned to Matt, who was suddenly quiet.

"Hey, Dad, what's up?"

"My God, son, I just can't get over what they put you through. I'm so sorry for putting you in that position. If I hadn't agreed to work with the DEA…"

Jason interrupted. "…No, Dad! Stop that! None of this is on you!

"The only people responsible for what happened to us are Morales, Jax, and their goons.

"I learned a long time ago that accepting responsibility for someone else's mistakes only makes you a doormat and enables criminal's to continue in their criminal pursuits and bad intentions.

"We can't make excuses for poor choices or allow ourselves to become scapegoats. People need to be responsible for their behavior instead of blaming everything and everyone for it."

Dean piped up. "I agree with that. People need to be made accountable for their actions regardless of the reasons behind them. No one should suffer when they've done nothing wrong.

"So, to make sure you don't have to pay for Jack's actions and decisions, I think we need to make sure a copy of this tape gets to the chief as soon as possible."

Kade was nodding, "Damn straight. This will definitely clear your name."

Matt nodded. "Agreed. But let me call Clay. I know he'll want to help us with this. And I think he'd smooth things out so you can get your job back, Jason."

***

At the DEA offices, Agent Thomas separated them into different interrogation rooms while Matt was debriefed.

Agent Emily Harris filled Becca in on what they knew about her sister's murder, and for the first time in five years, Becca felt like someone cared about what had happened to her sister.

Becca handed over copies of everything she'd uncovered during her five-year investigation. Most of the evidence she'd collected was against Jack, with testimony she thought might be used against Myers.

Agent Harris assured Becca that Detective Myers was being dealt with and would no longer be working in law enforcement.

In fact, she learned that they were building a case so that his next job would be assigned to him in prison.

Agent Harris reassured Becca that Joss Arianna Kennedy's case would be reopened, the cause of death reevaluated, and her killer brought to justice.

Dean and Kade explained their roles in Jason's investigation. Although their stories were similar, each had details the other didn't.

They also provided more details about what occurred at the compound while collecting evidence for Matt.

Jason handed over all the documents he'd gathered from his pack, along with the DVD and the bloodied files.

He gave a detailed account of everything he could remember since being told Matt was dead and everything he'd learned since he'd been put on suspension.

He ended his interview with an admission of guilt, stating that he was the one who broke Stryker out of the kennel to save him from what he felt was an unjustified order of execution.

When the debriefings were finished, they watched the video again.

This time on a big screen.

The DVD was duplicated and electronically sent to Chief Ron Thomas, Captain Alvarez, Lieutenant Bernard, and Sergeant Billings, along with the DEA Director's recommendations and advisements and a synopsis of Jason's assistance in the successful DEA takedown of several major cartels.

It was noted that the details were withheld until the cases were finalized in the courts.

Advisements included reinstatement for both Jason and Stryker to the Denver Police Department's SWAT/K-9 unit until such time as the canine is retired from the department and returned to his owner, Jason Colt.

In the Director's notes, she wrote, 'Let it be known that Stryker showed no signs of aggression during arduous and exigent circumstances, except when it was necessary to protect his team.

It should also be noted that Stryker has been cared for by Dr. Kennedy, who released him for active duty.'

Additional recommendations noted: 'It is the opinion of this writer that the highest awards or commendations be considered for officers Dean Fletcher Adams, Jason Maxwell Colt, and detective Kade Tanaka, in acknowledgment of their contributions in the biggest cartel takedown of the century.

This department will honor Matthew Braxton Colt, a retired special operations Marine Lieutenant and valuable DEA consultant, for his year-long sacrifice, dedication, and bravery.

Mr. Colt's contributions were vital in preventing a new substance from being released to poison our citizens and ensured the success of this department's mission.

Lastly, the Director recommended that Becca Ellawyn Kennedy be given the highest civilian award for her efforts in uncovering her sister's murderer.

Before they left, Becca requested a medical doctor examine Jason.

After a full workup, CT, and MRI, the doctor gave Jason an antibiotic and said, "I know you refuse to say, but whoever sewed you up did a bang-up job.

When it was finally time to go home, Jason filled the group in on his plan for the evening and they all headed to Matt's house exhausted but excited to place the last piece and complete the puzzle.

On the way, Jason called Charles and Desiree, Hiroshi and Emi and told them to be at his mother's house for dinner at six, stating that he had some big news that couldn't wait, and he needed to share it with the whole family.

He didn't mention that Matt would be there too, or that his name would be cleared. All he would say was that they definitely would want to be there.

As the sun slipped from the sky. Jason walked into his mother's house, calling for her. She replied from the kitchen, "I'm in here, son!

Standing at the stove, she was finishing the sauce on a large pot of spaghetti and meatballs.

As Jason, Dean, and Kade walked into the kitchen, Jason said, "Hey, Mom, I have a surprise for you, but you need to sit down."

After giving them all hugs, she said, "You know how much I enjoy you boys, but I'm trying to finish up dinner.

"I thought I might tempt you with spaghetti and meatballs.

"Dean… Kade, you absolutely must join us. I have more than enough here for an army."

Jason said, "That sounds great, Mom! Let's have a celebration! Just give me a few minutes, okay? The sauce can wait and I promise; you're going to love this."

Hesitating a little, she sat down on the kitchen island stool. "Well… okay."

Becca walked in and stood next to Jason. "Mom, this is Becca. Becca, this is my mother, Sofia.

"Mom, I think you'll be seeing a lot of Becca from now on."

Sofia looked at her son, a little confused. "Jason, I'm happy to meet Becca. She's a beautiful girl, and she's more than welcome to stay for dinner, but I just have a few more things to finish and…."

"No, you don't, Mom. Please. Just sit here for one more minute."

"Jason? I don't see why…."

Coming into the room behind her, Matt said, "Because we wanted to surprise you without giving you a heart attack, my love."

Sofia looked up at Jason as tears flooded her eyes, afraid to turn her head. "Jason?"

With a huge smile on his face. "It's okay, Mom, turn around."

As Sofia turned in her stool, she flew out of it, knocking it to the floor, and jumped into her husband's waiting arms.

She was shaking and crying. "Oh, my God, Matt?! Matt! Can it be? Are you real?"

She pulled away to look at him. Although scruffier than she remembered, he was alive. "Oh, my God! Where have you been? If I wasn't so happy to see you, I'd have to kill you… I've missed you that much!"

Laughing Matt said, "I know, I have some splainin' to do Lucy."

Embracing him and holding on for all she was worth, their happy tears mixed as they held each other.

That was about the time her temper caught up with her, "Matthew Braxton Colt, where have you been? We thought you were dead; do you know what that did to us?"

Matt pulled her close and kissed her until her fears and anger melted away. Then he held her close for a long time while he looked at his son, who was smiling with his arm around Becca.

"Damn you Matthew, I never could stay angry at you."

"I know, my love, and I'm sorry. I'm a scamp. But I promise I will make it up to you.

"But first, let us tell you a fantastic story that will explain everything. Then we can eat some of your amazing pasta and have some wine to celebrate our reunion!"

When the doorbell rang, Jason rushed to answer it. Exchanging hugs, Jason said, "Hey, family! Do I have a surprise for you? But first, cover your eyes."

They were such good sports, and covering their eyes, Charles, Desiree, Hiroshi and Emi allowed Jason to guide them into the kitchen.

Desiree sniffed the air, "Yum, I can smell your mother's amazing sauce. I sure hope that's part of the surprise."

Matt got into position right in front of them, and Jason said, "It sure is, but you might like this even more.

"Okay, you can open your eyes now."

"Matt?! Oh, my God—Matt?"

Dean and Kade were both smiling.

Life finally made sense again.

Watching Charles lift his lifelong friend off the floor in a huge bear hug brought tears to Jason's eyes which he quickly wiped away.

"But how? I mean, what the hell? How?" Charles cried.

"It's a long story," Matt said, smiling.

"Well, damn. I should have known that nothing could take you down, you old dog."

"Oh, my dear friend, I have so missed you! But please, put me down. We have so much to tell you all.

Even Hiroshi and Emi happily embraced Matt.

"Well, now that we're all finally back together. I say let's all get comfortable, shall we?

"I'll get some refreshments while my beautiful wife finishes our that delicious smelling meal.

"As I had started to explain to Sofia, we have an incredible—but relatively long, story to tell you.

"One that's both amazing and hard to believe.

"Even after you hear it, you might question if it's true.

"But trust me, sometimes even death isn't the end."

***

The full moon finally reached its apex, its brightness lighting up the yard, leaving him in full view of the men who'd ruined his life.

That's if they even bothered to look.

Watching from the corner of the house, he could barely contain his rage. Its intensity was so immense that it threatened to consume him in flames from the inside out, leaving what was left in ashes on the ground.

A wicked sneer was contemptuously held in place by the density of the hate that filled him while he seethed at the display of affection in front of him.

It had taken all of his tricks to escape the hospital.

The pain had made it more challenging than it would have been otherwise. But then again, to think handcuffs could keep him chained to a bed was idiotic!

He had escaped and had risked coming to kill the mother.

She was the last important person in Jason Colt's life, or so he thought.

He had believed that her death would destroy—the man who shot him—twice.

He wanted the discovery of the mother's body to be as gruesome and devastating as possible. He knew how to make the greatest impact on whoever found the body and that was to filet the woman.

But as he'd crept up to the glass doors, ready to catch her off guard while she was distracted cooking. The knife positioned securely in his hand, ready to strike, and his mind primed for punishment. As he reached for the handle, he was stopped a mere second before opening the door as three men entered the kitchen.

Stunned, he quickly pulled his hand away and watched the scene unfold.

It was bad enough that Jason was still standing, but moments later, when Matt walked into the room, he felt ill.

He'd escaped the hospital after surviving a punctured lung and the removal of a bullet that had pierced his left arm when Jason shot him with that puny gun he pulled from out of nowhere.

He wanted - no, deserved, retribution.

But how was it possible that Matthew Colt was alive?!

It would have been so much better if he could have cut up the mother—a little revenge before he headed south.

But even that little bit of retribution had been stolen from him.

They took everything: his employment, his creation, and his home.

With Morales gone and the other drug lords captured, he had nowhere to sell his extraordinary talents.

He was left to flounder on the streets like when he was a child.

To starve and pick food off discarded plates.

To wear discarded and dirty clothes.

And to live in abandoned buildings.

Then it hit him. Not only had he lost everything, but there would be no more playmates captured to pleasure him as his bonus. And that injustice shook him to his core.

They were laughing and celebrating at his expense.

At the ruin of his life.

He could smell the garlic and spices in the spaghetti sauce, which made his stomach growl. It was time to leave before he was seen and recaptured.

Before they could take his freedom as well.

He left through the gate, keeping to the shadows until he had made it to the street. Where a mad laughter bubbled up, emanating from somewhere deep inside of him, to escape through clenched teeth.

An insane sound, that burst out of him to ride on a current of the evening winds.

A whisper with a cold warning… "so help me, I will have my revenge!

"For I am the Wizard!"

~The End

Printed in the USA
CPSIA information can be obtained
at www.ICGtesting.com
CBHW021413220924
14609CB00003B/165